GRACE'S COURAGE

ANNEMARIE BREAR

It lies not in our power to love or hate,
For will in us is over-ruled by Fate.

- Marlowe, Hero and Leander

For my mother Betty Brear,

who I miss everyday

CHAPTER 1

*L*eeds, England
1870

MONTGOMERY WOODRUFF SCOWLED at the low, dirty clouds as though they had appeared just to torment him. He tugged at his lapels, jerking his greatcoat close as the wind tried its best to wrestle a way into his inner garments. The end of January had been unrelenting with blizzards, storms and freezing temperatures. Woodruff entered his carriage and yanked at the folded blanket on the seat, his impatience sending it sliding to the floor. With a muttered oath, he arranged the blanket to better suit his needs, ignoring his clerk who stood dithering in the elements waiting for last minute instructions. Woodruff sent him a withering glare before a curt command from his driver, Sykes, sent the showy black horses away from the three-storey Georgian building to merge with the traffic in the bustling streets of the great Yorkshire town.

Sighing heavily, Woodruff **stretched** his neck from the starched collar, trying to relax as they traversed around pedestrians and vehicles. Winter gloom and the cold sent most people hurrying home, shop keepers were packing up, women scolded children towards their own hearths while business men headed for the warmth and smoky atmosphere of expensive clubs.

Woodruff grunted, he also should be ensconced in his club, cradling a brandy and discussing world issues, but too many men wanted him for than his views on politics and such like, no, they wanted much more — money!

He rocked sideways as Sykes guided his ebony beauties out into the surrounding snow-topped countryside and towards home. *Home.* His precious gem, and the only thing he cared about. A cold sweat broke out on his forehead. He wouldn't lose it, couldn't lose it. He'd sell his soul to keep it.

Drifts of snow driven by the wind and the gray evening light reduced visibility. Sykes slowed the pair, not wanting to damage their legs in the snow-filled ruts. When a figure, robed from head to foot in a dark brown cape, lunged desperately for the nearest horse's bridle, the horses skidded in fright, dragging the person a few yards.

'What in Christ's name?' Sykes cursed, in a mixture of fear and surprise. He reined in hard and applied the brake, halting his horses to an uneasy standstill.

The wild jolting of the normally smooth ride sent Woodruff careening onto his side. He swore violently. 'What in hell are you doing, Sykes?'

'You, there!' Sykes threatened the staggering, shadowy figure. 'Leave go, before I wrap my whip around yer ear holes!'

For a fleeting moment, Woodruff wondered if he was being held up. His heart hammered, then blood pounded in his temples as his rage took over. *How dare someone rob me!*

'I must speak to Mr Woodruff!' A woman's voice beseeched from within the capacious hood.

He reached for the door, but it was wrenched opened. 'What the …?'

'Mr Woodruff, you must hear me!'

The hooded figure's desperate and needy manner instantly revolted him. 'Leave at once! Can a person not travel the roads without assault?'

'Please, I must speak with you!'

'I know you not, Madam.'

With a sudden flash of a slim white hand, the hood was thrown back revealing a pale, pinched, face with dark and imploring eyes.

'Olive?'

'Yes.'

Woodruff peered at his former mistress and sighed deep within his chest. It had been a while since he'd sampled her wares. Lately, he'd simply not had the time or energy. 'What possesses you, woman, to come out here in the depths of winter and throw yourself in front of horses?'

'You've not been near for months and I'm desperate.' Olive shivered as she spoke, but Woodruff refused to offer the warmth of the carriage. To do so would be to accept her as one of his own class and that would never do.

'If you need money, then I'm afraid I only give if I receive in turn,' Woodruff sneered at the frail figure. 'I assume you have gathered another customer or two by now, to keep you in comfort?'

'I wish I could, but I'm unable.' She snorted in contempt. 'It's not money, though of that I'm in need too. No, it's something more serious.'

'Are you sick? Good Lord, you haven't contracted a disease, have you?' Woodruff's skin prickled at the thought.

'No, of course not!' Olive glared. 'It's worse than a disease!'

'For God's sake woman! Spit it out. I have no time for riddles!'

'I'm with child! Your child!'

Woodruff fell back in his seat. Ice trickled beneath his skin. 'You think it's mine?'

'I've been with no one else.'

'And I'm to believe that, am I? Do you take me for a fool?'

'You know there's been no one else since you came calling. At one stage, you visited every night *and* during the day at times! How do you think I managed to entertain other men?'

Woodruff grunted. 'Go home, Olive. I shall call and discuss this matter with you tomorrow.'

She gripped his arm. 'You promise?'

He wrenched out of her grasp. 'Yes. Now go. I'm late for my dinner.' He reached over and slammed the carriage door, forcing her to hurriedly step back into the snowdrift on the roadside.

The carriage lumbered away and he leaned back against the plush upholstery. If she spoke the truth, Olive's news meant another burden he must bear. His fingers in many pies of business brought their troubles. Workers at his mill and factories had gone on strike against the low wages he paid. He refused to be held to ransom, to pay the dregs of society more money and give them better conditions! Oh, no, not he, Montgomery Clifton Woodruff. The thought of the unscrupulous working class bringing his small empire crashing to its knees nearly gave him a stroke. It wouldn't come to that of course! No, he was working himself through some very long days trying to right the situation.

With luck, in a week he would have sold his mill in Halifax and paid off one loan. It made better sense to shift the mill and dabble in other ventures. Roads and railways held his interest, and the navvies, mainly the Irish, working on those particular schemes were glad to have the work, never mind low wages. They possessed no grand ideas to better themselves and that's how Woodruff liked it.

He rubbed his forehead, his mind whirling. His bank manager sent him warning letters each week. He didn't know how he could delay meeting the man much longer, but if he went to him with a plan, then perhaps he had a chance. He could reduce his expenditure some more in some areas...

The carriage slowed to turn and pass through the wrought iron gates of Woodruff House. As always, the manor and surroundings filled him with a surge of pride. He doubted there was a finer home in all of England. He felt nothing for draughty castles and cold palaces, or large impersonal mausoleums pretending to be homes. No, Woodruff House was his ideal place in the whole world. Satisfaction filled him as the carriage drove down the impressive white granite-pebbled drive, bordered by tall graceful silver birch trees.

Movement at one of the windows caught his eye and Woodruff paused before descending from the carriage. *Yes, I am home, you lot of lazy good for nothing wasters!*

He heaved his considerable bulk out of the carriage and climbed the wide sandstone steps to admire the impressive bronze knocker in the shape of Woodruff's coat of arms decorated on the door. He checked it for smears but found none.

His old butler, Fernly, who'd served Woodruff's father opened the door, his face impassive. 'Welcome home, sir.'

The heat of the hall swept over him and again he nodded in approval. Divested of his outer clothes, Woodruff marched into the drawing room, hoping to catch his wife and children indulging in careless pastimes. He rubbed his hands together in glee at the thought of catching them out. It was a joy to harangue them for an hour or more on the benefits of their privileged life which he could squash at anytime he chose.

He detested his wife with a passion second to none and regretted the day he married her. He conveniently disregarded it was her money that drew him to her in the first place. Nevertheless, their marriage could have been a contented one, if she had delivered him the son he longed for. The dreams of filling this house with a dozen, handsome, intelligent sons, and being the envy of all who knew him, slowly eroded with each birth of a girl child. Seven daughters had supplanted the longed for sons. They were the very curse of his life.

No one occupied the drawing room, which nonplussed him at first. Quickly, he turned on his heel and strode into the parlour opposite. It too was empty. Annoyed, he stormed along the polished parquetry floor of the hall to the library. Here at last, he found one member of his family.

Curled up on the sofa, her slippered feet tucked demurely under the long skirts of her lemon organza dress and across from a roaring fire reclined Faith, the fifth and quietest daughter.

'Father, you are home,' she said, instantly putting her feet down.

'Have you nothing better to do girl than be idle all day?' He sneered.

Faith rose, slipping her book behind her back. 'I've done all I was asked, Father. I've visited the soup kitchens in town with Grace...'

'As if I care about that! Where *are* those other layabout sisters of yours?'

Faith blinked rapidly. 'I believe Heather took Letitia, Phoebe and Emma Kate to the milliners, while Gabriella is out visiting, and Grace is in the study.'

Woodruff glared at her. 'Don't let me catch you reading again. If you can't find something useful to do, then stay out of my sight!'

He crossed the hall and entered the study, eager for a drink. 'What the hell are you doing in my study?'

Grace slowly rose from behind the desk, her direct amber eyes meeting his furious scowl. 'I'm writing up the house accounts.'

'This is my room! The one room in this whole blasted house where I can achieve peace away from tittering females!'

'Very well. I shall continue my work in the library.'

At five-foot seven, Grace was as tall as he. Both she and Heather were the tallest of the girls and could eye him without having to look up. This annoyed him no end. 'I want those accounts reduced, do you hear?'

'I don't think anyone can accuse me of being frivolous.'

He stomped to the drink trolley. 'When is dinner to be announced?'

'At seven o'clock, as always, Father.'

'Well it better be edible tonight. Last night's meal was appalling!'

Grace paused by the door, one slender hand resting upon the brass doorknob. 'Every meal in this house is edible, Father.' She left the room before his tirade began.

WITH AN UNHAPPY SIGH, Grace went into the library opposite. She felt nothing for the man who sired her, except perhaps distaste. The library was her favourite room, with bookcases lining each wall from the gold embossed ceiling to the plush dark green carpeted floor. A large fireplace stood at one end and occasional tables of oak and beech were dotted between comfortable sofas and armchairs. By the large bay window, stood an impressive desk of walnut inlaid with burgundy leather. She ran her fingers over it as she gazed through the window, absent-mindedly watching a red robin skip from the branches of a rhododendron bush in the fading light.

Hearing noise coming from the hall, she closed her eyes momentarily. Her sisters' voices reached her even through the thickness of the library's walls. Grace rushed to quieten them before their father roared like an enraged bull.

She was too late. Her father entered the hall at the same time, freezing the smiles on the faces of the four young women.

'Why can you not do anything silently?' He said scornfully. 'Wasn't the money I spent on your governess enough to instil some sense of decency in you? Your mother has failed yet again, I see.'

Grace stepped forward. 'Take yourselves upstairs and change for dinner. You are late,' she ordered, though her eyes softened a little, taking the sting out of her words.

'Heather, my study,' Woodruff commanded.

Hesitantly she followed, giving Grace a surprised look.

'You might as well join us, Grace, for you will need to know what is happening and arrange things accordingly,' he added.

They followed him into the study and stood waiting while he sat behind his desk. He placed his hands over his extended stomach and rocked back in the chair. 'I have news regarding the dinner party we attended at the Ellsworths'. Amazingly, your mother performed her duty for once and made you all a social success.'

Grace raised an eyebrow. 'In all honesty, Father, your wife and daughters have been socially acceptable for many years.'

He snorted. 'With the local farmers? Do you think them to be acquaintances worthy of me?'

'I do believe our circle of friends are more than just farmers. I am sure we can count the odd alderman, a doctor or two, a solicitor, a Captain...'

'Don't be insolent, Miss!'

'Well, Father, you make the opinion that we do not venture into the correct society.' Grace tilted her head. 'Do you wish us to dine with nobility? Shall I send them our card?'

'Be quiet, you impertinent chit!' Woodruff flared. 'I will rise to dine in their exalted ranks eventually, and if I can't do it by marrying you lot into their lines, then I'll find some other way.'

'How ridiculous.' She crossed her arms. 'We are only second generation trade. Do you really expect a lord or an earl will come here and choose one of us?'

Their father's small round eyes narrowed as he grinned. 'No, not yet, although many nobles have little money. They will marry beneath them from time to time to gain wealth once more.'

'We have no fear on that account, sir. We've little compared to most.'

Woodruff bristled. 'Do you suggest I wish to remain so?'

Surprised, Grace frowned. 'Are you not content, sir, with all you have? We're very fortunate...'

'What do you know of finance?' He flung his short, fleshy arms wide to incorporate the whole house. 'All this requires a great deal of money. Position and status requires even more! The Woodruff name might not be linked to royalty yet, but I intend to have power and eminence one day, even if I have to buy it!'

'Surely, you are content...'

Heather stepped forward bringing the argument to a halt. 'What did you wish to speak to me about, Father?'

Woodruff settled back into his chair. 'I had a meeting today with Reginald Ellsworth. He has some business interests equalling mine. In fact, I own a profitable venture he wishes to take off my hands.' He waved in a dismissive gesture. 'I am giving him a good price and in return he affords me the opportunity to marry one of you into his pedigree. Of course your marriage settlement from your mother's money has greased the way a little.'

'No...' A cold shiver ran up Grace's back.

He held Heather's gaze. 'Ellsworth has granted a union between you, Heather, and his eldest son Andrew. I believe you may expect a call from Andrew tomorrow.'

Heather and Grace stood unblinking, trying to absorb their father's announcement.

'Come, come! No thanks? No gratitude, Heather?' Woodruff puffed himself up importantly.

'You-you cannot be serious, Father?' Grace hoped he was joking. He'd played evil tricks on them many times before.

He frowned. 'And why wouldn't I be?'

'Well, Heather and Andrew have only begun a friendship. To speak of marriage to cement a business deal is unjust.'

'Nonsense! It is commonplace.'

'I had hoped our family would be different. We have seen the evidence of a marriage made solely for business reasons.'

'Still your tongue, girl.'

'But there has been no romantic involvement yet, Father. Has there, Heather?' Grace appealed to her sister before spinning back to glare at him. 'Can you not let them grow to love...?'

'This has nothing to do with romantic notions you silly fool!' He roared, rising to lean over his desk towards her. 'This is two mighty families coming together. This is Heather's duty to me, and her family. She is the age of two and twenty and will be soon beyond her use if she doesn't find a husband willing enough to look past this error.'

Hatred filled Grace. She stepped closer to the desk. 'Her age has nothing to do with this. You simply want to use her as a pawn to infiltrate a society that sneers at you behind your back! They'll never accept you...' His stinging slap jerked her head back. Sharp pain bit at her cheek and she put her hand to her burning face. 'Heather,' she begged, 'say something please!'

Heather looked apologetically at her before glancing at their father. 'M-May I go now, Father?'

He spun away. 'Yes, of course, but make sure you look your best tomorrow.'

In the hall once more, Grace grabbed Heather's wrist. 'What's the matter with you? Why didn't you make any comment or simply refuse?'

'I'm sorry, Grace.' Heather lightly touched her cheek. 'Does it hurt very much?'

'Forget about it.' She shrugged. 'I'm more worried about this situation.'

'Please, don't be anxious. It's all right.'

'All right? He's married you off without even asking your preference!'

'Thankfully, I like Andrew enough.'

'Like?' Amazed, Grace stared into her sister's gray eyes. 'Oh, Heather, you must more than like!'

'Leave it, Grace, please. I know you mean well, but it's my choice...'

'No, it's not! It's Father's, obviously!'

'Andrew Ellsworth is a good man, and comes from a good respectable family. On past social occasions over the years I believe we got along well enough. I found we had much in common at the dinner party and although we have not met much since he came home from his tour in Europe, I'm pleased he's offered to marry me.'

'He might have been bullied into it too!'

Heather stepped to the plush red-carpeted staircase. 'Mr Ellsworth isn't father.'

'No, thank goodness!'

'Don't worry, Grace, please. I want to be married, I long for it actually.' She sighed. 'So, I am content. I'm not as choosy as you when it comes to acquiring a husband.' Heather smiled, her kind, generous temperament coming to the fore again, making Grace feel selfish.

Grace sighed, defeated. Of all her sisters, Heather was the one who felt the need to be married most, and realizing this, Grace knew any more argument would be fruitless. 'Very well, let us inform Mama.'

Together, they entered Diana Woodruff's suite of rooms. The rich, opulent decor of paintings, vibrant wall colours, numerous plants, abundant furniture, and plentiful ornaments were not to everyone's taste, but then not everyone had to live within these three rooms all the time. Diana Woodruff had turned away her husband's demanding attentions for the final time two years ago, when she suffered her last miscarriage at the age of forty-one.

Afterwards, Woodruff had gone abroad for six weeks and Diana recovered enough to move out of their bedroom and into another. A doorway was knocked through to the adjoining room and it became her sitting room to entertain visitors. She went downstairs only for dinner, and should they host a party. Other than that, her whole world centred in her three rooms, and she decorated them accordingly.

'Mama?' Heather smiled, entering the sitting room. A little colour tinted her cheeks and a sudden light entered her eyes, bringing a new beauty to her pretty face. Heather positioned herself closest to Diana. The importance of the statement made the middle sister, Letitia give her room.

Grace sighed at the transformation. She felt dejected at the thought of Heather marrying a man she didn't love just to escape their father.

'What did your father want, poppet?' Diana's cool blue eyes sparkled in anticipation. Her still youthful face, bearing few wrinkles, broke into a small nervous smile. Diana lifted her hand to silence her other daughters seated around her. She glanced up at Grace looking for clues.

Heather looked quickly around, seemingly for once wanting all her sisters' attention. She waited, taking a deep breath. 'I'm to marry Andrew Ellsworth!'

The sudden gasps broke the silence of the room.

Grace watched her mother. She knew her mother forced to keep the smile on her face, but it was difficult. She also knew her mother's thoughts as though she had spoken them aloud. *So, the mean scoundrel has kept to his word. He will marry them all off, one by one, leaving me alone in this enormous house. Leaving me alone with him!*

Within seconds, the Woodruff girls were hugging Heather. Their voices all joined as one, pelting Heather with questions she couldn't answer at once.

'Shh, shh!' Grace calmed them. 'We can talk after dinner, but it's late and Father will be displeased if we aren't at the table waiting for him as usual.' She ushered them out and towards their own bedrooms.

'Grace?' Diana halted her departure.

'Yes, Mama?'

'What do you think of this business?'

Grace raised her eyebrows and adjusted the lace cuffs at her wrists. 'It is exactly that, isn't it? Business.'

'Your father will do the same to all of you, you understand don't you? I want to see you all happily married, but only to the men you yourselves choose, not men who will further benefit your father's ambitions.'

'I know, Mama.'

Downstairs, the bell rang for dinner, causing Grace to groan. She hadn't changed her dress. 'If he complains I will say it was he who held me up!' Grace remarked, accompanying her mother downstairs.

'I doubt he will, my dear, for he has much to celebrate this night!'

CHAPTER 2

The next morning, Grace entered the breakfast room and said good morning to her sisters already seated at the table. She helped herself to the silver trays laden with eggs, bacon, kidneys and ham placed in warming stands on the sideboard.

'Will we all be bridesmaids, Heather?' Phoebe asked, flouncing into the breakfast room.

Grace shook her head at her youngest sister's deportment. At seventeen, Phoebe was the baby of the family and spoilt by them all. Her gray eyes, like Heather's, sparkled at the prospect of their first family wedding.

'Of course!' Heather smiled, sipping from her china teacup. 'I cannot be married without my sisters, can I?'

'When shall it take place, and where?' This came from Emma Kate as she nibbled her bacon.

'I'm not sure. I must speak with Andrew and Mama will speak to Mrs Ellsworth.' Heather added a drop more milk into her teacup.

'Oh, it's so exciting!' Phoebe grinned.

Heather laughed at her, caught up in her enthusiasm. 'Yes,

14

it is.'

Grace sat at the table and looked up at Partridge, the senior parlour maid, who filled her teacup. 'Has Miss Letitia slept late again?'

'Yes, Miss.' The maid nodded. 'She didn't stir when I opened the curtains in her room this morning.'

Grace frowned and turned to Heather. 'Letitia's behaviour is becoming increasingly odd of late.' She buttered her toast.

Heather sighed. 'I'll try to talk to her later, though her sullenness is beyond my understanding. She might confide in you about what is bothering her, she won't tell me.'

'I don't understand what the problem could be and Letitia confides in no one.' Grace shook the worrying thoughts of her middle sister from her mind and turned to Phoebe. 'Mr Booth will be here shortly for your lesson. I suggest you hurry.'

'Oh dear, I really wish he'd stop coming.' Phoebe sighed dramatically. 'Mr Booth scowls at me! I have no true gift for playing the piano.'

'Well, if you practiced more, he would praise you more!' Emma Kate chuckled, dabbing her napkin to her mouth.

Phoebe pouted. 'I must speak to Mama about it. We don't have a governess any longer, so why should we have a piano tutor? I've learnt all there is to know!'

Gabriella rose. 'I shall see if Father will share his carriage into town, does anyone want to join me?'

They all shook their heads.

Gaby placed her hands on her hips. 'I'd prefer not to as well, but Father's temper at the waste of using another carriage would be worse than sharing the fifteen minute journey with him.'

'Shhh, Gaby. Don't speak so.' Heather stared at her, appalled. 'Besides, Father has already left.'

'Damnation!'

'Gabriella!' Grace admonished. Her sister's outrageous behaviour and unladylike manners were at times too much. At twenty-one years of age, Gabriella was a mass of complexity underneath her tomboyish exterior. Of all her sisters, Gaby was the one to speak out of turn and be argumentative. Pretty like her sisters, her hair was a lighter shade of chestnut than the others, except Phoebe who was nearly golden blonde.

'I shall ride to Morgan's Farm then,' Gaby announced.

'Do you think that wise?' Heather fiddled with her napkin. 'I mean, Mr Morgan has no female living in his home, now his last sister has married, and people will talk.'

'Oh, Heather don't be so prudish! Rest assured I'll do nothing to diminish your chances with dear Mr Ellsworth. Not that anything would, Father will not allow it.'

'That was uncalled for!' Heather flashed back.

'Tell Mama I'll be home at noon,' Gaby called back on her way out.

Heather gaped. 'I find it amazing how easily Gaby can get away with offending someone and not be sorry about it.'

'To Gaby, words are simply words, they mean very little to her.' Grace pushed her chair back and rose. With her appetite appeased, she turned to the numerous jobs awaiting her attention. She walked to the window curtains to inspect their cleanliness.

'Well it is wrong of Gaby to be so thoughtless.'

'You know she is impulsive. She means no harm.' Grace turned to Faith, Emma Kate and Phoebe. 'Come along, all of you. Mama will want to discuss the wedding with you and I have work to do.'

Unsatisfied by the curtains' freshness, Grace left the room to speak to Fernly about it.

* * *

GRACE SIGHED at the slight tapping on the door. She would never get these blessed accounts done.

Partridge poked around the side of the study door. 'Miss Woodruff, I'm sorry to disturb you, but the butcher's new assistant has made a mistake with the order and he won't take it back. Mrs Hawksberry is nearly ready to strike him! I thought it best to come and get you, as I can't find Mr Fernly.'

'Very well, Partridge, I'm coming.'

As she followed the maid along the hall, she mentally listed her jobs still to do and the duties to assign to the staff. The linen needed checking for wear and tears, the flowers must be changed in the drawing room before Mr Ellsworth arrived, she required a meeting with the head gardener about the new hothouse being built, plus a number of other things she couldn't remember right now.

She turned right and stepped down into a narrower hallway leading to the service areas of the house. At intervals along the corridor were small rooms; the boot room where Johnny, the odd job boy, did most of his work; the gun room; a couple of storage rooms and finally the butler's and Mrs Hawksberry's personal quarters. Out of habit, she looked into each of the rooms to check what work was being carried out as she passed.

Grace thanked Partridge, as the maid held open the large blue baize door leading into the large kitchen. Walking down the three shallow steps, Grace was instantly assailed with warmth and noise.

In the middle of the stone-flagged floor stood a pine table measuring twelve feet by six feet. This table, nearly white from the daily scrubbing it received, was the main business area of the room. Maids chopped, diced, sliced, pounded, juiced, sieved and peeled all manner of vegetables, herbs, meats and dry goods supplied by the estate's own home farm and other merchants from town. The ceiling was high, twenty feet at the loftiest point in the middle where the timber rafters peaked and met in the vaulted ceiling. From these rafters hung steel storage baskets raised and lowered by pulleys and ropes. Mrs Hawksberry stood by the immense range, stirring a large copper pot with a wooden spoon.

Grace raised an eyebrow. 'Well, Mrs Hawksberry, what is all the fuss about? It must be important to have me interrupted.'

'Why it's nowt at all, Miss Grace.' Mrs Hawksberry replied offhanded.

Grace saw through the masquerade. 'And the butcher's assistant?'

'Gone now, Miss Grace.'

'What was all the fracas about?'

Mrs Hawksberry gave the evil eye to Partridge who stood cowering behind Grace. 'It were nowt, Miss. Partridge had no right to get yer. The kitchen is my domain, as you know Miss, and I run it how I see fit. You weren't needed to be bothered.'

'Well, I was bothered, so tell me.'

'A mix up with the order that's all, Miss. The new assistant tried to put one over on me. He's not used to my ways, but I soon sorted him out!' Her anger shook her great frame, wobbling her rolls of fat the same as when she laughed.

'You nearly cracked his skull with the wooden spoon just because he mentioned the account payment was late,' Partridge blurted out, from her spot behind Grace.

'Aye, and if I did then it's nowt to do with you, Norma Partridge! And to run tittle-tattling to Miss Grace! Well, I should be clouting you one an' all!' Mrs Hawksberry puffed, waving the wooden spoon in the air. Dollops of white liquid flew off the spoon like spittle off a rabid dog.

Grace frowned. 'What is this about late payment? No account should be paid late. I give my father the bills we receive in plenty of time for payment.'

'Aye, that's what I told the lad. He'd made a simple mistake.'

Grace nodded. 'Very well.' She turned to Partridge. 'Do not come to me again unless there is an immediate emergency, understand? I have enough to do without this nonsense.' She stormed from the kitchen, going back along the corridor until suddenly stopping. Through an opened door, she could see into the butler's pantry and found old Fernly bent over a table in the middle of the room.

'Fernly?' It was clear something was wrong with him. 'What is it? Are you ill?'

Fernly tried to straighten, but instead swayed, dangerously close to falling over. Grace took the old man's arm and helped him to a nearby wooden chair. 'Stay where you are, I'm calling for the doctor.'

'No, Miss Grace. I'm perfectly all right ...'

'Don't get up again. I'll be back in a minute.' She left the room and met Partridge in the corridor.

Grace had the doctor sent for and one of the outside workmen to come in and help put Fernly to bed. 'I want him looked after, Partridge. You mustn't allow him out of bed. His colour is not good.'

'But, Miss, who'll see to the front rooms?' Partridge's little brown eyes widened.

Grace massaged her temples. 'Er...where is O'Reilly?'

Partridge looked away back to the figure on the bed, before coming beside Grace to whisper the maid was ill.

'Ill? Does the doctor need to attend to her, too?'

Partridge shook her head. 'She's been sick all morning and was outside drawing fresh air into her lungs. She said something she ate disagreed with her. Shall I go find her?'

'Yes.' Grace sighed and rubbed a hand over her eyes as she headed back along the hallway.

It was not yet midday, but she'd been busy since first light. She must speak more forcibly to father about acquiring a house-keeper. Mrs McPherson, their former housekeeper, had retired and was sorely missed; though Grace was sure no one missed the old housekeeper as much as she. For it was she who'd stepped into the role of housekeeper, as well as a second mother to her sisters and at times a hostess for her father's parties when her mother feigned illness.

However, it was all becoming a little too much and Grace was weary of it. Her mother was mistress of this house not she, and both her parents were the caretakers of their daughters until they were married. So, why did all the work and worry fall on her shoulders?

Grace knew she was too indulgent with her mother, and Diana had happily relinquished the reins of the house and its responsibilities. Her father was equally selfish and assumed Grace would deal with everything. She received very little help from her sisters in the management of the house. They really didn't have the slightest notion of what it took to organize staff and run a home the size of Woodruff House, nor did they care. Each was happy in their own way and, as long as Grace held everything in place, then they were content to go along as ever.

Only Grace wasn't. She wanted the freedom they had, and the lack of responsibilities. They all assumed, even her parents, that because she wasn't actively looking for a husband she wouldn't mind taking care of the house. It was as if they thought she had nothing better to do with her time. They all envisioned Grace would remain an old maid, and looking after them would give her something to do. If only they knew her heart had been given since childhood.

Grace stepped onto the bottom tread of the staircase as Heather came out of the drawing room opposite.

'Are you going out?'

Grace paused. 'No, why?'

'Andrew will be arriving soon, and I'd be much more at ease with him if you were present.' Heather fiddled with the mother-of-pearl buttons on her pale blue dress.

'I have a lot to do, Heather. Mama can be with you, surely?'

'Please, Grace, you know how wonderful you are with people and I'm...' The clang of the front door bell interrupted her.

Heather looked at Grace in alarm. Movement from above their heads caused them to look up and see Phoebe descending.

'That'll be Mr Booth. He's over an hour late.' Phoebe haughtily stared at the door. 'Grace, tell him I'm busy now or out. I have no time for piano today.'

'I'll do no such thing,' Grace replied, as the bell clanked again.

'Where is Fernly?' Heather demanded to know, looking down the length of the hallway as though expecting him to appear out of the walls.

'He is ill, and Partridge is busy.'

'How inconvenient!' Phoebe muttered, turning to go back to her room.

'I'll answer the door, shall I?' Grace gave both her sisters a pointed look.

She was surprised to see their visitor was a young man dressed in the recent style, only the fabric of his clothes was of poor quality. He was quite handsome in a dusky-featured sort of way, with nearly black eyes, olive skin and thick curly hair, which sprang around his head now he'd taken his hat off.

'Good day.' He bowed. 'Is Miss Grace Woodruff at home? I wish to convey a message to her.' He spoke perfect English with a touch of a French accent.

'I am she.' Grace smiled as the information startled the young man. He'd obviously thought she was a servant answering the door, and the dark dress she wore did nothing to dispel his first impression.

'My name is Monsieur du Pont.' He grinned, revealing a dimple in his left cheek. 'My uncle, Mr Booth, is unwell and unable to make his appointment today.'

Grace, aware of Heather and Phoebe standing at her back, opened the door wider. 'Will you please come in, Monsieur du Pont?'

Grace waited until Phoebe had taken his hat and coat and rejoined them in the drawing room, before introducing her sisters. 'I'm sorry to hear of Mr Booth's indisposition. I hope it is not of a serious nature?' Grace said, when they'd taken their seats.

'No, not at all. Gout I believe.' du Pont gazed about the room then back to Grace.

She nodded. 'Oh, most painful.'

Phoebe edged forward on her seat. 'It will keep him from tutoring for some time?'

Grace nudged her with her knee.

'Yes, I think it may,' du Pont acknowledged. 'However, he has asked me to continue his work while I'm in England.'

'You too are a piano tutor?' Grace asked.

'No, not a tutor. I study music in Paris, but family circumstances now keep me in England for a short time.'

Grace switched her gaze from the young man to Phoebe and noticed her youngest sister staring at du Pont in a most embarrassing way.

Du Pont stood and from his inner breast pocket he pulled out a letter, handing it to Grace. 'My uncle asks if you'd want my services until he is ready to resume.'

Grace read the letter then looked at Phoebe. 'My sister Phoebe has recently told me of her desire to discontinue with her tutoring. She feels her talents are at level where Mr Booth can no long be of use. Isn't that so, Phoebe?'

Phoebe opened her mouth to speak then quickly closed it again. Her flustering made Grace raise her eyebrows. Booth was an old fossil, boring and unimaginative and she'd only kept his services to give Phoebe some discipline that their parents neither had the time nor wish to instil in her. Since the governess's dismissal, Phoebe had become a trifle unruly. Nevertheless, Grace's frown deepened, the alternative was to allow Phoebe and this charming young man to spend two hours every week side by side. Phoebe was young, and most certainly didn't have an intelligent thought in her head, but she might learn some decorum, and sensibility while under du Pont's instruction. Lord knows she never took a blind bit of notice of old man Booth.

Phoebe raised her chin to look down her nose at du Pont. 'I believe I would like to have Monsieur du Pont tutor me, Grace. I feel, as he's studied in Paris, he may have more to offer me.'

Grace rolled her eyes. 'Very well. We'll come to some arrangement.'

While Phoebe showed Monsieur du Pont the piano in the parlour, the doorbell clanged again and once more Grace answered it, as it seemed her staff had all but disappeared for the present. She welcomed Andrew Ellsworth, and after passing his outer clothes to the now apparently recovered maid, O'Reilly, she took him into the drawing room to where Heather waited nervously.

'I'll arrange for some refreshments and ask Phoebe and the Monsieur to join us, shall I?' Grace watched Heather and Mr Ellsworth gaze at each other. Both wore heightened colour in their cheeks.

'I will go!' Heather was out of the room before Grace could reply.

'Would it be bad manners to ask if Heather is as nervous as I am?' A shy smile lifted the corners of Ellsworth's mouth as he asked the question.

'Indeed, you are right, sir.'

'Please, call me Andrew. I believe plans are afoot for us to become family.'

Grace inclined her head. 'Then you must call me Grace.' She gestured for him to be seated. 'I hope you don't mind my saying I was made aware of the nature of this visit.'

A slight flush crept up his neck above his starched collar. 'I did not think it would be something kept secret for long.'

'Please do not think Heather broke a confidence. Our Father informed us together of his plans.' Grace swallowed and glanced at the doorway. 'May I be blunt?'

He nodded once.

'Is this what you really want?'

He let out his breath slowly. 'I am twenty-seven years old, Miss Woodruff. I feel the time is right for me to choose a bride.'

'But is Heather the bride you choose or was she chosen for you?'

'I did have some say in the matter, but of course my parents needed to be consulted.' He frowned. 'Do you think your sister is indifferent to me?'

'She hardly knows you.' Grace paused to pick the right words to say. 'Heather is a kind soul, Mr Ellsworth — Andrew. She is loyal and dependable. I know she will give you everything she has to offer. Should you earn her love, you will have it for life.'

'I ask for no more, Miss Woodruff — Grace.' He smiled in apparent relief. 'I believe this union will be most successful.'

'Despite our fathers' dealing?'

Shocked, he drew back a little, his smile faltered. 'It-it is not uncommon for two families to…to …'

Grace regarded him as he stuttered. 'Come, Andrew, I am not naïve to the world, but let us be clear on one thing. No matter what my father and yours decide in business, *you* will make Heather a fine husband or answer to me for the consequences.'

'But, Miss Woodruff…'

Grace held up her hand. 'I realize you must think me insufferably rude and certainly you must regard me as interfering, but my role for many years has been to safe-guard my sisters in every way. I do not apologize for my directness. Their happiness comes first. Always.'

'I understand this and admire you for it.' Andrew stood and held out his hand.

Grace rose and took it. 'Then we shall talk no more of this.'

The door opened, and Heather entered full of smiles and nervous excitement. 'Mama's headache has gone, and she has decided to come down to join us for tea.'

CHAPTER 3

*W*oodruff stomped his feet to keep them warm in the freezing hovel Olive called home. His nose was red and no doubt would soon drip. Olive pulled her shawl closer around her shoulders. The shawl's threadbare state did little to indicate it was once beautiful. Its colour had faded as her claims to looks and youth had.

'I'll not be drinking that, so don't waste your time.' He scowled at her as she carefully poured weak tea into two chipped china cups. 'Your money is on the bed. I don't care what you do with it, but don't ever come to me again, do you hear?'

Olive sighed. 'This is your child.'

Woodruff laughed with false humour. 'You have proof do you?' The tattered black skirt and jacket she wore barely covered the mound of her stomach. She was ill, with what he didn't know. The flesh seemed stripped from her bones. If the birth didn't kill her then the poorhouse would soon after. She had no way of earning a living now she was large with pregnancy and he had made it clear he wouldn't help her again after today. If he had complete proof the child was his, and a boy, then he'd take it the moment it took its first breath, but the chance that she was playing him for a fool kept him quiet.

'I went with no one while I had you.'

'You think I believe you?'

'I want you to take the baby when it's born. Give it to a good family who'll raise it well. You must know someone.' It was the longest she had talked since his arrival and the effort took its toll. She looked as though she hadn't eaten a decent meal in weeks.

He glanced away. 'Don't be absurd.'

'If you don't, it will die too. You want that? He may be a boy; the only one you'll ever have.' Olive stumbled and sat on her one chair.

'I'll not fall for that!' Disgust at her frailty filled him. 'You think you can make me a laughing stock?'

'No, I just want my baby to have a good home, a family, all the things I never had,' Olive whispered. Tiredness bruised the skin under her eyes. 'I don't mind what happens to me as long as the child is cared for.'

'I've given you all I'm going to give. Do *not* contact me again!'

'When the time comes I'll send word.'

'No!' Anger threatened to choke him. Why wouldn't she shut her mouth?

'He's yours.'

'Nonsense.' He took a step towards her, rage blinded him. 'Make trouble for me, slut, and I'll finish you!'

He hated being out of control and his hands shook. Olive glanced at the money on the bed. It taunted her, he knew. She may look like death rode her shoulder, but she would eat again soon. She would continue to live, if only for a while. In a moment of weakness, he took out his slim leather pouch and threw more gold coins onto the bed.

Leaving the dirty, damp room, Woodruff made his way down the dark narrow staircase of the tenement building. In the bleak alley, he shivered as a rat ran over his highly polished boots and scuttled away into a heap of snow-covered rubbish piled against the brick walls of a nearby building. Sewage ran down the cluttered gutters of the cobbled lane, making its own small dams. From somewhere in the recesses of the ugly building opposite, a scream shattered the stillness.

Woodruff paused and looked up at the soot coated walls. For a moment, the thought of his child living here angered him. That his conscience admitted Olive carried his child frightened him. *A boy child?* Shocked at his feelings, he strode, looking neither left nor right, to where his carriage waited him in the next street. He was uneasy having left Sykes alone, waiting around in back alleys where ragamuffins and urchins could set upon his expensive carriage.

In the past, he'd always hired a hansom cab to take Olive to some room in a local inn or his own cottage on the outskirts of town. This was his first view of where she actually lived, and his mouth turned down in disgust at the way people allowed themselves to exist. His journey into the slums of Leeds only reaffirmed his feelings about the lower classes and their filthy lives and habits. He made a mental note to stop Grace and the others from donating their time to the charities of the poor. He'd not have his money given to such scum.

* * *

LATER THAT EVENING THE FAMILY, except Diana, sat around the dining table. Grace mentally checked the room's presentation. Two silver candelabras set down the middle of the long, elegant table gave the dining room a warm glow, helped by the lamps on the serving dressers along the walls and the blazing fire at the end of the room. A bowl of hothouse lilies sat on the wine cabinet against the wall. The red damask curtains hung straight. Partridge and O'Reilly stood near the door ready to bring in the meal. Everything looked perfect. She let out a breath and nodded to the maids to start. Her father wouldn't find anything to complain about.

The meal progressed in silence, and, at intervals, Grace glanced at her sisters. As usual, the girls did not talk while eating, unless Woodruff asked them a direct question. Sometimes, depending on his mood, he would let them discuss his question or some other point of news as long as it interested him. He forbade all subjects of fashion, parties and friends. Only when guests dined did the Woodruff girls relax, knowing their father would control the conversation with their visitors, leaving the younger girls to whisper amongst themselves.

Her father poured himself a glass of wine. Over the bottle, he glanced at Heather. 'So, daughter, you and the Ellsworth boy come to an understanding. He called to see me at my offices later today to ask for your hand. I gave it, of course.'

'Of course,' Grace whispered under her breath.

Woodruff heard it and cast her a disparaging look, but didn't comment. Instead, he stared at Heather.

Heather smiled slightly. 'Yes, we came to an understanding. He is a good man and I think we will be happy together.'

'Has your useless excuse of a mother invited Jane Ellsworth to visit to discuss the setting of dates?' Woodruff drank deeply of the rich burgundy wine.

'I believe a letter was sent this afternoon,' interrupted Grace. She had done it herself on behalf of her mother who pleaded a headache. Grace, who knew her father so well, had written and sent the letter immediately so he wouldn't have reason to ridicule.

'Good. I want you married within six months. We don't want to give Ellsworth time to change his mind!'

'Six months? Surely a year is more appropriate?' Grace said, quickly covering her sisters' collective gasps of surprise.

'Blow a year! No, six months or less.'

Grace raised her chin. 'There is a lot to prepare, Father.'

'I'll let you have the whole trimmings, if you don't go mad with the expense, but I want Heather safely married into the Ellsworth family soon. I know Ellsworth declined an offer from Todd Jollings. He might be wealthy, but his daughter is as ugly as a shovel full of worms. Thank God you lot are worth looking at. Still, I want the deal done.'

Used to her father's lack of manners, Grace ignored his comment and indicated to Partridge to clear away. 'Neither Mr Ellsworth nor Andrew will renege on their promise, you know that. So, why the hurry?'

Woodruff peered at O'Reilly as she placed his dessert bowl in front of him. All colour faded from the maid's face and she leaped away as though he'd burnt her. He centred his attention back on Heather. 'I want to be a grandfather. Try to make me one as soon as possible, understand? Both Ellsworth and I want grandsons, lots of them. So, make sure you do your duty. I'll not have any daughter of mine being fussy about the marriage bed, you hear me?' He stared at seven shocked faces and cursed, 'Bloody women!' before throwing down his napkin and striding from the room.

Grace gazed forlornly at Heather. Tears shimmered in Heather's eyes, threatening to spill over. 'Don't cry, dearest. You know what he's like.'

Heather nodded, before bursting into tears.

'Go, all of you. Go and see Mama, but don't tell her what has happened. Say we'll be up soon.' Grace rose from her chair and walked around to her sister's side.

'Oh, Grace, he's so…so foul!' Heather sobbed.

'I know, but think of it this way, soon you'll be away from him and with the Ellsworths. Besides, you'll always have Andrew to care for you, and he won't let father speak to you so rudely. So, cheer up and forget him.'

'I cannot wait to leave here.' Heather wiped her eyes with a white lace handkerchief.

Grace nodded and sighed. *Yes, you will go, dearest Heather, like they all will, but I shall stay and forever bear the brunt of father's temper and mother's woes.*

* * *

GRACE STROLLED AROUND THE LIBRARY. She wished she could snap out of this awful feeling of bitter resentment. Family life was changing, as nature intended, but it didn't give her the joy it should. The world held no attraction, gave her no pleasure.

She shook her head at this apathy, but could not resist indulging in self-pity for a few minutes. In the last month, the family had busily prepared themselves for Heather and Andrew's engagement party, which her father, in his wisdom, decided would be held at Woodruff House, giving her more work. The recent passing of their elderly butler, Fernly, gave them some sadness. After all, Fernly was a part of the house, a part of their lives, even if they hadn't really appreciated him and his tireless work.

The butler's death had put her father in a fine mood. He ranted for days about how his personal belongings would be neglected now Fernly wasn't there to attend to them. As usual, Grace was given the task of setting things to right again. She glanced down at the newspaper folded on the desk. The advertisement she had written for a new butler was at the top of the first column. She nibbled her fingernails. She was to start interviewing this very day and wondered whether she could manage the task. A lot depended on the butler being the right person for the family.

Stepping closer to the window, Grace glanced furtively back at the door. Slowly, she pulled out a gold chain from under the high collar of her navy and white pinstriped dress. Suspended from the chain was a gold locket. Pressing the small catch, the locket sprang open and she smiled down at the miniature portrait staring back at her. William Ross, a distant cousin on her mother's side and the love of Grace's heart. She had not seen him in over five years, and received only one letter from him since.

Gazing out of the window at the lashing rain, she wondered where the years had gone. How had she managed to keep one man's name and face in her heart for such a length of time from just one perfect summer? She should be like Heather and the others and be interested in marrying, but something always made her shy away from any courteous attentions of eligible men at social gatherings. So much so, they were beginning to call her cold, stern, and an old maid, but she cared nothing for that. She wouldn't settle for anyone else simply because William wasn't meant to be.

Grace tucked the locket and chain back under her collar, cursing herself for being so ridiculous in keeping one summer alive. Who knew what William really thought of her, or even if he remembered her still? For all she knew he could be married with a nursery full of children by now, though she secretly doubted it. His mother, Verity and her mother had kept up their correspondence and Grace was always careful to listen to her mother talk of those letters and what was happening in the Ross family. Never once had a marriage been mentioned.

'Excuse me, Miss Grace, but the first applicant is here. I put him in the study,' Partridge announced from the doorway.

'Thank you.' Grace shook herself from her memories and followed the maid.

An hour later, Partridge showed the fourth applicant into the study, another two still waited in the hallway.

Grace smiled and beckoned the young man to a seat opposite the desk. 'My name is Miss Grace Woodruff. You are?'

'William Doyle.' He returned the smile.

Grace's head jerked at the mention of his Christian name. Having earlier thought of her own William, it sent shivers down her back and she silently reprimanded herself for such foolishness. It was a common enough name.

'I'm called Billy by my family though.' He grinned.

Grace nodded. He possessed good clean-shaven features. His velvety brown eyes appeared honest and his dark hair was cut short. He was the youngest butler she had interviewed, for he only seemed to be in his early twenties and she referred to this straight away. 'You are young for the post.'

Doyle's face became impassive. 'I was trained by my uncle, who is head butler at the Yallman estate, east of York.'

'I've heard of that estate. It's one of the grandest in Yorkshire.'

A wry smile lifted the corners of his mouth. 'Yes, apparently.'

'You don't agree?'

'It's not my place to say, Miss Woodruff.'

'But you have an opinion?'

'I lived there all my life. I know what is real, what is false.'

'I see you have a reference from Lord Yallman and the housekeeper there.' Grace picked up the papers he'd placed on her desk when taking his seat. 'Why did you leave? I presume you would have taken your uncle's position in due course?'

Doyle shrugged. 'Maybe I would have, but it was no longer to my liking.'

'Woodruff House is vastly different from Yallman, surely you could aim higher.'

'If I may interrupt, Miss Woodruff?'

'Yes?'

'I would like nothing more than to work for a family in a much smaller house on a much smaller wage, *if* it means I am left to my own devices.'

'Meaning?' She frowned at the strange question.

'That I do my job as a butler, nothing else.' Doyle was emphatic. His eyes turned from brown velvet to polished black stone.

'Undoubtedly you would be the butler, though here that also

means taking care of my father's personal belongings too. My father is a complicated man, and he has never been keen on the idea of a valet, so you would have to include his needs in your duties. Is that acceptable?' Grace looked sharply at him, for she sensed he was keeping something from her.

'Yes, Miss Woodruff.' Doyle held her direct gaze, but a pulse beat along his jaw. 'May I know something of the family I would be taking care of, should I attain the position?'

'There are my parents, myself and my six sisters, plus the indoor staff.'

'Six sisters?' His eyes grew wide.

Ignoring his reaction, she continued, 'Regarding the outside staff, there is a man who is in charge of each area, and they are answerable to my father or myself.'

Doyle frowned but said nothing. 'The number of staff?'

'There are two parlour maids, one upstairs maid, Mrs Hawksberry, three kitchen maids, a scullery girl and a boot boy.'

'Only one upstairs maid?'

'Yes, though that is to be rectified. Hopeland is a good worker, but she needs help since our other chambermaid married last month. I am yet to replace her.'

'I see.'

'Have you ever been in trouble with the law, Mr Doyle?'

Her directness startled him. 'No, Miss.'

'Do you drink spirits?'

'No, Miss. The odd ale on a festive day maybe.'

She tapped her fingernails on the desk. Mr Doyle was like a breath of fresh air. For so long the house had been filled with women and apart from her father, the only male had been old Fernly. Her father refused to hire permanent footmen, as he thought them too often impertinent, and did nothing but flirt with the maids. She wondered at her father's reaction if she hired Mr Doyle, a healthy and good-looking young male. Glancing at Doyle, she rose. 'Excuse me a moment, will you, please?' Grace walked to the door and look down the hall. Two men sat waiting, both upright, men of her father's age, exact replicas of the previous applicants.

Impulsively, Grace made a decision and a spark of defiant satisfaction made her grin.

Entering the study once more, she went to stand behind the desk. There was something about Mr Doyle that interested her. But was she about to make a big mistake? She lifted her chin. 'Mr Doyle, I am willing to give you a trial period of four weeks. If, at the end of that time, you or I find the situation not to our liking then your employment will be terminated. Agreed?'

'Agreed.' Doyle held out his hand and Grace shook it.

CHAPTER 4

*G*race! Grace!' Heather hurried into the drawing room where Grace stood directing gardeners, who were removing furniture.

Grace glanced at the slip of paper she held. Her list never seemed to diminish, and the sole responsibility of the evening's engagement party, rested heavily on her shoulders. The desire to run and hide from it all played seriously on her mind. 'What is it, Heather?'

'The extra flowers haven't arrived, and Mama desperately wants to make sure they are correct.'

'The flowers will be here at one o'clock, as I instructed.'

'Mama...'

'Mama will have to wait, Heather. I have enough to do. Father has invited far too many people, and space is a problem. Who would have thought a house with a large drawing room, parlour, dining room and library would be too small?' Grace rubbed her temple to ease the tension pulsing there. Weeks of preparations had nearly exhausted her. She received little or no help at all from her family. Her father wanted everything to be at its best without being bothered with details. Heather was too nervous for its success to be of use to anyone, and Diana was so terribly worried over her role as hostess to such a large gathering she was nearly insensible!

The anxiety in Heather's clear, gray eyes made Grace soften her tone. 'Everything will turn out fine, if you leave me to deal with it. The drawing room is empty now and when the carpets are removed, the floor will receive a final polish. We don't need many flowers in here since this is the dancing area, but I will have some of the displays put on stands behind the quartet.'

'Have all the extra staff arrived?' Heather wrung her hands. 'I noticed a young woman dusting near the banister. How many are there? Who will watch them to make certain they don't steal? And does Mrs Hawksberry have enough help? We don't want any disasters with the food. Oh, and you must speak to Letitia, she is acting strangely again. And Gaby refuses to wear her new dress! I assured her it looked wonderful, but...'

'Enough, Heather,' Grace snapped. 'You are sending me mad!'

Heather stepped back, her eyes filling with tears. 'Oh, I'm sorry. Please, forgive me.'

'Never mind all that now.' Grace dismissed her wearily. 'Go and appease Mama, while I check things in the kitchen, and let Gaby wear whatever she pleases!'

As Heather left the room, Doyle entered. He had been working at Woodruff House for three weeks and Grace wondered how she ever managed without him. No longer did she have to tolerate the petty squabbles or problems of the servants or delegate each and every task. Within a week of taking his post, he organized a formal meeting with all the staff one night and told them Miss Woodruff was not to be bothered and they should come to him with their concerns. He lightened the load for her and it revealed how inept Fernly had become before he died, poor man.

The lack of a housekeeper meant Doyle had control of the female staff, an unusual situation and one that must be addressed, but Grace marvelled at how easily he won everyone's confidence. She was shamed by her father's tight-fisted house money. He wanted his house run expertly but with only minimal staff. However, under Doyle's supervision, the staff worked better than ever.

'So Doyle, is everything all right?' Grace asked him.

'Yes, Miss Woodruff. I've supplemented the servants' quarters with more pallets and shown the hired staff where they are to sleep in the attics. The guest rooms are aired and made ready, leaving Hopeland free to assist the ladies in their preparation. The dining room is decorated, and the additional tables are set up, with only the hot food to come out later. The cases of champagne glasses are unpacked and washed. Hiring extra staff has made a difference all round. I've finished giving them their instructions for tonight. I'm confident they will do their jobs admirably.'

Grace acknowledged his professionalism with a nod. 'Good. I noticed the silver is looking splendid. The dining room is a credit to you, Doyle.'

'Thank you, Miss. When the flowers arrive, they'll add to the splendour of the house.'

'Yes, indeed. We are fortunate to have such a beautiful home. It may not be as grand as others, but I believe it has its own charm.'

'I agree, Miss.' Doyle gave her a wry grin.

She glanced down at her list. 'I will enquire in the kitchen to see if everything is organized.'

'I took the liberty, Miss. Mrs Hawksberry is charging along like a steamboat in a great swell.' He gave another ghost of a smile. 'No problems have arisen yet.'

Grace finally let herself relax. 'Thank you.'

'Perhaps you might find the chance to rest a while yourself, Miss. I'll call should you be needed.'

Doyle's concern made her sigh deeply as she went upstairs.

How was it this butler worried over her when her own family did not?

The noise of her sisters dressing assaulted Grace the moment she reached the landing. Gone was the feeling of harmony from minutes ago. She wondered whether her sisters knew what peace and quiet meant. Hopeland, looking harassed, darted from bedroom to bedroom at the mercy of the family's demands. Grace knew exactly how she felt. She weighed up her chances of reaching her bedroom undetected, but only took two steps when Phoebe came rushing out of her room and knocked straight into her.

'Phoebe!' Grace was too tired to put up with such nonsense.

'I'm sorry, but tell me, do Mama's pearls look better than Grandmama's rubies?' She held one necklace up at a time.

'They both are lovely, but the rubies aren't suitable for your age.'

Both Letitia and Emma Kate walked out of their rooms at the same time and, seeing Grace, they both started speaking at once.

'Grace, Mama wants you to...'

'Oh Grace, can you...'

'Stop!' Grace put up both hands to warn them off. The night had not yet begun, and she already wanted nothing more than to lie down. 'I cannot listen to you all at once. Letitia, you first.'

'Mama would like you to advise her on the shoes she wishes to wear.' Letitia tossed her black hair over her shoulder and gave Emma Kate and Phoebe a superior look.

Phoebe poked her tongue out and clutching the jewellery, spun on her heel and dashed back into her bedroom.

Grace raised a questioning eyebrow at Letitia, knowing all too well how her sister liked to rile the others. 'Tell Mama I'll be along shortly.' She watched Letitia saunter back to their mother's room before turning to Emma Kate. 'Yes?'

Emma Kate held out her stocking and showed her a slight tear in the silk. 'What am I to do? There isn't time to mend it and it's my last pair.'

'Come with me.' Grace sighed and stepped towards her own room. 'I have some to spare.' Sometimes, being the eldest was a heavy burden.

* * *

DOYLE STOOD by the entrance to the drawing room and appraised the efforts of his staff with a critical eye. So far, the evening was going well. Guests ate, danced, talked, and thankfully smiled. The speeches were over and many toasts drunk. Hired footmen circulated with trays of crystal flutes filled with bubbling champagne and he made a mental note to commend them all at breakfast in the morning. He only wished the extra staff could stay on as permanent fixtures. He pondered the reason why a proud man like Woodruff would allow his house to be run on limited staff. The man enjoyed his comforts, demanded them as his right. So, why the miserly administration?

A roar of wild laughter swung his gaze towards Woodruff, and his disdain for his employer rose another level. In the three weeks of his employment, there had been many a time when he wanted to pack his belongings and leave because he hated serving as Woodruff's personal valet. Really, both tasks were too much for one man. He wondered why Woodruff, with his pompous nature, didn't insist on a professional valet. Then he remembered the old butler had performed both duties, thereby saving Woodruff in wages.

Whatever the reason, Doyle wished his employer would relent, for he was a butler, a good one too, and had no desire to sort through Woodruff's smalls! The man was an odious brute and his lack of concern and respect for Mrs Woodruff and their daughters made Doyle's blood boil.

His experience at the Yallman estate, with men like Woodruff, with their greed and mental cruelty left a vile taste in his mouth. It was this, plus the Yallman women that made him wary of taking the job. However, he had soon learnt the Woodruff women were refined and respectable ladies. It was his concern for them and his high regard for Grace Woodruff, which kept him here when his principles would have normally told him to move on.

'Everything satisfactory, Doyle?' Grace came to stand at his side.

'Very much so, Miss Woodruff.' He gave her a slight bow, taking in her radiant loveliness. His heart thumped a rapid beat. *Why isn't she inundated with suitors?*

'Excellent.'

Doyle couldn't take his gaze off her as she walked away. The deep violet of her dress was skilfully cut to enhance her slender figure. Over the bustle at her back, the sleek taffeta material cascaded in silver lace-edged magnificence. Her rich honey-coloured hair with its red highlights was prettily arranged on top of her head with fragile tendrils hanging loose to frame her gentle heart-shaped face.

The clanging of the doorbell dissipated Doyle's daydreams and he wrenched himself away from the drawing room to answer it.

* * *

THE FLOWING music of a Johann Strauss waltz floated around the drawing room. Sitting next to Faith, Grace commented that Emma Kate and her dance partner made a lovely couple.

'Yes, they do. His name is Randolph Cahill, I believe.' Faith's gaze followed the couple. 'Andrew's friend.'

'Have you danced?'

Faith smiled. 'Yes, Andrew asked each of us.'

'He hasn't asked me.'

'You were busy in the dining room, I think. Andrew said he would capture you later.' Faith chuckled.

'I think we are lucky to have him as a future brother-in-law. I wasn't happy with the match at first, but Heather has quickly fallen in love with her intended. A marriage containing love has a better chance at success than a marriage without.'

Faith sighed, her face sad. 'Yes, I suppose if we are to acquire a brother-in-law, we could do worse than Andrew.'

They paused to watch Letitia weave gently by with a sallow skinned man. His appearance made Grace hurriedly cover her smile with her fan.

'Who is that?' Faith grimaced.

'I haven't the faintest idea. I think Father has invited every eligible man in the district,' Grace whispered, with a grin, wanting to lighten Faith's mood. 'I believe I wrote invitations to all the oldest and richest unattached men in the county.'

'Well, he has wasted his efforts on me.'

'Oh?' Grace raised her eyebrows. Faith was such a strange creature at times, so prickly and sour.

'I will not marry. Besides, having one sister marry is enough for now. Maybe father will leave the matter alone for a while.'

She turned to look at Faith fully. 'You sound as if you don't want any of us to wed?'

Faith twitched one slender shoulder while plucking at the pale rose material of her skirts. 'No, I do not. I abhor change. I like having my sisters around me.'

Grace's eyes widened in surprise and she sat back in her chair. 'I thought it was only I who felt that way.'

'Do you honestly think we want to marry just anyone to escape Father?'

'Of course not.'

'I know father rules us with a rod of iron, but *husbands* can be a lot worse.' Faith shuddered. 'The thought of the marriage bed fills me with horror.'

Grace softened. 'Come now, it cannot be all bad, especially if you love your husband. Some women find it less than a chore.'

Faith scoffed, 'Who? Whores? No decent woman would enjoy it.'

Surprised, Grace blinked. 'You cannot believe that.'

'Doesn't everyone?'

She'd never seen Faith react or speak so passionately about anything. 'I don't think of marriage as something detestable and neither must you. If you care for someone, you'd be pleased to share everything with him. Look at Heather. She is happy. How can that be bad?'

'Look at Mama and Father.' Her voice had risen and she glanced around to see if anyone had heard. 'Need I say more? Heather has no idea what she is becoming involved with. Husbands *control* you in every way.'

'I had no idea you felt this way.'

'If you took more time to talk to us then you'd appreciate we all feel the same. Well, nearly all.' Faith screwed up her face. 'No one knows what Letitia thinks.'

'*I* take more time?' She leaned forward, ignoring the comment about Letitia. 'When do you think I can manage more time? Who do you think runs this house? If any of you helped me a little, then I could have more time to sit with you!'

Faith's gaze darted around the room once again. 'Keep your voice down. You're drawing attention.' She straightened and adjusted her skirts, clearly showing Grace the conversation had finished.

Not trusting herself to speak, Grace stood and began making her way between the people milling about the room. *How dare Faith speak so?*

A guest stopped her to chat but Grace did not hear the woman's comment as a commotion in the entrance hall caught her attention. Excusing herself, Grace weaved her way into the hall. She halted and stared in surprise. Her mother hugged cousin Verity in the open doorway.

Verity Ross had visibly aged in the years since her last visit, yet Grace knew her immediately. The shock of seeing a Ross in their home again rendered Grace immobile. Snippets of conversation between Diana and Verity penetrated her dazed mind.

'... didn't think you were coming...'

'... the axle broke...'

'... you hurt?...'

'... no, but ...'

'... William with you...'

'... yes, we had to hire a...'

'...come inside, we'll warm you up in my sitting room...'

Grace blinked to clear her frozen mind as her mother and Verity climbed the staircase. If Verity was here, then was William here too? Movement at the door caused Grace to close her eyes. She couldn't bring herself to open them and see the one man she'd longed for since she was sixteen.

'Miss Woodruff?' Doyle inquired at her shoulder.

Startled, she spun to face him, but she was blind to him, blind to everything but the sensation of having William here. Crazily, she wondered if she would swoon like a maiden aunt.

Doyle's hand reached out, but he quickly tucked it behind his back. 'What is it, Miss Woodruff?'

Grace swallowed, feeling the fine hairs on her arms and nape prickle. *He is here.*

'Good evening, Grace.'

At the sound of William's deep velvety voice, her heart stopped beating, only to start again at a rapid pace. Her stomach clenched and her legs felt unable to support her anymore. Slowly, she swivelled to gaze into William's blue-green eyes and knew she was lost again.

William smiled his captivating smile. He had aged, no, matured since their last meeting. He looked leaner, but broader in the shoulders. There was an aura about him, something that females of any age wanted. He made all other men around him seem insignificant. A magnetism, a mystical air surrounded him, catching Grace in its clutches once more.

* * *

SEEING the quiet display of mutual attraction spring between Grace and the stranger, Doyle moved away back down the hall. The ache in his heart was a living thing. In the last few weeks he'd been able to silence it by simply being in her presence and telling himself he mustn't ask for more. Yet, somewhere in the far recess of his soul, he tormented himself with wanting her. He was the world's biggest fool! He knew she saw him as nothing more than a butler. Granted, they got along well. However, she was his employer and he, part of her staff.

He made it to the kitchen without realizing it, and the warmth and noise slapped him out of the misery he'd plunged into. The chaotic kitchen was like a nest of ants, all hurrying and scurrying to and fro, with Mrs Hawksberry in the middle as the queen. He made his way out of the back door and into the illuminated yard. Carriages, drivers and grooms littered the area, enjoying some of Mrs Hawksberry's fine food. He moved away from their small groups, seeking somewhere dark to tend to his wounded heart.

The cool night air sobered him, and he even managed a wry smile at his foolishness. He'd left his former residence because of the insistent advances of Yallman's daughter, and at times, his wife. From the age of sixteen, the daughter made his life a living hell by hiding in dark corners of the enormous ancient house and catching him unawares. Her antics were not of a lady, and definitely not encouraged. The times the noble family spent in London was his one relief, but as the seasons passed, he become conscious he couldn't continue to live that way. He'd been revolted by the brazen displays of both women and couldn't get away from the estate quickly enough. The irony of his present situation made Doyle chuckle without humour. Here he was, for once wanting his employer's daughter, only to find she was taken with another.

'Well, Billy boy! Shall we pack our bags?' he whispered up at the sky's diamond-peppered blackness.

* * *

THE MOMENT WILLIAM had gone upstairs to divest his coat and check on his mother, Grace ran for the study. Thankfully, her father wasn't in there showing off his expensive cigar collection. Grace turned the lock in the door to be safe from intrusion. She wasn't a heavy drinker, and found most spirits not to her taste, but now she headed for the drinks cabinet and poured herself a large measure of brandy.

The first swallow made her gasp, but the amber liquid soon had the desired effect making her feel calmer. With a ragged sigh, she stepped to the window and pushed aside the heavy curtains. The lighting in the room, provided by two gas wall lights, gave her reflection in the window. She stared into her own eyes and critically surveyed her appearance. *Am I enough to hold his interest this time? Can I capture his heart?* The tortured thoughts whirled through her head as the soft music from the drawing room filtered through.

They had first met prior to Grace's seventeenth birthday. He was twenty-eight then. His mother, Verity, recently widowed, longed to escape the memories of nursing a sick husband. She entreated William to take her away from their coastal home for a few months; he agreed. Letters passed between the Ross and Woodruff houses. It was finally decided the widowed Mrs Ross and William would summer at a gentleman's cottage close to Woodruff House. Verity and Diana spent hours reaffirming their childhood friendship and, as a consequence, the girls and William were also thrown together.

His age and worldly manner had been a barrier at first. Grace detested his arrogance and superiority. She thought him cold and distant, and his inclination to ignore them as silly girls who were beneath him irritated her. He treated them with as much tolerance as old dogs do to puppies, until one hot afternoon in late June, four weeks after his arrival.

Diana and the girls had gone to visit Verity at the rented cottage. Grace stubbornly refused to go with them. She'd endured enough of the silent reproof from Verity's tall dark son. The girls' governess was given the afternoon off and Grace tasted freedom. The warmth of the midsummer's day sent her outdoors with an apple and a book. In the orchard, she found a large tree to sit under and dream.

He found her reclining against the tree trunk crunching on her apple. Grace's nervousness at his attention was soon dispelled by their conversation of world events. They talked of the ongoing war in North America and the Maori rebellions in New Zealand among other things.

After she finished her apple, they walked through the orchard and into the open fields surrounding Woodruff House. As the afternoon wore on, she realized she liked his witty conversation and his cool character, which was still somewhat arrogant, but learning more about him showed her the true man, who had taste, sensibility and compassion. His handsome features helped to bring a flutter to her heart and a blush to her cheeks. She began to dream of his strong chiselled face and smiling blue-green eyes. She'd liked the way his rather long hair, raven-black, curled over his collar, and how he ran his fingers through it when he concentrated.

William, being the first man to take notice of her, began to burrow into her heart. Grace knew she was young and I, but she had also developed an early maturity that comes with being the eldest of seven. As the summer wore on, she no longer made excuses not to go to the cottage. She and William encouraged parties and picnics between the two houses. Grace hoped her father would mention something about their growing friendship, but nothing was said. There was to be no hint of William's feelings towards a future together.

At the end of that summer, the Rosses packed up the cottage and prepared to return home to Scarborough. Grace thought her heart would break clean in two without him, but was determined not to show her pain. At the last dinner party before their departure, William gave no promise to Grace that he would write, and unable to bear saying good-bye to him, she feigned illness and left the party early to retire to bed. Alone in her room, she cried until she was sick.

A week later, she received a letter from him, thanking her for her friendship. She wrote back saying it had been a pleasure and she hoped they would meet again soon. They hadn't.

Verity sent William's and her own tiny portraits to Diana the following Christmas. Grace felt she would die from the agony of seeing his face every time she entered her mother's rooms. Over the course of the next year, Grace managed to push his portrait further and further back on one of her mother's cluttered tables, until one day she simply slipped it into her pocket without anyone noticing. She took it to a jeweller's store in town. The end result was the locket that hung secretly around her neck.

Laughter outside the door startled her. She lifted her chin and straightened her shoulders. She wouldn't let propriety stop her from showing William what he'd left behind. He was here, in this house and this time she was older. She must make her feelings plain or he'd leave again for another six years. Wearing her most dazzling smile, she headed back to the party.

The string quartet struck up as Grace entered the drawing room. William stood beside her mother and Verity, but before she could make her way over, Letitia glided across to him and he took her elbow. She watched in frozen fascination as William held her sister and elegantly waltzed about the room. They made a handsome couple, as William towered above Letitia's petite frame.

When the dance finished Grace forced herself to smile and walk calmly to her mother's side. As the music rose to beckon new partners to the floor, William gazed at her and offered her his hand. Grace's heart fluttered wildly. Lowering her lashes, she soaked up the clean scent of him, every inch of her body aware of him.

'It has been some time since we last danced together.' William smiled.

'Yes, it has.' Her thoughts, her heart, her very soul was enraptured by this moment and being in his arms. She cared for nothing else.

'You are much changed.'

'Am I?'

'Oh, yes.' William looked down at her, his expression earnest. 'Tell me about yourself. I have a lot of catching up to do.'

Grace wanted him to be quiet, at least for a little while, to let her absorb this time with him. She didn't have the presence of mind to answer his questions while being in his arms. 'My life has been uneventful,' she murmured, closing her eyes.

The music stopped a short time later and they returned to their mothers. To Grace it felt like amputation when his hand left her elbow. She wanted the connection back and tried to make her hazy mind invent a way of staying with him.

* * *

DIANA WATCHED the attachment grow between Grace and William and frowned at Grace's obvious discomfort whenever William danced with another. She viewed her eldest daughter's attraction with increasing anxiety, for the previous conversation with Verity had revealed the news of William's recent betrothal. She tried in vain to be alone with Grace, but unfortunately, the opportunity kept slipping from her grasp. Saddened, Diana observed as Grace transformed into a glowing vision of happiness every time William looked her way. Grace's lack of propriety dismayed her. It seemed her daughter was intent on letting William, along with everyone, know her feelings. She couldn't understand this new Grace; where was the one they relied on for being sensible?

Little whispers became louder and more frequent as the night wore on. Diana hardly believed her eyes as Grace intentionally gave William all her attention. Panic bubbled in Diana. What could she do? Who could she turn to for help? She caught a glimpse of her husband through the crowd, but immediately dismissed him from her mind. He would be the last person she would ask for help.

'Mama, you must speak to Grace!' Letitia slid up to Diana from behind. She smelt of wine.

Diana placed her fan in front of her mouth so no one could read her lips as she turned her head slightly to Letitia. 'Control your temper, my dearest.'

'It is impossible when Grace monopolizes William! She has kept him eating and talking forever so no one else can dance with him!'

'Put William out of your mind, dear.'

'Why?' Letitia was all interest. She leant closer, stumbling a little.

Diana thought quickly. 'He is penniless. Your father wouldn't allow a union,' she lied.

Disgust etched Letitia's features. 'He's still penniless?' She shivered. 'If I have to marry, he'd better be rich.'

'No doubt he will be, dear.' Diana breathed in relief as Letitia left her. She didn't want to tell Letitia about William's engagement and knew her daughter would delight in passing such information on to Grace to spite her. Diana often wondered why Letitia took pleasure in being mean. It obviously was her father's trait. Diana shuddered. She found it hard to summon strong emotion where Letitia was concerned. She was the one daughter who most resembled her father.

When the party broke up at dawn, Diana lost sight of Grace for a while and when she checked her bedroom she found her daughter asleep. With a heavy heart, she closed the bedroom door and turned towards her rooms. As she passed her husband's bedroom, grunting sounds caused her to pause. The door was ajar. After a moment's hesitation, she gently pushed the door open. Diana clutched at her throat; Her husband's white buttocks filled her vision as he and a hired maid romped on the bed. In their haste, they hadn't bothered to smother the lights or close the door properly. The fine food she'd eaten earlier rose and she dashed for her rooms.

CHAPTER 5

*W*illiam sipped his tea and over the rim of his cup, eyed the daughters of the house, all except Grace who had yet to make an appearance. He grinned as Letitia hid a yawn behind her napkin. The harsh morning light was not kind to her. She clearly needed more sleep. She coyly fluttered her eyelashes at him while stirring her tea, but he refused to take the bait. She shrugged unperturbed. He wondered if her head ached as though a marching band played inside it. The amount of champagne she had drunk last night alarmed him. She drank more than was considered ladylike.

As the girls decided what to do today, they turned their attention to him, wanting his opinion. Squashing a groan, he forced a smile. 'Sorry, I have already made arrangements to meet with friends in Leeds.' He pushed back his chair and stood.

'Are you to be gone all day?' Phoebe asked.

'Phoebe, really! Show some manners!' Heather blushed. 'It is none of your business.'

William bowed slightly. 'I will be back later this afternoon.'

'Shall we have cards tonight or charades?' Phoebe asked. 'I refuse to give up. We must *do* something.'

'You decide, Phoebe. Good day, ladies.' William smiled. As he left the room, he heard their voices clearly.

At the staircase, he met his mother and kissed her cheek. 'Mother.'

'Good morning darling, or is it afternoon?' Verity chuckled.

'I think you've just made it, Mama.' He winked

'Are you going out?'

William paused on the third step. 'Yes. I wrote to Edward of my intention to visit him today. I thought I might while in the area.'

'Give him my regards will you, darling? It's been simply ages since I have seen him.'

'I will.' William took the rest of the steps in twos.

On the landing, he hesitated before Grace's bedroom. He had an awful urge to see her. With a deep sigh, he carried on his way, determined not to make the situation worse. He was quite aware of her fondness for him, since she found it hard to mask it last night. The difficulty was he too felt a resurgence of the old feelings he buried from that lovely summer years ago.

As it had been before, he was unable to offer Grace what she wanted. Six years ago, he had been a young man thrown into confusion by his father's death and the growing debts incurred on the family's estate and now, he was engaged to another. Felicity's face hovered a moment in his mind before he dismissed it. He did not love his intended bride, but did possess genuine warmth for her. No secret was made of why their union came about. Her father, a man descended from nobility, was immensely wealthy and well connected. Upon their marriage, William and his mother would once again live the life to which they were born, and he would save his estate from ruin.

William refused to feel guilty about marrying for money. He'd worked hard in recent years and endeavoured to pay off most of his father's debts. However, he needed more capital, lots of it, to restore the family estate and make it a profitable concern again.

His business ventures were limited at the moment, but with funds and his determination, they would grow and become successful. By marrying Felicity, it guaranteed his name being touted by all who mattered in the business world and his new enterprises would receive interested backers. His plan was a good one.

Only, his plan did not allow the added problem of becoming reacquainted with Grace. She'd been a wonderful memory thrust to the back of his mind in the hard years after that idyllic summer. Never once did he think she might still harbour feelings for him after all this time. Dear God! If he had known, he would have stayed away. Unfortunately, it was too late now. His attraction to her was stronger than before, simply because she had grown into a woman ripe for loving. Not only that, but she was beautiful, intelligent, kind and generous. All a man could want.

William took another step; he must leave here, today. It wasn't fair to Grace to stay.

'William? Is everything all right?'

At the sound of Grace's soft voice, he turned. 'Yes.'

'Are you leaving so soon?' Her amber eyes shone for him, he knew.

'Yes. I have friends to call on before I return to my London townhouse tomorrow.'

'I thought we might go for a ride, like we used to?'

William knew she tried to sound indifferent, but failed miserably. 'My friend is expecting me.'

Grace breathed in deeply. 'May I join you then?'

Surprised, he blinked. 'Join me?'

'Would your friend mind so much?'

He hesitated before his reply. 'No, he wouldn't mind. Shall we ask your sisters too?'

'Let's not.' Grace winked.

* * *

THE CRISP SPRING sunshine added to the cheerful atmosphere of the small gathering on the terrace of Edward Lotherby's house. William's friend and his wife happily welcomed William after nearly a year apart. Edward and William talked for an hour in the drawing room, before Alice Lotherby laughingly ushered them onto the terrace for tea and cake.

Grace found Alice to be a genuine and gracious woman and if Alice thought it odd that Grace was out alone with William, she said nothing of it. Not that Grace cared a jot for what people thought in any case. She wanted to be with William and if that meant flouting social conventions then she would do so. Besides, she'd rather have William than a good reputation.

Alice passed her another cup of tea and Grace smiled with thanks before turning to follow William's every move. She couldn't help it. His intentions to leave tomorrow filled her with dread.

Alice placed a delicate china stand of bite-sized pastries before Grace. 'I am told Woodruff House has magnificent gardens, Miss Woodruff.'

'Yes.' Grace's concentration flickered from William to Alice. 'We are indeed fortunate. Your home is quite splendid too.'

'Thank you. Shall we walk while our tea cools?' Alice was already rising, so Grace could not refuse.

They walked down the terrace's shallow steps and onto a white pebbled path, which swept through the garden. A cool breeze whispered through the treetops, but Grace saw no beauty in the new leaf buds opening towards the sun, or the fresh daffodil trumpets nodding in the dappled shade of the tall birch trees. The intricate layout of the garden design or the burgeoning blossoms in terracotta tubs recently brought from the Lotherby's greenhouses was lost to her gaze as she thought what she must do about William.

They'd talked little in the carriage. Grace felt he held himself back from her, but why, she didn't know. He'd look at her every so often with a quizzical gaze as if he wanted to speak but couldn't. His replies to her questions were stilted and forced, though she tried to look past this and still be her most delightful. She wanted their former easy friendship, but William was proving difficult today. Her belief in herself began to ebb. She was no longer sure she could attract William as she had before. She noticed Alice looking at her and then blushing. She wondered what went through the other woman's mind. Did Alice think her someone pathetic? She shrugged, unconcerned.

Alice daintily cleared her throat. 'You say you haven't seen William for some years?'

Grace smiled, remembering that summer. 'Yes, that is true. Last night was a wonderful surprise.'

'He is a good man, and a great friend to us.'

'I imagine he is a wonderful friend.' She thought of how her heart ached every time she gazed upon him. When he smiled at her, it was as though she was the recipient of a rare and precious gift. The sound of his voice sent shivers along her skin and with one look from his incredible blue-green eyes, she was his slave.

Alice stopped to admire an early spring primrose struggling to open without enough warmth from the sun. 'You must be delighted that William is to marry in the autumn?'

'Pardon?' Grace felt the warmth leave her face.

'I'm sorry, Miss Woodruff. I had hoped you knew.'

'I think you are mistaken, Mrs Lotherby. William is not engaged. He would have told me,' she said, though her tongue felt too big for her mouth.

'We are invited to the wedding, my dear.' Alice's sky blue eyes showed her concern.

'I wasn't informed ...' Grace swayed.

Alice rushed to put an arm around Grace's shoulders. 'I was right to think you have feelings for William.'

Grace nodded, blinking rapidly to forestall her tears from falling. Nausea rose in her throat. It couldn't be true!

'What would you like me to do?'

'Can you arrange for me to be taken home? I do not want to see William.'

'Yes, of course. Come this way through the side door, and when you have gone, I will tell William you felt ill, yes?'

Grace nodded.

* * *

BEFORE DAWN, Grace woke with a shiver. No fire glowed in her grate. It had burnt itself out hours ago when she cried herself to sleep long before the evening meal. Her memory of the day before was hazy, but her pain was sharp. She could not recall the drive home in the hired cab, though she clearly remembered asking Verity if it was true. Was William to marry? The affirmative answer barely registered before Grace rushed to her room and locked the door.

With a shuddering sigh, Grace nimbly got out of bed reaching for her dressing gown and slippers. She was thirsty, and, going to the water jug found it empty. She'd have to go down to the kitchen.

The house was in long shadows and the soft tick tock of the tall mahogany grandfather clock in the entrance hall greeted her as she stepped down the staircase. The tip tap of her slippers sounded loud in the quiet of the darkened house.

In the kitchen, embers gleamed like shy faeries in the range and she hurriedly added kindling to bring it back to life. When the fire was once again cheerful, she swung the large blackened kettle onto the hot plate to boil. From the larder she collected tea, sugar and milk, from the sideboard, a cup and saucer. Busy with her task, she jumped in alarm as movement from the corner of her eye caught her attention.

'I'm sorry!' William reached out a hand to calm her. 'I didn't mean to frighten you.'

'Well you did!' Grace barked. 'What do you want?' The sight of him made her shake. The tender hurt in her heart woke to ravage her again and she closed her eyes in weariness.

'I'm sorry.'

Grace thought she heard more than those simple words implied and turned from him back to the kettle as the tears rose.

'May I sit with you?' William's tone was gentle. He walked to the sideboard to collect another teacup and saucer.

Grace ignored him and poured the boiling water from the large kettle into a smaller china teapot. She refused to look at him as she brought the teapot over to the table.

'Can we talk, Grace?' When she lifted her tear-filled gaze to him, William groaned. 'I had no idea you owned such *strong* feelings for me.'

'It is nothing,' Grace whispered. 'I was being silly; holding onto something that was a memory. It's time I faced it. One cannot live by girlish dreams alone.'

'If I'd known...'

Grace gave a small tremulous smile. 'It no longer matters.'

'I want to explain.'

'There is no need.'

'I must.' He pushed his fingers through his hair. 'I was left with very little choice in regards to my future. My father's debts overwhelmed me, and I needed to make drastic decisions to safeguard the estate's future. Marrying Felicity is one of them, not that it's a bad thing. She is a good woman.'

'Do you have to marry her?'

'Yes. Her father is helping me with the rest of the estate debts, plus other things and marrying Felicity is part of the agreement.'

'Isn't there any other way? Can you not take out a mortgage?'

'I already have. No, there is no other way. I've tried to do it alone for years. I need the money he is offering and his contacts to make more, but I must marry his daughter to access his money. I have no other choice. Felicity is a better prospect than other offers I've had.'

Grace nodded. She understood his needs, but that didn't take away her pain. 'I would marry you even if you lived in a cave,' she whispered.

William stared at her, obviously surprised by her frankness. 'I'm honoured, Grace, really I am. If things were different I would ask you to be my wife, but I cannot go back on my word.'

'You never thought of me.' Emotion clogged her throat. She sniffed unladylike, wishing she had a handkerchief.

'I did in the months after we returned to Scarborough,' William admitted.

'You should have thought of me recently. My father has money.'

William looked away. 'He doesn't have enough. I've heard he's in the market for wealthy young men to marry his daughters. He claims to support any man who has political ambitions.'

Grace dashed away a tear. 'I, for one, will never marry now.'

'Oh come, Grace, someone as lovely as you will never be an old maid.'

This hurt, coming from him. 'I'll not marry to further my father's ambitions.'

He shrugged. 'He is determined. I've heard he is ploughing more of his money into making his name known in the business world.'

'At this moment what my father does concerns me little.' What was the matter with him? She didn't want to discuss her father. She wanted to curl up in a cupboard and die. He sat there talking about money and business when the entire time her heart was breaking. Her tears fell faster.

He reached for her hand. 'I'm sorry. Please don't cry. Your tears shimmer like diamonds set in gold.'

A lone, hot tear slipped down her cheek and she turned her head away. 'Huh! What nonsense you talk.'

'You have beautiful eyes.'

She jerked to her feet. 'I must go.'

William stood also. He reached for her when she went to walk away and pulled her into his arms. 'I know this is wrong and you may despise me after, but I have the urge to kiss you until you can no longer stand.'

Grace had no time to reply as his mouth descended on hers and swept away all reason. She was glad he held her tightly for her legs went weak and breathing was impossible. A rapid fluttering in the pit of her stomach grew as his kiss deepened. His tongue darted between her lips, forcing her mouth to open. Grace arched into him, desperate to feel the entire length of his body against her. She now understood the needs of the flesh, for her own body was ablaze. Only, this new awakening was bittersweet as William abruptly put her away from him. He groaned deep within his chest.

Blinking rapidly to clear her mind, Grace realized he wasn't completely in control of his emotions either. The physical connection between them was alive like a wildfire and she felt a sudden surge of power as William struggled to regain his composure.

Her damaged pride refused to be ignored. It hurt and angered her that he was willing to throw away their future for money. Pain and rejection ate away at her insides like a demon feasting on an angel. 'I am pleased to see you are not immune to me.'

'No, I am not immune to you,' his reply was strained.

Grace tilted her chin and contempt flared in her eyes. 'Think of me when you are with your new wife, William.' She walked closer to him, watching as his eyes widened in anticipation. 'Will she leave you breathless, I wonder?'

With a strength she didn't know she possessed, Grace walked out of the kitchen and away from her love.

CHAPTER 6

A cock pheasant, its feathers gleaming shades of emerald and copper, flew out from beneath the roadside's hawthorn hedge causing Grace's horse to toss his head as the bird's cry rent the air. She made a soothing noise in her throat to steady him as they turned into the drive of Woodruff House.

The day was the year's warmest so far, enticing the gardens to bloom into fragrant and colourful magnificence. Spring always gave her a sense of renewal as though the resurgence of plant and animal life was a sign to her saying; open your eyes, look at what is here for you to enjoy. Only, since that stirring kiss in the kitchen, four weeks ago, she had spiralled into despondency and wondered if she would ever laugh again.

An argument with her father last night did nothing to alter her unhappiness. His refusal to hire a housekeeper drove her to despair. Not that *he* cared. He blatantly told her he would not force a husband upon her if she took care of the house; thus allowing her to remain a spinster. She challenged him, telling him people thought him mean in taking such advantage of her, but he just laughed.

When she'd argued her sisters' right in choosing husbands of their own he simply dismissed her concerns. The girls would do as he said or be sent to his elderly aunt in Devon, who was a little unhinged and kept chickens in her front parlour. The situation was desperate and hopeless. She had to protect the girls. Not every man Father found would be another Andrew.

At the front steps of the house, Grace slid down from the saddle and handed the reins to one of the grooms, who came running at the sound of hooves on the gravel. Mounting the steps, she looked up as the front door opened and Doyle stood there with a tender smile. She should feel uncomfortable with Doyle's devoted attentions, but instead she welcomed them, needed them and felt selfish because of it.

'How was your ride, Miss Woodruff?' He took her riding crop, veiled top hat and soft kid gloves.

'Fine, thank you, Doyle. The day is warm.'

'Shall I pour you a drink, Miss? I recently brought a bottle of ginger ale from the cellar.'

'Yes, thank you. Has my father left for the day?' She was determined to accost her father at every opportunity.

'Yes, Miss. He informed me he'd not be home until tomorrow.'

'I see.' Grace nodded. 'I shall take the refreshment in the study, thank you.'

Settling herself behind the desk, Grace stared at the books on the table. She had accounts to view and wages to make up, but she couldn't summon the interest to do it. Last night's confrontation with her father also revealed his refusal to hire more desperately needed lower staff. Neither would he increase the current staff's wages. Furthermore, he informed her of his intentions to cut her mother's and the girls' dress allowances. Naturally, he left that piece of news for Grace to impart to them.

A tiny bud of doubt over father's finances wended its way into her thoughts. *Is there a hidden reason why he is cutting expenses?* Sometimes, she wished her mother didn't come from a connected bloodline. Then her father couldn't use it as a bargaining tool to entice rich industrialists who had money but no pedigree. She knew he sought power. He wanted to be a man remembered, a man of note. Woodruff couldn't do it on his own. He had to marry his daughters to remarkable men who could advance him. Yet, if no gentlemen asked for one of her sisters, would father use his money to buy them husbands? He failed to sire a son, therefore an influential son-in-law and future grandson would have to be his compensation.

Grace's gaze lifted when Doyle entered carrying a drink tray. His movements were quick and precise, a gifted butler. With this in mind, she looked keenly at his face, noticing the fine arched eyebrows above his rich brown eyes. His features were strong and well proportioned, in all, a handsome man. She frowned as she studied him, then realized he watched her as intently.

'I'm sorry, Doyle.' Grace shook her head. 'I didn't mean to stare. I don't know what is wrong with me some days.' She smiled tentatively, hoping he wasn't as embarrassed as she was.

'Don't apologize, Miss.' He handed her a tall glass of ginger ale. 'If I may, there is something I wish to discuss with you?'

'Yes?'

'Maureen O'Reilly is with child.'

'Really?' Grace's eyes widened. She thought the maid a decent girl. 'She is to marry shortly then, I presume?'

'No, she isn't and she'll not disclose the father's name either.'

Grace sat back. 'Does anyone have a notion who it might be?'

Doyle looked away, his fingers tracing the edge of the tray.

'Doyle?'

He straightened and looked her in the eye. 'No one knows.' He paused. 'She begs us not to send her home, for she says her father will beat her.'

'I see.'

'I think we should let her stay and work for as long as she can.'

The passion in his voice made Grace uncomfortable. Normally, she would have felt the same way, for she enjoyed flouting restrictive social boundaries. She bore a tolerance for the poor, unlike most of her class, and found charity work thoroughly rewarding. Her mother's friends talked and whispered that she was turning into an eccentric, or worst of all, a reformer! She understood how most young girls got into trouble through broken promises from men who cared little of their actions.

Not so long ago, she too had fervour and enthusiasm for exciting schemes to help those more unfortunate. However, now, the fire in her was doused. Her heart held nothing but ashes. She no longer possessed visions of righting the world, hopefully with William by her side. The thrill of making a statement, and being counted for her time on earth, had gone. At twenty-three years old, she felt as tired and dispirited as an old woman.

Rising, she walked to the window to stare aimlessly out of it. 'I do not think it is a good idea for her to remain here. Mama won't allow it.'

'Would *you* allow it, Miss Woodruff?'

'I have maiden sisters and staff to think of, Doyle. You know it is impossible.' An edge came to her voice. *Was he testing her?*

'It can be done, so as not to arouse suspicion. She can work in the laundry, away from the house.'

Grace faced him. Again, she wished they had a housekeeper to deal with these situations. 'And what kind of example does that show to others?'

'She was taken against her will!'

'How do you know this?'

'She told me.'

'And you believe her?'

'Yes. She wouldn't lie to me.'

A tight knot of ownership gripped Grace's stomach; surprising her. She didn't like the thought of her butler being a young woman's confidante. She lifted her chin. 'Then I am sorry for her, but it's your duty to remain detached from the female staff's personal problems. You have to be above such things. They should see you as their leader not a shoulder to cry on. They must go to Mrs Hawksberry or come to me.'

'How would she come to you with such a problem?'

'Better me than you!'

'I'm glad they see me as their friend as well as their leader.' Doyle raised one eyebrow in defiance.

Anger built in her chest. An urge to smash something consumed her. Doyle portrayed her as someone cold-hearted and bigoted. She was neither. Her ire left her as quickly as it came. Wiping a hand wearily over her eyes, she waved her other hand towards the door, dismissing him.

Alone again, Grace sat heavily, laying her head upon her folded arms. She needed to take hold of herself and contain her emotions. All too often in the last few weeks she was prone to anger or tears; such weaknesses she found abhorrent in herself. Her mother tried to talk to her about William's engagement but Grace forestalled every attempt. The agony of knowing he was lost to her sometimes drove her close to madness. She wanted to rant and rave, scream and cry. Only, in the end, what good would it do? William and her beautiful summer memory was a falsehood and all she had left to look forward to was a lonely spinsterhood running her father's house.

* * *

GABY SAT astride her bay horse, gripping the reins until her knuckles showed white. The wave of nausea receded a little as she sucked in mouthfuls of fresh air. The day's warmth, which had been welcoming an hour ago, now brought out a fine film of sweat on her forehead. Tremors flowed along her limbs and she wondered dazedly if she would faint.

She cursed the fates that brought her to this state. *Why me?* Why did a few moments of excitement lead her to this?

'Damnation!' Gaby dashed at the tears threatening to spill.

She wouldn't give in to helpless emotion. Taking a deep breath, she lifted her chin. She had to conquer this. For a moment, she wondered if she should tell Grace, but shook her head at her own folly. To see Grace's disappointment would be too painful.

Curlews and jays flittered from tree to tree. Early wood anemones framed the bottom of tree trunks like a pretty garland. The odd bluebell played peek-boo through the tall wild grasses. After a few minutes of sitting still, Gaby gently nudged her horse into the cool shade of Saw Wood, for both she and it were tired. She had departed Woodruff House at dawn and ridden until her horse stumbled in weariness on the far side of Roundhay, miles from home. Would such furious riding do the trick? She waited with baited breath for any result.

* * *

IN A SMALL ROOM off the crowded, smoky taproom of an ancient inn situated on the Roman made road to York, Woodruff swallowed the last of his ale. With a violent oath, he slammed his fist on the stained tabletop and rose to gather his coat and hat.

A short, barrel-chested man breezed into the room, tapping cigar ash onto the worn timber floor as he did so. 'Woodruff, dear fellow, going so soon?'

'I've been waiting two hours,' Woodruff growled, flinging his belongings back on a nearby chair. 'I never wait for anyone.'

'Business kept me, dear fellow, business!' The newcomer smiled, showing a gold tooth set in amongst yellowing ones.

'Don't presume to play me for a fool,' fumed Woodruff. 'I, too, am a busy man, Horton.'

'Too right! Now, have you eaten?' Horton sat his bulk down comfortably at the low table. He unbuttoned his expensive, tailored suit-coat to accommodate his stomach. A thick gold fob chain looped across his embroidered waistcoat.

'No.'

'No? Well, what a fine state of affairs!' Horton turned to the opened doorway, yelling for the innkeeper to serve them his best food and plenty of it.

'Why in God's name are we meeting here?' Woodruff scowled, wiping a speck of dirt off his trousers with a white handkerchief. 'Surely your gentleman's club in York or mine in Leeds would be better than this rat-infested hole?'

'Don't be so fastidious man!' Horton laughed. 'Tell me, can you talk honestly in any gentleman's club without eavesdroppers? Of course, you can't!'

'But at least there we don't leave covered in flea bites!'

Horton's roar of laughter only deepened Woodruff's sour temperament.

Their food, when it came, consisted of steaming bowls of beef broth, plates of buttered thick brown bread, pickled pork, chutney, boiled eggs and foaming jugs of hot ale.

Woodruff had not eaten in several hours and his mouth watered at the aromas. Both of them ate without comment until they were replete.

Horton belched loudly then wiped his mouth with a strip of linen the innkeeper passed off as a napkin. 'So, Woodruff, you wish to invest in my new venture?' He picked his teeth with a fingernail.

'I won't deny it sounded interesting when we last met.'

'I've gained further ground since then. I've got buyers for the cargo coming back from the Indies. I managed to buy a few favours within the ranks of some parliamentary leaders, so the tax levy is, shall we say, nonexistent? However, I've no wish to spend my days in London fighting noble causes, which is what they want in return for their selective blindness.' He paused to grin wickedly. 'But apparently you do? The country isn't good enough for you anymore. You want to be the one shouting the odds in London's elite clubs? You want to gain the ears of influential men, dine at great palaces and make some money on the side?'

Woodruff squirmed. He hated others knowing his weaknesses. Yes, he wanted to be in London and he'd do whatever it took to get himself there. If he had to sell his daughters or make bribes with the very devil to do so, he would. If he possessed sons, he would've pushed them into Parliament or bought them a commission in the military. Through them, he would have become known. Only, he had daughters.

Horton refilled his glass. 'Am I right?'

Woodruff paused, scowling, buying himself time to gather his argument. He didn't like Horton much. The man was low born, but due to a combination of luck and some illegal activities, the fellow had heaved himself out of the gutter and was now immensely rich, much richer than himself and that rankled, but he would use Horton to his advantage. Horton's wealth bought him friends in high places, such places Woodruff couldn't reach without a leg-up. 'I am agreeable to London. Will you back me?'

Horton leaned back in his chair wearing a dubious expression. 'Aye, I might. Depends on what you offer in return.'

Woodruff relaxed. He knew Horton needed a fine young wife, plus the man wanted sons, lots of them. 'To some men money isn't worth its weight in gold unless they have a son to inherit.' Woodruff let the thought enter Horton's mind for a moment. 'Flesh of their flesh.'

'Go on.'

'Take yourself for instance. You have more money than you can spend. Yet, you're all alone with no one to share it with. That monstrous house you've built near York is as empty as a barren woman. Have you never thought of sons, man?'

'Of course, I have!' Horton scoffed.

'What are you doing about it?'

'Well ...'

'You need a wife to give you sons.' Woodruff rubbed his hands, smug. 'For my input in this deal you may choose one of my daughters to marry. You've seen their beauty. They've got exceptional breeding. Diana's line goes back to Saxon nobility. What do you say?'

Horton wiped his podgy hand over his thinning hair. 'If I recall correctly, your eldest daughter is a bit of a spitfire.' A cunning smile lit his face. 'I distinctly remember her digging her nails into my hand when it strayed under the dining table the one time I stayed at Woodruff House.'

'Grace is the intelligent one, Horton. You'll not tame her. It is best you pick another, one that will be passive and not likely to challenge your every decision.' A tight knot of possession gripped his belly. He'd not relinquish Grace, for he knew her value and required her as hostess for Woodruff House; her beauty and poise would remain under his roof. She was the only one he was proud of.

Horton shook his head with a laugh. 'I cannot remember them clearly, you have too many! But one is as good as another as long as she's pure and doesn't come empty handed. I want some dowry in return, man, for I can buy myself women aplenty should I chose.'

'Ellsworth took a chunk of my wealth to keep him sweet about Heather. He wasn't too keen on the match at first. But despite his superior attitude, he was quick to take what I offered. The man is all show. I doubt he has two sixpences to rub together. '

Horton snorted. 'Typical aristocrat.'

'Come to dinner next week. It will give you time to choose one. We can then draw up a contract.'

'Very good, excellent in fact!' Horton bellowed. 'One of your fine daughters is bound to provide me with many good-looking sons!'

Woodruff rose, collecting his things once more.

'Speaking of sons, why hasn't the lovely Diana been brought

to her birthing bed in the last few years?' Horton quizzed. 'Are you past it, old man?'

'Damn woman is worthless!' Woodruff spat.

Horton laughed. 'Has she denied you your rights? Imagine having a beauty like Diana under your roof and being unable to touch her. You should concentrate on begetting her a son or two, instead of finding rich husbands for your daughters!' Horton's laughter followed Woodruff out of the inn.

On the journey back to Leeds, Woodruff's mind turned over Horton's words. Yes, there was still time to have sons of his own. That bitch Diana was still young enough to carry them! Being over forty and still bearing children was a normal business, and by God, she would continue to do so or die in the attempt! He had been patient enough with her.

DIANA SIGHED TIREDLY and closed her book of poetry. It was late and Heather had exhausted her with wedding preparations until her head was spinning. She'd sent all the girls to bed so she could read in peace. However, she soon lost interest in the verses. Too many worries crowded in on her. She agonized about Grace's despondency over William, Gaby was never home, Heather would soon be lost to them and Letitia's behaviour simply frightened her by its extremeness. She prayed the other three would do nothing untoward for a while until she gathered strength to deal with them.

Diana reached over and turned down the gas lamp by her bed. With the room plunged into a dim light, she nestled more comfortably under the blankets and closed her eyes.

The door handle turned with soft click. Diana peeped through one eye. Hopeland or Partridge must have come to check the fireguard; forgetting that no fire burned due to the surprising warmth of the spring night. The figure loomed closer to the bed. Bulky and breathing heavily, it was definitely not one of the maids.

Diana struggled into a sitting position, but the shape was onto her quickly. A stubby hand covered her mouth. Her scream died in her throat.

'Be quiet, you stupid woman!' Woodruff whispered savagely. He stripped off the bedcovers. His strength overpowered Diana as he pinned her beneath him.

Fear made her eyes widen when Woodruff gripped both her wrists in one hand while with his other he pulled up her night-gown. She struggled. 'Get away from me!'

'Oh no, wife, I've been patient enough with you. You're not too old to bear more children.'

'I am too old! I lost the last three.' She tried to jerk free.

'I want a son!' He panted.

'Not from me.' She ripped one hand free and grabbed his hair to wrench his head back. 'Never from me!'

'If you don't then I'll send you back to your family.' He paused to peer at her, his little eyes glinting. 'That shut you up didn't it? Don't like the thought of leaving your comfort here to go back to a noble, but poor family.' His laugh grated on her strung nerves. 'Or maybe you don't like the thought of going back to the society of an uncle who likes to grab you in dark corners? Is that it?'

Fury filled her. 'You are no different to him.' She spat in his face.

Against her breast, he wiped her saliva off his cheek. 'At least anything you beget of me is legal and normal. Off him … well, who knows how many heads it would have?'

She went to slap him, hating him for dredging up the old memories. 'Get out! I won't have you near me.'

'You, my dear wife, aren't going to deny me my rights anymore. You've a duty to me by law. I want a son and you're going to give me one even if it kills you!'

'I would rather be dead than have you touch me.'

He chuckled. 'I wish you were. Then, I could marry a younger woman and start again.' He cocked his head to one side. 'Maybe I should divorce you?'

Her stomach clenched, she swallowed.

'No, you wouldn't like that would you? The scandal would be worse than lying with me. Am I right?'

'You are evil.' She wriggled under him, trying to free herself, but found he enjoyed her thrashing. His wicked grin stilled her.

The door opened and light from the gallery flooded over them. Diana gasped as Letitia stood in the doorway. 'Mama? I heard noises?'

Woodruff swore. 'Get out, for God's sake!'

'Mama?'

Diana closed her eyes, heart thumping. 'Go, Letitia. It's all right.'

The door closed plunging them into dimness.

Diana's cry as he entered her was muffled and ineffective for Woodruff's wet mouth enveloped hers. She closed her eyes, willing her mind to think of something else as he violated her body, knowing all the while that only death would release her. Now, he had started coming to her again he'd not stop. Her two years of respite from his attentions were over. A single tear slipped down her cheek.

CHAPTER 7

*G*race raised her goblet as another guest toasted the happy couple. She fought the faint sadness lingering in her heart at the thought of Heather not being at home with them anymore. It was the beginning of the end.

Emma Kate, sitting next to Grace, leaned over. 'The Ellsworths have spared no expense for the wedding breakfast. Heather is lucky to be marrying into such a family.'

Grace nodded. 'I'm happy Heather will want for nothing. Her position in the community is secure.' But her voice trailed off as an idea formed. Heather's new status as an Ellsworth would give her a powerful ally against their father.

Emma Kate sat down opposite them. 'It was wonderful watching Heather say her vows, and doesn't Andrew look splendid?'

'Home will not be the same without her,' Faith cried, close to tears again. She had wept throughout the service and her sodden handkerchief represented her misery.

Letitia drained her champagne. 'Well, if Father has his way another one of us will soon follow Heather.' She hiccupped.

Grace frowned at her. Letitia was on her way to being decidedly drunk.

The sisters turned as one to stare at their father, who laughed raucously with Mr Horton at another table.

'Why was he invited?' Emma Kate scoffed. 'He is not a gentleman.'

Laughing, Letitia refilled her glass from the bottle near her plate without waiting for the footman to assist. 'Father does not care a whit as long as Mr Horton can advance him.'

'Let us not discuss this now,' Grace murmured.

Letitia drank deeply. 'I heard Horton and Father talking.' She swayed. 'I imagine Father has offered him one of us as an inducement.' She laughed and then spluttered. 'We are so unfortunate, aren't we? If Mama's family hadn't disowned her on marrying father, then they would have helped to find us substantial husbands. Instead, we have Father's inconsiderate offerings.'

'I will not marry *him* or anyone!' Faith declared.

Emma Kate toyed with a flower from the table's central display. 'You may want to be an old maid, Faith, but I certainly do not, not after today.'

Faith huffed. 'Being an old maid is preferable to marrying Father's friends.'

Emma Kate shrugged. 'Horton is a bad choice, granted, but Heather has an Ellsworth. We might do as well as her.' She grinned. 'I want to be a bride to a handsome and dashing army officer!'

The others agreed except Gaby, whose gaze lingered on Horton, her brow puckering. Grace looked from her to Letitia, who again refilled her glass, and back to Gaby. *How am I to keep them all safe and happy?* The situation was fast spinning out of her control.

Phoebe hurried over to their table, her face aglow. 'Mama says we're travelling to London in September.'

Grace looked at her in confusion. 'Mama made no mention to me. Are you certain?'

Phoebe waited for the footman to pull out her chair and then sat. 'Yes, it was decided this morning when Mama received William's wedding invitation. It's been two years since we were all in London. I wish father would let us go there more. I wonder if he'll rent the same townhouse near Kensington Palace?' Phoebe tapped her lips with one finger. 'Anyhow, Father wishes to stay on after the wedding for a week or so, but we'll return home.'

Grace closed her eyes momentarily. William's wedding. *I will not go.* She could not possibly stand in a church and watch William marry another. She would die before doing so.

'Why aren't cousin Verity and William here today?' Phoebe asked. 'If we are invited to his, surely they were invited to Heather's?'

'Mama received a letter yesterday from cousin Verity,' Faith supplied. 'William's intended in-laws have an estate in Nice. They are spending part of the summer there.'

Letitia motioned to a passing footman for another glass of champagne. 'They are in France?' She slipped sideways in her chair and knocked over her glass.

Grace stood. She wouldn't sit listening to another word about William and Letitia's behaviour drew attention. 'It's time we said our farewells to Heather and Andrew.'

* * *

THE POIGNANT STRAINS of *Chopin* drifted on the warm breeze out through the gardens. Grace lifted her head to smile at Phoebe's giggles as she made a mistake and was corrected by Monsieur du Pont.

Grace bent and cut a rose's stem. A wicker basket sat at her feet filled with long stemmed roses and blue-purple irises. She enjoyed being in the garden and ventured there whenever she could. The heady scent of the blooms filled the air, inciting Grace to bury her nose in a salmon pink rose. She inhaled until she felt light-headed.

Cutting off new buds, her thoughts returned to her father's latest news. He informed her only this morning that Mr Horton had chosen Emma Kate for his intended bride. Grace could not allow it to happen. Horton might be wealthy, but he was also revolting. The thought of him touching her darling sister sent ice-cold shivers down her spine.

The soft, lush lawn cushioned her footsteps, but Diana made her presence felt by calling from the next garden bed.

'What is it, Mama?' Grace asked, taken out of her tortured thoughts.

Diana, holding up the skirts of her bronze-coloured dress, marched like an indignant hen. 'I've just passed the laundry and noticed the parlour maid, the Irish one.'

'Maureen O'Reilly works in the laundry now, Mama.' Grace collected her basket and averted her gaze.

'She is with child! I could see quite plainly!'

Grace stepped to the next rose bush, but paused to delicately untangle her sky blue skirts caught on a thorn.

'Well? What do you have to say about this?' Diana narrowed her eyes. 'Did you know?'

'Yes, I knew.'

'Is that why she was demoted to the laundry? I wasn't aware she even married! I find it most inconsiderate of you to not inform me of the staff's movements. I know I keep to my rooms a lot and you've taken on the responsibilities...'

'Mama, please!'

Diana scowled from under her wide brimmed straw hat.

Grace sighed. 'Maureen is not married and yes, that is why she is now in the laundry.'

'Not married?' Diana's tone was icy.

'Correct.'

'And you have allowed her to stay on here?'

Defiant, Grace raised her chin. 'She has nowhere to go.'

'That is not our fault! I want her gone from this house today!'

'I took pity on her, Mama. She was taken against her will.'

Diana tossed her head. 'You do not accept such lies, do you? They all say that, but in truth they are immoral and wicked.'

'Tell me you do not believe such nonsense.' Grace stared at Diana. Letitia had told her what she witnessed between their parents the other night. 'You of all people should know how she feels.'

Her mother avoided her gaze and blushed. 'It doesn't give you the right to let her stay.'

Grace softened her tone. 'I gave my word she'd have a home here.'

Diana's head jerked up. 'No! I won't allow it. I refuse to have her flaunted before me.'

'She is hardly flaunting herself. This is not something she wishes to promote.'

'Think of your sisters' sensibilities if nothing else.'

'I'd hope my sisters had compassion.'

'I want her removed from the estate.'

Out of patience, Grace threw her hands up. 'If you wish her gone, then *you* dismiss her.'

'I most certainly shall not!'

'Mama, you must either allow me to run this house as I wish, or return to your duty as its mistress. You can't have it both ways.'

'How dare you speak to me in such a manner!'

'I dare, Mama, because it is I who must deal with everything when you choose to ignore matters that you find distasteful.' At Diana's astonished gasp, guilt immediately dampened her temper. 'I'm sorry, Mama. I didn't mean...'

'I want her gone from this house by dusk. See it happens! I'm appalled by your lack of concern towards your family and your lack of respect towards me.'

Diana stormed off, leaving Grace shaking her head at her mother's idiosyncrasies.

Her pleasure in the garden vanished and unhappily she strolled to the side of the house and into the glass-domed conservatory leading off from the parlour. Yellow canaries twittered in their wire cage by the doorway, but Grace paid them no heed. She placed her basket on a table tucked away behind tall palms and ferns.

She hadn't meant to hurt her mother, but Diana's lack of authority over her daughters' future irritated her. Never did she voice her concerns about his attempts to marry them off to men like Horton. Why did her mother not fight for their happiness?

* * *

ANOTHER SULTRY MORNING gave way to rapid thunderstorms typical of a hot summer's day. The last few weeks of continual heat had sent a wave of lethargy throughout the estate. Animals and humans alike slowed and waited for the weather to break.

Grace climbed up the library ladder and replaced a book she had finished reading last night in bed. Peering along the row, she gently touched the leather-bound volumes of Chaucer, Trollope and Wordsworth. The books were her grandfather's collection, inherited by her father, though she doubted *he* had ever read one in his life.

Suddenly, she saw Letitia pass by the window on her left. Grace lifted her hand to knock on the glass, ready to make a silly face at her, except her hand stilled mid air when Letitia stumbled, straightened and then staggered again.

Shocked, Grace grabbed the ladder for some security as Letitia drew a wine bottle out from beneath her cape. Claps of thunder made Letitia raise her head to look at the angry sky. Then, she slipped around the side of the house and out of sight.

A horror so unreal filled Grace's mind. *She is drunk again.* Why is she behaving like this? What is driving her to such depths? Grace thought of the cellar and its hundreds of bottles. Only she, her father and Doyle had the keys to it. Had Letitia stolen a set? Rubbing her forehead in thought, she made a mental note of all the rooms that held a liquor cabinet. Were they locked?

Sighing, Grace stepped down from the ladder intent on finding Letitia, although she knew Letitia would deny everything and become argumentative.

The clanking of the front door bell sounded between the rolls of thunder. Doyle, passing the doorway, paused to gaze at her a moment before continuing on. Since the business last week with Maureen O'Reilly, he'd hardly spoken to her.

She walked into the hall to see Doyle pull the heavy door open. Immediately, a figure fell inwards and on impulse, he caught it before it crashed to the floor.

The figure shot out a thin, white hand to grasp his sleeve. 'Help me,' came the hoarse whisper from within the folds of the hooded cape.

Grace hurried to him as he lurched with his burden to a nearby chair. Doyle pushed the stranger's hood back to reveal a woman's small, pinched face. 'Are you hurt?'

The woman groaned.

'Do you know her, Doyle?' Grace bent down in front of the woman.

'No, Miss.'

'She needs help.'

'I must insist you step away, Miss. She is ill and could be contagious.'

The woman, huddled over, groaned while holding her stomach and at the same time, her dirty cape parted revealing her large stomach.

'Good God!' Doyle's eyes widened. 'She is birthing!'

'We'll have to make her more comfortable.'

'I'll call Partridge, Miss. You shouldn't be involved. If she'd gone around to the back of the house, you would've been spared this.'

'What nonsense!' She glared up at him. 'Besides, she is in no fit state to know where she is, never mind walking around to the back entrance. Now help me.'

They removed the woman's cape and Doyle rushed into the drawing room to pull the bell-rope. 'Where shall we put her?' he asked, returning.

The woman cried out and Grace looked up at the staircase in alarm of her mother hearing and descending. 'In your rooms for now. Come, you take her other side.' Grace pulled the woman upright. 'My mother or sisters cannot see her.'

The woman groaned again as another pain seized her. Unable to walk, she whimpered as they moved her. She had no strength to stand and was as limp as a rag doll.

Doyle scooped her up into his arms and carried her down the hall.

As Partridge came into the hallway, Grace took her to one side. 'Send for the doctor and get Mrs Hawksberry.' They parted outside Doyle's door and Partridge scurried away towards the kitchen.

Grace took a deep breath. *Why did the woman come to our door?* Closing her eyes, she prayed for strength. Raising her chin, Grace entered the butler's domain going through to Doyle's own bedroom.

'She's awfully frail, Miss. Did you send for the doctor or a midwife?'

'I have, and I have also sent for Mrs Hawksberry. She has ten children and has helped to bring countless others into the world.' Grace stood by the bed as the woman tossed in agony. Her skirts were stained, with wet patches. She had lost one shoe and her black stockings were torn. A well of sympathy flooded Grace as the woman struggled with another pain. 'The poor dear.'

'What brought her here, though?'

Grace shrugged, knelt by the bed and took the woman's hand. 'I don't know, but I cannot have Mama and my sisters knowing there is a woman off the streets giving birth in the butler's bedroom.'

Doyle shook his head. 'What else could we do? Surely they'd understand our helping her?'

'Yes, they might, but Father will not.' Grace stood, went to the water jug and dipped her handkerchief into it. Then, once more, she knelt by the bed and dabbed the woman's flushed face. 'Once the baby is delivered, we can move them both to wherever they live.'

The woman murmured and groaned. Her cheeks reddened as she drew her knees up and strained to expel the child. Blood seeped onto the blankets like a slow moving river. The amount of it frightened Grace and she glanced at Doyle, who stood frozen.

Grace leaned over her. 'We'll help you, do not worry.' She dabbed the woman's brow. 'Do you have family we can send for? Are you far from home? What's your name?'

'Olive.' Her whisper was barely audible. She reached out a claw like hand and gripped the bodice of Grace's dress. 'Woodruff...'

'Yes, you are at Woodruff House.' Grace struggled to smile as the woman, in anguish, twisted the material of her dress pinching her skin.

'Tell him... I had to...' The woman's breath was taken from her as she pushed down. Her face turned crimson with the effort. More blood gushed forth.

'Hush now, save your strength.' Grace held her hand. Her gaze lingered on the ever-growing pool of blood. She rose and peered over Olive's bent legs. She jumped as the baby's head emerged. 'Oh, my lord.'

Doyle started forward and Grace turned on him. 'Find Mrs Hawksberry immediately!'

'Good God.' Doyle gulped, but didn't move.

'Woodruff, the child ...' Olive's tormented eyes pierced Grace's heart. 'He owes the child ... Tell him!'

'Who am I to tell? I don't understand.' Grace frowned. 'What do you mean?'

'Woodruff ...' The child slipped into the world and Olive shuddered then went limp.

Grace and Doyle stepped back in shock as the mewling baby lay amongst its mother's skirts and blood.

'Oh, my.' A wave of dizziness overcame Grace as she stared at the motionless woman.

Mrs Hawksberry, with Partridge right behind her, bustled in carrying a jug of steaming water and towels. Her largeness instantly made the room seem smaller. 'Now then, what do we have here?' She frowned as a stream of blood still flowed from the woman. After placing the jug on the bedside table, she examined the woman. 'This poor woman is dead.'

'Can you not help her, Mrs Hawksberry?' Grace begged.

Mrs Hawksberry's craggy face softened. 'No, pet, it's too late for that, but this little mite looks all right.'

Doyle gently took Grace's arm to move her from the room, but she refused and stood staring at the thin, hollow-featured face, who a few moments before had talked to her. She dragged her gaze to the small baby waving its scrawny arms.

'Mr Doyle, I think Miss Woodruff needs some brandy,' Mrs Hawksberry said from the end of the bed. 'And when the doctor arrives have him give her something to make her sleep.'

'Yes, certainly.' He took Grace's elbow. 'Come, Miss.' She shook her head and after hesitating a moment, Doyle left to get her a brandy.

Grace watched, mesmerized, as Mrs Hawksberry cleaned the

dead woman and Partridge soothed the baby now wrapped in a warmed towel.

Mrs Hawksberry tutted. 'She's all bones, poor lass. How did she think to survive a birth in her state?'

'Maybe she had no choice.' Partridge said, cradling the baby.

'Aye, likely as not.' Mrs Hawksberry scoffed. 'Well, we'll need to find her family. This little lad needs a home.'

'There are infant clothes in the attic trunks,' Grace informed them, surprising herself how normally she'd spoken when all she could think of was that a dead woman and a newborn baby was in the butler's bedroom.

'Nay, Miss Woodruff, we can't be usin' the family garments.' Mrs Hawksberry nodded to Partridge and took the baby from her. 'Sit Miss Woodruff down, she's in shock. Women of the gentry never see this kind of business unless they're married.'

Partridge led her to a chair as Doyle returned bringing a tot of brandy. Grace drank it gratefully. The fire it lit going down her throat and the punch it gave her stomach brought her out of the dazed state she'd slipped into. She felt better but still out of control. She tried to think clearly. Her father would be home soon. She groaned inwardly at thought of his reaction to this situation.

'Well, this little feller needs someone t' feed him, Miss,' Mrs Hawksberry crowed. 'Partridge's sister, Lydia had a bairn last week, didn't she, Partridge?'

'Aye, Mrs Hawksberry, she did.' The maid nodded vigorously.

Mrs Hawksberry inclined her head to Grace. 'I think Lydia would be the best one for the job until something is sorted out more permanent like, what do yer think? It could take the doctor some time to find out this woman's family.'

Grace blinked. 'Yes, Mrs Hawksberry, that would do very well.'

'Right then, Partridge, when the doctor's been yer can take him into Leeds.'

Grace scowled, not understanding. 'What do you mean, Leeds?'

'Like I said Miss, Partridge will take the little lad to her sister's house. Her sister is a clean woman, I'll vouch for her,' Mrs Hawksberry spoke slowly as though to a small child.

'You are not taking him!' Grace sprang forward and plucked the child from Mrs Hawksberry's arms.

'But he needs to be fed.' Affronted, Mrs Hawksberry stood with her hands on her wide hips.

Grace gathered the baby close to her chest, gazing down at his little face and soft downy head. A unique and surprisingly strong bond seized her heart. A sensation so powerful her knees threatened to buckle. She turned to Doyle, who stood solemnly by the doorway. 'Doyle, I ...' She paused not knowing what to say.

Doyle was instantly by her side. 'What do you want, Miss?'

'She ...' Her gaze strayed to the dead figure. 'The woman said something ...' Grace closed her eyes trying to make her stupefied mind focus on the woman's last words. 'She said Woodruff.'

'Yes, Woodruff House.'

'No, she said *he* owes the child.' As realization dawned in Grace's mind, her eyes widened. She bit her trembling lower lip. 'She meant that he is the father!'

Mrs Hawksberry, Partridge and Doyle all looked from the woman on the bed to the child in Grace's arms.

'She could have just said that, Miss, you know?' Partridge whispered.

'I don't think she was lying.' Grace rocked the sleeping baby. 'Why would she?'

'Many do, Miss,' Mrs Hawksberry said in a superior tone. 'Usually, they're after money.'

Grace shook her head. 'No, I think not. I believe that woman knew she wouldn't live.'

'What shall we do then, Miss?' Mrs Hawksberry asked, indicating the child. 'This is a fine predicament and no mistake.'

'He is staying right here.' Grace decided. 'Where he belongs.'

Doyle ran his fingers through his hair in agitation. 'You can't, Miss. You have no proof this baby is your father's child.'

'We are miles from the nearest village and that poor woman there,' she waved towards the bed, 'managed to walk here in great pain so her child could be born at Woodruff House.' For Grace, the proof was mounting and she took courage from that. Everything fell into place. She looked down at the baby's face and saw familiar features of her father and Letitia. This child was a Woodruff.

Doyle cursed under his breath. 'And what will your father say when he comes home?'

'Never mind that.' Grace dismissed his concerns, feeling stronger. She knew what she had to do. 'Mrs Hawksberry, arrange for a wet nurse, one who can live in. Partridge, go up to the attics and bring down the old nursery things. I know the nursery is now the painting studio but there's a baby in the house again, my sisters will have to paint elsewhere. Have Hopeland help you.'

Mrs Hawksberry shifted from foot to foot. 'Miss Woodruff?'

'Please do as I ask.'

The two women, though shaking their heads in bewilderment, went to do as she wished.

'Your mother will never allow it.' Shocked, Doyle hovered beside her. 'You cannot hope to keep the child here.'

Grace rounded on him. 'He is my half-brother. Do you expect me to send him away?'

'Well, yes. Your father will go mad the minute he's through the door!'

'Let him!' Grace spat, as the child suddenly cried. Grace flung out one arm pointing to the waxen-faced woman on the bed. 'Look what my father has to answer for!'

Doyle's gaze flickered from Grace to the figure and back again.

'My father is a murderer!'

'Murderer?'

'Yes! He had his pleasure and then threw her over when not needed anymore. Do you think she'd be so thin and dressed in rags if she was still his mistress?' She thrust the child into Doyle's frozen arms. 'Take him into the kitchen. I must speak to Mama.'

CHAPTER 8

Grace burst into Diana's sitting room where her mother and sisters sat discussing the music festival to be held next week at Leeds Town Hall. 'Mama, I must speak with you, it is urgent. Can we go into your bedroom, please?'

Diana frowned, put down her embroidery and rose. 'Can it not wait, my dear? We are planning what to wear to the festival. I think if we alter the lace on our hats and add ribbon, we may not need to buy new ones.'

'Mama, please!' Grace took her elbow and led her into the bedroom.

Grace knew she could only impart her news coherently by maintaining a complete detachment from the event which had just occurred downstairs. She concentrated on her mother's face. 'A short time ago, a labouring woman came here looking for help. We, Doyle and I, took her to his rooms and there she gave birth to a baby. Unfortunately, she died immediately after.'

'Well, what an affront to come here. Have people no decency?'

'Mama, listen to me. Before she died, she spoke a few words, effectively telling me that Montgomery Woodruff is the father of the baby.'

Diana closed her eyes, swaying a little. 'Oh dear sweet Jesus,' she whispered tearfully. 'Are you certain?'

'Yes.'

Diana paled. 'How dare the slut come here?'

Grace bit her bottom lip. 'That hardly matters now.'

'What are we to do?' Her mother clasped her hands to her breast. 'Why? Why does he continually insult me?'

Shaking her head, Grace wiped her hand over her eyes. 'I've sent for the doctor. He must declare her legally dead, I think,' she frowned, 'then the undertaker must be summoned. I've organized Partridge to make the nursery ready.'

Diana gripped Grace's arm. 'The nursery? Whatever do you mean?'

'The child, Mama, needs to be cared for.'

'Not here it won't!'

'Yes. It will.' Her tone was as cold as steel.

Panic widened Diana's eyes. 'How can you be sure she was speaking the truth? It could be anyone's!'

'Why would she travel all the way here during a thunderstorm, while in labour? She knew this house and she knew Father. She said Woodruff owed the child.'

'That could mean anything,' Diana cried, pacing the bedroom. 'Oh dear God. I cannot bear much more.'

'I will get the truth from Father.' Seeing her mother's distress, Grace softened her tone. 'If she was his mistress, then he should be horsewhipped for his treatment of her. She was all skin and bones, Mama. She had no strength for the birth.'

'We need proof first!'

Grace folded her arms across her chest as her temper rose. Her world was spiralling into chaos and she could do nothing to stop it. 'Then I will obtain it, but in the meantime the baby stays here.'

Diana froze. 'No! No, Grace. I won't allow it! I will not have your father's bastard here. How can you even suggest such a thing?'

'He may be Father's bastard, but he is also my half-brother. I will not let him be farmed out to some family who could mistreat him.'

'Do not be naïve, girl.' Her mother's face flushed in annoyance. 'Do you think your father will want it?' Diana laughed harshly. 'He'd likely throw it into the nearest cesspool.'

Grace shook her head and remembered the feel of the baby in her arms. It was the first baby she had held since she was a child and her heart had swelled with love at first sight. She folded her arms across her chest. 'No, he will not. I won't let him.'

'Think girl! Think of the scandal! Your father wants to further himself, even enter politics. Do you think he'll want his bastard to taint his image? Money will only buy him so many favours and he won't thank you for ruining it for him.'

'I care nothing for father's plans. He fools himself thinking he can become a member of the aristocracy! They know him for what he is, the grandson of a merchant.'

Diana clutched Grace's arms cruelly. 'Think of your sisters then! Of me!'

'And what of the innocent baby downstairs?'

'This will destroy us! *You* will ruin us if you do this. How can you do this to *me*?'

Grace wrenched her arms out of her mother's grasp. She wanted Diana's help and support, not her censure. 'He now has a son. You should be grateful; he may leave you alone now.'

Diana gasped. 'Still your outlandish tongue! You know nothing of what I've endured. And you're wrong to think a bastard child will be sufficient for his needs.'

'The child can be recognized as a Woodruff. Father must provide for him.'

'No!' Her mother's face twisted in anguish. 'Do you think that child is the only bastard he has? There could be dozens more. Are you saying you want them all to come here?'

'What does it matter how many there could be? We know nothing of them, but it is this child, born here today in front of me, under this roof, that I am concerned for.'

'If this becomes common knowledge no one will want your sisters, except men like Mr Horton, have you considered that?'

Grace felt an ice-cold band encircle her heart. 'Are you forcing me to choose?'

'There is no choice! Bastards are born all the time. Some are secretly provided for, others given away. It is a common enough thing to happen. We need not flaunt what has happened to us in public. No one need know.'

'We hold his future in our hands. I cannot allow this child to be cast aside like some unwanted puppy. I couldn't live with myself not knowing of his fate.'

Diana blinked rapidly. 'We can be kept informed.'

Grace backed away. The whole idea repulsed her. 'Mama! He looks like Letitia.'

An agonizing whimper came from her mother as she staggered towards the bed as though Grace were a fearsome enemy.

'I'm sorry, Mama, but the thought of sending him away distresses me so much. I cannot do it. He's my half-brother.'

'Then you are no longer a daughter of mine!' Diana threw herself onto her large canopied bed, wailing.

This sound brought in the others, who, chattering like a cage of birds, crowded onto the bed to give solace to their mother.

Grace stood back. It seemed as though she was not in the room, that she looked on the scene from a distance. All that was familiar now became strange, foreign.

Over the noise of Diana's weeping, Letitia confronted her. 'What have you done? Why did you upset Mama?'

'Be quiet, Letitia,' she whispered, hating how her sisters looked at her in accusation.

'What a demanding shrew you've become, Grace,' Letitia scoffed.

Appalled and frustrated that her sister should think about her like that caused white-hot fury to run through her veins. 'Out, all of you!' Grace tugged Phoebe's arm, then Emma Kate's, wanting them all gone so she could think. 'Mama, pull yourself together!'

Letitia strode around the bed to stand but inches from her and Grace smelt the alcohol on her breath. 'I'm tired of you telling us what to do. I know you spy on me. You're nothing but a mean spirited hag! I hope Father persuades Mr Horton to pick *you* as his bride!'

'He has already decided,' Grace retaliated before looking regretfully at the person in question. 'It's to be Emma Kate.'

Emma Kate slowly rose from the bed, dismay written on her face. 'No! No, I won't do it! Not him. He's old and *ugly*.' Emma Kate looked wildly at them all before running out of the room crying, her mother's wretchedness forgotten.

'Why must you make everyone's life a misery, just because you have been thwarted in love?' Letitia's sneer made Grace want to slap her pert oval face.

'Come with me, Letitia.' She turned to leave the room, knowing her sister's curiosity would send her following.

'No, Grace!' Diana struggled off the bed in a tangle of copper-coloured skirts. 'Stay here, Letitia.'

Grace ignored her mother's outburst and Letitia's furious scowl and continued out into the gallery. She didn't want to take them out of their safe, comfortable world and thrust cold, harsh reality in their faces, but she must. She was tired of handling everything alone. They needed to carry their share. They did nothing but wait for someone else to tell them what to do, whether it be herself, their father and no doubt eventually their husbands. She loved them too much to let them be blinded to life outside this house. Serving at soup kitchens wasn't enough.

At the top of the staircase, Diana caught up and frantically grabbed her arm, halting her. 'No, Grace, I beg of you. Protect them.'

'Protect them from what, Mama? Death? Life? Father? I simply cannot keep guarding them from everything! I've tried but it's not possible. All their lives I have tried to keep them safe from harm and the harsh realities of the world outside this house, but in the end what good will it do if Father sells them to men like Horton? Life is not knights in shining armour and castles in the clouds.'

'What is happening?' Gaby asked from the bottom of the stairs. Her soaked riding habit clung to her skin.

'Everyone is getting a lesson on life and death, Gaby.' Grace shook off her mother's restraint and carried on downstairs. 'Do you wish to join us?'

'Have you gone mad?' Diana's screech echoed off the walls.

Doyle ran into the hall to stare up at them in amazement. He made a move toward Grace, but her words forestalled him.

'Ahh, Doyle. Do tell my mother and sisters what's recently occurred in this house. What we witnessed.' A sudden, high hysterical laugh sprang from her.

The girls and Diana huddled together at the top of the staircase, crying softly at the sudden upheaval.

Doyle met Grace on the stairs and gently took her cold hand in his warm one. 'Miss Grace, let me take you to the study and pour you a brandy or some tea, yes?' His soft, dark brown eyes implored her to allow him. 'You've suffered a shock, but I'll help you.'

She sagged against him. 'Tell them, Doyle. Tell them what Father has done!'

Gaby came up the stairs to her side. 'Dearest, come with Doyle and me.'

Grace nodded. The pain in her chest threatened to suffocate her, while everything else became numb. Supporting her between the two of them, they led her down to the study and sat her down. Doyle placed a small brandy in her hand. She shook violently and spilt the liquid down the front of her lilac linen dress. The sips of brandy breathed fire back into her body. She watched, dazed, as Gaby and Doyle whispered in the corner until a tentative knock on the door had them glancing her way before leaving the study.

Alone, the silence crowded in on her mind. Tiredness crept slowly over her like a morning mist. She ached to close her eyes and sleep and hope that when she woke it would all have been a nightmare.

When Gaby returned she knelt in front of Grace. 'Darling, the doctor has arrived to see to the poor woman. He knows her, apparently. Dr Bambridge whispered some information about her to Doyle. And from what I can gather from Doyle, she was Father's mistress.'

'So, it is true then,' her voice wobbled, 'the baby is our half-brother?'

Gaby nodded. 'I'm afraid so.'

'I knew it. Something gripped my heart as soon as I saw him. I watched him being born, Gaby. I held him when he was only minutes old.'

'Yes, dearest. Doyle told me.' Gaby sighed. 'Father once asked Dr Bambridge to see Olive one other time to rid her of a child. Dr Bambridge was alarmed to see Olive here, as he knew her to be ill. He wonders how she even made it here in her state.'

'Poor woman.' Grace shook her head, sad the woman had suffered so. 'And what of Father?'

'He has been sent for. Do you wish to go up to bed and rest?'

'No. I am better now.' With one hand, she tidied her hair. 'I don't know what came over me.'

'It was the shock, dearest. It's not every day a woman gives birth and then dies right before your eyes.'

'I thought I was the strong one.' Grace smiled a little, feeling faintly recovered.

'You are. But sometimes, you need help too. You think you have to do everything on your own, but you don't.' Gaby kissed Grace's forehead. 'I must go up to see Mama. The doctor has given her a sleeping draught to soothe her.'

'Poor Mama. I was dreadful to her.'

'No, you weren't, under the circumstances. She has suffered at father's hands too.'

'It will not stop as long as he's alive. I hate him, Gaby, for everything he has done.'

Gaby stood, her voice flat. 'Don't we all? Emma Kate is threatening to run away.'

'Things will change now.' Grace rose also. Her shaking had ceased. She took a deep breath.

'How will they? This scandal will haunt us forever.'

'Indeed, and it'll also show father that his ambitions to be an influential member of this community are lost.' Grace tilted her chin, regaining her old self once more. 'No more will Father rule us as if we are animals to be sold off to the highest bidder. We may not make wealthy marriages, but there is a chance we may make happier ones to men who care for us.'

Gaby walked to the drinks cabinet and poured herself a good measure of their Father's whiskey. 'Do you know what people say about Father?'

'No, what?' Grace frowned as Gaby drank the glass dry in one swallow, the distaste showing clearly on her pale face.

'That he has no breeding and if he hadn't married Mama, then the Woodruffs would still be merchant traders. Mama's bloodline and money is all that keeps society calling on us.'

'Such is common knowledge and we're still accepted. Why is it coming out now?'

'Because they say father is reverting back to type by selling us off one by one. Father acts like the big man of the town but they still see him as a merchant's grandson.' Gaby gave a mocking grin. 'Only, no one will say it to his face.'

'Well, now they will have more to talk about. The news of Woodruff's old mistress dying after giving birth to his bastard son in his own house will do the rounds of drawing rooms for months to come.'

'Plus the rumours of his financial circumstances.'

'Really?' Grace was instantly alert. 'What have you heard?'

'A few whispers. Mama's money was spent years ago and now a few of his investments have gone badly. Gossip has it he is near bankrupt.' Gaby shrugged. 'At least Heather married well.'

'The first and maybe only one to do so.'

'Poor Mama.' Gaby sighed. 'All she has got out of her marriage is a husband that spent her money and daughters she can't marry off. It doesn't bode well for the sanctity of marriage does it?'

A tap on the door preceded Doyle. 'He is home.'

Gaby placed her glass on the desk. 'We shall tell him together.'

They left the room to greet their father in the hall.

Woodruff handed Doyle his coat and hat. He stopped mid-stride as he saw them. 'What is the emergency? Why was I sent for? I've had a dreadful day and I must be in Leeds for business so it had better be important!'

'Father.'

'Well? What is it? I have enough worries without being brought home over some trivial nonsense. Is the house on fire? No, and nothing else would cause me a moment's concern, I assure you.'

'We must speak to you, Father. An event has occurred today.' Grace raised her voice. 'A shocking event needing your immediate attention.'

Woodruff glowered at her before walking into the drawing room. 'Doyle! Brandy!'

Doyle went to the spirit trolley by the window.

'Father?' Grace waited for him to acknowledge her. Gaby linked her arm though hers for added support.

'Hurry up and get to the point, then leave me in peace, damn you!' Woodruff roared, flinging his bulk into a wide, wing-backed chair near the fireplace.

Grace felt Gaby tremble, but she didn't know if it was anger or fear. 'There is something you must see.' Grace swallowed. She had her strength back and now a deep rage simmered.

Woodruff picked up a small, delicate figurine from a rose-wood ornamental table beside his chair. He studied the porcelain figure for a moment before suddenly throwing it in the direction of Grace's head.

With reflexes she didn't know she owned, Grace ducked the flying object and pushed Gaby away to the side. The shattering fragments rebounded from the wall behind them to land in splinters on the polished floor.

Doyle strode to Grace's side his fists clenched.

Grace grasped Gaby's arm, holding her sister upright as she swayed to near fainting. 'You can smash every article in this room for all I care. Nevertheless, I still have something you need to see.' She would never know how she managed to make those words sound unconcerned when inside she shook like a leaf in a stiff breeze.

Woodruff bellowed like an enraged bull. Doyle moved closer to Grace to protect her, but in the event Woodruff stood and scowled at them. 'Show me.'

In Doyle's bedroom, Woodruff barely glanced at the prone form, covered in a white sheet, on the bed. 'What is this?' he sneered at them. 'You brought me home because a serving wench has died?'

Grace trembled as she gently lifted the sheet back.

'Olive?' Woodruff's eyes bulged and his face lost all of its ruddy hue. 'What ... I ...'

'Yes, your mistress is dead, Father, and your newborn son sleeps upstairs in the nursery.' Her eyes narrowed in disgust.

He turned for the door, staggering blindly. He shot out a hand to steady himself, beseeching Doyle's help. Doyle turned away but Woodruff clasped his sleeve as he slumped to his knees gasping for breath. Wheezing noises escaped him, as wordlessly he begged for aid from his daughters.

Such was the display, Grace and Gaby stood unable to move. They watched their father keel over onto his back clutching at his chest.

CHAPTER 9

*D*oyle sat at his small desk positioned by the only window in his private sitting room. In front of him lay the bills from food and fuel merchants of the town, all needing his attention and none receiving it even though Grace asked him personally to attend to them. He leant back in his chair to stare absently through the lace curtains. Outside, summer was at its height, promising a good harvest for the farmers. The gardens of the house never looked better and it was a shame no one, except the gardeners, took note of their splendour.

The last month had seen Woodruff House disintegrate into a place reeking of despondency. The family's visitors dwindled to a small group of Diana's genuine friends.

With a deep sigh, Doyle rose and stood by the window over-looking the service areas of the estate. Grace, as always, came to the forefront of his thoughts. His gut twisted in agony of wanting her. They lived in the same house but were further apart than if they lived in different countries. *I'm the biggest fool to stay.* Yet, he knew he couldn't leave her, would never willingly leave her.

After tapping on the door, Mrs Hawksberry wobbled in, wincing in pain. He knew her thick legs, swollen with fluid from standing on stone floors since she was a nine-year-old scullery maid, made walking difficult. 'I've news, Mr Doyle.'

Doyle pulled out an arm-less chair for her to perch her ample behind on. 'You should stay off those legs, Mrs Hawksberry.'

'Nay, who'd run my kitchen?' she asked tartly.

'They'd cope for an hour or two I'm sure. If you don't rest, those legs of yours will have you bedridden before long and then we'd be in a fine pickle.' Doyle winked.

Mrs Hawksberry granted him a scraping of a smile. 'Do yer want me news or not?'

'Of course.'

'The maid, Maureen O'Reilly. The poor lass hung herself yesterday. They found her hangin' from a rope in a barn.'

Doyle closed his eyes.

'They say her father treated her real bad. Apparently, he thumped her black and blue when she first went home.' Mrs Hawksberry struggled to her feet. 'Well, the lass is free from it all now.'

'Yes.'

At the door, Mrs Hawksberry turned back to him. '*He*,' she nodded towards the ceiling above, 'has a lot to answer for, by God!'

'No doubt he'll get his judgment.'

'He should have died when he had his attack. He's bringin' all those lovely lasses down. Miss Grace hardly eats or sleeps, Miss Gaby looks fit for the grave and as for Miss Letitia, well, I can't find the words!'

'I know, Mrs Hawksberry, I know.'

* * *

THE BABY'S soft gurgling brought a tender smile to Grace's face. She sat on an old wooden rocking chair, humming a tune, the baby cradled in her arms. The air in the small room was close, even though the short square windows were open to allow any stray breeze to enter. The warmth of the day magnified in the rooms at the top of the house, made Grace as sleepy as the baby.

In the five weeks since his birth, she had spent most of her time in the nursery. She was his primary caregiver and had hired a local girl, Janey, as a live-in wet nurse.

Grace put him into his cot and then went through to the main room of the nursery. 'He's asleep now. I'll come back in a little while.'

Janey bobbed a quick curtsey. 'Yes, Miss Woodruff.'

Downstairs, she found Faith in the library reading a Dickens novel in honour of his recent death. Faith gave her a small smile before burying her nose back into her book. Grace faltered, wondering whether she should speak, but decided against it. Her relationship with her all sisters, except Gaby, had deteriorated greatly. They blamed her for the family's plunge into social obscurity. Her insistence on keeping the baby brought howls of protest from everyone, Diana worst of all, who'd taken to her bed and stayed there.

Their father's attack, culminating in a stroke, had rendered him bedridden, his left side paralyzed. Grace employed a stern-faced woman as his nurse since Doyle refused to have anything to do with him. She knew her sisters cared nothing for the state of their father's health, nevertheless, in their eyes he was still the head of the house. Now, as the scandal still reigned supreme in drawing rooms, gentlemen's clubs and other social places where the gentry gathered, the name Woodruff was an embarrassing hindrance.

Grace searched the library shelves for a tempting book to take her mind off her troubles and the accounts awaiting her attention.

The door opened, and Doyle entered. 'May I have a word, Miss Woodruff?'

'Certainly.' She followed him out to the study.

'What is it, Doyle?'

'News has been given to me of Maureen O'Reilly.'

'Oh?'

'She was found hanging in a barn close to her village.'

Grace's shoulders sagged. 'How extremely sad.'

'Yes, a terrible end she didn't deserve.'

'Have a basket sent to her family. Mrs Hawksberry will know what to put in it.' Grace slumped onto the leather chair behind her father's desk.

'A basket of food. Not much for a life, is it?' A mutinous glare lit his eyes.

'Pardon?' Grace frowned.

'Your father's habit of ruining people's lives continues.'

'I don't follow you.' Grace tilted her chin, fearing his next words.

'Your father was responsible for O'Reilly's condition ... Miss Woodruff.' He deliberately added her name as an afterthought. He was defying her, goading her even. He did this on occasion. Why? He had no idea, but some inner stubbornness and maleness inside him longed for her to recognize him as a male, a partner. However, today she didn't rise to his taunt, for his last bit of news had obviously devastated her and he was instantly sorry. Never would he purposely hurt her; he loved her too much. Nevertheless, he ached for her to turn to him as a man, not as a butler. His jibes were a covering for her unknowing rejection of him.

His sweet Grace held her head in her hands, though she did not cry.

'Miss Grace, I am sorry. I should not have told you. You have enough to deal with.' Doyle bent over her. His tender love shone through his words and he could have kicked himself for his vicious thoughtlessness. He knew she couldn't endure much more. For the last few weeks, he had watched her shrink inside herself whenever her sisters rebuked her advances, when her mother refused to see her and when her father mumbled his sickening curses at her.

'I would have found out sooner or later,' Grace spoke wearily, lifting her head to gaze at him.

Their faces were close and for a moment, Doyle had an acute urge to touch his lips to hers. Just once, he would like to rest her head against his shoulder and comfort her. She wore her loneliness like a cloak and it was more of a tragedy for being in a house full of people.

The air between them was taut with sizzling tension and Grace closed her eyes and involuntary leant towards him. Desire surged through him in a tingling rush. He sucked in a breath, anticipating the silken feel of her. She heard his sudden intake of breath and her eyes flew open. With a jerk, she leapt up and ran from the room.

'Christ!' The ornate ceiling echoed Doyle's strangled oath.

* * *

GABY SLIPPED DOWN from her horse and looked around the deserted farmyard. She headed for the plain two-storeyed house made from the same stone as the barn.

'Gaby!'

Slowly, Gaby turned back to watch John Morgan rattle into the yard on a flat-topped cart. She waited until he clambered down and walked to her, hobbling slightly. In the summer, his bad leg, a reminder of his efforts in the Crimean War, didn't hurt so much and so his limp was less pronounced.

'What yer doin' here, lass?' His gentle, green eyes smiled at her. He took off his hat and the sun glistened on his greying black hair.

'What do *you* think? To see you, naturally.' Being frightened hardened her tone. She hated being out of control. Her condition haunted her every thought.

John Morgan squinted in the sunlight. 'I haven't seen you for a while.'

'I do have other matters to attend!' She snapped.

'Aye, I guess you do,' he murmured.

Gaby bristled. 'So, you have heard about the child?'

'Hasn't everyone?' His look was full of concern. She hated it when he looked at her with kindness shining from his eyes. She didn't want his kindness, well, she did but she couldn't afford to say so. He was a tough Yorkshire man and they didn't fall in love at his age, or so he said, and they certainly didn't fall in love with the local toff's daughter.

Gaby bowed her head. She was tired, so very tired of worrying and being strong. John softly touched her arm and she sprang back.

'I'm tryin' ter weigh up yer mood, lass.' He grinned. 'Yer as unpredictable as a young filly and sometimes yer need a gentle hand.'

'I've enough to concern myself with, John Morgan, without being compared to a horse!'

He folded his arms across his chest as though waiting for her to finish. She knew he took none of her nonsense.

'Are yer comin' in fer a cuppa tea then?'

Gaby shook her head. 'I must get back. Grace needs me.' Her voice was husky, full of repressed emotion.

'Nay, lass, come in fer a minnit.'

'I'll come again soon.' She turned in the direction of her horse.

'Right. Well, yer know where I am.'

Pausing, Gaby looked over her shoulder. She swallowed the tears clogging her throat. She had to be brave like Grace. 'Morgan ... John?'

'Aye, my lass?'

'Don't put three spoonfuls of sugar in my tea. It's disgusting.'

John Morgan held out his hand and smiled; it crinkled the corners of his eyes.

* * *

GRACE STOOD at the end of her father's large bed and looked on without pity. Her father struggled to sit and speak, but she and the hired nurse, Gibbons continued with their conversation.

'I know you're busy, Miss, but I would only be gone for two days. I haven't had any time off since coming here. I wouldn't ask if it wasn't important.'

'I understand, Mrs Gibbons. You deserve to attend your niece's wedding,' Grace said.

Woodruff turned puce in his frustration to get the two women's attention. His right hand, the only hand to move, twitched and grabbed at the bed sheets. Drool dribbled down his chin to hang suspended before plopping onto his nightshirt. The look in his eyes burned hatred at them. 'B ... Bee ... Bitches.'

The nurse and Grace, ignoring his struggles and curses, left the bed and went to stand outside the bedroom door.

'You will leave tomorrow?' Grace asked.

'Yes, Miss, and I'll be back on Sunday evening.'

'Very good, Mrs Gibbons.' Grace dismissed the nurse and walked down the gallery towards her own room.

A door opened to her right and Letitia came out of her bedroom. She glared at Grace before turning her nose up and marching by as if she had seen something repulsive. Grace sighed and continued on her way, only to pause at the sound of weeping coming from Phoebe's room. She opened the door.

Phoebe lay across her bed, her shoulders heaving with each sob. Grace hurriedly crossed to gather her into her arms.

'Oh, Grace!' Phoebe wailed.

'What is it, darling?'

'I hate it! Hate it, hate it, hate it!' She cried louder with each word.

'What, dearest? What do you hate?'

'This! This life we now have to lead! How will I marry well, when we don't receive callers any more? Everything is ruined.' Phoebe's sobs increased. 'Am I to remain a maid like you?'

Grace pulled away from Phoebe so she could see her better. 'Listen to me. You are a beautiful young woman, and you *will* marry, I promise you.'

'How? We go nowhere?' She wiped her nose with a sodden handkerchief. 'All our invitations have stopped. I want to have fun. We have missed so many parties and I have not worn my new hat yet.'

Fishing for her clean handkerchief in the pocket of her blue muslin dress, Grace's mind worked overtime. '*We* will have a party.'

'A party?' Phoebe's eyes widened. 'We couldn't possibly.'

'And why not? We have nothing to be ashamed of!' Her impulsive decision surprised her, but she warmed to it.

'Mama will not allow it. She will be outraged at the mere suggestion.'

'Then Mama can stay in her rooms.' Grace shrugged.

'You wouldn't dare, Grace,' she whispered.

'Both Father and Mama are incapable of running this house, therefore I am in charge and if I want to order a party, I will.' Grace stood and walked to the door.

'Will people come, though?' Phoebe was worried. 'Who will we invite?'

'Of course they will come!' Grace forced a bright smile to her face. She prayed it would be so. 'And we'll invite the whole town if need be.'

That evening, Grace was the last to enter the dining room for dinner. She had barely sat down at her place before Letitia fired questions at her.

'Is it true what Phoebe has been telling us? Are you suggesting we host a party?'

Grace held Letitia's stare with ease. 'You obviously do not like the idea.'

'You are a fool to think we can even give an afternoon tea, never mind a dinner party!'

'Then I am a fool,' Grace answered, smiling at Doyle who bent to fill her wine glass. It pleased her that he gave a hint of a smile in return, dispelling some of the awkwardness that plagued them whenever they were in each other's company.

'Grace, it would be shameful to do so with Mama in her rooms and Father ill,' Faith murmured.

'Nonsense. Father and Mama will attend. There is nothing wrong with Mama, and Father can be put in a chair to watch the proceedings.' Grace smiled.

'Mama won't leave her rooms,' Emma Kate said. 'She is easy to tears since ... well, since the child.'

'And Father should remain in his bed.' Gaby cringed. 'I nearly brought up my meal at the sight of him lying there jabbering and drooling. We don't wish for visitors to see that, do we?'

Grace sighed. 'Do you all want to find husbands or remain here forever? Since the invitations have stopped coming to our door, then, we must send them out.' She paused to watch their reactions. 'We shall have a dinner party a fortnight hence, then a summer garden party the week following. Obviously, father will not hold his usual hunt and shooting weekend this year. However, I see no reason not to have a picnic or a musical soiree.'

'It is simply bad taste!' Letitia spat, waving her half-empty wine glass in the air. 'It would only invite more gossip.'

'We have nothing to be ashamed of.'

Letitia nearly choked on a sip of wine. 'Nothing to be ashamed of! Are you insane? Upstairs sleeps some whore's bastard who you claim is our brother!'

Grace glared at her. 'Shut your filthy mouth. *He is our brother.*'

'Only on some tramp's say-so.'

'No, on Father's!' Anger and resentment burned like acid in Grace's throat. *Why did they not understand her?* She took a calming breath and felt better when Gaby gave her a small smile of support.

Letitia scoffed. 'Well, he'll never be my brother and his presence ruins us.'

'Many known families have raised half-siblings, Letitia,' Faith said. 'It's not as uncommon as you think.'

'Be quiet. What would you know?' Letitia sneered.

Grace raised her chin, ready for another battle. 'The other alternative, Letitia, is for you to take Mama to Scarborough for the rest of the summer.' She shrugged. 'You can spend lazy days with cousin Verity. There you may find a husband amongst Scarborough's society.'

They all looked at each other, weighing up this last statement.

Emma Kate picked at the tablecloth. 'I believe a change would be good for us all. So, why should only Letitia go with Mama?'

Grace couldn't say she wanted Letitia gone because she was a thorn in her side. 'You can all go if you wish.'

'I will stay,' Gaby said. 'You cannot remain alone, Grace.'

'How will I be alone in a house full of servants?' She grinned, trying to remain unruffled.

'Nevertheless, I'll stay,' Gaby said.

Grace looked at the others.

Phoebe pouted. 'There will be no parties if we go to Cousin Verity's, Mama will never allow it.'

'No doubt Verity will host some social gathering while you are there.' Grace finally made a start on her soup.

'Cousin Verity doesn't socialize much, she told me.' Emma Kate frowned.

'Simply a thought.' Grace ate more soup.

Letitia held up her wine glass for Doyle to refill. 'Why should I be the one to suffer? Mama and Verity will sit all day bemoaning their children's courses in life!'

Grace quickly looked up from her soup. 'Why would Verity have reason to complain about William?'

A sly look passed over Letitia's face. 'William has announced he is to live in France after his marriage.'

Grace lowered her spoon, ignoring the flash of satisfaction on Letitia's face.

'Scarborough is not as exciting as London,' sulked Phoebe. 'Mama says we aren't to go to William's wedding now. I was so looking forward to it!'

'Why aren't you going to the wedding?' Grace asked.

'I'll accompany Mama to Scarborough,' Faith spoke, as the tension rose in the room.

Tears shimmered on Phoebe's eyelashes. 'Mama says the scandal will have reached London as well by now.'

'What twaddle!' Grace snapped. 'As if London would care about what is happening in a country house near Leeds! Mama is over-reacting.' With a suddenness that made the others jump, she scraped back her chair before Doyle could help her.

'What are you doing?' Gaby asked, her spoon poised mid air.

'I need to talk to Mama.' Grace left the table and strode to her mother's rooms. With a loud, preceding knock on the door, she entered Diana's sitting room to find her mother dining at a small, round table.

'Grace!' Surprised, Diana recovered to show her irritation at being disturbed. 'What do you want? I have nothing to say to you!'

'Oh, well I have much to say to *you*, Mama.'

'Leave me at once!' Diana's bottom lip quivered.

'Not yet.'

'How dare you!' Diana scrambled in her dress pockets for a handkerchief.

Grace hardened her heart towards her mother's distress. Diana had always taken the coward's way out. 'Mama, I've decided to host a few gatherings in the coming weeks, and I need you beside me.'

Diana gasped and held her white lacy scrap of linen to her

chin in readiness for the tears she could conjure at the slightest provocation. 'No! Oh, no, Grace! Why such a thing is incomprehensible!'

'It's not, Mama. In fact, it is exactly what this family needs. We need to show everyone we are still worthy. Do you not care that we're no longer invited to certain receptions given by people who once claimed us as friends?'

'I care! But whose fault is it we are shunned?'

'I'll not accept blame, Mama. The child has no one but us to take care of it.'

Diana stood, angrily throwing down her napkin. 'How do you think I feel having *his* bastard under this roof? Have you no feelings for me?'

'Yes, Mama, you know I'd do anything for you, but I'll not send this child to an orphanage.'

Diana walked to the window and looked blindly out into the darkened sky. 'Then I think you and it should leave this house.'

Astounded, Grace took a moment to understand. 'If I should go, who will run this house? Who will look after you all? You, Mama? Will you suddenly return to your duty as hostess? A duty you have conveniently denied doing for years.'

'We have Doyle. He can take care of us.'

'And what about your husband?'

'He has his nurse.'

Grace took a step towards the door, and then looked over her shoulder at her mother's cold stance. She nearly laughed at the irony of her mother finally standing firm on an issue, only for the issue to be about her. 'Very well, Mama, I … we'll be gone in the morning. Good night.'

CHAPTER 10

*G*race entered her bedroom where Hopeland was packing clothes into trunks. 'Are you nearly finished, Hopeland?'

The maid sniffed. 'Yes, Miss Woodruff, though the task has been a sad one.'

Grace patted her shoulder before leaving the room to cross the hall and enter her father's bedroom.

He sat in a chair by the partially opened window so he could watch his estate workers go about their business. She knew it would irritate him beyond belief that he couldn't be out there. He had no control over anything. The irony of the present state of affairs was not lost on her. Now he might understand the frustration at being a pawn to another's whims.

As Grace neared his chair, he turned to frown at her. 'You.'

'Yes, Father?' Grace watched as he struggled to speak. A task he could only do if he spoke individual words instead of sentences. The whole lengthy process clearly infuriated him.

'You... Go?' He managed to make his lopsided mouth spit out.

'Yes, Father. I am going today.'

'Boy?'

'Yes, the baby is coming with me. He isn't wanted here.'

'Di...ana, bitch!'

'No, Father, she is merely thinking of the others. It's my choice. I chose the baby.' Grace moved closer to look out of the window. Below the magnificent gardens of Woodruff House bloomed in the summer sun. 'I understand the situation will not work the way it is.'

'You...not...go. I...master!' Drool dribbled down his chin. 'Boy...stay!'

Grace looked down at him. 'No one is calling, Father, the girls aren't happy. You know what scandal can do to a family.'

'You... stay!'

'And what will happen to us all? Because of you, and now me, we are social outcasts. But if I leave, society will eventually welcome Mama and the girls back into the whirl again; even pity them. They might not marry as well as Heather, but they may find someone suitable.'

'I better...soon!' Woodruff banged his good hand on the arm of the chair.

'We cannot wait.'

'You go...my...h...ouse...Leeds.' He puffed, the strength leaving him.

Grace frowned. 'I wasn't aware you owned a house in Leeds.'

'Eight.'

Grace shook her head, not surprised at this admission. She would never know him, nor did she care to. He'd never shown them love or induced his family to foster affection towards him. It was too late in the day to seek the obligatory respect due to one's parent, and he deserved none.

She let out a breath. 'I chose York to give us some distance. The scandal will die a natural death without us in evidence, but perhaps we can live in Leeds if we are quiet and unobtrusive.'

He nodded.

'Well, let me have the best one, Father, as your son will be raised there.' Grace played her trump card.

'Raised...here!'

'Not until the girls are married. They must be given a chance first.'

'Humph!' Woodruff grunted.

Grace laid her forehead against the cool glass of the window, her heart heavy. She had no wish to leave her home and face the unknown with only a baby and a nursemaid for company. Many a night in the last few weeks, she'd lain awake looking up at the stars in the black velvet night hoping to find some answer to the misery enveloping the house. However, try as she might, nothing came to her which would help. She wanted her sisters to be happy, but that wasn't possible while people thought she was flaunting the baby in their faces. Only, she couldn't give him up. How would she live with herself if she did?

'You. Only...one...I like.'

Grace glanced down at her ageing father. His balding head held only gray hairs now and the lines around his mouth had deepened. She sighed. 'I wish I liked you.'

Woodruff chortled at her honesty.

* * *

SWEEPING DOWN THE STAIRCASE, Grace held her head high and the baby close to her chest. Janey followed her.

Waiting for them at the bottom of the stairs was Letitia. 'Mama told me you are going today. Now.' Her pale face added to the worried look in her red-rimmed eyes. 'The others don't know. They're all out; you must wait for their return.'

'I'm sure you will delight in informing them for me. I've left them all letters. They can visit me whenever they wish.' Grace sailed past and out into the bright sunshine. At the foot of the steps stood the carriage loaded with luggage.

Letitia scurried after her. 'You cannot go, Grace, what will happen to us all? Who'll take care of us?'

'Ask Mama.' Grace handed the baby to Janey so she could enter the carriage. She wondered where Doyle was.

'How can you do this?' Letitia pushed past the wet-nurse. 'You're so selfish!'

From within the carriage, Grace looked at her and for once felt detachment. 'Perhaps I am selfish, Letitia, but no more so than any other in this house.'

'You have always said you care about us more than anything or anyone else in the world.'

'True, and it's the reason why I'm leaving.'

'Liar! Now we know you as you truly are, a self-centred liar!'

Grace turned away and once Janey was settled, she gave instructions to Sykes to depart. Sudden rocking movement had Grace frowning, she leant out the window to see Doyle climbing up beside Sykes as the carriage rolled down the drive. 'What *are* you doing?'

'Coming with you, Miss Woodruff,' he called down as the carriage gathered speed.

Grace stared bewildered, but said nothing for the moment. Her mind was too occupied to worry about his actions. She would deal with him later.

They travelled through Leeds town centre and out to the other side before turning into Old Woodhouse Lane and headed towards the countryside again. Before long, Sykes halted the horses outside a small, neat cottage.

Grace sighed in relief as Doyle helped her down from the carriage. Head held high, she stepped along the path to the front door and knocked.

A tall woman answered, her eyes narrowing in her thin angular face. She wore her greying hair scrapped back into a tight bun and an unadorned dark gray dress.

'Mrs Winton?'

'I am, Miss Woodruff.' The older woman's clipped tone matched her cold eyes.

'Oh, good, you received my letter then. I'm sorry for the short notice.'

'No mind, I'm always ready for visitors. Mr Woodruff and his guests used to call at odd times.' Mrs Winton stood back allowing Grace to enter.

Only a coat stand and a wooden chair furnished the narrow and dark hall. A long woollen rug ran the length of the stone-flagged floor.

'You are the only servant?'

The housekeeper nodded and then waved towards the room on the right. 'This way, if you please, Miss Woodruff.'

Grace made a quick tour of the cottage. The parlour, study and dining room were small and clean as were the bedrooms. The brightest room was the kitchen.

Standing on the back doorstep, Grace viewed her surroundings. A wooden barn, including a horse stall, stood vacant at the side of the house. The length of the back yard was deceiving due to the open fields beyond it. Farmer's wheat grew high and golden as far as she could see.

'Miss Woodruff?' Mrs Winton cleared her throat, her primness evident in the tilt of her head and the straightness of her stance. 'The man, girl and child?'

'The wet-nurse is called Janey and the baby is my brother, Daniel Thomas. Give them the largest room. A cart will be arriving soon with nursery furniture.'

'And the man?' Mrs Winton's back was stiff with displeasure.

'He is returning to Woodruff House.' Grace walked back along the hall and into the parlour where Doyle stood waiting. 'Sit down, Doyle.'

He perched on the edge of the chair. His gaze never left her face.

Grace folded her hands in her lap and gave him a small smile. 'You have to go back.'

'No!' He sprang to his feet. 'I will not leave you.'

She stayed him with her hand. 'Listen to me, please.'

His hands clenched at his sides. 'I won't stay there without you.'

'I need you to be there in my place,' she pleaded. 'I left so my sisters could continue to live in the way they were meant. The scandal has taken away their opportunity to be selected by good husbands. I don't want to be responsible for more unhappiness. With my father incapacitated, my mother can guide the girls into suitable, if not exciting marriages. However, Mama will need you to run the house.'

'Can she not employ a housekeeper?'

Grace shook her head. 'I would prefer it if you were there. I trust you to take care of them in my place.'

'But what about you?'

'The baby and I will be well and happy here.'

Doyle gazed at her and conflicting emotions crossed his face. He sighed wearily and sat back down.

Grace reached over and clutched at his hand resting on his knee. She broke a social rule by doing so, but she had learnt not everything could be ruled. Besides, she knew this sweet man would give her anything; do whatever she asked, because it was she who asked him. He showed his feelings for her in his warm brown eyes. 'I know having you at the house will help me to live here without complaint.'

He leaned closer as if to take her in his arms. 'But who'll look after you?'

'I can take care of myself. However, I would like it very much if you would come and spend Sundays with me.'

Doyle's eyes widened in surprise. 'Sundays?'

'Yes. Can you come here every Sunday and bring me news? And while you are here, you might as well have a meal with me.'

He shook his head. 'If people were to find out, the scandal would surpass the last one.' He sighed. 'I don't want to hurt your standing in the community any more than it is.'

She raised an ironic eyebrow. 'Somehow I don't think I'm on anyone's seating list at the moment.'

'It's not right. I am your butler. I can't dine with you.'

'You are my friend too, I hope.' Grace rose and walked to the door. 'I will see you on Sunday then?'

Doyle followed her. 'Miss Woodruff...'

'Sunday?'

'Yes.'

Upstairs the baby cried. Suddenly, tears pricked her eyes, but she swallowed them back. She'd never been apart from her sisters until now. She had to be strong and firm on her decision. This was the right thing to do and she must believe it.

'Shall I inform your mother and sisters of this arrangement?' Doyle asked, hesitating on the step.

'Yes, if they inquire.'

He hesitated. 'You'll send a note should you need anything?'

Grace nodded.

He walked half way up the path and then turned around. 'Until Sunday, then.'

'Yes.'

* * *

DIANA PACED HER SITTING ROOM, kicking out her navy skirts impatiently on every turn. She held the letter received two days ago from Verity, informing her of their intended visit to Woodruff House.

William's wedding was in two weeks' time and Verity promised to spend a few days with Diana before continuing on to London. The door opened and Diana turned expectantly.

'Mama, a carriage is coming down the drive,' Emma Kate said, coming into the room.

'Where are the others?' Diana asked, putting a hand to her hair.

'Phoebe is having her lesson with Mr du Pont, Faith is walking in the garden, Gaby is riding, and Letitia is in her room.'

'Go down and have cousin Verity brought up immediately. Have Doyle put her luggage in the blue guest room.'

'Doyle is away today.' Emma Kate blushed. 'Remember? It's Sunday.'

'Blast.' Diana slapped the letter in her hand. She waved a dismissive hand to her daughter. 'Have it seen to, Emma Kate.'

'Yes, Mama.'

Diana continued pacing, waiting for her cousin's appearance. Lord knows, she needed someone to talk to. She doubted she could cope alone for another day. The requirements of the house and her daughters were too much for her. Doyle's return did ease the condition a little, for he could be relied on to keep the house in order, but keeping her daughters cheerful was impossible. They were in no situation to entertain and invitations were few and far between. *How did I come to this?*

She paused by her writing desk and looked in disgust at the correspondence lying there. Begging letters to her family had received cruel missives in reply. Pride had kept her from writing to them since her doomed marriage to Montgomery, but she had thought, naively perhaps, that now he was incapable of being a husband and father, and literally gone from society, then her family would take pity on her and forgive her past mistakes. How wrong she'd been.

She sighed as Emma Kate entered with William Ross.

'William!' Diana's mouth fell open.

He strode into the room and kissed Diana's cheek. 'Good day, Cousin Diana.'

'Where is your mother?'

'Mama is still in Scarborough. A slight chest illness and persistent cough delays her departure for a few days.'

Emma Kate stepped closer. 'Shall I order tea, Mama?'

'Yes.' Diana waved her away and invited William to sit. 'What brings you to this part of the country so close to your wedding?'

'I thought I might be of assistance. I believe Mr Woodruff is bedridden?'

'Yes, he is.'

'The situation must be daunting?'

'Situation?'

'The child. Mama told me of the child and of Mr Woodruff's seizure, but circumstances such as these can be overcome.' William smiled in reassurance.

'We are ruined! That is not *overcome* easily.'

'Not ruined, Diana. Many families have bastards somewhere in their lineage. The gossip will die, people will forgive and forget.'

'Not a Woodruff scandal. No one ever forgets what the Woodruffs were, William; they let it slide under the carpet for a time and then bring it out again to amuse themselves when life becomes dull.' Diana stood, agitated. 'The girls receive very few invitations and now, because of Woodruff's cruelness, he refuses to use his money to give them good dowries to entice a gentleman's offer. He knows his chances of advancement are lost and doesn't care a whit about the girls.'

'To a wealthy man, your bloodline will be enough to induce him. Not everyone can claim their bride has an Earl for a great uncle.'

Diana dashed away the rising tears. 'I thought with Grace and the child living away, we would have a chance of resuming our lives, but it hasn't happened. The scandal continues to rage.'

William frowned. 'Grace is living away?'

'Did you not hear?'

'Where is she?'

'In one of Woodruff's houses in Leeds.'

'Why?' William's tone hardened. 'Her place is here. This is none of her doing.'

'She refuses to listen to me about the child. I'll not tolerate it under this roof.'

'So, you banished her?' William stood, his impressive height dwarfing her.

'What else was I to do? The girls need my protection.'

William made for the door as it opened with Partridge coming in carrying a tea tray. He glanced over his shoulder. 'Where is your husband?'

'In his rooms, of course. William...' Diana huffed in vexation when he ignored her and went along the gallery.

William knocked, then opened Woodruff's bedroom door. He entered, preparing to see the odious man propped up in bed, but instead, he sat on a chair at the window, a rug covering his knees. A nurse read to him.

Woodruff turned to the newcomer, surprise registering on his dour face. 'W ... William.' He turned and dismissed the nurse with a lopsided sneer.

'Good day to you, Woodruff.' William went to stand by the window. Feelings at his return to this chaotic house churned within him. With each day bringing his wedding closer, he thought more about Grace and the choices he had made. 'Things cannot continue as they are, Woodruff. Grace must to be brought back. I'm astonished this state of affairs has become so out of control. Her place is here.'

'Yes.'

'Good. I'll see to it.' He drew in a deep breath. 'Although it is another problem which brings me here today. Reports of certain share prices. Of these particular companies, I'm aware you hold key investments. Did you read *The Times* today?'

Woodruff nodded. With his good hand, he indicated the fallen newspaper by the bed.

William frowned. 'Have you lost much?'

'B...Bloody fortune. Bastards...Lot of them!'

'Can you recover from it? The rumours are Siltorn's Shipping will not rise again. They've lost too many ships and valuable cargo. They cannot secure any more finance or insurance.'

Woodruff's cheek twitched. 'Poured...much into it. That and...Kendleton Coll'ry.'

He jerked. 'Kendleton Colliery? Are you mad? I read reports of a cave disaster killing twenty men only last month. I didn't know you were involved.'

'Must...pay hundreds...of...pounds.'

'Why buy into it in the first place?' William paled. This was incredulous news. 'It has a history of flooding.'

'Good...seams,' Woodruff said slowly.

'But unattainable.'

'I'll...make it...greatest...mine...in England.'

'From your chair? Have sense man!'

Woodruff reddened at the insult. 'What...you know? Puppy!'

'It's doesn't take a fool to know Kendleton Colliery is prone to flooding and cave-ins. Pull out while you can, Woodruff. Sell to your other shareholders.'

'No shareholders.'

William's eyes widened. 'No shareholders? You own it solely? My God.'

'It won't...flood. I...better each day.' He paused to suck in a breath. 'Soon be...about again. Got ideas.' Obviously tired from the effort, he slumped.

'I'll go to see Grace now. Then, when I return we'll devise a plan to pull you out of the mess you're in.' He turned for the door.

Woodruff straightened. 'Don't need...help!'

William spun back to him. 'Don't you? Funny, I imagined you did. Your whole family is ostracized and your money is diminishing by the minute. I'd say you need more than my help. Do you have anything left?'

'Some.'

'Will you be bankrupt?'

'No!'

'Good.' William stormed from the room and bumped into a startled Diana, who portrayed the guilty look of someone listening at the door.

'William! Is it true?' She pulled at his lapels. 'Have we lost our money?'

'Cousin Diana, *please*.' William released her hands from him.

'I thought you'd come to see *me*, in my time of need, not *him*,' she spat.

'I came to help you all. Woodruff told me, when I was here last, of his investments. When I saw the shares plummet I came to see if I could help him.'

'Are we ruined?' Diana hugged herself.

'Not yet. I'll do all I can.' William reassured her, making for the stairs. 'I need to see Grace. I'll have your driver take me.' He ran downstairs.

Diana hesitated for a moment, letting her anger, frustration and fear build before marching into Woodruff's bedroom; the first time she had entered it for over two years. 'You!' She screeched into Woodruff's pale face.

Woodruff's lips turned back into a snarl. 'Get... out!'

'You aren't happy just to foist your bastard onto us, but now you take away our security too! You always were a *stupid* man!'

With a roar, Woodruff propelled himself out of his chair to latch his good hand around her throat. She managed a hoarse scream, which brought Mrs Gibbons running.

'Mr Woodruff!' Mrs Gibbons grasped his arms. 'Leave go of your wife!' She turned and yelled for help, as Woodruff, in his madness, squeezed tighter with an almost inhuman power. Hopeland and Partridge, followed closely by Letitia and Emma Kate ran into the room. Diana's eyes bulged as she struggled against his demonic strength.

'Father! Let Mama go!' Emma Kate cried, though she and Letitia were too scared to actually step closer to help her.

Hopeland and Partridge wrestled their master's stranglehold from their mistress's neck. They managed to free her from his grip and she slumped against the wall, gasping for breath.

Her daughters crept closer to her, all the while looking fearfully at their father, lest he should spring for them too. Crying, they led her back to her own rooms.

Woodruff, his rage now spent, flopped back against his chair puffing and wheezing. Taking advantage of his weakened state, Hopeland and Partridge dragged him back to his bed. Shaking, Mrs Gibbons settled him under the bedcovers. He was asleep soon after.

'Ye Gods,' Partridge whispered, shaking her head at the grotesque man who nearly committed murder minutes ago.

* * *

GRACE GATHERED the skirts of her green and white pinstriped dress with one hand, and held out her other to Doyle for help over the stile. They had walked further than last Sunday's stroll. But the glorious weather would soon end and days sauntering in the fresh air, passing fields in full harvest would be no more. The city of Leeds was visible over their shoulders, only a mile away. However, if one turned to face north, to gaze over the surrounding countryside, they could imagine they were far from civilization.

She swatted a hovering fly with a small leafy twig carried for such a purpose. This was the third Sunday Doyle had visited with news of the family. Each time he declined dining with her, accepting only a cup of tea. Last week, as today, Grace invited him to walk the country lanes with her. They spoke little on these ambles, being happy to walk and enjoy the innocent delights of the countryside. She found herself comfortable in his presence, though she didn't question why. For now, it was enough to have a friend. His status was of no consequence.

In the distance dark clouds gathered, though not yet close enough to warrant concern. Her thoughts returned to the baby. Again, he had been unsettled most of the night. Again, she and Janey had walked the floor with him. Since their move to the cottage, Daniel Thomas hadn't thrived. Her scant knowledge of babies worried her and left her feeling inadequate. 'Shall we turn back?' she asked.

'Yes, of course, Miss Grace.' Doyle turned, and then swooped down to pluck a long-stemmed grass leaf. He twirled it between his fingers. His jacket hung over his shoulder.

'This is pleasant, isn't it?' she asked him, feeling guilty at her lack of conversation.

'Very.' He turned smiling eyes upon her.

Birds ducked and dived above their heads. By the path, wild scabious, bellflowers, moon daisies and many more meadow flowers ran riot. Grace picked at them, adding them to the growing bouquet she held. She smiled in thanks as Doyle snapped one and gave it to her.

They reached the cottage's long back garden and went through the gate.

'I enjoyed our stroll, Doyle.'

'As did I, Miss Grace.' He opened the backdoor for her.

'Would you care for some tea before you leave?'

'That would be grand, Miss.'

Grace left her flowers and straw hat on the kitchen table and led Doyle through the hall to the parlour.

William Ross turned from the window. Grace jumped in surprise, her face drained of colour.

'How are you, Grace?'

Just a few words, but they were enough for Grace to falter and close her eyes in acute pleasure and pain. *He is even more handsome than before.*

Doyle pulled his jacket on. Misery etched his tone. 'I'll leave you now, Miss Woodruff.'

Grace blinked and half-turned to him. 'Yes. Yes, very well. Thank you for coming.' Her gaze flickered from him and back to William.

Doyle bowed his head and turned to leave.

'Oh, Doyle, you'll return next Sunday with any news?' Grace asked, not actually requiring a reply. She couldn't stop staring at William. He was the very last person she thought to see.

By the doorway, Doyle hesitated. 'Yes, of course, Miss Woodruff.'

Grace swallowed and nibbled her bottom lip.

William looked at her in fascination as they heard the front door slam. 'That poor man is in love with you.'

'Nonsense! Why are you here?' Grace stepped further into the room. Her heart thumped against the bones of her chest. Her reaction to him made her vulnerable and angry.

William's gaze softened. 'You look very beautiful today. The scent of fresh air and flowers emanates from you.'

'Your charm is wasted on me.' She lifted her chin. 'Again, why are you here?'

'I could ask you the same thing.'

'You already know, otherwise you wouldn't be standing in this cottage.' Grace walked away to stand by the unlit hearth. She fought the urge to run to him and beg him to love her.

'I'm here to help.'

'Help us? We need no help, nor are we your concern. You're soon to be married, and I believe, to live abroad. Take your concern there.'

William took a step towards her. 'I didn't come here to cause you pain, Grace.'

'You cause me none,' she threw at him. 'My infatuation with you is over.'

He lifted one eyebrow at her words, and didn't believe them.

'So, what exactly brings you back to Leeds?' Grace stood stiffly, as if to ward off possible hurt. Having William in this small room sent an ache spreading out from her heart to consume her whole being.

'May I sit?' William asked.

'Please do.' They sat opposite each other, the low occasional table between them. Grace waited for him to speak.

'I heard reports, while in London, that certain investment shares were plummeting. I had reason to believe your father held a good amount of those particular shares. I came to offer him assistance.'

'I gather my father could well ride out a fall in any of his shares. He holds a good number in many companies.'

'Perhaps. However, he once told me himself the depth of which he had invested with Siltorn Shipping.'

Grace's brow puckered. She rose, crossed the hall to the study, and returned with a newspaper. As she sat once more, she tossed it onto the table, the headlines of the shipping collapse in full view. 'How much has he lost, do you know?'

'I'm not sure yet. I will discuss it at length with him when I return to Woodruff House.'

'Surely, it cannot be too bad? Besides, his other investments will cover the losses.'

William ran his fingers through his hair. 'His other investments, that I am aware of, are not substantial enough to recover everything. He's been playing the field, taking high risks from what I can gather. If he isn't careful, there could be dire consequences.'

'We will see it through, no doubt.' She rose again, bringing his visit to an end. It was torture to have him so close.

William stood. 'Grace, this is serious.'

'Of course, it is, but it is none of your business.'

'You are family.'

'We've never been high on your list of priorities before.' Grace willed disdain to show on her face.

'I could never sit back and do nothing in your time of trouble.

Your father is incapable of taking care of it himself at the moment.'

'You detest my father.'

'I don't consider him a friend, true. However, I wouldn't rejoice in his downfall because it would mean suffering to you, your mother and sisters.'

'He has managers and such, William, they'll see him through this. Run along back to London, and your fiancée. I'm sure she needs you more than we do.' Grace gave him a strained smile as at the same time a cry came from above.

'Grace...'

'I have other duties, William. Good day.' She left him and went upstairs.

* * *

By EVENING, William longed to be away to London. Only, he couldn't until after the visit from Woodruff's solicitor in the morning. So he was left to bear dinner with the women, who appeared lifeless. He noticed the stark difference in their behaviour from previous visits, Letitia most of all. She drank more than was considered desirable for a lady. William took note of how little they ate, and as soon as possible all disappeared to various rooms to follow their usual solitary occupations. Even when Woodruff had been hale and hearty and at ease to torment them, they had appeared more animated. Now, no healthy glow adorned their faces, and Gabriella looked positively woeful.

Late into the night, William sat in silence by the library fire-side, drinking brandy. He heard the clock chime eleven, and sighing deeply, he rose to retire. He was met at the library door by the butler.

'Is there anything you need, Mr Ross?'

William looked at the man with pity. 'No, thank you.'

Doyle bowed stiffly and turned for the kitchen.

'Er, Doyle?'

Slowly, Doyle turned back again, his gaze direct. William exceeded him in height by two inches, but the man stood proud and defiant. William hesitated, not knowing the words to speak, only aware he had to say something. 'Your devotion to Grace is admirable.'

Doyle stiffened.

'I feel relieved that she has someone who cares for her.'

'And you don't?' Doyle snapped.

He ignored the man's impertinence. 'Yes, I do. However, I'm not in a position to act on my feelings.'

'A *man* must make decisions and take the consequences.'

'Indeed, and if I only had myself to please then I would. But I do not.' William nodded once in respect, and walked away.

'Tell me what is more important than her?'

William glanced back to stare at him. 'You could not possibly understand.'

'I know I'd do anything for her. Would you?' Doyle scoffed.

'Unlike yourself, I'm not one man alone. I've family and estate responsibilities. I will help Grace and her family in whatever way I can that is within my limits.'

Doyle laughed mockingly. 'Then I pity you, sir.'

'Pity me?' Astonishment made his voice high.

'Well, yes. You see, to me, nothing would be more important than Grace, not estates not family, not anything.' Doyle bowed with a touch of arrogance. 'Good night, Mr Ross.'

CHAPTER 11

$\mathcal{T}$he following day, Woodruff sat on his chair at the round table brought into his spacious bedroom. He ignored William who sat opposite; after all, this was his doing. He had no wish to let others see his finances. Outside, slate gray clouds blanketed the window suiting his mood.

The door opened and Doyle ushered in a stooped, white-haired man. 'Mr Swindale is here, Mr Woodruff.'

With his lopsided mouth, Woodruff snarled as best he could when his solicitor entered, carrying a worn leather satchel which no doubt held condemning documents. He watched Swindale bow to him and then shake hands with William.

'Good of you to come at such short notice, Mr Swindale,' William said. 'I am certain that between us we can sort this mess out.'

Swindale's slight smile did not reach his watery eyes. 'We can but try, Mr Ross.'

For twenty minutes, Woodruff looked on helplessly as his money and commercial ventures were openly discussed. Anger mounted in him that the control of his interests was no longer his, but as the other two men thrashed out his dwindling estate and business empire, he vowed to show them all he wasn't finished. It'd take more than a shipping line to collapse to bring him down.

He moved his good foot and then tried to lift his paralyzed leg, but nothing happened except his big toe wiggled. He gritted his teeth in irritation. The nurse said it would take time. Only, he didn't have much of that. He needed to get better and leave this bedroom if he was to ever reclaim his dream of high standing, not only in the community, but the whole county.

'As I see it,' William said, lifting a document up, 'there is no other way. You must sell your townhouse in London, warehouses in Leeds, Kendleton Colliery, the candle factory and the tannery in York. With these changes, you can hopefully refinance this house.'

Woodruff placed a shaky hand to his forehead and felt the sweat beaded there. 'I tell…you, I ride…it out.'

'Mr Woodruff, you must do as Mr Ross suggests.' Mr Swindale pushed his steel-rimmed spectacles further up his nose. 'Your expenses outweigh your present income. Buy no more hunters, art, or anything not absolutely necessary, and you may, *may,* come out at the other end of this with the estate intact.'

'Blah!' Woodruff snorted. 'You … know nothing!'

Ignoring the insult, Swindale stood and passed Woodruff a paper to sign. 'Give Mr Ross the authority to oversee your finances in the event of your health deteriorating. It's the only way.'

'Blast!' Woodruff pushed the article away in a fit of temper. 'I better…soon!'

'What if you aren't?' William asked. 'What would happen should you have another attack and be rendered dumb? Who would take care of you, your family, or your home? Have sense man!'

The heat of frustration scorched its way up Woodruff's neck. He tried to breathe normally but it proved difficult.

Hatred burned inside him at the fates that had dealt him this blow. Wasn't it enough not to have a legitimate son? He clenched his good hand into a fist. He thought of the baby boy Grace cared and an idea ignited. It took hold and he grinned. 'Boy.'

William frowned. 'Boy? What do you mean?'

'Grace...boy...son.' He willed himself to calm down so he could make them understand. His plans grew in his mind like a fever.

'Your bastard son?' William's eyes narrowed. 'What about him?'

'He has...everything.' Woodruff watched for their reaction. His heart raced, and he sucked in a deep breath.

Swindale leant closer. 'Are you saying you want the boy to be left everything in your will?'

He nodded once.

'What about your daughters and wife?' William snapped.

'Nothing.'

William reared back, eyes wide. 'You cannot!'

'Can...and will.'

Swindale cleared his throat. 'Mr Woodruff, you must wish to provide for them in some way? Your estate can give them a home after your demise.'

'Estate for boy. Write... it.' Woodruff glared at the man. 'If boy...dies...Grace...estate.'

'And your wife and other daughters?' William jerked to his feet and glared at Woodruff. 'Diana and the girls are to live here with a small annuity until their deaths or they marry, yes?'

Woodruff shrugged one shoulder and looked away, unconcerned.

'Damn it, Woodruff, you evil baggage!' William banged his fist on the table. 'Agree to this and my placement as their guardian!'

'Give!' Woodruff indicated the document Swindale was quickly scrawling on.

A few moments later, the amended paper held all three signatures.

* * *

GRACE SAT on a blanket under a tree. Daniel Thomas slept in the perambulator beside her. In her lap, Mr Dickens' book, *A Tale Of Two Cities* lay unread. The prose could not capture her interest as her thoughts flew across the fields in the direction of Woodruff House.

'It's a beautiful day.'

Grace twisted around and looked up at William. She closed her eyes in weariness. She didn't need the added burden of William's close proximity when her life was so wretched. Why did he not go away and stay there? Did he not see the strength it took her to stay sane in his presence, when all she wanted to do was cry in disappointment? It was enough of a torment to think of him night and day, without having him physically near.

William crouched. 'I wish you nothing but happiness, you know that, don't you?' he asked softly. His tender gaze crumbled the fragile walls she'd built around her heart.

'I wish you the same.'

'May I sit with you?'

'Of course.' Grace tucked the long length of her duck-egg blue skirts under her legs to give him room. 'Tell me, how are things at home?'

'Not good, I'm afraid.'

She gave him her full attention. He looked tired.

Folding his arms on his drawn-up knees, he searched for words. 'If you thought moving here would bring happiness back to your family, I fear it was a wasted exercise.'

'It'll take time. However, Mother's old friends are like bees, they swarm in when someone has stirred the nest.'

He tilted his head, his face serious. 'The girls are unhappy. Have they visited you?'

'Hardly. Mama has even insisted I attend a different church so we don't come into contact. Though Gaby writes me little notes for Sykes to deliver.' Her voice dropped to a whisper. 'She comes in secret tomorrow.'

'Your mother told me little has changed in regards to invitations.'

Grace gazed past William to the open fields beyond. The summer was at an end, the fact heralded by the flat harvested fields. Where yesterday waist high wheat grew, now stood stubble and that too would be burnt within a few weeks and ploughed back into the ground for the winter snow to cover. Further away, men, women and children bent working the fields, while birds did their best to swoop down and peck at the fallen grains before being frightened off. It was an idyllic scene to those who knew nothing of the backbreaking toil.

William's gaze softened. 'Grace, your father gave me authorization to control his finances should he die or become mentally inept.'

Grace swung back to him. 'You?'

'There is no other. He has no close male relations, as you know.'

'But I could do it!'

'Come, Grace, you know of your father's intolerance of females. Do you think he would willingly hand it all over to you before his death?'

Sighing in acceptance, Grace nodded. 'Will there be notable changes?'

'Yes, I'm afraid. The base of your family's wealth is no more. The shipping collapse took much of your father's money. Selling his surplus assets will repay most of his debts and stop the drainage of his remaining capital. The estate will survive, albeit, on a smaller scale.'

A humourless chuckle escaped her. 'No wonder father was trying to marry us off to rich men.'

'Yes. He is finding out what it's like to step in the quicksand of a failing business empire. He's the prey now, not the predator.'

'He obviously thought he could play with high stakes because he was to marry his daughters into money. Yet, where are these rich, powerful men now father is bedridden? Have they come to offer help?'

'Bad news spreads faster than good. No one will commit to a deal with Woodruff now. His business is unstable and so is his health.' William took her hand. 'And as lovely as you girls are, you are tainted by your father's actions.'

'And my mother and sisters?'

'They'll have to curtail their expenses, but should your father die they can live at the estate until they marry or die themselves.'

Grace heaved a deep sigh. 'My sisters long to marry as most women want to do. I think for them to achieve that, they might have to lower their standards. A good but poor husband is better than no husband at all.'

'You could be right. Their marriage settlements are now much smaller, and your father's financial situation is not enticing. He was fortunate to make a good arrangement for Heather. Ellsworth was only too happy to barter over her dowry, acquiring a cotton mill in Liverpool while your father received the prestige of being related to the Ellsworth family, which he could trade on just as well. Ellsworth wishes for Andrew to enter parliament and your father promised to support him.'

She closed her book. 'Thankfully, Heather was happy to marry Andrew.'

William touched her cheek. 'I am sorry my news is not what you wanted to hear. However, I'll do my utmost to make certain your mother and sisters are taken care of should anything happen to your father.'

Grace nodded. 'Thank you, William.' She gazed into his eyes

and welcomed the warmth that entered her heart as he lifted her hand and kissed it. Where his lips touched her skin burnt a fiery trail straight to the pit of her stomach and she bit her lip to stop a moan of wanting.

He must have read the desire in her eyes for he groaned and gathered her into his arms. She closed her eyes as his lips rained light kissed across her temple and over her nose. When he kissed her fully, she greeted it tenfold. Reaching up, she entangled her fingers into his black hair and pulled him closer. A want, a throbbing pain of yearning gripped her with such intensity, she dragged him down onto the blanket. His tongue probed the depths of her mouth, but it wasn't enough. He bent to kiss her neck and Grace threw her head back to give him better access. His hands slid around to her back and he began undoing her dress's row of buttons as she pulled his shirt out of his trousers.

A sudden cry shattered their obsession with each other. Grace stilled as Daniel Thomas let out another bellow. Her sanity returned bringing with it the shame. She had thrown herself at him. Grace blinked to clear her mind. *What have I done?* Instantly, she was on her feet, rushing to the baby.

Her hands shook as she picked him up. 'There now.' Heat scalded her cheeks. What had possessed her to behave like that? She closed her eyes and placed Daniel Thomas over her shoulder. She couldn't face William. Never had she acted in such a way, but the need, an animal need, was so strong, too strong for her to ignore. Even now, her skin tingled from his touch and deep inside she felt unfulfilled. The throbbing dwindled to a dull ache.

'Grace.'

With a weary sigh, Grace turned and went back to the blanket. Avoiding his eyes, she collected her things one-handed, as Daniel Thomas snuggled into her neck. Clouds blocked out the sun. The afternoon had grown cool in more ways than one.

'Grace, look at me.'

She heard the longing in his voice and smothered a cry. She

straightened and forced herself to sound indifferent. 'When do you return to London?'

'Tomorrow, but...'

'And in two weeks, you are to marry.'

'Yes, only...'

'The next time I see you, you will be married.' An ache squeezed at her chest.

'Grace...'

'Take care, William.'

His eyes begged her. 'You know...'

'Yes, William, I know.'

He tenderly stroked her cheek. Grace captured his hand and kissed his palm. She would never touch him again after this day. 'Do not come back, please. I cannot bear it,' she whispered against his skin.

William briefly closed his eyes. 'Good bye.'

* * *

FOR THE UMPTEENTH TIME, Grace went to the parlour window to peer up the road. Gaby was late. Rain came down in a soft mist, obliterating the surroundings beyond the garden wall. The small clock on the mantle struck two, and Grace wondered what kept her sister. Maybe something at home stopped her? Had Mama found out and prevented her from visiting? Had the weather put her off? The thoughts whirled as she restlessly moved around the small room. This delay showed her how much she had anticipated this visit.

The minutes ticked by. The greyness outside matched her mood and she shivered. Impatiently, she swept the lace curtain aside to achieve a better view, and was relieved to see a hackney cab appear through the gloom. She rushed into the hallway.

Mrs Winton opened the door.

'I thought you weren't coming!' Grace enveloped her sister in a tight embrace.

'So sorry I'm late.' Gaby kissed her cheek.

Grace blinked in surprise to find a man in a dark brown suit standing on the doorstep

Gaby stepped back to beckon him forward. 'You remember John Morgan, from Morgan's Farm don't you?'

Holding out her hand to him, Grace smiled, hiding her puzzlement. 'Yes, of course. It has been some time since we last met at church. How are you, Mr Morgan?'

'Well, thank you, Miss Woodruff.'

Gaby removed her outdoor clothes, her movements jittery. She wore a woollen dress of pale gold shot through with silver. Her hair was piled on her head in a torrent of highlighted chestnut curls interlaced with silver velvet ribbons. She looked wan but very beautiful.

'Come through, please.' Grace turned for the parlour. 'Tea and scones, thank you, Mrs Winton.'

Mrs Winton sniffed, narrowing her eyes at the visitors.

Once seated on the sofa, Gaby's smile appeared strained. Grace itched to ask why Mr Morgan escorted her. She turned her attention to him. 'How does your farm fare, Mr Morgan?'

'Well, thank you, Miss Woodruff.' He sat on the edge of the chair as if ready to run at any moment.

'And you have finished harvesting?'

'Yes, last week.'

'You must be pleased, seeing as the weather has turned. Many will be caught out.'

'Indeed, Miss. I always like to get my fields in early.'

She looked from the tense Mr Morgan to her sister.

'I have news,' Gaby blurted out.

'Oh?' Grace smiled expectantly, as Gaby pulled off her lace glove and held up her left hand; on her third finger shone a plain gold band. The smile slipped from Grace's face. She swallowed with difficulty.

'We were married this morning,' Gaby fluttered her hand for a second more, then hid it in her lap.

'I don't know what to say...'

The amazing words 'we were married' hung thick in the air.

Gaby's frozen smile didn't falter as she glanced at her new husband and back to Grace. 'I know it must be a surprise.'

'Yes ...' Appalled, Grace sagged.

'We kept it a secret due to the family problems.'

'Did ... did you not think this would add to them?'

'No, I thought...'

'You did *think*, did you?' She asked unbelievingly. 'I'm all amazement.'

'There is no need for sarcasm.' Defiant, Gaby raised her chin, it quivered traitorously.

Anger, hot and pulsing, surfaced like a boil needing to be lanced. How could Gaby have done such a thing without telling her first? Grace rose and paced the floor in stilted movements. Her gaze darted to John Morgan. 'Did you ask my father? No, obviously a silly question.'

'Gaby advised me not to, because of his health.' He shifted on his chair. 'I wished to nevertheless.'

'Oh, Gaby.' Grace wrung her hands in torment. 'Why?'

Gaby turned to her new husband. 'Would you mind leaving us for a moment? Perhaps go into the kitchen and have something to eat? Or...another room somewhere?'

Morgan stood, and with a nod to both women limped out.

The moment the door closed behind him, Grace sat back down as though her legs could no longer support her. 'Tell me, Gaby, what made you marry our tenant farmer? Mama will be inconsolable! Heaven knows what father will do!'

'It was either that or give you another bastard to care for.' Tears brimmed in her eyes.

Grace jerked back. 'No...'

Gaby nodded, as a single tear slipped down her cheek. 'I'm sorry.'

'But why? Why did you do it?'

'I hated the restrictions of our home life, and the way father controlled us. Farm hands have more freedom than we do.' She glanced away. 'I wanted to know what the relations between a man and woman were like. I was curious.'

'We're all curious!' Grace couldn't stop her blush as she recalled the scene between her and William the day before.

'I guess I wanted to defy Father and his stringent rules. I don't know.' She shrugged. 'It never occurred to me that my actions would come back to roost.'

'Why not wait for marriage?'

'What excitement is there in that?' Gaby gave a false laugh.

Grace couldn't speak. She had no right to preach on the matter, for if Daniel Thomas hadn't woken when he did yesterday, who knows how far she and William might have gone?

Gaby tossed her head. 'Besides, I never thought I'd marry, I still find it hard to believe the deed is done. I didn't think it would come to me, at least not to a man of my choosing. When I realized I was with child, the thought seriously came to mind about marrying Horton. But I couldn't. I would rather be poor and married to a man of decency, than live richly with a scoundrel like him.'

'I cannot believe you have married John Morgan.' Grace felt ill.

'Oh come, Grace, you're the last person I thought would care about social standing!'

'It's not his position in society I worry about, not really.' Grace argued. 'However, can he care for you? Will he treat you well?'

'You really are a snob underneath all of your charitable qualities!' Gaby flared.

'Not true. I wish to see my sisters settled, but being a farmer's wife wouldn't always be happy and comfortable.'

'So, you think living a wealthy existence would deem you happy ever after?'

Grace wiped a shaking hand over her eyes. 'No.'

Gaby fiddled with her glove. 'Morgan is not without means, though they are modest.'

'Do you *love* him?' She asked, desperate for confirmation.

'What is love?' Gaby tossed her head.

'Gaby…'

'Leave it be, Grace. I married him because I was caught out. Simple. Yes, I like him. In fact, we have much in common and enjoy each other's company.'

'He's a farmer, Gaby. He pays rent to our father. Do you have any idea how your life will change from now on?'

'Like yours, you mean?'

'Yes, like mine. I don't recommend it. Being shunned by my own family and friends is not a favourable way to live.'

'*You* will visit me.' Gaby impatiently wiped away the tears that refused to cease.

Grace hurried to hug her sister. 'Try and stop me.' She smiled through the numbness of shock. 'You should have come to me.'

Gaby gazed at her. 'I couldn't bear you being ashamed of me.'

'You're my sister. I could never be.'

'I don't regret it, Grace.'

'I hope you never do.' She stood and crossed to the desk. The feeling of discontent rose in her. *Have I done the right thing in moving here?* Stuck in this house she was unable to rescue her sisters from their own actions. But just as quickly came the thought that Gaby's exploits had been happening for sometime right under her nose and that made her feel worse. She sighed. 'Mama will cast you adrift.'

'Yes.'

'Thankfully, Father, being so ill, is in no position to make difficulties. We might be able to keep him in ignorance for the present.'

'Poor John, I pressured him awfully.'

'To marry you?'

'Not to marry me, no, in that he was quite willing once he knew about the baby. It was the act of ... bringing me down, that caused him strife.' Gaby smiled the secret smile of one who knew the physical act of love.

'Oh?'

'He refused to do it, you see. I begged him and still he wouldn't. So, I let nature take hold. By instinct I touched him in ways I never knew a person could touch another. I behaved like no lady.'

Grace's face flamed at her sister's words. 'Oh, Gabriella!'

Gaby rose from the sofa on hearing crying coming from above. She took a deep breath. 'How is Daniel Thomas?' she asked easily, the subject over.

Grace wondered if she ever really knew her. Gaby's capability to switch from one mood to another always surprised her. Shaking her head at the absurdity of the situation, Grace frowned. 'He cries a lot.'

'I shall find out all too soon about such things, won't I?'

Grace gripped her hands together. 'I still cannot believe you have done this. How will you manage, living on a farm?'

'Oh, you know me, I'll survive well enough.'

'Two sisters married,' Grace wondered aloud.

'It is no celebration like Heather's.'

'No.'

'Heather and Andrew return home next week,' Gaby said, as a knock came upon the parlour door and John Morgan stuck his head around.

'Come in, John.' Grace watched him gaze at Gaby and the way her sister tentatively smiled at her new husband. Grace hoped they would survive the gossip and one day be truly happy. The tender way John looked at Gaby gave promise of a strong bond between them. She hoped Gaby wouldn't throw it back in his face. Her stubbornness was a factor he must deal with, alongside her unruliness.

John came to stand before Grace. 'I'll protect and care for Gabriella with all of my being. I'm a simple man with simple needs, but I honour the vows I make.'

'I trust you, John,' she said and meant it. 'Our families share a long acquaintance, since my grandfather's time. You have a friend in me while ever you treat Gaby as she deserves.' Grace linked her arm through his. 'Come upstairs and see Daniel Thomas. No doubt he's in need of fresh faces to smile at.'

* * *

EARLY THE NEXT MORNING, Grace sat eating breakfast in the dining room and read *The Times*. More news reports of share prices plunging after Siltorn's collapse made her shiver in dread. She needed to talk with her father about this.

Sudden knocking at the front door gave her pause. She listened as Mrs Winton greeted the visitor and haughtily inquired the newcomer's business. Within moments, the housekeeper stood stiff before Grace, informing her a Mrs Woodruff waited in the parlour.

'Have tea brought in, Mrs Winton,' Grace instructed, rising. Her mother would be here for one reason only; Gaby. She prayed for patience.

'Miss Woodruff, I believe your mother is a trifle upset.' A disapproving frown accentuated Mrs Winton's apparent scorn of the distraught woman.

Grace rolled her eyes in weariness; she was certain her mother found turmoil a perverted comfort. She glanced at Mrs Winton and it occurred to her the woman was always frowning about something. Both of them were an excellent pair of miseries.

In the parlour she found her mother huddled on the sofa wearing a large navy cape over a dress of rustic brown. Her small black hat held a double layer of veil.

'Good morning, Mama. This is a surprise.' Grace sat opposite, hiding a smile at her mother's attempts of concealment. Why she bothered was anyone's guess, for no one of their acquaintance lived along this road.

'It's certainly not *good*.' Diana lifted her veil to wipe her red, tear brimmed eyes with a handkerchief.

'Is this about Gaby, Mama?'

Diana shot her a venomous look. 'Do not dare speak of her name in my presence!'

'Mama...'

'Did you know of this? Did you encourage such outrageousness?'

'No!'

'Can you believe the audacity of that Morgan man, to actually think he can marry her?'

'He has married her, Mama.'

'A tenant farmer! *Our* tenant farmer!'

'At least we know of him.'

'Oh!' Diana fell back against the sofa in a near swoon. 'I cannot bear it. To think of my daughter having stooped so low.'

Grace resisted the urge to comfort her mother. Her own hurt at Diana's hands was too fresh. 'He's not a bad man, Mama.'

Diana wrung her sodden handkerchief between heavily ringed fingers. 'How could she? How could they? Oh, Grace.'

'Do you know everything, Mama?'

'If you mean Gaby's condition, then yes!' Diana's temper flared again. 'He should be shot for taking such advantage!'

'No, Mama. Gaby was the instigator.'

'Nonsense. Even if it was so, he should have shown restraint.'

Grace gazed in pity at her mother, but nodded. 'It's done now. They made a commitment to each other and I hope they'll be happy.'

'Happy! How can you say such a thing?' Diana was forestalled in saying anything further as Mrs Winton brought in a tea tray. She gave Diana another haughty glance before departing.

'Your housekeeper appears rude, Grace.'

'Indeed she does, Mama.' Grace lifted the teapot. 'Tea?'

Diana peered about the room for the first time. Her eyes took in little things of interest.

'Why did you come here, Mama?' Grace murmured.

Obviously startled by the question, Diana waved her handkerchief, searching for the answer. 'Because of Gaby.'

Grace looked directly at her. 'I thought it your wish to never see me again?'

'I… Well, you must understand that I had to think of your sisters.'

'That you did. Also, you might have thought of me.'

'It was your choice!'

'No, Mama, you gave me no choice. Yet, for you, there was.' Grace swallowed the lump of emotion in her throat.

'I cannot have…*it* under my roof.' Diana's tears flowed once more. 'I simply cannot.'

'His *name* is Daniel Thomas.'

'He is a bastard, and always will be. You have ruined your life because of him!'

Grace nodded. 'I understand that, Mama. But still, I should not be made an outcast by my own family. If you feel visits are not acceptable, then maybe letters will suffice?'

'Letters would be totally suitable,' Diana agreed, giving Grace a sidelong glance.

'And Gaby?'

Instantly, Diana stood, readying herself to leave. 'She is no longer my daughter.'

Grace sighed. 'Sit down, Mama and have your tea.'

Diana paused, as if to weigh the idea, then she sat and took her cup. 'You have always been bossy.'

'I've had the need to be.' Grace added sugar. 'William told me of Father's finance troubles. Things will be difficult for some time.'

Flustered, Diana spilt her tea on the saucer. 'It's all too much!'

'Simple living will ease the burden, I'm certain.'

'Simple living! We might as well emigrate to the ends of the earth, such will be our life now.'

Grace bowed her head to gaze into her tea. She had forgotten how exhausting her mother was.

* * *

A WEEK LATER, Grace stood dazed and uncertain outside the bank. The busy Leeds traffic passed by without notice as she tried to absorb what the bank manager had said only minutes ago. His words brought home to her the true financial mess her father had blundered them into. *How can I cope with no money?*

Grace hailed a hackney cab from the other side of the street. Soon, she was trundling towards Woodruff House. A headache throbbed behind her eyes and she felt sick with the swaying of the cab. *I have no money. I have no money.* Her thoughts played in time with the wheels crunching over the road.

As the cab turned through the gates of the drive, her stomach clenched in anticipation of being back home again. The feeling intensified on noticing a gig waiting in front of the steps. Quickly, she bade the driver to take the cab along the side drive to the back of the house.

Alighting, Grace had no time to gaze around at things familiar. She didn't want to risk running into her mother and whoever was visiting so she strode into the kitchen, nearly giving Mrs Hawksberry a heart seizure in the process.

Mrs Hawksberry pressed her hand against her large bosom. 'My word, Miss Woodruff, you could have knocked me down with a feather, seeing you walk in like that.'

'I'm sorry, Mrs Hawksberry. I never meant to alarm you. I'd rather not disturb Mama with her guest.' The kitchen held an aroma of roasting meat and spices. Its warmth was always welcoming on cool days such as today. 'How are you all?' Her smile encompassed the kitchen maids; she had missed them.

'We aren't too bad, Miss,' Mrs Hawksberry sighed, 'but upstairs is in an uproar. The only visitor here today is the doctor.'

'Why was he summoned?'

'The master's had another seizure this morning, not as bad as the first, though.'

'I must go.' Grace hurried from the room. She made it into the hall unnoticed, and was halfway up the main staircase when Doyle appeared at the top.

'Miss Grace?' Doyle's delight showed in his eyes before he quickly masked it and became professional.

'I have come to see Father, Doyle.'

'How did you know?'

'I didn't. Mrs Hawksberry informed me. I came to see him on other business.' Grace joined him at the top of the stairs. 'How is he?'

'Grace!' The sudden shout from Phoebe gave her little warning before her youngest sister hurtled herself into her arms.

'Phoebe, dearest, how are you?' Grace tried to pull away to look at her sister, but Phoebe hung on tightly. A few moments later, Emma Kate and Faith surrounded her too, hugging and crying.

'Are you here to stay?' asked Phoebe, her eyes large in her pale face.

'No, dearest. I've come to talk to father about something.'

'You'll find it difficult. He is worse you know.' Phoebe shuddered.

'Will you take tea afterwards?' Emma Kate asked, as the three sisters walked towards the stairs.

'Yes, I will.' Grace turned for her father's room. She gave Doyle a small smile as she stepped inside. Stale, sick room odour assailed her nostrils. The drawn curtains darkened the room. A gas wall sconce by the bedside shadowed the walls with the doctor's profile. He glanced up as Grace stepped closer to the bed.

'Ahh, Miss Woodruff.'

'Dr Bambridge. How is Father?'

The doctor straightened. 'Not good, my dear, not good. He tries to do too much before his body is ready.'

Grace moved closer to gaze down on her father. He looked old and shrivelled, no longer the terrifying ogre who had once frightened them.

Gathering his instruments back into his leather bag, Dr Bambridge gazed over the top of his spectacles. 'He'll be well in a day or two.'

'What brought it on, do you know?'

'A visit from his solicitor, I believe.' The doctor picked up his bag from the bed, indicating for Grace to leave the room with him. 'Also, in secret, he's been trying to walk with the aid of a walking stick, against my advice.'

Mrs Gibbons came along the gallery carrying fresh linen. The nurse listened to the doctor's instructions before he and Grace went downstairs. Thanking him, Grace showed him out.

Emma Kate, Faith and Phoebe waited anxiously in the drawing room. They greeted Grace with apprehension flickering in their eyes. Tea was poured and handed around.

'Has Heather returned yet?' Grace asked, tea in hand.

'Yes, late last night.' Faith replied. 'Mrs Ellsworth sent a note this morning.'

Phoebe leant forward to impart her news. 'Heather has a bad cold and is in bed. Mama and Letitia ventured to see her despite

Mrs Ellsworth's advice to stay away. Mama was cross to be told that, and decided no cold would keep her from Heather's side.' She stifled a giggle. Her youth enabled her to sway from despair to happiness in moments

Grace shook her head at Phoebe. Would the girl ever learn restraint? She listened to their varied woes and did her best to put them at ease. However, their situation wouldn't be easily overcome while father lay ill upstairs. They told her bits of gossip, gleaned through the odd letters they received from friends.

'Were is Letitia?'

All three looked guiltily at each other.

Faith added more tea to her cup. 'We don't know what Letitia does most of the time. She is never home. She argues with Doyle a lot because he tells her there is no more wine left in the cellar.'

'Oh, no!' A feeling of utter helplessness filled Grace.

'Could we not come and visit you, Grace?' Phoebe pouted.

'Quiet, Phoebe!' Faith nudged her with her knee. 'Mama told you it is out of the question.' She looked sadly at Grace. 'I'm sorry. We do miss you.'

'And I miss you all, too.'

'Well, I think it barbarous to not see *two* sisters!' Phoebe sulked.

Grace rose, placing her teacup and saucer onto the tray. 'I'll not turn my back on Gaby. You are all adults and free to make up your own minds.'

'I doubt that.' Emma Kate muttered.

'Gaby is married now. John Morgan is a good man. He may not be socially acceptable, but he was Gaby's choice and he'll look after her. Aren't you happy she is settled?'

'Yes, if it's truly what she wants,' Faith said.

Phoebe pouted. 'At least she'll not be an old maid, like the rest of us.'

'Tell me,' Grace frowned at her sisters, 'what exactly are you doing with your lives? Are you content to sit here into old age?'

The three sisters seated looked at her like circus monkeys awaiting orders. 'What can we do?' they chorused.

'Go to visit friends, window shop, take drives into the country, go on picnics.'

'We couldn't possibly,' Faith was aghast. 'We must think of Mama, and Father is so ill.'

'Being a dutiful daughter is a credit to you, Faith, but it is up to you to find happiness.'

'Not all of us can up and leave when the mood suits us,' Faith muttered.

'Do you think it was easy for me?' Grace demanded. 'It's time you all matured a little in your ideas.' She walked into the hall in readiness to leave. Her sisters trailed her like ducklings after the mother duck.

'Don't go yet. Come back and sit down,' Emma Kate pleaded. 'We long to talk more with you.'

Grace kissed her and Phoebe goodbye. 'I must get back.' She turned to Faith and gave her a long look. 'Don't settle for half a life, Faith. Learn from me.' She kissed her and was thankful when Faith held her tight. She turned for the door, and as Doyle opened it, she caught his tender gaze. Swallowing her tears, she raised her head and left them.

CHAPTER 12

The little bell over the door tinkled as Grace left
Henson's jeweller's. Her reticule now held money,
where before it had held pearls. She hoped her face had lost its
red flush of humiliation at selling her jewellery. Dodging the
traffic and steaming manure deposits, she crossed Briggate and
set about paying accounts at various shops. An hour later, with
her fund diminished to a few shillings, she chose to walk home,
instead of hiring a cab. Thankfully, her kid leather boots had only
a small heel and were comfortable.

She hadn't gone far when she heard her name called above the
rumbling of carriage wheels. Turning, she lifted her head to scan
the busy street.

'Grace!' Heather leant out of her carriage window.

Grace managed to wait until the carriage slowed before
rushing to it. Heather flung open the door and leapt down with a
squeal.

'How I have missed you,' Grace said, gripping her sister's
gloved hands.

'And I you.' Heather looked her up and down. 'You're still
wearing that dress? It's two seasons old. You should have seen the

fashions in Paris and Rome.' She glanced at the cosy teashop behind them. 'Let us have tea. Yes?'

Grace nodded, ignoring the comment about her dress. 'Have you the time to stop?' She noticed Heather wore expensive silk and a hat so large Grace was frightened it wouldn't fit through the teashop door.

'Oh, yes. What does it matter if I'm late for my appointments? I'm desperate to tell you about my glorious honeymoon.'

They picked a quiet corner inside and Heather ordered tea and cakes with so much confidence Grace couldn't help but stare at the transformation of her once quiet and shy sister.

Heather selected far too many sandwiches and cakes from the stand and before long Grace's full plate looked like a miniature pyramid.

'Now, I'll pay, so don't argue.'

'I wasn't going to.' Grace bit into an apple tart topped with cream, grinning like a child. She'd not eaten something this sweet since leaving home.

She studied her sister, recognizing the change. Heather looked more mature, more knowledgeable and fashionable. 'Is Andrew well?'

'Of course. I believe he never had an ailment the entire time we were on the continent. Nevertheless, we shall talk of him later. First, there is our family to discuss. Mama wept for an hour as she regaled me with the happenings of the last few months. I cannot believe the events.'

Grace sighed. 'Would you have expected me to give up our brother to strangers?'

Heather shook her head. 'I honestly don't know. It's so difficult to think of such a thing as a baby half-brother.'

'It was a shocking time, the day he was born, though I feel no sympathy for Father.'

'Yes, Father. What a terrible burden he has placed upon this family.'

'And then there is Gaby.'

'Oh, a shock indeed.' Disdain transformed Heather's pretty features. 'Her behaviour is deplorable! I never imagined it of her.'

Grace frowned and drew back as the waitress poured their tea and departed again. 'Are you saying you shan't visit her?'

'I have yet to discuss it with Andrew.'

'Discuss it with Andrew? Heather, she is our sister. Besides, you have come to see me, why not Gabriella?'

A slight crease appeared on Heather's forehead as she tried to express herself. 'You have done nothing wrong, Grace. Others may think it strange, the strength of your devotion to the child, but you have done nothing morally wrong. It is commendable to give your life away to care for the boy. I am sorry for you.'

'Indeed?'

'Whereas Gaby has married beneath her, *and* was in a compromising situation when she did marry him.'

'So, you think, as Mama does, that because she has gone against our class, she should be ignored?'

'Well ...' Heather toyed with a macaroon. 'I am fiercely disappointed she behaved so. To marry Father's tenant is not acceptable. My in-laws are perfectly horrified, as all our society is.'

'She's still our Gaby.'

'No. She is now Mrs John Morgan, a farmer's wife.'

'Her status is of no importance!'

'Of course it is important!' Heather frowned. 'I can't help but speak the truth, Grace.'

Frustration simmered inside Grace's chest. 'Not so long ago, this family was equal to the likes of John Morgan, remember that. Grandfather Woodruff was a merchant.'

'A highly successful and rich merchant!' Heather glanced around as others stared their way. She leant forward to whisper. 'And Mama's family are descended from noble lines.'

'What does that matter?' Grace suddenly wanted to slap her.

'It matters a great deal when one is an Ellsworth. I have

standing among the ladies of this community now. I have married into a worthy family. Do you think I'll let Gaby ruin it?'

'Are you telling me that if Father is declared bankrupt you'll have nothing more to do with us? Simply because you married an Ellsworth?'

Heather's eyes widened. 'Is it really as bad as that? Mama mentioned something, but I had no idea.'

'How could you know?' Grace shook her head. Heather had changed since her marriage and not for the better. 'There are still plenty more changes coming to Woodruff House and they'll not be pleasant.'

Heather wrinkled her nose as if she had smelt something distasteful. 'The whole family has fallen in the eyes of our society. I am lucky to have made my marriage when I did.'

Grace stared at her and something died in her as she watched Heather stir her tea. 'Yes, you are fortunate. It also allows you to help us.'

Heather snorted. 'How is that possible, now?' She dropped her spoon as though it were repulsive. 'No, there is nothing I can do. I told Mama the same.'

A cold band encircled Grace's heart. She jerked up from her chair. 'I'm disappointed in you, Heather.'

'Oh Grace, please, you must understand I have a position to uphold. I am an Ellsworth, I must think of my husband.'

Grace looked down at her. 'Your loyalty to them is admirable, but remember you were a Woodruff first.' She left the tearooms and strode down the street, eager to get back to the simplicity of the cottage on Woodhouse Lane.

* * *

ON THE SUNDAY of William's wedding, the sun over Leeds sent out its last crescendo of heat before the crisp, cool autumn claimed its title. The air was fresh, the breeze light and the sun streamed down from a cloudless blue sky.

Grace woke with a restlessness that kept her edgy all morning. Her pent-up energy, her constant flitting from one room to another was sending Mrs Winton mad. When at last Doyle arrived at two o'clock sharp, Grace had him out the backdoor and walking with her towards the open fields before he could take his coat off. She had expected to spend the day in tears at the thought of her beloved marrying another, but instead her mind seemed heedless of her breaking heart.

This whole mood of denial surprised her and obviously worried Doyle, who stared at her as she nearly skipped down the dirt lane skirting the fields. She wore a dress of white linen underskirts overlaid with sprigged peach faille split at the front and gathered around to her sides in two deep scallops, then trailed over the bustle into a torrent of silken flounces. In an act of rebellion, she left her long chestnut curls to tumble down her back in wild abandon. No hat or parasol covered her face from the sun, and she didn't care if freckles claimed her nose. Grace felt more like a young girl of fifteen than a woman of nearly twenty-four. She liked how Doyle's amazed gaze never left her.

They walked on towards a cluster of buildings making up a nearby farm. They heard music on nearing, and, feeling extremely cheeky, Grace grinned at Doyle and led him into the farmyard. A large, festive group of people confronted them as they rounded the corner.

Doyle pulled back. 'Oh no, Miss Grace, we mustn't.'

'Nonsense, Doyle. Come, they won't mind.' She tugged him into the throng.

A florid faced man with a large stomach and smiling eyes hurried to them. 'Good day there, are thee lost?'

'No, sir, not at all.' Grace flashed a smile. 'We were wondering if we could join your merriment?'

'Well, course thee can, lass. A harvest party is for all,' the farmer roared with good humour. In a moment, the whole party knew of the late guests.

Grace beamed at Doyle, and he could do nothing but laugh back at her. Another cheerful farmer slapped a tall, frothy ale into his hand, spilling it over his fingers. Grace was given a plate of cold meats and a glass of elderberry wine, while the band struck up a fast paced tune.

'Here lass, thee know how ter dance?' Another man of uncertain age asked Grace, taking the plate of food from her to place on the nearby trestle table. 'We don't stand on ceremony here, me dear,' he added, guiding her into the melee of vivacious dancers.

'I'm not sure I know this,' Grace called to him above the din.

'Nay, lass I'll tekk care of thee!' With a suddenness that left her breathless, the man grasped her in a tight embrace and swung her around the yard with undisciplined vigour.

Overcome with helpless laughter, Grace danced in a way she'd never done before. For two hours Grace danced, drank, ate and laughed with a recklessness totally unsuited to the worry-burdened, serious woman she'd been at Woodruff House.

Doyle stood by the side, conversing with the local villagers who'd all helped with the surrounding harvest and were now enjoying the abundant rewards of a good year's return. Every now and then, his gaze would stray to her and they'd laugh as she was clasped within the arms of some burly farmer or spotty youth.

By nightfall, colourful lanterns were strung, lighting the yard in a rainbow hue. They carved a roasted pig and more food replaced the emptying plates. The party continued as the farmer tapped another keg of ale. Someone put a torch to a large bonfire, its sparks drifted high into the clear black sky.

'So, Miss, how are you keeping on your feet?' Doyle smiled at her, as she drank deeply from a large tankard. 'I don't think you've sat down for more than ten minutes since we arrived.'

'And nor shall I, until you have danced with me!' She dragged him by the hand behind her.

'Oh no, I can't!' Doyle resisted, half-heartedly.

Grace giggled. 'Come, you're not frightened of me are you?'

The somewhat drunken band members, revived again after consuming a plate of pork and pickle, washed down with fresh ale, gathered their instruments and delved into a rowdy jingle. Grace thrust herself into his arms, grinning into his face.

Taking a deep breath at their closeness, Grace gave Doyle no time to think of it, for she purposely infused him with her gaiety. For one night, she didn't want either of them to think.

'Seeing you like this is simply breathtaking,' he managed to whisper into her ear.

'Thank you, kind sir.' She chuckled and then stumbled. Doyle's quick actions kept her upright, and she giggled some more.

'I think you, dear Miss Woodruff, are drunk.' He shook his head with a wry smile.

'Who cares, Doyle? I wish to enjoy myself tonight like no other!'

Eventually, the music settled down to a slower pace and couples suited their movements to the gentler tones. Doyle automatically gathered Grace close. She instinctively nestled her head against his shoulder with a sigh. Abruptly, the air was thick with straining awareness of animal attraction.

Grace raised her head to peer at the handsome man holding her. Her finger traced a line from his dark brow to his well-defined jaw. His body stiffened, his eyes widened as he gazed at her. He loved her, he wanted her. Grace knew this and, for a moment rejoiced in it. For somewhere in a distant town, but under the same moon, her love was now bedding another. The pain cut deep, and she needed to stem the flow of hurt. He was lost to her now, but she needn't be alone.

She stopped swaying to the music and led Doyle from the party into the shadows. Music drifted on the still night air, following them as she guided him behind a barn. The ground sloped slightly as they neared a grove. Winding through the trees, the half moon shed them little light, but Grace liked the silvery glow. Underneath her feet, a thick carpet of late summer flowers offered up their crushed scent. Suddenly, she sank to her knees.

'Grace…' Doyle's voice thickened.

She looked up at him and held out her hand. 'I want to be loved, Doyle.'

'Not by me.' In the half-light, his pale face showed her his anguish.

'Tonight, I want you.' She took his hand and kissed his palm. 'Do I have to beg?'

He groaned deep in his chest. 'This is wrong…'

'I am on my knees…' She kissed each finger of his captured hand. A coil of longing twirled deep in the pit of her stomach.

'Don't do this to me, Grace.' Doyle reached down to haul her up, but she grabbed his arms and leant back, pulling him down beside her.

'Why fight it?' she breathed into his ear. 'Kiss me.'

She grinned when he rejected all sense of reason and surrendered to her plea, crushing her to him. His demanding kiss re-ignited the fire that William had started. She welcomed his urgency, rejoiced in his fumbled attempts to undo the ivory buttons down her back. He spun her around to make the task easier and with a cry of triumph, he slipped the material off her shoulders.

Grace unclipped the front fastening corset and flung it away before stripping off her chemise. She leant back against his chest as his hands cupped her breasts. Her nipples throbbed and she arched in need. She twisted in his arms and faced him. With quick jerks, she assisted him in shedding his jacket, waistcoat and shirt. His chest had a light covering of curly dark hair, and she ran her fingers through it before bending to flick her tongue against his nipple.

His groan rumbled in his throat as he laid her back on his discarded clothes and searched for the ties of her of her bustle, but she knocked his hands away and hitched up her skirts for him to pull down her undergarments. He kissed her neck and shoulders, burning a path along her skin up to her face. His tongue traced her lips as his fingers gently made patterns around her nipples.

'Grace, sweetheart...'

She felt the front of his trousers and the bulge pressing against her thigh. Within moments, she had freed him from his restrictive clothing and held him in her hand. He was hot and silky. Doyle's ragged breath fanned her as he moved over her, and, with a deft movement of his knee, had her legs apart. He sat back between her knees and bent to kiss the softness between her legs. The sensation shocked her, and she gasped. He lifted his head and gazed at her. 'Are you certain?'

Grace nodded, unable to speak. A fever of desire gripped her and took her to another place. She wanted him more at this moment than she wanted air.

He gathered her up against him as he entered her, kissing away her moans. She wasn't sure what to expect but there was no pain, only fullness. Doyle moved slow and steady, gentle rhythmic strokes. Heat grew in her thighs and somewhere in her inner core. Her fingernails dug into his buttocks as she rose to meet him.

'Grace...' He paused to kiss her deeply and she wriggled beneath him to make him thrust again. 'Say my name ...'

Grace frowned, she didn't want to talk; she wanted the fulfilment her body craved. A thrust of her hips silenced him. She raked her nails up his back to urge him on. She wanted completion. The need that threatened her sanity had to be satisfied. He gathered her closer, smothering his face into her neck as his body raced for the ultimate goal.

She threw her head back as their bodies joined in a spiralling climax. The wondrous feeling amazed her. Closing her eyes, she lay with her breathing suspended in her chest. Her limbs went soft and lethargic.

The sensations pulsing through her body gradually eased to be replaced with the consciousness of what she had done. Grace bit her lip and turned her head to the side. She didn't feel ashamed. However, happiness didn't seize her heart either. In truth, confusion and numbness reigned. For a short space of time, she had been wanted, and she liked the feeling. 'Marry me,' she whispered, surprising not only Doyle, but herself.

He held her for a second more before rolling away. The pale moonlight shadowed him as he stood to adjust his trousers.

'Marry me.'

'You've had too much to drink. It's time to go.' Doyle's Adam's apple jerked in his throat.

'You are refusing me?' Grace's tone hardened, for she meant every word.

'You don't realize what you're asking. Stop talking nonsense.' Doyle took her hand and helped her to her feet. He went behind her to ease up the top of her dress.

'I know exactly what I'm asking.'

'And you think I'll be content always being second choice? Or do I not rate at all in your heart? Am I just convenient? Simply a diversion to keep you occupied in your cottage?'

'You think so little of me?'

'I think too much of you, that is the problem.'

She took a deep breath. 'I asked you to marry me, what is your answer?'

Doyle's voice sounded wretched as he fastened the buttons of her dress. 'Please, let us go back.'

'Are you not man enough to answer me?' She half-turned to stare at him with a quirked eyebrow.

His jaw tightened at her insult. 'I am man enough to answer you.'

Grace raised her chin in readiness for his words. 'Yes?'

'No, I won't marry you.'

* * *

THE FOLLOWING DAY, Grace woke late. Her head ached with a thumping not human. Groaning, she rolled out of bed and staggered for the water jug placed on a tallboy by the window. The first glass of water took away the furry taste of stale alcohol. Pouring her second glass, there was a tap on the door before it opened to reveal a frowning Mrs Winton. 'I see you're up, Miss?' She sniffed disapprovingly.

'Indeed.' Grace went back to her bed.

'May I ask, Miss, what am I to do with Mr Doyle sitting in my kitchen?' Mrs Winton folded her arms across her flat chest.

Grace turned to stare in bewilderment. 'Mr Doyle?'

'He slept on the sofa last night, since it was too late for him to return home. And now he refuses to leave until he's spoken to you.'

Closing her eyes, Grace sighed. 'I'll be down in a moment.'

The disagreeable housekeeper pulled the door shut as she left Grace to dress. She washed in cold water to freshen her sluggish mind. Next, she selected a pale pink skirt and matching mid-waist jacket with a cream blouse. Her hair she could not bother with and after a few brushes left it down in a riot of long curls. She descended the stairs in apprehension of facing Doyle.

He stood instantly when she walked in. 'Good morning, Miss Woodruff.'

'Don't call me that,' she muttered, going to put her hands out to the fire glowing in the grate.

'Don't call you, Miss Woodruff?' Doyle frowned.

'You must call me Grace if we are to be engaged.'

'I told you no.'

'And I refuse your answer.'

'You really want us to marry?'

'Of course.'

'Please don't think you have to go through with this. I understand you were not yourself last night. It won't go any further.'

Grace faced him, her stance proud. 'Do you mean it when you say you don't want to marry me?'

'I'm saying, you don't have to go through with it. I understand why you said it.'

'Do you?'

Doyle sighed at her prickly mood.

His patronizing angered her. 'My life has changed, Doyle. I want to be married, whether it be to you or someone else. I would prefer it were you, since we rub along well enough, but if you are unable to come to the task, I'll understand.'

'What nonsense you talk woman!' Doyle strode to her and grabbed her arms. 'Do you think any man will want to marry you when you ache for another?'

Grace's head jerked at this. 'What do you know of such business?' she threw at him.

Doyle flung her arms away and marched to the door. 'I know what it's like to love someone, to want someone so badly it eats you alive, for I live it every day! But I won't be used, Grace, even though my heart aches for you. I won't be second best.'

Grace stared at him. *What a man he is.* Something in the proud way he stood, and the truthful words he spoke, awakened a fluttering in her heart. 'I would be a good wife to you.'

Doyle took a step towards her, his face tortured. 'Do you know what my name is?'

Grace blinked, her mind faltered, she couldn't think. *What was his name?* She always thought of him as Doyle.

'My name is William.' Doyle's tone was as cold as ice.

'I... Well, that is...'

'So, you would be married to a William, but the wrong William, yes?'

She found it hard to swallow and was sure her head would split in two from its throbbing. She fumbled her way to the sofa and sat in stupefied silence.

Doyle, his anger spent, sat alongside her. 'You need to get him out of your heart,' he said gently.

'I could, with your help.' She looked at him, agonized.

He groaned and pulled her to him. He kissed her brutally, crushing her to him with a force that left her mindless. It was act of ownership, his stamping of authority. Relaxing, he deepened the kiss and his grip softened into a tender loving embrace that sent the blood rushing into her veins making her light headed. They parted but he didn't let her go. Grace leaned into his shoulder.

'How soon can you arrange a special license?' He joked.

Grace chuckled and ran her fingers through his brown curls. 'Oh no, nothing like that. It's going to be a proper wedding.'

He looked at her straight. 'And what do you plan on calling me?'

'My darling Doyle.' She grinned at him.

The smile slipped from his face. Hastily, he rose. 'No, Grace. It'll never work. You'll always see me as your butler, Doyle. But I am William, or rather, Billy. A man who has nothing but his pride.'

Stunned, she watched him walk out. A few moments later, the front door closed and he was gone.

* * *

WOODRUFF WATCHED with suppressed anger as the nurse manhandled his body with indifference. 'I ... not...baby!' He growled out between his loose lips.

'Indeed you ain't, Mr Woodruff. But neither can you wash yourself,' she replied fitting a clean nightshirt over his head.

'Whore.'

'Not recently, sir,' she said, 'I'm a bit past it at my age.' She went chuckling out of the room carrying his soiled linen. No sooner had the door closed behind her, than it was opened again, and Diana stood there with a look of disgust.

Woodruff snarled at her and awkwardly turned his upper body away.

'I sold the hunters,' she announced. 'They do nothing but eat. You'll not be riding them anymore, and the girls never wished to.'

'Sell ... hunters ... I ... kill ... you.' He spoke his words steadily, each one well meant.

Diana blanched, but, knowing he could not reach her from his bed, she lifted her chin. 'A man comes for them today. I managed to obtain a decent price for them. The stables will be reduced to the carriage horses and Emma Kate and Phoebe's horses. Faith insisted I sell hers, too. This reduced state will mean I can let go of two grooms, leaving Sykes, Potter and one stable boy.'

'You...'

'Taking Mr Swindale's advice, I've let go two gardeners as well. The two remaining can do what work is needed.'

'No!'

'Yes!' Diana took a step away from the door. 'You've caused this, *you*. However, we can still live in this house quite comfortably if we reduce our expenditure. I'm fully aware of the circumstances now, and will do my utmost to see that we don't slide any further down into the pit of debt you dug.' Diana tilted her head regally. 'Now, if you'll excuse me, I must dress for a ball at the Ellsworths'. Through Heather, we may still regain our place in society.' She turned for the door, but spun back to him again. 'Oh, and I'll do my best to marry our daughters off to whoever they happen to find attentive. Thankfully, the Ellsworths' have a higher class of society that do not include the types like Horton.' She left in a flounce of trailing purple skirts.

With his good arm, Woodruff reached over and rang the bell pull. Presently, Partridge entered to stand some feet from the bed. He flung back the bed covers and lifted his good leg over the edge. Woodruff looked at her and pointed to a cane leaning against the dresser. 'Fetch.'

'The doctor said…'

'Fetch!'

With the cane in his good hand, and leaning heavily on Partridge's strong shoulders, he heaved himself from the bed for the first time since his second attack. A wave of dizziness enveloped him but he fought it. He was weak, frustratingly so, but with Partridge's help he made it slowly to the chair by the window. A whoosh of air escaped his lungs as he sat down, but he was grinning like a child who'd successfully stolen a chocolate.

'Meat.'

'Pardon, sir?' Partridge bent low to hear him better.

'Meat. Wine. No…more…Baby…slops.' His thoughts turned nasty as he planned his recovery.

* * *

WILLIAM ROSS LEANED against the wall by the large window to look out over the city of Paris, as he had done every night for the past fortnight. Below him, the Seine flowed majestically, carrying watercrafts to different points along its banks. He watched a group of people disembark at a small jetty further down the street. They wore beautiful clothes of lavish colours, which dazzled in the evening twilight. A dog ran in front of a passing carriage, the horse pranced and reared, scaring the group of revellers.

A noise behind him brought him out of his study. He turned his head as his wife entered the drawing room of their rented apartment.

'I thought you would be out until late?' she said, gliding towards him with a smile.

She was an attractive woman, nearly as tall as he with long

midnight black hair and laughing blue eyes. Although spoilt and headstrong, she was a fine hostess and intelligent. Her pedigree proclaimed distant relations with French royalty, and her family's immense wealth would make any man pleased to call her his wife, any man except William. From the moment he had said his marriage vows, he knew he'd made the most dreadful mistake of his life. 'I finished early,' he told her.

'Did everything go well?'

'Yes. I now own one of Paris's greatest houses.'

Felicity grinned, and reached up to kiss him on the cheek. 'You are so clever.'

He pulled away from her gently. Her eyes narrowed at his withdrawal, but he couldn't help it. 'Not really. Your father pointed out to me the value of such an investment.'

'And are we to live there, darling?' She moved away towards their bedroom, Parisian lace and Chinese silk streaming out behind her.

'No, I shall lease it. The French government pays good money to have great places to work from, or entertain in.' William poured himself a brandy, dreading the coming night. He had consummated the marriage in haste, glad to have the act done, but since then Felicity's attentions had left him cold. Grace tormented his mind the whole time and nothing he did could blot her image from behind his eyes. Sharing a bed with Felicity made guilt rip at his insides, while his burdened heart refused to release him from a woman living with a baby in a cottage on the outskirts of Leeds.

Felicity paused in the bedroom doorway. 'When shall we go south?'

'I've rented these rooms for another two weeks.'

'Let us go sooner, darling. The autumn maybe kinder down there. Today was terribly cold; then we can go on to Italy.'

'I have business to attend to, Felicity, I cannot simply dash around the continent.'

'Pooh to that, William, you know my father will take care of everything, and no doubt make a heap of money on your behalf.'

William scowled. 'I do not wish for your father to make me money. I can manage well enough myself.'

Felicity's tinkling laugh grated on his taut nerves. 'Come now, we both know how well my father does it. It was the sole reason we married, and he so enjoys doing it for you now you're his son-in-law, the son he never had. Therefore, there's no point in you working too. You can simply sit back and spend your energy entertaining me.' She disappeared into the room before he could answer.

He threw back the rest of his brandy and poured another generous amount. Pride burned his chest as much as the brandy did. *What have I done?*

* * *

DANIEL THOMAS LAY hot and fevered in his crib, unaware of the two anxious faces hovering over him. Janey wrung a cold cloth over a water basin and placed it gently over his little forehead. 'Oh Miss, when's t' doctor comin'?'

'Soon, I'm sure, but as he said yesterday, there's nothing he can do but apply poultices to his chest.' Grace nibbled her fingertips, watching her sweet baby brother struggle for each breath. She felt so useless at not being able to ease his suffering. For the first time since his birth, the overwhelming responsibility placed upon her struck home. His welfare, his survival rested on her shoulders, and the weight of it seemed oppressive at that moment. Apart from a nursemaid and a housekeeper, she had no one to share her fears over him.

The door opened and Mrs Winton came in carrying a steaming bowl of hot water. 'Right Miss, this will help the little fellow.' She placed the bowl on the floor by the crib. 'I've got two more to bring up. We'll keep them topped up and see if it helps clear his chest.'

'Thank you, Mrs Winton.' Grace smiled faintly. 'You've been a tremendous support in the last few days.'

'Well, we can't have the little lad suffering now, can we?' She gave the closest evidence of a smile ever shown.

Grace grabbed her hands and squeezed them. 'You're a good woman for all your prickles.'

Mrs Winton stiffened. 'I'll bring more bowls up.'

The day passed by in anxious anticipation. The doctor called and examined his patient for ten minutes before shaking his head and informing Grace there was nothing more he could do. Daniel Thomas must weather this storm alone.

Angered by such insipid advice, Grace spent the next twenty-four hours by her brother's side. She walked the floor with him for hours. She repeatedly washed his red hot body, and spent endless hours trying to coax drops of water between his parched blue lips. Exhausted, she finally slept on the old rocking chair brought from Woodruff House. The same chair in which her mother had rocked each of her daughters.

The twittering birds outside the window roused her from sleep before dawn the next morning. Grace stretched and yawned as she stood. Apprehensively, her gaze rested on Daniel Thomas, hoping to find his fever gone and him sleeping with ease. Stepping closer to the crib, she saw he slept peacefully, only not of this world. With her breath suspended between a sob and a cry, Grace bit her lip and gently reached over to touch the tiny, motionless body. She stroked his still warm cheek. *I'm so sorry, darling boy. I could not help you when you needed me.*

Two tears ran parallel down her cheeks, as outside, the country woke to herald a new day.

* * *

'WHAT DO YOU PLAN TO DO?' Gaby asked some hours later after rushing to the cottage on receiving Grace's note.

'What do you mean?' Grace tried to focus on Gaby, but her mind refused to work.

Gaby placed her teacup back on the table and moved to sit on the arm of Grace's chair. She rested Grace's head against her chest. 'You must go home. Your time here is finished. Go back and bring some accord into the house again.'

'Is that all I'm good for?'

'No, but you know what I mean.'

'I cannot go back there,' she replied, her tone dull. 'Besides, Mama wouldn't want it.'

'Mama has no idea what she wants. But the rest need you.'

'Do they?' Grace brooded. 'I think they can manage rather well without me.'

'Well, if you don't return, what shall you do?'

'I honestly don't know. I'll decide after the funeral.'

'When is it to be?'

'In two days. He'll be buried with his mother ...' Grace gave herself a mental shake and looked up at Gaby. 'How are you finding married life with John Morgan?'

A thoughtful expression appeared on her sister's face. 'It is suitable. Naturally, there was, and is, a lot of adjusting to do. But we find that we enjoy married life considerably well so far.'

'No regrets?'

'Not yet.' Gaby grinned, then her face altered a little. 'Well, maybe a few. It would be nice for the family to come visit me or I them.'

'Has Heather called?'

Gaby lowered her gaze. 'No.'

Grace rose, tired and desperately sad. 'Come for a walk with me, the day is not so chilly, and I need to breathe fresh air.'

They put on their cloaks and gloves, and then walked through the house to the kitchen. There, Grace paused to inform Mrs Winton of their intentions.

'Mind how you go, Miss Grace,' the housekeeper replied. 'I'll have a nice pot of soup ready for your return.'

Grace smiled at her, for it was the first time the woman had offered such a blessing. *Maybe she is thawing after all?*

The crisp cool air brought a blush of delicate pink to their cheeks. Linking arms, they set a good pace until Gaby complained of a stitch and the baby's kicking, Grace slowed to accommodate her.

'I asked Doyle to marry me,' Grace suddenly spoke into the comfortable silence between them.

Gaby jolted to a stop. 'What?' Her eyes were wide. 'Why on earth would you do that?'

'Because the thought of spending my life alone fills me with dread.'

'You have time to meet someone of worth, Grace.'

'I'll be twenty-four on my next birthday, Gaby; who'll look at me now? Anyway, Doyle is worthy.'

'But you're beautiful! Many men of our acquaintance would dearly like to court you, they always have done. However, you always remained aloof, and beyond forming friendships like the rest of us.'

'I didn't mean to be. But for the last few years, I've always had so much to worry about. When Mama retired to her rooms, it became my responsibility to guide the rest of you. When did I have time to think of a beau?'

'Except William Ross.'

She lifted her gaze and stared out over the barren fields. 'Yes, except William.'

'And now he is married.'

'Yes.'

'So, now you want to marry the butler.'

'He is a good man, Gaby.' Grace glanced at her sister before looking into the distance once more.

'I agree, and he's very handsome, but is he the one to marry?' Gaby persisted.

Grace stopped to watch a flock of birds wheel overhead. The trees were sending their bronze coloured leaves to lie gently on the ground below. Somewhere in a field close by, a cow bellowed. The lane she walked, the sights she saw, were familiar, for she came this way with Doyle every Sunday. *Is he the one to marry?* The thought echoed in her mind like a shout into a cave. She didn't have the answer.

Gaby took her arm again and they turned back. 'If you marry Doyle, where will you live? And Mama will not accept him or you. You will live simply like me, and like you have been at this cottage. It is enough for me, because I am developing feelings for Morgan, but is it enough for you? Daniel Thomas has gone, you can reclaim your old life now, if you want it.'

'I think so differently now than I did only this time last year. Our lives were uncomplicated and ordered before, now we are scattered like seeds on the wind. Nothing is the same.'

'No.'

'I had one dream, to marry William.' Grace's voice caught with emotion. 'That dream was torn to shreds and it seems my whole family life with it.'

'It will not be easy, but you must do what you think right.'

'I shall marry Doyle, and I shall live at Woodruff House,' Grace said with determination.

'How?'

'I do not know yet, but I will.'

'Do you love him?'

Grace's smile struggled. 'I care for him. He will be good to me.'

'Is it enough for you?'

She stared over the fields into the distance. 'It will have to be.'

CHAPTER 13

*D*iana sat like a stunned rabbit trapped by a fox while Letitia directed a mutinous glare at her eldest sister.

The silence, after Grace's statement that she wished to marry the butler, continued as the women in the drawing room gazed at each other in utter surprise.

'What have I done to deserve such ungrateful daughters?' Diana managed to babble. 'You cannot mean it, Grace?'

'Do you want to me to come back home, Mama?' Grace asked, from her stance by the hearth.

'Well, having you back would be lovely, indeed, but as for you marrying Doyle, I will not allow it.' Colour drained from her mother's face.

'You have no say in the matter, Mama,' Grace informed her. 'I am simply asking you whether you would like me to come back home, even though I will be married to Doyle. If you do not, then I will leave here today and never return.'

'You are not with child, are you?'

'No, Mama, I am not.'

'Then, why?'

Grace sighed. 'Because I wish to be married to a good and

decent man and have a family of my own. There is no one in our society I admire and if I wait much longer no one will want me.'

'Nonsense! You hold your age well. There would be plenty of men wanting your hand.'

Grace ignored the slight. 'Thank you, Mama.'

Letitia sauntered over to the drinks cabinet and poured herself a sherry from the only bottle there.

Diana scowled. 'Letitia dear, it's a little early in the day, don't you think?'

'I've received a shock, Mama,' she replied lightly.

Diana turned her attention back to Grace, her worry over Letitia's drinking evident in her agonized eyes. 'Why must you do this to us, Grace? We are only now regaining some respectability in society. What do you think will happen to us when this is known?'

Letitia snarled at Grace. 'You were always so high and mighty, yet all the time you were lifting your skirts for the butler. I have two whores for sisters now, have I?'

'Letitia!' Diana cried.

As the others gasped, Grace raised an eyebrow. 'I am no whore, Letitia, nor is Gabriella.'

'Really?' Letitia laughed, her eyes over bright. 'Do the lower classes have a certain way with them that our class does not? I might try one myself.'

'You have filthy tongue, sister,' Grace told her.

Diana banged her hand on the arm on the chair. 'Stop this at once!'

'Do you love him?' This sudden question came from Phoebe, whose eyes shone with tears.

Grace smiled at her. 'I think him a fine man, dearest, and I know of no other who would make me happy now.'

Phoebe glanced at their mother and back again. 'You are not bothered by his low status?'

'No, *I* am not.'

Phoebe nodded and then looked under her lashes at Faith and Emma Kate. She rose and kissed Grace's cheek. 'You deserve to be happy.'

After Phoebe left, silence once more settled on the room.

Diana wiped a shaky hand over her face. 'Will you at least not rush the decision and think it over some more? For my sake? Can you not return here and let everything settled down before causing more upheaval?'

'Very well, Mama, I will say nothing more on the subject for a little while.' With a deep sigh, Grace walked towards the hall. 'I'm going up to see Father. I believe he has been improving very well lately.'

In the hall, she found Doyle waiting for her by the stairs. He shook his head. 'I won't marry you.'

Grace paused on the first step, turning to look at him. 'Why?'

'I won't be the cause of you again being estranged from your family.'

'I already am.'

'You have a chance to come back and live your life as you should.'

'Can we talk about this later?' Grace asked, mounting the stairs. 'I am about to visit Father.'

'Grace,' Doyle took the stairs after her.

She stopped and turned to him. Gently, she put a hand to his cheek. 'Why deny us both?'

'You don't understand, it will not work. You'll never see me as your equal.'

'You are wrong.' She smiled. 'I already do.' Gathering up her skirts, she quickly went up the stairs.

In the drawing room, discussion of Grace's announcement gathered momentum again before petering out until all remaining felt exhausted.

Diana knew her life was over; society would never reclaim her if Grace married their butler. The shame bowed her shoulders, and she asked Faith and Emma Kate to assist her to her rooms.

Left alone, Letitia finished the remaining sherry quickly, knowing Doyle would confiscate the bottle now her mama had retired. Staggering, she ascended to her room, where a hidden bottle of gin waited for her. She closed her bedroom door and turned the key in the lock before rushing over to her writing desk. Pulling out the third drawer, she pushed the papers aside until her fingers found the small, sinful bottle. Eagerly, she drank until she choked. Coughing and gasping, she stumbled over to her bed and sprawled across it. Without any shred of dignity, she finished the small bottle in record time. Annoyed her craving wasn't sated, she hid the empty bottle under her bed and then searched the room and adjoining dressing room to find any of her previous hiding places. After many minutes of fruitless hunting, she sat red-faced and puffing on her bed. With a sudden jerk, she rang the bell pull by the bed.

Patience had never been her virtue, and she became more irritated waiting for Hopeland.

At the maid's knock, Letitia opened the door. 'Ahh ... Hopeland. I feel a triflish unwell.' Letitia felt herself slipping sideways and gripped the bedpost. 'I believe a nip of brandy will settle me. Just to be sure bring the bottle.'

'Yes, Miss.' Hopeland bowed her head and closed the door. Lifting her skirts, she ran lightly across the gallery, down the servant's staircase and along the corridor to knock on Mr Doyle's open door. Doyle looked up from the accounts laid opened before him and beckoned her in. She went to stand by his table.

'Yes?' he asked her.

'It's Miss Letitia again, Mr Doyle. She's asking for brandy this time.'

Wearily, Doyle replaced his pen in its stand and closed the books. 'Is this the third time this week?'

'Yes, sir. Though, Partridge found an empty wine bottle

hidden behind the curtains on the gallery landing, so that makes it four.'

Doyle took a bunch of keys out from his pocket and unlocked a liquor cabinet in the corner of the room. He selected a bottle of brandy and poured a small measure into a crystal glass on a silver tray.

'Shall I take it this time, Mr Doyle?'

'No, thank you, Hopeland. I'll take it, but you wait outside her door in case she becomes loud. Miss Grace is still in the house and knows nothing of Miss Letitia's growing problem.'

'If you pardon me for saying so, Mr Doyle, I think you should tell her.'

'Miss Grace has enough worry with the baby's death, without this to add to it.'

They made it up the back stairs and to Letitia's door without interference. With a light tap on the door, Doyle entered the room to find Letitia pacing wildly. He left the door open.

'It took you long enough!' She snapped, hurrying to the tray he held. She stopped short on seeing only a small glass and not a bottle. In a fit of anger, she knocked the tray from his hand. It clattered across the room. 'Where's the bottle?'

'There are no more bottles, Miss Letitia. You must understand money for extra luxuries has been curtailed by your Father's solicitor.'

'Damnation, man, I asked for a *bottle*!'

Doyle turned for the door, but Letitia flew around him and slammed it shut, she turned the key in the lock and then popped the key down her dress front. 'If you want to get out, come and retrieve the key,' she purred, sensual and rhythmic.

He and other staff members who knew of her dependence on alcohol had witnessed this change in mood before. That her family members remained unaware of her predicament was not surprising, for she had become clever at disguising her longings, and sneaky in her ability to acquire bottles from the cellar without being noticed. But *he* knew, and had known for some time. It tore at him that he must keep it from Grace; he wanted to shield her from further hurt. But he was out of his depth now. He couldn't hide what he knew any more.

'Miss Letitia, open the door, and I will get you a bottle from the cellar,' he murmured, watching as her eyes widened a little at his offering.

'Oh yes, you *will* get me a bottle, but first I want you to kiss me.' She laughed at his look of disgust. 'No? You don't want to kiss me? Why ever not? Surely one sister is as good as the other?' She sashayed closer to him, stopping inches from his chest. He held his breath as she moistened her fingertip and placed it against his lips. 'I will let you do whatever you wish,' she whispered, standing on tiptoe to kiss him. 'I can whore myself as good as Grace or Gaby.'

Doyle carefully placed his arms around her, and she grinned as he pulled her close. Slowly, he turned her around so her back was resting against him. She groaned, sliding her hands out behind her to touch him. He ran his hand over her shoulder and then swiftly down her dress front and fumbled for the key nestled between her chemise and corset. With a cry of triumph, he pulled out the key and pushed her away. He ignored her cry of protest and went to the door, unlocked it and quickly escaped.

'Oh, Mr Doyle, I was so worried,' gushed Hopeland, fidgeting with her apron. 'I was only going to give you a few more minutes before going for help.'

'You weren't the only one worried.' He winced as articles smashed against the door. He shook his head at the disaster Letitia would create.

'What will we do?' Hopeland wrung her hands.

'What's happening?' Grace walked down the gallery.

Doyle rubbed a hand over his eyes. 'There is something you should know.' He turned to dismiss Hopeland then led Grace back along the gallery to the landing by the staircase. He indicated for her to sit on the window seat.

An unreadable expression came to Grace's face as she listened to his account of Letitia's habit. 'This is my fault. I left here knowing she indulged. I should have done something about it before now, but with everything else on my mind...'

'It is not your fault. You are not responsible for everyone all the time.'

'But I knew!' She stood and paced before him. 'I could have helped her, but I was selfish, wanting my own way all the time, thinking and believing my way was always the correct way.' She thrust her knuckles into her mouth to stop the moans escaping.

'You cannot blame yourself. I won't let you.'

'I can't bear it, Doyle. This is my doing. All of it. Letitia, Gaby, Daniel Thomas. I failed them all!'

'Stop this!' He held her tight but she pushed him away.

Wide-eyed, Grace stared at him. Pain and misery etched her face. 'Don't you see? I'm doing it to you too! I'm taking, not giving. Always demanding.'

'Grace, enough.' He ran his fingers through his hair. 'You have given too, don't you understand? You have set aside your youth to care for this family. You gave your mother the chance to selfishly stay in her rooms while you ran the house. As for me, you've given me much.'

'Yet you don't want to marry me?' Her face crumpled. 'Why?'

He took her hands and kissed them. 'I can't, my dearest heart. It wouldn't work. I want you, body and soul. You don't love me, there is desire, yes, but it wouldn't sustain us in the years to come.'

'It might, and I could come to love you. I know I can.'

He sighed deeply, burdened with sadness. 'I believe somewhere there is a man who will take your heart and claim it as his own. No, not William Ross, that was a girl's dream left to linger longer than it should.'

His words weaved themselves into her suffering and she nodded, acknowledging them as truth.

He straightened his shoulders. 'Come, I will stay with you while you speak to your Mama about Letitia.'

Grace wiped her eyes with her handkerchief and let him guide her to her mother's rooms.

Diana, seated up in bed sipping tea, scowled as they neared. 'What are you both doing? What do you want?' She shrank away from them.

'Mama, we've come to discuss the future, all our futures.' Grace gathered her strength and employed a no-nonsense look at her mother.

Her hand shaking, Diana placed her cup back on the tray by her bed. 'I cannot deal with this, Grace. You are wicked to put me through such sensations. You give me no thought.'

Grace took a step closer. 'Yes, I do Mama. I love you deeply.'

'No, you do not.' Diana pouted like a petulant child. 'You wish to send me to an early grave. Haven't I suffered enough at the hands of your father?'

'Yes, Mama, but we shall discuss the calamities father has inflicted upon us later. First, we must talk of Letitia.'

'What of her?' Diana's eyes became wary.

Doyle stepped forward and Diana's gaze shifted to him. 'I have reason to believe she is dependent on alcohol, madam.'

'Nonsense!'

'Listen to him, Mama.' At Grace's instruction, Diana listened to the harrowing tales of Letitia's desperation.

Eventually, after much shedding of tears and more cups of tea, Diana declared herself too tired to discuss the matter further. She asked Doyle to leave; she needed to talk to Grace alone.

'Yes, Mama?' Grace asked, on Doyle's departure.

'Please do not marry him, my dear.' The tears glistened in Diana's eyes. 'You were never one to covet marriage, what has changed you so much that you must insult us by marrying our butler?'

'I...'

'You are so selfish!' Diana broke into fresh sobbing.

'Mama...'

'Do you care for any of us?' Diana shrieked. 'Isn't it bad enough to have Gabriella marrying beneath her, an outcast from us? And for all our money to be recklessly gambled away by your repulsive father, plus now the added problem of Letitia?' She paused to catch her breath before adding, 'Am I to carry these burdens alone, and must you add to them?'

'I am not going to marry, Doyle, Mama. He won't have me.'

Stupefied, Diana sat back against her pillows. '*He* won't have *you?*'

'No.'

'How dare he? Not have you?' Her mother's eyebrows nearly shot up to her hairline. 'Why, he's not fit to wipe your shoes.'

'Stop, Mama. I cannot take much more. We must concentrate on the family now. Letitia needs help and the other girls need our guidance.'

Diana nodded. 'Yes, you are right. We must turn to each other in our times of need. We require no others.'

'Much has changed, Mama. It will take time to find our way again. I know nothing of what Faith, Emma Kate and Phoebe have been doing in the months I've been gone. I shall need to visit Mr Swindale too.' She sighed. 'We'll talk more tomorrow. Good night, Mama.' She kissed her mother's cheek and left the room.

Doyle waited for her on the landing. 'How did it go?' he asked, taking her hands in his.

For a long time, Grace looked into his brown eyes. 'I am returning here to live.'

'Good. This is your rightful place.'

Tears spilled over her lashes, racing each other down her

cheeks. 'I am the eldest, and it is up to me to take care of them all. This time I shall do a better job of it.'

Tenderly, Doyle lifted her hands and kissed them. 'I have you back under this roof. You'll never go short of support.'

'I wish I could give you more in return, but I cannot. I know that now.' She swallowed her tears.

'Your friendship will maintain me. I'd rather that than nothing at all.' His eyes glowed for her.

With her heart wounded and her mind numb, Grace left Woodruff House to return to the cottage. Mrs Winton met her at the door. Rain had begun to fall and the cottage seemed gloomy and dismal. With the baby gone and Janey returned to her family, the quietness echoed in every corner.

Grace sat on the sofa as Mrs Winton added more coal to the fire. 'My father has given me this cottage, Mrs Winton. However, I am returning home to live, so I shall be letting it.'

'Very good, Miss.' The housekeeper sniffed.

'I was wondering if you would care to work at Woodruff House, as its housekeeper?' Mrs Winton stared at her as she continued, 'Of course, your wage will not be as high as you may receive at other establishments. You are aware of my family's financial difficulties. But the offer is there for you, should you wish to take it.' Grace rose to leave the room.

'Miss Woodruff?'

'Yes?'

'I'd be happy to work as your housekeeper, but what of Mr Doyle?'

'Mr Doyle is quite happy to share his work load, I assure you.'

* * *

THE RELOCATION BACK home proved to be of little consequence. The family and servants welcomed her enthusiastically for the first day, and then soon fell back into the old routine of everyone wanting a part of her. Grace found the first week so busy her head was spinning, but then she settled down to a schedule that suited her. Mr Swindale visited twice to speak to her father and herself. The money situation was no better, but no worse either, for the moment.

Grace shook her head at her mother's foibles. Diana took pleasure in the notion of having Mrs Winton employed. She enjoyed being able to converse with her returning friends about the fundamentals of a good housekeeper, even though they couldn't afford her.

But money concerns paled in significance compared to Letitia's problem. Grace sought Dr Bainbridge's help. However, when he arrived to examine her, Letitia denied all knowledge of her behaviour and called them foul names in a fit of temper. Shaken by the outburst, Grace listened to the doctor, who believed rationing her consumption of spirits would mean he could eventually wean her off them all together.

As the days folded into one another, the family and servants endured hell, as Letitia swayed between moods of melancholy, bouts of crying, and rages fit for Bedlam.

Slowly, amidst the mayhem, Grace reclaimed her sisters' trust and friendship. Together they went for many walks through the gardens as the weather turned cool. Often their talks would touch upon their father's gradual recovery. Most days, with the aid of a cane, Woodruff moved around his room. His volatile temper worsened with every improvement, and Dr Bainbridge warned him of placing stress on his weakened heart.

The thought of the master back in command again made the servants edgy. Grace tried extra hard to keep the house running smoothly, while reassuring her sisters she'd not let him rule them so harshly as he had done previously. But to have her father once more in charge of them filled her with dread.

CHAPTER 14

*G*aby puffed as she carried the bucket of pig slops out of the back door. She wiped a hand across her forehead. Her large stomach jutted out over her feet and she hid a yawn with her fingers. Sleep did not come easy for her now.

On the doorstep, she breathed in the cool November air, for the heat from the kitchen was stifling. She arched her back to ease the ache from it. Stretched out before her, over the top of the farm buildings, were the green fields of her husband's land. Dotted about the landscape, flocks of sheep and some milking cows offered a sense of peace and tranquillity.

Abel Trotter, Morgan's old labourer, rounded the side of the house, carrying logs in his arms. 'Mornin', Mrs Morgan, can I be tekken that fer thee?'

'Thank you, Abel.' Gaby smiled. Just in time, she remembered to call him by his first name. John had explained that here, last names were for strangers not for people who worked and lived with them. It was the way of his people, and she was content to acquiesce to his rules. The customs of her family's society were quickly forgotten when living on a farm. Nevertheless, she wasn't about to relinquish them altogether. Her children would be brought up as gentlemen and women wherever they lived.

'I'll place this lot down in't cellar and be away wirrit.' Able nodded at the bucket.

Gaby moved back inside the scullery to allow him to pass, and then proceeded into the kitchen. Ruth, the Morgans' maid of all work, was busily taking out fresh bread from the oven. Gaby knew she wouldn't have lasted a day here without the maid, for how was she to know the fundamentals of running a kitchen? Governess Pringle had done a remarkable job in teaching the Woodruff girls to sew, sing, embroider, speak French and dance, yet none of these skills were useful for a farmer's wife.

'Ere, Madam, sit yersen down, yer look all done in.' Ruth bustled Gaby into a chair by the table. 'Mr Morgan would never forgive me if owt happened ter yer.'

Gaby smiled. 'I'm fine, Ruth, honestly. I just need to rest a moment, and then I'll try my hand at making those tarts you showed me last week.'

Ruth laughed. 'I wonder if they'll turn out like those scones, hey, Madam?'

'Oh, nothing could be as bad as the scones, Ruth.' Gaby joined the maid in her laughter. 'Why, John thought he could skip them across the duck pond, they were so hard.'

A sudden knocking on the front door had Ruth wiping her hands on her apron. 'No, doubt it's fer you, madam, fer no tradesmen goes ter front door.'

Gaby eased herself up from the chair and straightened her hair, which was roughly tied up in a loose knot at her nape. On hearing Ruth welcome the visitor in, Gaby took off her apron and dusted spilt flour off her dark gray skirts. She walked down the hall to the sitting room at the front of the house.

Her heart nearly burst with delight as Grace, and joy of all joys, Phoebe, rushed to hug her. Eventually, Gaby released

Phoebe and spun to clasp Grace's hands in thankfulness. 'I cannot believe you brought Phoebe with you this time.'

Grace grinned, her eyes moist. 'Phoebe asked to come with me. It was her doing. They all know I come here once or twice a week.'

Gaby turned to Ruth who stood in the doorway. 'Bring some tea, please Ruth?'

'Aye, of course, madam.' Ruth left the sisters to smile at each other.

Phoebe held Gaby's hand and stared in wonder at her large stomach. 'My, how big you are, Gaby! When is the baby due to be born?'

'Today, hopefully, I'm tired of carrying such weight,' she joked.

Phoebe's eyes widened in fright. 'Today?'

Gaby and Grace laughed. 'No, not today, dearest one. Next week, maybe,' Gaby said with a grin before looking at Grace.

Phoebe jiggled on the edge of her chair, her eyes full of mischief. 'You will never guess our news!'

Gaby grinned. 'What news?'

'Emma Kate has acquired a beau.'

'No, really?' She looked at her two sisters.

Phoebe nodded. 'His name is Oliver Vincent, a cousin to Andrew on his mother's side. Twice now, he has called for tea. Heather invited Emma Kate to the Ellsworths' to stay for the weekend while Mr Vincent visited. A sure sign there is approval for the match on both sides.'

'And is this man young, old, a poor artist or gentleman?' Gaby wished to know.

'Oh, he's a gentleman indeed, Gaby, though only a third son, would you believe. That vexed Father greatly, but Emma Kate does not care a jot. His family own land to the north of York. They have a townhouse in London and large house on the Scottish border.'

'Really?' Gaby smiled over at Grace. She had missed Phoebe's excited prattle.

'Yes,' Phoebe went on, 'and we think Mr Vincent has a fortune of his own, even though he is a third son. His family must be very wealthy, don't you agree?'

'Indeed, I do,' Gaby replied, as Ruth brought in the tea tray. 'I hope it is a great success for Emma Kate. Does she hold him in high opinion?'

Phoebe nodded eagerly, pouring the tea for Gaby. 'Mama is beside herself with happiness, but feels sad that Emma Kate may live so far away from us.'

'Hold on, Phoebe,' Grace interjected. 'Mr Vincent has not asked for Emma Kate yet, and he may not at this time. He leaves for London on Wednesday, and who knows when he'll return?'

'But surely, he will? I cannot imagine why a man would pay so much attention to a lady and not show his hand.'

'How is John, Gaby?' Grace asked, changing the exhausted subject.

'Quite well. He's gone to Leeds today. There is a beast market on, and he wishes to sell some of our sheep and maybe buy a new ram for our own is becoming old.' Gaby laughed. 'Goodness, I'm sure you didn't wish to know that.'

Grace swallowed a bite of a light sponge cake. 'Of course, I wish to know such things.' She grinned. 'I want to know about your life. It beats thrashing over new silk colours as Mama's friends do.'

'Are they calling more now?' Gaby asked, serious once more.

Grace nodded. 'Ever so slowly, life is returning to normal.'

'Letitia is not normal. She is an embarrassment!' Phoebe huffed.

'Phoebe!' Grace admonished. 'It wasn't to be mentioned.'

Gaby frowned. 'Tell me.'

With a sigh, and a dark look at Phoebe, Grace told Gaby of

Letitia's problem and the burden she was placing on the tenuous grip the family held on to respectability.

'Why did you not say so sooner?' Gaby demanded, affronted at being left out.

'I'm sorry, Gaby. I have meant to every time I call, but I keep hoping she will change.'

Phoebe snorted in disgust. 'How is that possible? She is violent and sneaky.'

'She's in trouble, Phoebe.' Grace looked at Gaby. 'I think she needs to be sent away to one of those places which help the troubled with their problems. There are asylums catering for people like Letitia, but Mama won't hear of it.'

'And nor should she!' Phoebe stood and walked to the window to gaze out of it. 'Imagine what people would think.'

Gaby looked from one sister to another. 'What is to be done?'

'Nothing for the moment, unfortunately.' Grace shook her head sadly.

'You appear weary, Grace. You must take care of yourself too.'

'I try.' Grace replaced her teacup and saucer on the tray. 'The doctor's bill is enormous from his attendance to Father, Mama's feigned sicknesses and now the demands of Letitia. I dread the sight of Mr Swindale visiting; he's so full of doom and gloom about our money problems. He puts the whole house into misery the moment his hat is off. I doubt the man will allow money to be spent on Letitia's stay in an asylum.'

'The horrid man says we are to buy no more dresses in the next year.' Phoebe scoffed from the window. 'Stupid man, as if we can last a whole year without new dresses!'

'We will manage, Phoebe,' Grace told her.

'Indeed, you will,' Gaby added. 'I know I shall not be needing half of my ball dresses, so why do you not take them? You could cut them up, add new lace or braid, and so on.'

Phoebe pranced over to hug her. 'Wonderful idea, Gaby. You'll never need your silks again living here.'

Grace shook her head at her tactless sister and changed the subject once more. 'Did you find the nursery furniture I sent suitable?'

'Oh, yes, very well. Though John was a little proud at first to take them. I reasoned with him on the silliness of refusing what we need. In the end, he enjoyed arranging it in the baby's room. We bought new linen and curtains too.'

'I think your husband is looking forward to having a child. Yes?'

Gaby enjoyed the happiness that lightened John's eyes every time he gazed at her. 'Indeed, yes. I believe he thought it wouldn't happen to him at his age.'

'How old is he?' Phoebe asked.

'Seven and thirty.'

Phoebe rolled her eyes. 'Good Lord, positively ancient!'

'Aren't you excited?' Grace inquired, sharing a grin with Gaby over Phoebe's words.

Gaby shrugged her shoulders. 'Actually, I wonder how I will cope. Ruth is wonderful and does everything for me, but still she cannot be everywhere all the time.'

'Can you not afford to employ another girl?'

'Oh, I'm sure we could, and I must discuss it with John, but he is so busy, and the farm takes all his time. I think he forgets how useless I am at domestic arrangements.'

'I'm sure you are being too hard on yourself.'

Phoebe refilled their teacups. 'I think it's romantic to live in such a house and work side by side with your husband,' she said in a dreamlike tone.

'There is nothing romantic about it, Phoebe,' Gaby swiftly answered. 'Farming is exhausting, ceaseless work and not for the faint hearted.'

'True,' Grace nodded.

Phoebe pouted. 'I didn't necessarily mean farming.'

'John is lucky I am not the type to turn my nose up at hard

work,' Gaby continued. 'I could have made his life a living misery. However, I happen to think that when anyone makes an informed decision they should summon all strength to see it through with honour. I chose this life, knowing the pitfalls, and I refuse to sit and whine about the unsatisfactory aspects of it.'

'He is indeed fortunate,' Grace agreed, smiling. 'I surmise, dear sister, that you enjoy your simpler life.'

Gaby grinned ruefully. 'In all honesty, you are correct. Though, an extra servant or two would be convenient.'

* * *

WOODRUFF LEANED HEAVILY on his cane and the banister as he made his way downstairs. The effort it took to dress and make it down to breakfast cost him plenty, but seeing the astonished faces of his family rewarded him. The fact that he was back on his feet sent Diana back to her rooms to stay there, which suited him handsomely, for she needed to be put in her place. Lately, she had gained too much control of the house and his affairs. The moment he learnt of her bending Swindale's ear caused him to hasten his recovery.

Before he sacked his nurse, he'd spent hours with her exercising his limbs and gaining strength back into his left side, plus he read aloud every day to improve his speech. Never again would he let anyone control him or his money.

Now, as he sat at the head of the breakfast table, he looked around at the five daughters left at home. His eyes narrowed as he weighed up their potential. Emma Kate, hopefully, would snag the Vincent fellow, which gave him the opportunity to wring as much money as he could out of that union. All he had to do was secure the other girls with men of wealth. He peered closely at Letitia and saw she appeared ill with a sallow face and dark shadows under her bloodshot eyes. 'Letitia!' He barked, making the girls jump. 'Are you unwell?'

Letitia slowed turned her blank gaze to him. 'Yes, Father, I am.' Her hands shook as she replaced the teacup she had been nursing.

'Get to your room then, stupid girl!' he roared. 'Do you think we all wish to succumb to it too?'

She slowly moved her chair back. With Doyle's help, she left the room.

'Father,' Grace turned to him. 'I must speak to you about Letitia's health.'

'Am I a bloody doctor?' He sneered. 'I have no wish to be informed.'

'But...'

'Today Horton arrives. He is to stay but one night. See his needs are met.' Woodruff smirked as the girls blanched at the news.

Grace dabbed her napkin to her mouth. 'I wish you would give me more notice, Father. I'll have to consult Mrs Hawksberry.'

'Consult who you wish,' he muttered.

His daughters left the breakfast table, all sickeningly obvious in their eagerness to be away from him. It pleased him his presence unnerved them. They never knew what went on in his mind, and even when they did, it usually wasn't to their benefit.

* * *

LATER, as the clock's chimes struck eleven, Doyle opened the door to Horton's summons. Rain cast a gloomy grey shade over the house and grounds. Doyle showed him into the drawing room, where Woodruff waited. The two men laughed and greeted each other.

'Ah, Doyle, pour some whiskey for my guest,' Woodruff commanded from his chair by the fire. 'You might as well leave the bottle close by,' he added, as Doyle brought the drink.

Doyle masked his irritation at having to order spirits into the house. His employer cared nothing if he flaunted the evil liquid in front of Letitia at meal times.

Horton accepted the drink without thanks and supped a mouthful, before inquiring about the daughters of the house.

'Damn useless females,' Woodruff grumbled.

'Well man, how am I to pick one if they aren't in front of me?' Horton bellowed with good humour.

This announcement caused Doyle to look sharply at both men, before silently departing the room to look for Grace. He found her in the conservatory. She must have sensed his worry or seen his concern clear on his face, for she left her potting bench to cross to him quickly.

'What is it? Letitia?' Panic clouded her eyes.

'No. Horton has arrived.'

Distaste changed Grace beautiful features. 'Filthy man!'

'I know the nature of his business.'

'Oh?'

'He is here to pick a bride.' He watched her eyes widen, then close.

She turned from him to sit on the love seat by the palms. 'Father knows of Emma Kate's attachment to Mr Vincent; surely he would have the sense to know that he is far wealthier than Horton.' She raised tortured eyes to him. 'So, he means to marry one of us who are unattached.'

'Not you. I won't let it happen.' Doyle rushed to assure her.

'Don't be ridiculous, it won't be me,' she snapped. She rose to pace the floor, chewing her bottom lip in anxiety.

'Grace...'

She abruptly stopped her pacing. 'Go back to them, find out all you can. I need to be prepared.'

'Grace...'

'Go, and stay with them for as long you can. Report back to me with anything relevant.'

'I'm not your...'

'My what?'

His jaw clenched, he shook his head sadly. 'Very well, *Miss* Grace, as always I'm here to do your bidding.' He bowed stiffly, but she had already turned from him. She missed the sarcasm and pain piercing his heart. Once more, she had unknowingly put him in his place.

CHAPTER 15

*T*he polished dining table glowed in reflection from the tall candelabra and silver ware. Using her fork, Grace moved the food on her plate around in circles. The knot in her stomach tightened every time her father and Horton laughed. From under her lashes, she glanced at each of her sisters, who were all there except Letitia, who rarely left her room. Emma Kate kept her head bowed as she ate, and Grace's heart turned over in sympathy for her. Once before, Horton had named her as his preferred choice, but nothing more had been mentioned since her father's illness. Now Grace wondered if his plans had resumed with her father's return to society. Frustratingly, Andrem's friend Mr Vincent had grown cold in his intentions, much to Emma Kate's despair. The man had gone travelling to Ireland in recent weeks and not one letter had arrived from him.

Phoebe gave a small cough behind her napkin and Grace looked at her, conveying her thoughts through her eyes. The girls wanted to leave the table, despite the fact dessert hadn't yet arrived.

Horton laughed at something her father said and turned to

grin at the girls, his gold tooth glinting in the light. His eyes narrowed on Emma Kate and Grace shrivelled inside at the man's vulgarity. Her mind whirled in an effort to find a way to prevent him making a claim on one of her sisters.

When Woodruff belched loudly, Grace could stand it no more and rose. 'Please excuse us, Father, Mr Horton. We shall leave you to your cigars and port.'

Before their father had a chance to reply, the girls stood as one. Like whipped dogs, they scuttled from the table and out of the room.

At the door, Grace paused near Doyle and whispered, 'Miss Letitia?'

'Quiet. For the moment.'

She smiled at him, and then quickly followed her sisters upstairs to their mother's rooms, where Diana sat on a velvet sofa, embroidering, and waited for her chicks to settle themselves around her.

Listlessly, Grace walked to the window and pulled back the curtains to gaze up at the night sky. A half moon showed between cloud scuds. Idly, she wondered whether William looked at the same moon. She waited for the familiar pain to squeeze her heart and found it did less than ever before. She snorted and bit her lip to stop a wry smile. What irony. Even her accustomed pain was no longer hers to enjoy.

'Well, Grace?' Diana asked, her needle poised midair. 'What do you know?'

'Nothing, Mama.' Grace replied.

Faith took up a book, and flipped through its pages, her mind clearly not engaged to read. 'Will we know at breakfast, do you think?'

'Horton leaves in the morning, so he may give Father an answer then.' Grace dropped the curtains and turned for the door.

'You aren't staying with us for a time, dear?' Diana asked.

'No, Mama. I feel restless.' In truth, she felt utterly miserable. She gave a small smile of reassurance to them all before leaving the room.

Grace turned for her own bedroom when suddenly a loud crash sounded from further down the gallery. Startled, she hesitated. Another clamour came. *Letitia.* The thought jerked Grace into motion and rushed along the gallery.

At Letitia's door, she hesitated. Silence. Her heart hammered in her chest. Slowly, she inched open the door. A scene of destruction greeted her. The remnants of Letitia's belongings lay scattered about like the aftermath of a wild storm. She stared in shocked silence at the curtains which hung in tattered strips, as did long pieces of wallpaper torn from the wall. Ripped clothes and bedding littered the floor. Shattered perfumed bottles intermingled with the other contents of her dressing table. The strong, undiluted scents stung at her nostrils and throat. It took a moment for Grace to register what she saw. Time stopped. She stood frozen in the doorway.

Slight movement to the right caught her stunned attention. Letitia. Grace crept forward, crunching on broken glass with every step. The slender woman curled up in a ball, shaking beside the upturned bed, was not the sister she knew. Letitia's hair resembled a bird's nest. She had taken scissors to it and hacked away chunks of the long dark tresses. With either her nails or again scissors, she had rent her dress and petticoats into limp rags. Slowly, so as not to frighten the afflicted creature, Grace knelt down and tentatively touched her shoulder, but she flinched, turning tormented eyes to her.

'Darling pet, rest easy,' Grace crooned. 'No one is going to hurt you.' When no response came, Grace looked up at Partridge who now stood in the doorway. 'Find Doyle. Tell him to send for the doctor.'

'Yes, Miss, and will you be wanting laudanum?'

'It might be best, yes. Quickly now.' Grace moved closer to Letitia. 'Come, darling, let me help you.'

'Grace?' Letitia frowned, her eyes unfocused.

Gently, Grace took her hand and rubbed it between her own. 'You're cold, dearest.'

'Cold.'

Tears spilled over Grace's lashes. Blame ripped at her soul, for she had been too harsh and uncaring in her treatment of this illness that cursed Letitia. The poor girl needed her sympathy and understanding, but she had shown only annoyance and temper at having this thrust upon her at a time when she found it difficult to control her own life. How could she have not foreseen this? What kind of sister was she to abandon Letitia when she, out of them all, needed her most?

Movement at the open doorway had her craning her neck around the end of the bed. She expected Doyle, but was shocked to see Horton standing there with a sneer on his face.

She swallowed. 'I think, sir, privacy is required here,' she hinted in a harsh whisper.

'No wonder Woodruff is eager to marry his daughters off to the highest bidder.' Horton's eyes narrowed with sourness. 'He wants them off his hands before the truth is known.'

Grace frowned in puzzlement. 'The truth?'

'That lunacy runs through the family.'

'What a falsehood! Letitia is ill,' she spat. 'I think you should leave, Mr Horton.'

'Oh, I'll be leaving all right, and I'll be telling your father his little trick hasn't worked. I wouldn't touch any of you for a King's ransom!' He marched from the room, just as Doyle reached the door. 'You!' Horton roared, his temper fully up. 'Have my man bring the carriage round. I must be gone from this place immediately!'

Doyle swung back to Mrs Winton, who came along the gallery. He asked her to arrange Mr Horton's departure, before hurrying to Grace's side. 'What happened?'

'I'm not sure. She's suffered some kind of rage. Help me to take her to my room.' Grace cradled Letitia to her. The raised voices had her trembling violently.

Diana appeared in the doorway as Doyle lifted Letitia into his arms. She stood blocking the way, shock rendering her immobile. Her mouth opened and closed like a gasping fish. Like a stunned mute, she waved her handkerchief, struggling to find the words to express her horror.

'Go back to your rooms, Mama,' Grace murmured. 'I'll be along shortly.'

'What ...? How ...?'

'Mama, please.' Grace took her mother's arm to move her back into the gallery. Doyle went ahead with his burden, indicating for Hopeland, who had come upon the scene, to open Grace's bedroom door.

Horton left his guest room and bore down on them, a small luggage bag clamped in his hand. He glanced at Doyle and Letitia before Grace's bedroom door was closed to him. 'You, Madam Woodruff!'

Diana blinked rapidly, her hand grasping Grace's. 'I ...'

Horton halted some feet from them. 'I don't like to be made a fool of, nor do I enjoy being used. Be rest assured, Madam, I'll do my utmost to prevent your husband from making fools of anybody else.'

'W ... what do you mean?' Diana stammered.

'I mean to tell the whole district that madness runs through this family.'

'No!'

'I may be low born, Madam, but at least *my family* aren't ready for Bedlam unlike yours.'

'I don't understand.'

Grace pulled at her mother, glaring at Horton. 'Come, Mama, he talks nonsense.' She nudged Diana in the direction of her rooms and then turned her ice-cold fury on him. 'Your carriage is waiting for you, Mr Horton. I suggest you leave, before I forget myself and behave as no lady should.'

'What in Hell's name is happening here?' Woodruff roared from the top of the staircase. His knuckles showed white where they gripped the banister. His breath came in short puffs.

Horton advanced on him. 'You have a hide to ask!'

Woodruff's beady eyes went from his family to his enraged guest. Abruptly, he changed his tone to a simper. 'My dear fellow, whatever wrong has been done to you, we can put right.'

'Bah, you're a bigger fool than I thought you were!' Horton made to charge past him.

Woodruff clasped his coat sleeve. 'Friend, surely...'

'I'm no friend of yours. You think I am so desperate for a wife I'll gladly become tainted with bad blood? Never!' Horton glared inches from Woodruff's pale face. 'You thought you could hoodwink me into marrying one of your daughters while madness ran in their veins!'

'Madness?' Woodruff frowned. 'What madness do you speak of, man?'

'Consider yourself fortunate one married well, but you'll not be successful with the others when I'm through with you.'

'Come, Horton,' wheedled Woodruff, still clinging to the man. 'Let's us go down for a drink. We can discuss this...'

Horton pushed past. 'Leave go!' He yanked himself free.

Woodruff, caught off balance, and combined with his unsteadiness on his feet, swayed dangerously. His hand reached back for the banister, while the other hand waved his cane about like a muddled conductor. It all happened so fast, yet so slow. Woodruff stumbled, his free hand missed the banister grasping at nothing but air. He pitched sideways to lunge for the railing. The cane was thrown upwards as Woodruff fell back a long way before, sickeningly, his body hit the staircase hard halfway down. He bounced bodily, a few more steps, before slithering and rolling the rest of the way to the bottom. On the hall floor, he lay as limp as a straw Guy Fawkes.

For seconds, no one moved. One of the girls, now all gathered in the gallery, screamed. Diana fainted. Grace felt a rush of wind as Doyle flew past her and down the staircase, while Horton stood with his hands up, as though in surrender, his back pressed flat against the wall muttering it wasn't his fault.

Grace ignored him, calling for her sisters to take their mother, who was regaining her senses, back to her rooms. She gathered her skirts and hastily descended the stairs to look down upon her shattered father. His head lay at an awkward angle; clearly, his neck was broken. Montgomery Woodruff, the father she never loved, was dead at her feet.

* * *

FOR THE FIRST time in many months, all seven Woodruff daughters were under one roof. In the subdued atmosphere of the drawing room, the only sound came from the logs crackling in the hearth and the rustle of black taffeta and crepe the women wore. In the corner, Dr Bainbridge and Mr Swindale chatted quietly. All the women were dry eyed and pale. They drank tea, nibbled on scones, and wondered what would happen next to this seemingly blighted family.

'I'm not sure Gaby can stay much longer, Grace,' John Morgan mentioned, on coming to stand by her. 'Her pains are likely to start at any moment, and I would like her home to rest.'

Grace gave him a small smile. 'Yes indeed, John, take her home. But please, send word the minute her time begins. I want to be there, if it's all right with you?'

'Yes, of course.' John nodded.

'Oh, before you go, I wish to ask you something.'

'Yes?'

'I have talked the matter over with Mrs Winton, the house-keeper,' Grace paused, hoping John would not be offended with her suggestion. 'I would so like it for Mrs Winton to go to you and Gaby. She is quite willing, for she finds little here to keep her occupied, as Doyle runs everything so smoothly.' She paused again to assess his reaction, then hurriedly continued, 'Besides, you would be doing me a great favour.'

'A favour, how?' John's look was direct.

'We cannot afford her, and although I am loathe to lose her, I would rather she went to you and Gaby than to turn her out with no other employment to go to.'

John tapped his hand softly against his trouser leg in thought. 'We've talked about hiring another girl, but Mrs Winton is hardly that, is she?'

'No.' Grace smiled. 'But she is a good worker. Between her and Ruth, Gaby wouldn't have to trouble herself. She could devote her time to you and the child.'

'You have given this much thought, I see.' John raised his eyebrow. 'I'm not an unkind man, Grace. I know it's been hard for Gaby to adjust to life on the farm. It's vastly different to all this.' He nodded indicating the splendour of the room.

'She doesn't want all this, John. She is happy with you, do not doubt it. I'm only suggesting this to help you both, but if you feel it's not in the best interests for either of you, then no more will be said.'

'Can I give you an answer tomorrow?'

'Of course.' Placing her teacup and saucer on a side table, Grace glided over to Gaby. 'Dearest, John wishes you home, and I agree with him. We mustn't have you overtiring yourself.'

She glanced up with a cheeky grin. 'I doubt I can manage to get up out of this sofa, Grace.'

Faith, seated beside her, quickly stood to help Grace haul Gaby to her feet. 'It's been lovely to see you, dear sister,' she admitted, as they walked out into the hall. 'I was wrong to shun you; I apologize.'

'None of it matters now, dear Faith.' Gaby kissed her cheek. 'Come visit when you can.' She glanced up at landing. 'Shall I go up and see Mama?'

'Best leave it for now,' Grace whispered. Diana still refused to accept Gaby's marriage.

The four sisters stood in the hall and kissed Gaby goodbye. They waved her away from the steps of the house, until she was out of sight, and then turned as one back into the relative warmth.

'I'll go and sit with Mama,' said Faith, mounting the stairs.

Grace smiled her thanks and re-entered the drawing room with the others. Immediately her gaze flew to Letitia, but she still sat where they had placed her on returning from the funeral. The cup of tea held in her lap had gone cold, and Grace gently took it from her stiff fingers. Letitia raised her eyes. 'Can I go upstairs now?'

'Yes, dearest, let me help you.'

'No,' Letitia rose with poise, knowing every pair of eyes were upon her. 'Maybe Doyle can help me?'

'Yes, pet, and Hopeland will be waiting for you.' Grace turned to catch Doyle's attention from where he was pouring a drink for Mr Swindale and Dr Bambridge. He instantly finished his task and came to her side. 'Please assist Miss Letitia upstairs.'

'Come now, Miss Letitia, take my arm.' Doyle guided her out into the hall.

Grace gazed in pity, as did the others, at the sight of a beautiful young woman reduced to such a state.

'The house is in mourning for more than one reason, Miss Woodruff,' Dr Bambridge said.

With a sigh, she agreed with him, though he wasn't to know

they mourned more for Letitia's ruined life than that of their father. She regarded Mr Swindale. 'The reading of the will, Mr Swindale, when will it be done?'

'As soon as I receive word from Mr Ross, Miss Woodruff. There is so much to consider now.'

'Surely, things will carry on as before?' Grace wondered.

'In some cases yes, but Mr Ross has to be consulted in all matters now. Together we must capitalize on what money is left to keep you all in the comfort you're accustomed to.'

Grace nodded and excused herself. She was in no state today to ponder their situation. Crossing the room, she noted Heather and Andrew were to depart also. 'You are not leaving yet, are you?'

Heather gazed nervously from her to Andrew and back. 'Yes, I'm sorry.'

'Aren't you going up to say goodbye to Mama?'

Andrew stepped forward. 'No. It'll only upset her. She wants us to stay the night but, unfortunately, we cannot.'

Grace raised her eyebrow. Andrew had fallen in her estimation. Both he and Heather had limited their contact with the family. His true feelings had come to the fore; he didn't want to associate with the Woodruffs now they had no money.

Heather placed one hand on Andrew's arm, a new diamond ring glinting on her finger. 'I've told Emma Kate that if I hear news from Mr Vincent I'll contact her immediately. I know she is desperate for some word from him, but we are leaving for London tomorrow and we might not see him.'

'London?'

'Yes. We are staying there until the new year.'

Grace frowned at the news. 'This is sudden.'

Andrew cleared his throat. 'Dear Grace, I have business to attend there. And while in town, Heather and I can enjoy the season.'

'We are in mourning.'

Unease filtered through his manner. 'Yes, of course; we shall be circumspect, naturally. Nevertheless, one must take advantage of all opportunities. This will be Heather's first time in such society. Mother's sister, the Viscountess Sherrington, wishes to meet Heather. We've been invited to spend a week in Kent at her home.'

'I hope you enjoy your time there, as we struggle here.' The coldness of her tone ripped the excitement from Heather's eyes.

'Really, Grace, it's hardly our fault strife haunts this house.' Heather dabbed a handkerchief to her dry eyes.

Hidden in the folds of her black skirts, Grace clenched her hands in anger. 'Strife?'

An embarrassed blush stained Heather's cheeks. 'Grace, please …'

'I never thought you capable of turning your back on us, Heather. Obviously, marriage changes things.'

'Yes, it does,' she hissed back. 'I told you before, I have to think of my new family now. Andrew is my husband and he comes first.'

Grace's eyes narrowed, her emotions ran high, but she tried to keep them in check. 'Certainly. However, I thought better of you. Have you any understanding of what we are dealing with here? Must I carry it alone, can you not lend your support?'

'You have my … our support.'

'And what of Letitia?'

'I have no answers for Letitia's plight.' Heather's fingers played fretfully with her black lace collar. 'You must act according to your own conscience.'

'Why am I always alone in such things?' Grace shook her head, closing her eyes to hide her pain and disappointment. 'Go to London, go to Kent and forget us, your family.' She walked away.

'Grace, please …' Heather made to move after her, but Andrew held her arm.

'No, my dear. We have to think of our future. We discussed this, and you agreed distance is needed. I feel sorry for them all, but we mustn't become involved.'

Grace glanced back at them both and felt that Heather was as good as dead to her.

CHAPTER 16

*G*race strolled with Letitia along the gravelled path between the sleeping garden beds. Warm in their woollen capes, they felt disinclined to chat. It had pleased Grace when Letitia agreed to accompany her on this walk, even if she had done it under protest, having no desire to be out on a cold, crisp day ambling the gardens.

In the silence, Grace's thoughts wondered. No evidence had turned up that her father held a secret hoard of money. She had turned out every drawer in the study, his bedroom and dressing room, and nothing. Not a farthing. Once a week, the accounts were given to Mr Swindale to pay and balance. He now did the job she had done for nearly three years.

William was in control of their finances, the estate, of their very future. Hopelessness overwhelmed her. She would see him often, for naturally he must visit her to discuss the Woodruff estate. A dying light of old love flickered, but there was no answering spark to feed it and she was glad. She knew she could see him now and not be stricken dumb with unrequited love.

With a deep sigh, Letitia paused to turn back for the house.

'Where are you going?' Grace asked, concerned. 'Is something wrong?'

'I wish to go back.'

'We've only been out for a few minutes. Can you not walk some more? The fresh air will do you good'

'Why?'

'Because you are closeted in your room all day, every day. I thought you needed a change and might enjoy a stroll.'

Letitia wore an expression of utter boredom tinged with wariness. 'Leave me alone, Grace.'

'I wish to help you, Letitia. Let me, please.'

'Help me or control me?'

'Do you relish being in the depths of despair?' Grace tried not to aggravate her, but needed Letitia to understand she wasn't her foe in all of this.

'You cannot help me.'

'I can try, if only you will allow it.'

'What can you do?' Letitia scoffed. 'Taking away all the drink in the house will not fix the problem. I still want it, whether it's there or not.'

Grace paled. 'If you trust me, I know we can win this battle.'

'Maybe I'm a lost cause.'

'Never.' Shaking her head, Grace linked Letitia's arm through her own. 'You are young, beautiful and clever. I won't let you fade away, hiding in your room like a monster.' They walked on in silence for a while before Grace broached the subject again. 'What makes you desire it?'

Letitia shrugged her shoulders. 'I have no idea.'

'When did it start?'

'I'm not sure really. One more glass of wine with dinner, and then somehow it became a regular habit to partake of something during the day also.'

'So, there was no actual event that triggered it.'

'Well, it didn't help matters when father started bringing our name into disrepute.' Letitia gave a withering look. 'His mistresses were known by everyone but us, did you know? I would hear the maids gossiping about him. I'd see their fear at the mere thought of him looking at them as though they were only there to serve his lust.'

'Letitia!' It hurt Grace, seeing so much pain and disgust on her face. But once she started, Letitia couldn't seem to stop the words.

'His gambling away our family fortune, the strict way of life he imposed, and finally the arranging of our marriages simply filled me with such despair, such anger. I know we aren't free to do as we please, not like girls of the lower classes, yet, he denied us so much joy.'

'Yes, he did.' Grace paused. 'You have thought much about this, haven't you?'

'I've had no choice. I've never fitted in with the rest you.' She glanced away. 'I used to watch other families, other fathers with their daughters and saw love and respect. We grew up with fear and loathing.'

Grace frowned, alarmed by Letitia's bitterness. 'Mama loves us.'

'Mama loves herself more.' Letitia stared out over the lawn. 'Mama would have let him marry us to anyone he pleased so long as he stayed away from her.'

Grace couldn't argue with the truth. She hoped Letitia purging her mind might have helped her a little, but the coldness in her eyes told another story. 'Without question our lives have been difficult. However, we have to think positively. There are others a lot worse off than we are.'

Letitia reared back. 'What are you saying? That we should be thankful for what we have?'

'Well...'

'Thankful for an abusive father? Thankful to be hated because we aren't boys? To be pawns in his play for power?'

Grace grasped her hands. 'I meant to be grateful to have a nice home, food on the table.'

'Huh!'

'You mustn't let the things beyond your control destroy you!' Grace sighed and tilted her head back to stare at the overcast sky. 'Was it so bad that you had to succumb to drinking to dull the pain?'

'For me, yes. I haven't your strength. But don't you see?'

Grace brought her gaze down from the sky and back to her sister's pale face. 'See what?'

'We all have used our own traits to escape father. Heather's was marrying the first man to look kindly at her. Gaby's was John Morgan, our tenant. Faith's is to read and lose herself in another world. Emma Kate's is to cling to Mama, and Phoebe's is to think only of herself.'

'And my trait to escape?'

'First it was dreaming of William Ross, then managing Woodruff House and finally it was Daniel Thomas.'

Grace swallowed. 'And now?'

Letitia's eyes softened for the first time in many months. 'Now I think you're as lost as me.'

* * *

GRACE STEPPED DOWN THE STAIRCASE, adjusting her petite black hat. Below, Mrs Winton waited with a small trunk at her feet. Movement in the drawing room caught Grace's attention as her mother rose from the writing desk and bustled into the hall.

'Grace?'

'Yes, Mama?'

'Are you going somewhere?' Diana averted her gaze from the housekeeper.

'Indeed, yes. I'm going to see Gaby, and Mrs Winton is

sharing the carriage with me, since she starts her employment at Morgan's Farm today.'

Diana jerked her head forward as though pulled on a string. 'Pardon? I do not understand.'

Grace pulled on her gloves, indicating at the same time for Mrs Winton to go out to the carriage. 'Gaby and John need another woman to help in the house. So, Mrs Winton is filling the role.'

'But she is *our* housekeeper,' Diana said in a strangled tone.

'Doyle controls the house very efficiently. Mrs Winton feels, as I do, that her talents are wasted here. Besides, we cannot afford her.'

'No!'

Grace turned to her mother with a sigh. 'I'm in no mood to put up with tantrums today, Mama. I'm sorry, but you've no say in the matter and Mr Swindale insists we keep expenditure low. Now, I'll be back at midday.'

'*I have no say?*' Determination entered Diana's voice. 'This is my house!'

Grace gave her a cool look. 'It is *our* house, which I run. When you take over *all* responsibilities, then you'll have a right to decide what happens within it.'

An angry flush stole across her mother's cheekbones. 'I'm your mother! The mistress of this house!'

'It is I who keeps this family together and this house running smoothly on nothing but a minimal allowance.'

'Don't you dare speak to me in such a way, Miss!'

A hardness darkened Grace's tone. 'I will speak in any way I wish. I have earned the right, wouldn't you agree?'

Grace walked out of the door, but heard her mother follow her. Without giving Diana time to utter another word, she spun back, nearly colliding with her. 'I advise, Mama, that you take a long hard look at the state this family is in, and concentrate on that instead of writing letters to *friends* who whisper cruelly behind our backs.'

Grace entered the carriage and steeled her heart against the distraught woman left standing on the steps. She refused to feel sorry for her mother. The last week had again proved to her that Diana's selfishness could harm the family as much as their father's had. Her mother ignored Letitia's plight as though it didn't exist. She neglected the other girls at home, doing nothing but taking herself off to bed at the slightest provocation. Diana no longer encouraged the girls in useful endeavours to occupy their minds, and they were left to fill their days as they pleased. Most times, Grace didn't even know where they were.

Sykes turned the carriage into Morgan's Farm before Grace was aware of it. She gave Mrs Winton a reassuring smile.

The front door opened, and Ruth came out to greet them. 'Good mornin', Miss Woodruff,' she said, dipping a quick curtsey.

'Good morning, Ruth. I've brought Mrs Winton to lighten your load.' Grace grinned.

'Aye, Miss, she's sorely needed.' Ruth laughed.

Once Mrs Winton alighted from the carriage, Grace made the introductions. A few spots of rain sent the women inside. In the entry, Grace took off her cloak while inquiring after her sister.

'Well, Miss Woodruff, if that bairn don't come out soon, it never will. She's awful late with it.' Ruth chuckled good-naturedly, not noticing Mrs Winton's scowl of disapproval.

'Is Mrs Morgan in the parlour?'

'No, I'm up here,' Gaby called from the landing. Slowly, she plodded down the staircase, wincing with each step. 'Welcome to Morgan's Farm, Mrs Winton.'

'The pleasure is mine, Mrs Morgan,' the housekeeper replied.

'Poor Ruth has been left to deal with everything. So, no doubt she'll enjoy having you here too.' Gaby's face screwed up in pain.

'Dearest?' Grace went up the first few stairs to take Gaby's arm. 'What is it?'

'Nothing. I've had an awful backache all morning.'

'Come, back up and into bed.' Grace glanced back over her shoulder. 'Have tea brought up, Mrs Winton.'

'Certainly, Miss.' The two servants headed off for the kitchen. Grace could hear Ruth chatting amicably to Mrs Winton as if they were already the best of friends. She hid a small smile at the thought of such opposites working under the one roof. Gaby was in line for some interesting times with those two.

'Oh, Grace,' Gaby suddenly bent against the railing, puffing hard.

Grace paled. 'Is it the baby?'

Gaby nodded. 'I think so. Help me.'

'I thought you said it was back pain? How long have you been like this?'

'I woke at dawn with it.'

'Dawn? You've had pains since dawn? Oh my!' Grace leant over the banister. 'Ruth, Mrs Winton!' She turned and put her arm around Gaby's waist. 'Come, darling, can you walk?'

'Noooo …' Gaby drew the word out on an agonized breath, and then crumpled onto the stairs.

'Gaby!' Grace knelt beside her as Ruth and Mrs Winton bounded up the stairs together. 'Send for a doctor quickly!'

'No, Mrs Jamieson, the midwife from the next village,' Gaby said, head bent. 'Tell John or Abel, they're in the fields.'

'Run, Ruth,' Grace demanded, putting her hands under Gaby's armpits and heaving her up to her feet. Mrs Winton assisted, and between them, they managed to make it to the bedroom door before Gaby gave a deep groan and lowered herself to the floor.

'Darling, we must have you in bed.' Grace nibbled her lip in worry.

'No.' As a pain ripped at Gaby's body, she held onto Grace's hand with a force that nearly broke the bones in Grace's fingers. Grace bit back a moan of complaint even though her hand throbbed. When the contraction was over, they lifted Gaby to her feet and put her onto the bed.

'We'll need to get her out of these clothes, Miss, and into a nightgown,' said Mrs Winton.

Grace blinked, trying to think coherently. 'Yes, yes of course. And water, hot water, and …' Grace's words were drowned out by a guttural moan from the bed. Gaby reared up, arching her back as though possessed. The two women watched in amazement, as nature took hold.

'I'll go and heat some water for the midwife,' Mrs Winton said, eagerly disappearing out the door.

When Gaby relaxed once more, Grace approached the bed. 'Gaby dear, we have to get you out of your dress, all right?'

Gaby nodded. 'Take the sheets off and put on the old blankets in the wardrobe there.'

As quickly as possible, Grace undressed her and fitted a loose nightgown over her. While Gaby dealt with another contraction, Grace stripped the bed and placed the old, but clean, blankets upon the mattress. Sweat beaded her upper lip when she had finished.

'Open the window, I cannot breathe,' Gaby panted from the bed.

'But it's raining,' Grace replied hesitantly.

'Open the damn window!' Gaby's face grew red as she gritted her teeth against the pain tearing at her.

Grace flung open the windows letting the cool air flow inside the warm room. Ruth rushed in with reports that Abel had gone to the village for Mrs Jamieson, and Mr Morgan was having a wash then coming up.

'Not in here, surely?' Grace asked.

'Yes, in here,' Gaby replied. 'He's to see what I go through.'

'But Gaby, it's no place for a man. Is it Ruth?' Grace turned to the maid.

'Nay, don't be asking' me, Miss Woodruff.' She quickly left the room.

Grace was about to argue further when Gaby took hold of her knees and began to strain. The sound she made hurt Grace's ears.

A few moments later, Gaby rested back against the pillows, gasping. 'Get John.'

'The midwife will be here soon and ...'

'Grace!' Gaby growled with impatience. 'Get John now!' Grabbing her knees, she cried out the pain.

* * *

TIRED OUT, Grace stepped down from the carriage. The door opened before she reached it. She grinned at Doyle. 'Gaby had a baby boy and I was there to see it. John delivered him before the midwife arrived. It was so beautiful. The baby is wonderful.'

He didn't return her smile, but took her elbow and pulled her into the parlour.

'What is it?' Grace demanded, her smile slipping.

'A telegram arrived,' Doyle sneered. 'From *him.*'

'Who?' She frowned, balking at anything that would sour this glorious day.

'Who do you think?' Doyle huffed, dropping her elbow as though it would contaminate him. 'Contacted him, did you? Brought him running back from his honeymoon, did you? Have you realized a wife will be in tow this time?'

William. Grace raised her chin, pinning Doyle with her stare. 'Nothing, I mean *nothing,* ever gives you the right to speak to me in such a way, do you understand?' She twisted away. He had never shown such bad temper before and she was shocked.

'Have you no heart?'

She spun back. 'How dare you! If William returns, it's not at my bidding, but more likely from Mr Swindale's letter concerning my father's death. And as to my heart? Well, I have one, and it's been trampled on enough!'

'God, why do I stay, when I mean so little to you?' Doyle shook his head with a humourless smirk.

'You know how much I care for you.' She made for the hall, now was not the time to discuss the issue. She wanted to see her mother and sisters, to tell them of the baby.

'I can't stand this much longer, Grace.' Doyle sagged and bowed his head. 'I've tried to handle our situation, but it's so hard seeing you and not being able to touch you.'

Grace returned to place her hand on his arm. 'I'm sorry that I … turned to you for comfort. It was wrong of me. I acted self-ishly, impulsively. However, I cannot keep apologizing and asking for your forgiveness.'

Doyle's face screwed up in disgust. 'You want my forgiveness? That's funny; I thought it was my body.'

Her face flushed at his crude words. They were true of course, as they both knew, but for him to throw it in her face shamed him, and her. She wished she could utter a witty retort to silence him, but her mind was numb. Lowering her gaze, she inclined her head and left the room.

CHAPTER 17

For the umpteenth time, Grace lost concentration on the row of figures before her. She heard the front bell, and in relief gladly put her books away and left the room.

Doyle came swiftly up from the service areas to answer the summons and she waited in the drawing room for him to announce the visitor. Over the fireplace, hung a gilt-framed mirror and she adjusted the black ribbons in her coiled hair, and then smoothed the bodice of her mourning dress. In the mirror's reflection, she saw her guest. Her heart thumped a faster pace, as William's blue-green eyes held hers.

'Good day, Grace.' His deep voice sent shivers of familiar pleasure down her spine, but thankfully, the overwhelming rush of love didn't swamp her as it used to do. But, even so, she had missed him.

Slowly she turned around to greet him. 'William.'

'The midday meal will be ready in ten minutes, Miss Woodruff,' Doyle said, making his presence known.

Grace glanced in his direction. 'Thank you, Doyle. Have Mr Ross's belongings sent up to the room he usually occupies.'

Doyle inclined his head, but pinned Grace with a stare that spoke volumes. She chose to ignore it.

William's gaze seemed to devour her. A look of longing came to his face before he quickly masked it. 'You look very well.'

'And so do you.' Grace indicated for him to sit as she did and wondered at the peace she felt. He looked older. Grey now streaked the hair at his temples.

'I was sorry to hear of your father's death. This plunges the family into more difficulties.'

'Thank you, and yes, it does. Mr Swindale is eager to speak with you.'

'Diana and your sisters are well?' His tone was businesslike.

She replied in the same vein, 'Yes, very well, thank you. Mama finds it hard that we cannot live as she is accustomed to. Since Father's death, more bills and gambling debts have found us. It seems Father gambled and invested unwisely all the way up and down the country.'

William shook his head, his expression cold. 'I'll do all I can to help, but it'll not be easy. Mr Swindale and I tried our best before, but your father found it difficult to be honest with us. I'm not surprised he didn't reveal all.'

'I believe he always thought he would resume his normal life. Indeed, the evening he died, he was in fine spirits. He'd been exercising and successfully walking with a cane.'

William nodded, and the air between them became taut with unspoken words.

Grace fiddled with her lace cuff. 'How long are you staying?'

'A few days only. I came straight from Dover.'

The thought of his wife suddenly entered her head. 'Is your wife well?'

'Yes. Felicity and I parted at Dover. I travelled the rest of the way alone. She has gone on to London to her parents' home.' A muscle ticked along his strong jaw.

The arrival of Diana, Emma Kate, Phoebe, and Faith eased the strained tension between them and with a sigh of relief; Grace fell silent as her mother took control of their visitor.

Diana's chatter and endless questions about William's wedding and honeymoon accompanied them into the dining room for luncheon.

In the hall, Doyle caught up with Grace. 'Miss Grace, may I have a word?'

She looked at him and waited for the others to sit before stepping to the door. 'Yes?'

'Are you all right?' Doyle whispered roughly.

'Yes, I am, actually.' She heaved a deep sigh. 'I don't know what I feel, but I do know it isn't as it once was. Please don't worry about me.'

'It's my duty.'

'Thank you.' She smiled. 'I must return to the table.' She turned back as a loud smashing sound of splintering glass echoed throughout the house.

For a moment, she wasn't sure where it had come from. She had a horrified thought of Letitia, but Doyle had dashed into the drawing room. Gathering her skirts, she ran after him.

Doyle squatted amongst the broken glass, in his hand a large rock crudely wrapped in paper.

William, after a quick glance at her, marched over to Doyle and surveyed the damage.

'What is it? What happened?' Diana burst into the room followed by the girls, who all chattered at once.

William took the missile, and everyone watched in silence as he untied the string holding the paper, and then read the note. Head bent, he raised his eyes to Grace, and flickered a look in the direction of the others.

Instantly understanding him, she turned with forced brightness to her parent. 'Come, Mama, do not let some silly children's prank disrupt your meal.'

Diana hesitated. 'Is that all it was, dear?'

'Yes. William and I will speak with the outside staff. No doubt, the vegetables have been raided, too.'

'Well! What a disgrace.' Indignant, Diana glared at the doorway as though they would be inundated with poor children any moment.

Appeased, and never once thinking what Grace said was untrue, the girls re-entered the dining room, with Diana issuing her thoughts on suitable punishment for all wayward children.

Grace returned to William and Doyle. 'Well, what does it say?'

'*Burn in hell.*' William sighed deeply.

The blood left her face as she looked from the note to William.

Immediately, he took her hand and squeezed it tenderly. 'I'll get to the bottom of this, I promise.'

'But who would do such a thing? It's never happened before.'

'You understand your father left many men unsatisfied with his business practices.' He frowned and looked at Doyle. 'Have the carriage brought round, please.' Doyle left the room reluctantly, and William gave Grace a gentle smile. 'I'll call on Swindale. We'll work together to clear your father's debts.'

'It cannot be done overnight, William.' She sighed as they walked into the hall to gather his coat. She watched him prepare to leave, as Diana came out to them.

'Where are you going, William?'

'Into Leeds, dear Cousin. I must meet with Mr Swindale this hour.'

'But your meal…?' Diana waved in the direction of the dining room.

William kissed her cheek. 'I shall enjoy my dinner more for the wait.'

* * *

It was late evening when Sykes pulled the horses to a halt by the front steps. Wearily, William stepped down as light flooded him from the opened door. Doyle took his hat and coat, eyeing him with suspicion. William ignored him; with more important issues pressed on his mind, he had no time to feel sorry for the benighted butler.

Walking into the drawing room, he found Grace and Diana sitting up waiting for him. The others, he presumed, had retired.

'You missed your dinner, William.' Diana paused in her embroidering. 'Your mother will never forgive me for such neglect.'

'My apologies, Cousin Diana. It could not be helped.' William eyed the empty drink trolley and frowned.

Grace blushed. 'I'm sorry we cannot offer you something suitable to quench your thirst.'

Diana bent towards him full of concern. 'Would you care for some tea, dear boy? You look much worn.'

'No, thank you. I have drunk tea all afternoon with Swindale.'

'And did it go well?' Diana asked lightly, resuming her needlework.

William gave a false laugh. 'No, not really.'

Grace placed her book on the occasional table beside the sofa. 'Tell us, please.'

With a restless sigh, William leant against the mantelpiece. 'Bankruptcy is looming, and you must prepare yourself for it.'

'No!' Diana's sampler fell to the floor. 'Surely you are mistaken?'

'Is there nothing else that can be done?' Grace asked.

'We are trying all we can, but much was sold off to pay for the earlier debts of imprudent investments. With those companies' profits now lost, it puts pressure on those businesses still retained.'

Diana became puzzled. 'But if we've some business still belonging to us...'

'You must understand, Cousin, the businesses left need capital, for improvements and to keep with the current markets, and it's money which they aren't receiving nor will do so in the foreseeable future.'

'What do we have left?' Grace sat rigid, her face drained of all colour.

'Not much. The combined profits of the remaining factories cannot sustain the estate for long.' William marvelled at her strength. She had accepted her father's foolishness had depleted their finance considerably, but to lose everything would be a tremendous shock. 'And the estate cannot sustain itself if we have to sell the rest of the land.'

'Can we not obtain a loan?' Diana asked.

'You have no way to pay it back,' he answered. 'I have already used some of my money to cover a few debts, but I cannot maintain it all.'

Long tears ran down Diana's cheeks and she scrabbled in the pockets of her black skirts to find a handkerchief.

Grace helped her to her feet. 'Go up to bed, Mama. We'll talk some more in the morning. Maybe William and I can think of a way out of this mess before you wake.'

'Yes, dear, that would be wonderful for how shall I face my friends with such news?' At this thought, Diana wailed even more as she left the room.

Grace paced between the sofa and the door. 'Thank you, for paying some debts, William. I wish I could prevent you from doings so, but that would be churlish. Are you certain we cannot keep the house? Why can't the income from the remaining tenant farms be enough to keep it?'

'That is what we have yet to discover. I'm hoping it will be, but the house and grounds are large. It will mean another cut in staff, plus much more. In the winter, rooms will have to be closed off, and so on.'

'The alternative is to sell?' Grace shuddered.

'Perhaps, yes.' William took her hands. 'And there is more.'

She took a deep breath. 'Oh?'

'Kendleton Colliery is for sale, but as yet there has been no interest. The mine is treacherous, full of flooding shafts. Naturally, money is needed to keep the mine safe, but there is none. The miners are threatening strike action because of the terrible conditions they endure.' William swore softly under his breath. His mind scrambled to find answers. 'We, Swindale and I, would rather they did strike, because that would keep them out of the dangerous mine. But, it also means whatever money the mine was producing will be lost.'

Grace bit her lip. 'If they strike, families will go hungry.'

'Yes. Already they are angry. They will be more so when there's no food on their tables.'

'Was it a miner who threw the rock?'

He nodded. 'A few inquiries soon provided the answer.'

'Then tomorrow we must travel to the mine and talk with the workers.' Grace decided.

'And say what exactly?' William asked stunned.

'We'll explain our circumstances, and ask them to be patient.'

William laughed without humour. 'They'll not care! To them you are the image of the rich. They will not relate to you or your troubles.'

Grace bridled. 'I can show them I am sensitive to their needs.'

'No, Grace. It is madness to suggest such a thing. They're volatile. A raw angry mob.'

'Are you going to come with me?' she challenged, her chin raised for battle.

'I must insist that you do not undertake such a plan.'

'I shall go alone then.'

'Don't be ridiculous.'

She stared at him with fiery golden brown eyes, and longing washed over him. *What a bloody mess!* He nodded. 'Very well. We'll go tomorrow. Though, what answers you can give them will be interesting to witness.'

* * *

DOYLE OPENED the front doors the next morning, and Grace braced herself against the dawn's cold wind. Clouds scudded across the sky as though chased by an invisible demon.

William paused on the top step on seeing the dairy cart waiting. He scowled. 'Where is the carriage?'

She tucked her scarf in under her black coat and pretended innocence as she descended the steps. Sykes handed her up onto the cart's bare seat. The wind buffeted her on the unprotected transport, and she hid a smile as William marched to her side.

'What are you doing?'

'Well, if it's all about representation, then arriving in the carriage emblazoned with the family crest is wrong. Seeing me so humble might make them more receptive to my words.'

'Very well.' William hoisted himself up into the back of the cart and sat on the hard wooden bench that ran down the middle of it.

The journey to the colliery took them through shallow valleys and beautiful, but winter bleak countryside. Whitewashed cottages dotted the rolling hills. The distant slopes were now bare of sheep and cows, as the farmers brought their livestock down to the fields closer to home for shelter from the harsh winter snow.

On nearing the mine, the landscape changed to become an unsightly scar scratched into a once glorious valley. Slag heaps blotted the view. The height of some older piles made new hills, as nature tried to grab a foothold once more and swathed the ugliness with weeds.

Grace had never been to a mine site before, and gazed ahead with interest as Sykes negotiated the steep track into the valley bottom. Dirty ragged youths, men and women plodded along the edge of the track, going either to or from the pithead. They looked at the passing cart with little interest, until they noticed the occupants. Word passed quickly between the extended lines, so when the cart halted in the middle of the filthy, black yard, a small gathering awaited them.

The mine manager left his hut to greet them, but on seeing the growing rabble, hurried back into its safety. He peeped out of a murky window to watch the proceedings.

'Don't get down from the cart, Grace. Just stand up to speak,' William whispered, helping her to stand.

Nerves in her stomach made Grace feel sick. The crowd around the cart grew noisy. She stared into the red-rimmed eyes of countless coal-blackened faces. 'My name is...'

'Speak up, luv, can't hear yer!' A voice called from the back.

Taking a deep breath, Grace raised her head to shout, 'My name is Grace Woodruff. I have come...'

The enormous hiss and booing from the people drowned her words as the name Woodruff bounced around the valley.

William raised his hands to calm them. 'Let her speak! Let her speak!'

'We don't want no bloody Woodruff 'ere!' yelled a faceless voice.

'Have yer come ter show us yer money?' called another.

'Aye, 'ave yer come t' fix t' bloody pumps down below? We ain't bleedin' ducks!' The calls and jeers carried on for some time, until Grace's nervousness gave way to temper.

'Now, be quiet for a minute!' She stood hands on hips. 'I understand your concerns. My father neglected you, but he has gone now, and the mine is for sale. I am sure the new owner will make this mine safe once more...' Again, they shouted her down, as each in the crowd tried to have their say.

A small man completely coated in coal dust pushed his way to the front. 'So, lass, while yer waitin' fer the sale, 'ow are we ter survive in a pit full er watter?' He crossed his brawny arms over his barrel-like chest. 'We lost two men last week ter cave-ins. Can yer say we'll not lose any more?'

She looked down at the man in sympathy. 'No, of course I can't guarantee that. But my cousin and I believe it wise to only work half the number of seams, to lessen the risk...' She stopped talking as the mob erupted into a frenzy at her idea.

'An' who's gonna pay me fer stayin' at 'ome, yer silly cow?' a man cried at her, shaking his fist.

Grace shifted her position slightly to talk to the man, but suddenly a heavy dirt clod was thrown at her. It smashed against her black shirts, teetering her off balance. She stumbled, and both Sykes and William reached for her. More clods flew into the cart, barely missing them. Shouts filled the air before being swept away by the wild wind.

Grace straightened, frightened at being assaulted and also very furious. 'Listen to me, *please! I want to help!*' She ducked another missile. 'We can come to an agreement, I assure you! Let me try, I beg you.'

'Quiet!' William thundered to no avail. Clods hit his legs and chest.

The objects thrown were no longer dirt clods, but lumps of coal and rock. Sykes had a difficult job of controlling the frightened horse. The noise grew into a deafening roar. Even the reserved workers became caught in the ferocity of the onslaught. Words no longer carried weight for the miners, for they were tired, hungry and worried people living a hand to mouth existence.

'Turn around!' William ordered Sykes, pulling Grace down to her seat and trying to shield her with his body as best he could.

'No, William, no. I must speak with them!' Grace pushed him away. 'I must show them I will listen.'

'They're past it, Grace. For God's sake get down!'

She refused him, and struggled to stand. A rock hit her in the shoulder, but she merely flinched and raised her chin higher. 'Stop this at once!' she screamed.

A tall man at the back called for quiet. Amazingly, the crowd lowered their arms, but kept their objects clutched in tight fists. The man walked forward and the people parted for him. He paused in front of the cart, and his dark green eyes pierced Grace with their quiet authority. 'We're not bad people, Miss Woodruff. We simply want to be safe as possible while we work an honest day's living.'

'I understand.' Grace tried to look beneath the coal dust covering his face to see his features but his cap, which he did not remove for her, shadowed his face.

'I hope you do understand, Miss, because this is their livelihood and if it was lost to them, they face eviction from their cottages, which come with mine employment. It's not unknown to us, that when a colliery closes down, whole villages became redundant, finished. Homeless families, with young children and the elderly are forced to walk the roads, sleeping in hedgerows until they have trudged the miles it takes to the nearest city. There, if lucky, they might find low paid hard work and housing in the shape of disused cellars in rundown tenement buildings. Is it any wonder they use whatever means necessary to keep their jobs? All they want is an adequate wage for honest work done in decent, if perilous, conditions.'

The man's eloquent speech lingered in the quiet and goose bumps rose on Grace's skin as he stared at her. The man possessed a silent power that fascinated her. She nodded to him. 'Thank you.'

She forced herself to look away to the others. 'Please let me finish what I have to say, and then I'll leave you to discuss my proposal. You can choose representatives to come to my home to speak to me and my family.'

'Grace!' William hissed behind her.

'It's all right fer yer ter talk of less workers, but you'll still want t' same profits, no doubt,' jeered a fellow somewhere to the right.

'No, you're mistaken.' Grace waited for the murmurs to die again. 'All money made from this mine as of today until it is sold, will be spent on new equipment for the mine. I'll instruct the mine manager to issue me with a list of what you need. However,' Grace held up her hand to quieten their mutterings, 'those who have more than one family member working, will stay at home, or find work elsewhere until the new owner is found.'

'Nay, I can't feed me family of ten on one wage!' An older woman spat in disgust.

'Then you must economize, madam, as I have learnt.' Grace inclined her head respectfully.

'Econ what?' another jested, scratching his baldhead.

William stood. 'We understand your anxiety and your fear. You work every day in hazardous conditions, and we wish to alleviate your worry. Miss Woodruff and I shall do all that is possible to keep the mine open and safe while a buyer is sought. Think on this offer. Good day.' He indicated for Grace to sit, and for Sykes to turn the cart around.

The crowd parted for them and the cart passed by the tall man who made the speech. Grace stared at him. He stood with his feet planted square, but his face showed no emotion behind his mask of dirt.

CHAPTER 18

*I*n the days after her trip to Kendleton Colliery, Grace tried to keep busy with her usual duties, but the events at the mine continually came into her thoughts. She and William discussed the dilemma at length each evening, hoping to find a resolution that benefited everyone. Grace cursed her father's lack of judgment. His foolish, money-grabbing ideas had fallen flat, and she was left to pick up the pieces one more time.

No more rocks came through the windows. Nevertheless, reports filtered through that once again the miners were losing respect for the manager. Grace waited each day for a week for the arrival of the equipment list. It never came.

As the first flurries of winter snow touched the dormant gardens of Woodruff House, Grace paced the drawing room. William had left three days before to visit his mother at Scarborough. He generously included Diana and Faith in the visit to his cliff-top home. With her mother gone from the house, serenity settled on those remaining. Grace declined all invitations and sent none herself. Their evenings were calm and the days spent in useful occupation. Letitia was moody and at times troublesome, but overall, better. They rarely saw Phoebe as she spent her spare time window shopping in Leeds, walking the woods or visiting Gaby. Emma Kate mooned around the house, waiting for every mail delivery. She did her best to act unconcerned when no note arrived from London, and continued to ply Heather with long letters about Mr Vincent.

Walking to the window, Grace looked at the growing whiteness beyond. Shadows moved in the strange grey light cast by the heavy clouds overhead. Peering closer, she watched a figure coming down the drive and thought it only a yard servant, until the figure stumbled and nearly fell. Some instinct sent her hurrying into the hall.

Emma Kate came out of the parlour opposite. 'What is it, Grace?'

Grace flung open the doors, and without pausing to collect her coat, ran down the steps and onto the gravel drive in her house slippers. Snowflakes coated her hair as she lifted her black skirts and raced down the drive. The cold air stung her face and bit deep into her lungs. She skidded to a stop in front of the huddled shape kneeling on the gravel.

A boy looked up, his face white underneath the slight dusting of dirt. He clutched at the brown scrap of blanket covering him. 'Yer must come.' His voice sounded wooden, lifeless. His staring blue eyes did not blink.

'Yes, I'll come.' She placed her arm around him and helped him up. In his shock, he did not protest.

They stumbled towards the house where Doyle met her halfway and took the boy from her. He frowned at Grace. 'Who is he? What does he want?'

The boy suddenly halted, turned to the side and vomited. The action sent the blanket slipping off his head, revealing blood-matted hair. When he righted himself, he shook violently.

Alarmed, Grace took his shoulders. 'Come inside.'

The boy looked at her. 'I had ter tell yer. Yer said yer'd help us, I 'eard yer that day. I walked all the way...'

'I'll help you, I promise.' His lost expression made her want to hold him tight. 'Tell me what has happened.'

'All gone...'

'Wha s gone?'

'Water everywhere, freezin' water...' His staring eyes seemed dead. 'I got out by an old shaft...' The boy smiled grimly. 'I use ter hide in there when I were rabbitin'.'

Grace tried another tack, for it was cold outside, but the boy refused to walk any farther. 'What is your name?'

'Joe.'

'Where do you work, Joe?'

'Kendleton pit.'

Grace closed her eyes momentarily at the realization. 'Has there been an accident there?'

The boy screamed and didn't stop. He flung himself onto the snow-covered gravel, screaming for them to run. Doyle went to him, but the boy pushed him away swearing and punching at him, saying that he was getting out first. A sound slap to the boy's cheek from Doyle reduced him to a crying heap in the middle of the drive. Gently, Doyle pulled him to his feet and with soothing tones, took the child inside.

In the hall, Grace issued rapid instructions to Partridge, Emma Kate and anyone within hearing that she wanted food, everything Mrs Hawksberry had. She sent for Sykes and the carriage, as well as the doctor.

Doyle closeted the boy in his own rooms, leaving Partridge to mother him, before returning to Grace as she donned her thick woollen cloak, scarf, gloves and boots. 'What are you doing?'

'Going to the mine.'

'Don't be ridiculous!' He scoffed, as though she were a wayward child. 'What can you do there, besides giving them a target to vent their anger?'

'It is my responsibility, I must accept the blame.' She pinned a black velvet hat onto her head. 'I should have closed it down!'

* * *

THE SNOW STOPPED FALLING as Sykes sent the horses bounding towards the mine. Grace sat squashed into a corner of the carriage surrounded by such baskets of food from the kitchen as they had been able to spare. She prayed no one had been killed in the accident.

The full enormity of the situation did not hit her until they slowed to make their way down into the valley. Thin lines of darkly clothed people walked, some hurried, over the hills towards the mine head. News of the disaster had spread. They swarmed like a disturbed ants nest, seeking their loved ones.

The lean covering of snow, which did its best to coat the ugly manmade landscape with virgin whiteness, was quickly turned into gray murky sludge. At the pithead, where the miners and coal tubs came out of the earth, a natural meeting place formed.

Leaving the carriage, Grace headed for the tall man who had made the speech to her, and who seemed in charge. Unlike her last visit, this time the gathered crowd stood in silence and moved aside for her.

Teams of men were handed water bottles, picks, shovels and rope. Grace waited patiently while the man gave orders to the team ready first. When they had entered the black hell, he moved onto the next team, and it was then he saw her. The look he gave her she'd remember for the rest of her life. It was the look of a man condemned, who had seen and heard too much of death.

Summoning all her courage, Grace stepped before him. 'What happened?'

'Cave in. The bottom seams are flooded.'

'The injured?'

'Are being tended to over there.' He pointed to the manager's office.

Men and boys sat or stood in and around the hut. Bloodshot eyes stared out from coal-black faces. Some looked stunned, others shook their heads not believing their luck. A few wept. Women, wives and mothers fussed around them, tending to their injuries.

Grace swallowed and glanced back at the man beside her. 'A boy came to me. He had escaped through a disused shaft, maybe others have as well?'

'Some did, but now the entrance to that shaft is underwater.'

Grace bowed her head. Guilt, frustration and helplessness swamped her. 'This is tragic. I'm at a loss to know what to say, Mr...?'

'Walters. And there is nothing you can say, Miss Woodruff.' His expression held the censure his voice didn't.

'Please, tell me what I can do to help.'

'Pray, Miss Woodruff.' He turned away from her, back to his important tasks, but she took another step.

'I have brought food. What else is needed to ease the suffering?'

His eyes of green narrowed. 'Tell the wives and mothers you are sorry, and that you plead for their forgiveness.' He walked away.

Pushing her way back through the people, tears stung her eyes at his harsh words. Impatiently, she dashed at them with the back of her hand and returned to the carriage. She instructed Sykes to help her unload the baskets and then to return home for as many blankets as possible.

'Would yer like a hand, Miss Woodruff?' A young girl had appeared at her side unnoticed. With a small smile, Grace nodded and told her to distribute the food to those needing it.

For an hour, Grace walked between the humble, waiting families. As she gave a piece of pork pie to a little girl, a gentle murmur in the crowd began. Pausing, Grace craned her neck to see what was happening at the mine entrance. Movement at the front of the gathering set her feet moving before she was aware of it. She nudged her way through in time to see two men stagger out of the black opening. They were wet, shivering and only their red-rimmed eyes showed in the black grime encasing them.

Walters rushed to them. 'Nay, lads, you're all right now,' he murmured, guiding them to an overturned box. They sat down together, their arms still locked around each other's shoulder.

A scream from behind Grace, gave her warning before she was roughly pushed aside. The woman threw herself onto the two men seated, howling and thanking God. The crowd became animated. If two men had walked out alive, then how many more could do so?

Slowly, at intervals of ten minutes or so, the rescue teams came back up from the depths of Hell. Once or twice, they held within their strong arms the moaning figures of survivors; other times, they carried the limp forms of the dead. The afternoon grew long. Shadows and hope began to fade.

With the many blankets Sykes had brought back, Grace helped to wrap the elderly, the frail and the young against the cold. The women whose families were safe, having not worked that shift, went home to make large pots of tea for the ones still waiting. They built fires around the yard for lighting and heat. A storage shed became a temporary hospital as the village doctor arrived, along with the vicar.

Grace wandered restlessly about, offering what comfort she could. But she knew words were empty to those who had lost, in some cases, more than one family member. Her eyes scanned faces etched with the devastation of loss. As the hours passed, rescuers brought out fewer men alive. A heavy weight settled on her shoulders and heart.

Wheels rumbled down the track to the yard. Grace gave a steaming cup of tea to an ancient miner and glanced up. In the dwindling light of approaching evening, she watched the driver leap from the gig. His height, his walk, she knew. William. He spotted her as she made her way through the throng of crying people, fires, supply crates, coal piles and numerous other articles that litter yards of a mine site. He opened his arms to her and she stepped into them gratefully.

'I've been worried to near madness about you,' William said, his tone grim. 'I came back earlier than expected, because I had a feeling something wasn't right. And when Doyle told me what had happened, I couldn't believe it.'

'It's been awful, William.' Grace straightened, trying to be brave and not cry, but the weight of responsibility was heavy.

He kissed her forehead. 'These things always are.'

'But to see men and boys dead and broken.'

William swore under his breath. 'Come, there is still much to do before I take you home.'

They walked back through the yard, until Grace found the leader, Walters. She had learnt he was a shift foreman and a union man. He fought for the men's rights in a mine that had become a working coffin. Kendleton Colliery had been allowed to slip under many regulations for the last few years. The numerous strikes the men organized did not have the desired effect on the previous owner, and, like him, her father had refused to heed the men's concerns.

William shook Walter's hand as an equal. 'William Ross.'

'George Henry Walters,' he replied with a nod.

'I'm told you're in charge?'

'Aye, along with other shift foremen.'

'The manager?'

'At home, sick since yesterday.' The look on Walter's face conveyed his disgust. 'Word's been sent to him, not that he'll come runnin'. Frightened to show his face, I expect.'

'How bad is it?'

'Fourteen dead, twelve missin', twenty-one injured.'

William shook his head in sympathy. 'Do you know how it happened?'

'The men broke into a new seam yesterday. We pillared and posted it, concentrating on that area and leaving smaller teams in the other levels. Then earlier this morning, in level thirty, they must've cut into an underground stream. It flooded the bottom three levels within ten minutes.

'Christ.' William took off his hat and scratched his head. 'Pumping?'

'Yes, been at it solid since the accident.' Walter's sighed. 'Only now, the pump engine has seized. We can't get the water level down until it's fixed, unless it finds its own way out, but by then it's too late.' He shrugged his shoulders as if to suggest there was nothing more to say.

'It will be investigated.'

'And the families taken care of,' Grace interrupted them, 'I'll see to it personally.'

Walters turned his damning gaze on her. 'There's nowt you can do to replace good men.' His tone clearly stated where the blame lay. He left them to organize more rescue attempts.

'He's right, of course. It is my fault.' Grace hugged her arms about herself in cold misery and helplessness.

'No, he isn't. You and I weren't to know the extent of the neglect here.' William took her hands. 'Either the manager didn't reveal it all or your father refused to listen to it.'

'All these people have no jobs to go to tomorrow, William. How will they survive? No sane person will buy this troublesome mine now.' She looked at the people nearby who wouldn't meet her gaze.

'We'll get through this.'

She lifted her chin. 'I have hardly a penny to my name, yet I am determined to help these people. I know I can do it.' She didn't know how she could accomplish such a mission, but the purpose gave her new strength.

* * *

LETITIA PUSHED BACK the bedcovers and lowered her feet to the thick mat. She listened for any sound of her family. Hearing nothing, she quickly crossed to her small dressing room. From a drawer in the oak tallboy, she took out a hidden velvet purse. Unwrapping it, she saw the jewels shimmer in the soft moonlight that shone through the gap in the curtains.

Breathing rapidly, Letitia discarded her nightgown and reached for a chemise and corset from within the dark interior of the large wardrobe. Her shaky fingers found the eyelets of the corset impossible to manage. In frustration, she flung the article away. She'd do without the damned thing. A sound she couldn't identify rang distantly in the far reaches of the house. A fine sweat lined her upper lip. She hurriedly dressed in her black clothes and donned her boots. After so many years of being tended to by others, the effort it took to dress by herself made her dizzy. She steadied herself a moment against the doorjamb before slipping the velvet purse into her cloak pocket.

She inched to the bedroom door and rested again. Her head was slow in clearing from the numerous potions the doctor insisted she take each day to cure her from the wretched curse raging in her body; but the doctor's ministrations had no effect on her, other than to make her drowsy. Biding her time, she knew her strength and endurance against the restrictions placed upon her would be rewarded. Tonight, she would claim her reward.

Suddenly, she laughed in the stillness of the room. The sound echoed in the silence and she swore at her foolishness. Nevertheless, she grinned again at the thought of outwitting Grace and the others. They thought her better, her need gone. Her mother left for Scarborough believing she was in control of herself once more. She grinned again. *Oh yes, Mama, I am in control.* A burst of excitement filtered through her. In the aftermath of yesterday's disaster at the colliery, Grace and the newly returned William had no time for her. *Well, bugger them! No longer will they deny me!*

The door opened easily at her touch; its well-oiled hinges gave no clue of her flight. Creeping stealthily from shadow to shadow thrown along the gallery, Letitia made her way down the staircase. She hadn't ventured downstairs for two days, and she wondered briefly if Grace had allowed liquor back into the house. A fleeting glance into the drawing room showed the empty drink trolley. Annoyed at being thwarted, Letitia turned for the door. She quickly displaced the three locks, and taking a deep breath, opened the door without noise.

Outside, the moonlight reflected off the white-gravelled drive as though lighting a way to freedom. The snow was gone, washed away by a heavy shower, but the night embraced the cold, turning everything to ice. Freezing air slapped at her face. She lifted the cloak's hood over her head.

She stood poised on top of the steps like a baby bird teetering on the end of a branch, readying itself for its first undertaking of flight. A calmness settled over her. Her skipping heartbeat slowed and stabilized. Lifting her chin, she felt a desire to cry out into the icy purple-blackness of the night; to tell the world she was alive and free. But another cry rang out first, that of a male fox on the prowl. Its eerie call sent shivers up her arms, and gave wings to her feet.

Skirting the drive, knowing the crunching gravel would give her away to one of the few remaining estate gardeners should he be walking his rounds, she ran along the grass beside it. Under the tall silver birches lining the drive, she ran all the way up to the gates. There, she stopped, gasping for breath. She hadn't managed much physical activity for many months and that burst of energy left her shaking and giddy. She sucked in gulps of air.

After a few moments rest, she stepped out onto the road, the road to liberty. Above the bare trees, the clouds drifted, one moment she was in shadow, the next in grey light. Turning slowly, she gazed back down the drive as silvery moonlight lit the house and gardens. A smile lifted the corners of her mouth.

CHAPTER 19

*G*race was woken early as she had instructed. Hopeland brought a light breakfast, followed by hot water for her to wash with, and after helping Grace dress, arranged her thick chestnut hair into a tight French roll.

'Is anyone else awake, Hopeland?'

'No, Miss,' the maid mumbled, with hairpins sticking out of her mouth.

'Let Miss Letitia sleep this morning; her days are long enough as they are.'

'Yes, Miss.'

'I'll not be at home today, nor will Miss Phoebe or Miss Emma Kate. So, she will be alone for most of the time. Try to encourage her to eat, will you?'

'I'll do me best, Miss.'

Downstairs, the house stirred awake. On her way to the kitchen, Grace paused to smile in encouragement at Partridge, who sleepily set the fire in the drawing room. Grace felt guilty that the poor woman had to perform such tasks when she was head parlour maid. The situation would not get better either. More staff layoffs were imminent.

In the kitchen, Grace found Mrs Hawksberry seated in her chair by the range drinking a cup of tea. Two other kitchen maids busily organized breakfast.

Mrs Hawksberry rose quickly to her feet, despite her bulk. 'Good mornin', Miss Grace.'

'Good morning, Mrs Hawksberry. Are the baskets ready?'

'Aye, Miss, they are.' Mrs Hawksberry crossed over to the baskets covering the servant's breakfast table in one corner of the room. 'I've put the same amount in each, except the last two. They've got more fer't bigger families.'

'Thank you.' Grace smiled.

Mrs Hawksberry gave a final inspection of her handiwork. 'Well, Miss, I'm sure those poor souls will thank yer.'

'I don't expect their thanks, Mrs Hawksberry.' Grace turned from the table. 'Has Johnny come in from the stables yet? I want him to load the baskets into the cart. The earliness of the hour is to catch the pit women before they walk to the village market.'

'Yer've enough ter do here, without botherin' with those miners.' Mrs Hawksberry frowned. 'They'll get by, lass, they allus do. They're medd of strong stuff.'

'I know they are. Only, I feel responsible. I need to do this. However little it is.' With a sigh, she stood.

The back door opened and young Johnny entered. He snatched off his hat on seeing Grace. 'The cart's ready, Miss. Early like you said.'

'Good, then start loading the baskets.' Grace turned back to Mrs Hawksberry. 'Can you let Doyle and Mr Ross know I'll be home later? And Miss Phoebe and Miss Emma Kate are calling on our sister at Morgan's Farm today, so Miss Letitia will be alone. I'll try not to be too long.'

'Aye, Miss.' Mrs Hawksberry nodded. 'Don't worry yer head about it.'

The door leading into the kitchen from the corridor opened,

Doyle checked his step as he saw Grace standing there. 'Miss Grace?' He strode to her side.

'Good morning, Doyle.' Grace went outside to the cart with Doyle hot on her heels, muttering his disapproval.

Johnny packed the last of the baskets, as Sykes handed Grace up into the seat. He was about to climb aboard too when she forestalled him.

'No need to trouble yourself, Sykes, thank you. I'm quite capable.' Grace took up the reins.

'But, Miss, I can't let yer go on yer own!' The old carriage driver stared at her as if she'd lost her mind.

'Of course you can, Sykes. I can drive this cart with one hand.' Grace scoffed, giving him a superior look.

Sykes stood as straight as his old frame would allow. 'Aye, I know yer can drive the thing, for it was me who taught yer when yer were no higher than me knee!'

Grace gave a cheeky grin. 'My sisters will need you today. I can manage.' He tramped away, muttering under his breath, back to the warmth of the stables.

'Grace, is *he* going? And if he's not, then I'll ride with you.' Doyle glared up at her. 'I won't allow you to go alone.'

'Grace!' William called from an upstairs window. 'Where are you going?'

She swore softly under her breath and then shouted up to him, 'To the pit rows.'

'Wait, I'll join you.'

'No, I'm going alone.'

William banged the windowsill with his hand. 'Are you mad?'

'Quite possibly!' She looked from one to the other and addressed them both. 'I have always done things alone, long before either of you started to claim you know what is best for me.'

Grace sat tall in the seat, averting her gaze from Doyle's

torment. She clicked her tongue for the horse to walk on. Dealing with those two took more fortitude then she was prepared to spare. There were others who needed her more, others to focus her energies on.

The lane to the colliery forked off from the main road between the villages of Scholes and Barwick. Then the track forked again. Grace steered the horse to the pathway on the right that led over the valley to the rows of miners' houses. Her stomach tightened the closer she ventured to the little settlement. Would the people, still recovering from the disaster, receive her? Or would they stone her out of the valley like some medieval witch?

Atop the three rows of terraced houses, sat a common. On one side of the common, or The Green as the inhabitants called it, stood a small hut declaring itself a public house but which was really no more than a dirty hovel attended by only the desperate. Men who worked the nightshift at the colliery, were making their way home. Some of the levels in the mine were being worked, while other crews did their best to pump water from flooded areas. This arrangement had caused her to protest at first, until William explained that the men needed to keep working. They needed to still feel like they were doing something worthwhile.

Grace drove down the first row of houses. The front door of each house opened onto the dirt road. The row was unattractive with small windows and rough stonework. She halted the horse and climbed down. From the back of the cart, she lifted out the first basket. Taking a deep breath, she went to the first door in the row. A black ribbon nailed to the door, showed it was a house in mourning. Grace knocked.

After a pause, it opened to reveal a large woman in a brown dress and apron. 'Aye?'

'I have brought you a basket of food and essentials.' Grace

handed the basket over to the stunned woman and stepped away. With a nod of respect, Grace went back to the cart for another basket. These tough, plain-speaking women didn't want her small talk, wouldn't want to pass the time of day with her. Grace didn't wish to linger and give them the opportunity to fling the basket back in her face. Her hands shook, but she repeated the exercise all the way down the row.

By the time the cart was half-empty, a gathering of people waited at the end of each row. Grace was beginning to tire, but doggedly refused help from any of the men. No one was pleased to see her, and no basket of goods would change that, but the mood against her wasn't hostile. As she made her way up the last row, towards the empty cart, a man stepped out from the crowd. Grace bowed her head, hesitated in passing him. She didn't want trouble.

'Is this to be a regular thing?' he asked.

She jerked up and stared at the man. 'I will try to make it so, yes.'

'Have you found a buyer?'

'Not as yet.'

His green eyes narrowed. 'Four families have left, gone to the cities to find work.'

'I hope they succeed.' Grace gave a shimmer of a smile.

'They will die in the *gutter*!'

Grace stepped back, alarmed at his contempt.

'Have you offered jobs at the estate?'

'No, we are not in any position to do so,' she whispered. She could feel his frustration and anger. 'I wish I could do more.'

'You will never be able to do enough!'

'Perhaps not, Mr Walters. However, I'll continue trying. Please, excuse me.' Grace walked past and heard him swear softly.

'Miss Woodruff?'

She turned slightly back to him.

Walters rubbed his hand wearily over his tired face. 'I'm not a harsh man. I thank you for your effort this morning. You didn't have to.'

Her gaze didn't waver. 'Yes, I did.'

* * *

FROWNING, Doyle hurried down the steps to open the carriage door. They weren't expecting visitors today and, he hoped whoever it was would soon depart again, for the house was in enough turmoil regarding Miss Letitia's disappearance without attending to callers.

Extending his hand, he saw the large hat first. The feathered creation of dove gray and plum purple swamped his vision as the lady descended the step. She straightened and looked about her. Finally, she turned her face to him.

He swallowed. 'Welcome to Woodruff House.'

'Will it be a welcome, do you think?' came the saucy tone, surprising him. She glided majestically up the wide steps and into the house. Pausing in the hall to slowly remove her fur-trimmed gloves, she frowned at the surroundings. 'Rather provincial.'

Doyle could not take his eyes off her. She carried herself as though she were an empress. He took her gloves and fox fur stole.

She left the enormous hat on and strode into the drawing room unannounced. The empty room made her turn back to Doyle as he followed her. 'Is my husband in residence?'

'Mr Ross? He's gone to Leeds, I believe, Madam.' Doyle couldn't help but feel a sense of impending doom.

'Leeds?' Felicity Ross strolled around the room, taking little interest in the paintings and ornaments on display. The bored look upon her face showed such things were not worth her regard. 'He is due back, when?'

'He and Miss Woodruff didn't mention a time, Madam.'

Felicity gave him a sharp look. 'Miss Woodruff is accompanying him?'

'Yes, Madam.'

'They are looking for Miss Woodruff's sister, who has been missing for some eight days now.'

His eyes widened. She continued her inspection of the drawing room. 'Yes, I know the reason that keeps my husband here.' Her tone was as cutting as her piercing blue eyes.

'Would Madam care for some refreshment while you wait?'

Ignoring him, she went to the window and moved the curtain. 'Is *everyone* looking for the missing delinquent?'

Doyle's dark eyes widened at her words. He knew her kind. She was exactly like his previous mistress and her daughter. 'Mrs Woodruff is returning from Scarborough with one of her daughters …'

'The mother is returning only now?' She interrupted him with a mocking look.

'The mistress was too ill to travel. The news was a great shock.'

Felicity's tinkling laugh stopped him. 'What has William got himself mixed up with?' She turned, raising her arms to her hat and pulling out the pins securing it. The action brought his attention to her thrusting bust and slender waist.

His stare was steady. 'Refreshments, Madam?'

'Ah, why not?'

'Would you prefer a light meal while you wait?'

'Tempt me, my good man.' Her voice suddenly dripped silk and honey.

He wasn't going to play her game. With a slight bow, he left her

* * *

GRACE PEERED out the carriage window at the passing streets. Sykes knew his instructions and kept the horses' speed to a walk. Both she and William searched people's faces as they walked along the cold city streets, but the one face they longed to see never materialized. For over a week, they had trawled every road and alley in Leeds. They offered money to anyone with scant knowledge of where the homeless and desperate gather, but each piece of information returned nothing. The police helped them a little, but they could not devote all day every day to one missing young woman, a woman who left home of her own accord. In Wellington Street, the carriage slowed to a stop outside a disused warehouse, now doubling as a soup kitchen. Stepping down, with William's help, Grace stared at the soot-covered buildings. Behind her, along the road to the right, was the goods station, and to the left was the first of many textile mills that ran parallel to the River Aire. Low clouds and no wind allowed the thick layer of smog to hover. The thousands of chimneys throughout the town spilled forth their choking pollution, coating every surface with grit. She felt it on her cheeks.

'This is the last place for today, Grace,' William said, guiding her through the muck masking the cobbles to the other side of the street. 'You've had no rest since seven o'clock this morning.'

'There is still daylight left, William. We shall keep looking.'

He stopped her at the entrance to the soup kitchen and turned her to face him. 'I'm worried about you. You've not rested a moment since Letitia left. There will be no more night searches until you've had a whole night's sleep.'

Her worry and exhaustion ignited her temper. 'I can never rest until she's been found!'

'Making yourself ill will not help her!'

An elderly woman in a black dress and white apron interrupted their debate. 'Miss Woodruff!' She rushed to Grace, her winkled face showed her urgency.

'Mrs Bates! Do you have news?' Grace had volunteered her

time at this soup kitchen on many occasions and respected the older woman's tireless efforts for others.

'No, I'm sorry.' The old woman's lace cap wobbled dangerously as she shook her head.

Grace sagged. 'You'll keep a look out for her?'

'Of course.'

William took her hand, helped her back into the carriage and kept hold of it as they rumbled through the traffic. 'When Letitia has been found, I need to speak to you about other matters.'

'Other matters?' Grace sighed and nodded. 'We've ignored Mr Swindale all week. He sent a letter to the house late last evening expressing his need for us to come to his office as soon as possible. I believe he is rather annoyed at coming out to the house and finding us gone every day.'

'I don't mean Mr Swindale.' He stared straight into her eyes. 'I am divorcing Felicity.'

His words astounded her. For a moment, she didn't think she had heard correctly. 'Divorcing Felicity?'

'Yes. I made a ghastly mistake.'

His revelation overwhelmed her. 'You have only been married...'

'I married her for the wrong reason. I...'

'You have grounds to do this?'

'No. Not yet.'

'I don't want to hear this now!' She ripped her hand out of his clasp. 'Have you any idea what you've done to me? I waited for you for years. I went through hell when you married another!'

'I know, I know, and I'm sorry. It was never my intention to hurt you. I love you.' His blue eyes were full of wanting.

Grace slumped. He spoke the words she'd longed to hear since the age of sixteen, but the timing was all wrong. The feeling was all wrong. She no longer loved William. He was too late. 'Do not divorce her on my account.'

'What are you saying?' He jerked back in shock. 'Soon I will be free to give you comfort, to give you everything you need.'

'Thank you for the offer, but you are mistaken, because I don't need you anymore.'

'Grace.'

'No, William. No more.'

They kept their gazes from each other as the Leeds city streets passed by in a blur. Once on the outskirts of the city, William turned to her. 'Tomorrow, I shall call at the pawn brokers again. Letitia's jewellery may have turned up. We might find a lead there.'

She nodded and looked away.

At Woodruff House, Grace opened the door and stepped down before Doyle had descended the wide steps. She went straight into the house with William close behind. She didn't take off her outer clothing but continued up the staircase.

'Darling ... you have returned.' The silken tones drifted up the staircase. Grace faltered. Slowly, she turned and stared down at the vision of loveliness wrapping her arms around William.

'Felicity!' William untangled his wife from him. 'Why did you not notify me of your intentions?' His voice held censure.

'I missed you, sweetie. I was all alone in London.' She pouted up at him, but her blue eyes glinted with grievous intent.

'I don't like surprises, Felicity.' William glanced up at Grace and she saw his stricken face.

Grace slowly made her way down the stairs. Squaring her shoulders, she greeted William's wife. 'How do you do? I'm Grace Woodruff.'

'A pleasure to finally meet you in person, Miss Woodruff.' Felicity inclined her head. Her blue eyes burned with hostility. 'I trust you have cared for my husband well?' She gave William an adoring look.

'To the best of our ability, Mrs Ross, but William *is* family. Woodruff House is his home as well as ours,' Grace replied, amazed this frozen beauty was William's wife. Poor William. The two women locked gazes. With a slight bow to Grace, Felicity anchored her hand on William's arm and guided him back to the drawing room, talking of her father at the same time.Grace turned for the staircase again. In doing so, she caught Doyle's wink and for the first time in a week, her smile was real.

CHAPTER 20

Grace played with her food, unable to do justice to Mrs Hawksberry's creations. The food stuck in her throat at every sound Felicity made. The woman was purposely goading her, she was certain. Of course, it was done subtly. No one at the dining table could actually say she was being anything other than a doting wife. Only, Grace saw beneath her polished veneer. Felicity's high laughter and chatty conversation earned her the attention of all present, even Phoebe, who had come into the room solemn, but was now laughing with ease. Felicity's promises of shopping sprees for her sisters made the difference, Grace had no doubt.

She chanced a quick look at William. He didn't welcome his wife's sudden appearance. Grace admitted Felicity had all a man would want in a wife; looks, poise and wealth. However, watching her carefully, Grace was surprised to find the woman's mask slip now and then. Often during the afternoon and subsequent dinner, she had seen expressions of contempt and anger on the other woman's face. The interaction between William and his wife was interesting indeed.

As Grace sipped from her wine glass, Partridge entered the

dining room and whispered in Doyle's ear where he stood by the serving bench. He nodded and came to Grace's side. 'Miss Woodruff, your mother's carriage is coming down the drive.'

'Thank you, Doyle.' Grace used her napkin and then rose from her chair with Doyle's help. She turned to the others as Doyle left the room to greet the carriage. 'Mother has returned.'

'Wonderful!' Emma Kate clapped, and she and Phoebe ran from the room.

Grace saw Felicity's haughty expression at her sisters' exuberant behaviour and sighed.

In the hall, her mother's aggrieved voice rang distinctly over the noise of baggage being brought in. With pleasure, Grace noticed Cousin Verity, who must have been persuaded to return with Diana. Hugging them all in turn, Grace forestalled her mother's urgent complaints about the journey home, by guiding them into the drawing room.

'And Letitia? What of my dearest girl?' Diana cried plaintively as she sat.

'No news yet, Mama. William is hiring a private investigator tomorrow. Hopefully, he will succeed where we have failed,' Grace told her as William and Felicity joined them.

Verity, delighted to see her son and daughter-in-law, kissed them both. 'How thankful I am to have made the journey, especially since you are both here.'

Felicity sparkled in front of an audience, all the while holding William's arm possessively. 'It is good to see you, Mother Ross.' She turned to Diana. 'I am so very pleased to meet you, Mrs Woodruff.'

'What a joy it is to have you here, my dear. I hope your stay is pleasurable, despite our sad circumstances.' Diana's face quickly fell into a decent show of sadness.

Grace rolled her eyes at her mother's performance and wondered if Diana cared at all about Letitia's fate. 'Mama, shall I accompany you upstairs while you change after your journey?'

'Why, thank you, dearest. I do declare I'm completely exhausted. Darling Verity was a wonderful diversion for the journey, was she not, Faith?'

'Yes, Mama.' Faith inclined her head and excused herself from the room. Grace's gaze followed her. Something was wrong there too, but she had to deal with Diana first before she took on more problems. She would talk to Faith later.

Diana regaled Grace with tales of her stay in Scarborough as they went to her rooms. Once inside Diana's sanctuary, Grace dismissed Hopeland who was unpacking the trunks, before cutting into her mother's flow of words. 'Mama, are you not at all worried over Letitia?'

'Worried? I'm ashamed! That's what I am. Ashamed!'

'Mama!'

'How could you let this happen? You were looking after her. How did she escape? Like a thief in the night?'

'Yes, something like that. She took the few jewels she hadn't already pawned last year, and I think she has taken some of yours too.'

'*My jewels*?' Diana face turned an ugly shade of burgundy. 'How dare she!'

'Well, thankfully you took the majority of what you have left with you.' Grace sighed. 'None of this matters. Finding Letitia is our primary concern.'

Her mother's eyes narrowed. 'To be honest with you, I feel giving her a taste of the unsavoury aspects of this world will make her rethink her conduct at home. I'm rather tired of the way my daughters selfishly behave!'

Grace stared in amazement. 'Mama!'

'Well, it's true.' Diana stormed over to her bed to trifle with a dress laid across it. 'Your father was the bane of my life, but you girls are quickly making his efforts childish in comparison.'

'Letitia is sick! She is alone somewhere needing our help.'

Tears welled in Diana's eyes. 'Letitia, like Gaby, has ruined our reputation.' She turned away. 'I no longer have a daughter called Letitia.'

'What utter nonsense!' Grace raged. 'You cannot keep disowning us when we do something you don't like. You are our mother, and it's time you started acting like it.'

'You have no right—'

'I have every right!' Grace walked across the room and thrust her face before Diana. 'From now on, you'll do your share! Starting tomorrow.'

'Tomorrow? What do you mean?'

'You will spend the day searching the streets for your daughter.'

'No.'

'Yes.' Grace walked to the door. 'Then, on our way home, we shall call and visit Gaby and you will meet your grandchild.'

'Grace!'

'Goodnight, Mama.' Grace left the room and walked along the gallery to her room. It was only early yet, but the thought of spending the evening with Felicity was abhorrent to her. She entered her room and closed the door with a sense of relief.

* * *

FELICITY SAT FUMING at the breakfast table, sipping tea. She had risen early so as not to miss William, should he decide to leave the house before the others. His rejection of her last night still rankled and she wasn't going to make it easy for him today. She wouldn't be ignored just because the holier-than-thou Grace Woodruff was under the same roof. Felicity knew where William's heart lay. A rage simmered inside her chest. She'd not be made a fool of, not by him and definitely not by a scandal-ridden penniless descendant of a merchant trader! All her life she had had her own way; nothing would stop her now.

The door opened and her husband appeared as she expected.

They might have not been married for long, but she was a keen observer. She smiled at his surprise on seeing her up so early. 'Good morning, my darling,' she said in a loaded tone.

'What reason has you from your bed at this hour?' William poured some tea before seating himself opposite her.

'I thought I would make the most of my day with you.' Her reply was as sweet as sugar.

'I cannot entertain you today.'

'That is where you are wrong.' Her eyes narrowed. 'As your wife, I take precedence over this provincial family.'

William pierced her with a look. 'No, you don't.'

For a moment, pain sliced Felicity. 'Don't make me angry, William. It isn't pretty. All I ask is for some of your time. Our honeymoon was cut short by this family and I refuse to let them monopolize you.'

'I've a duty to them. Besides, I wish to find Letitia. At this point in time, she is my main priority. Go back to London, please.'

'How dare you order me about like some servant!' Incensed, she rose from her chair to sneer across the table at him. 'Make me unhappy and my father will make your life a misery!'

'I care little about your father and what he can do to me.' William rose also and made for the door. 'And you may tell him that on your return.'

'I won't let you do this to me!' Felicity flung at his back.

He turned in the doorway. 'And you can also tell your father I want to divorce you.'

'Never!' She grinned wickedly. 'You will remain married to me until one of us is put under the ground.'

Her words sent him thundering to her side. He grabbed her arms painfully. 'I want a divorce and I will get one!'

'Why? What's changed since our marriage?'

'Me! I've changed. I have realized the enormity of what I've done.'

'Well, too late!' She spat. 'You shan't shame me in front of my friends. My father will not tolerate it.'

'Bugger your father.' His face was inches from hers.

She gave him an insolent glare. 'My father holds you in his hand. You are nothing without him.'

'Not so.' William eased his grip on her arms. 'Your father only gave me the means to make money. I have made substantial sums on my own. I don't need your father's influence any more.'

'Oh, you think you're big enough to go alone now?' Her laugh was derogatory.

'I only ever wanted enough to bring my estate back to its former glory. Unlike your father, Felicity, I am not greedy.'

'No, but you are a leech. You used me and my father.'

William stepped away. He wiped his hands over his face tiredly. 'No, that's not true. I went into our marriage with the proper intentions. I truly wanted it to be happy. The thought of marriage appealed to me.'

'But you married the wrong woman, didn't you?' She congratulated herself on keeping the desperation out of her voice.

'I didn't realize at the time.'

She gave a disgusted snort. 'How pathetic you are.'

'You divorce me, then.' William placated her with an uncaring shrug. 'I'll give you the grounds with which to do it, if you want. Make me out to be a blackguard, I don't care.'

Acting as though she was thinking the idea over, Felicity tilted her head with a frown. 'And the child?' She revealed her trump card.

William scowled in puzzlement. 'What child?'

'Our child.'

He reared back from her as though she had stuck him. 'No.'

She smiled serenely. 'Oh yes, dear husband.'

* * *

DIANA SAT on the edge of her chair, her back ramrod straight. The Morgan's maid added coal to the fire, but the cheery blaze did not comfort her. The maid bobbed in her direction before leaving her alone.

'Mama.' Gaby glided into the room with her head held high. 'I was so surprised when Mrs Winton came into the nursery and announced I had visitor. I was feeding the baby.'

'Gabriella,' Diana kept her tone formal.

'Is there any news of Letitia?'

'No, none.' Diana sniffed.

Gaby frowned. 'Then, what is the reason for your visit?'

'I wish to see my grandchild.'

'Why?'

Diana blustered. 'Because. Because, I just do!' She stood and gathered her things. 'I see I have wasted my time.'

'Did Grace ask you to come?'

'What does it matter?' Diana said from the doorway, as Mrs Winton came in carrying a tea tray.

'Sit down, Mama.' Gaby sighed and indicated for her to sit. 'Ruth has made a batch of fresh scones and they're delicious.'

Diana sat and accepted a cup of tea from her former housekeeper. 'Do you like your new employment, Mrs Winton?' It still annoyed her that she'd lost the housekeeper to Morgan's Farm. What did Gaby need with a housekeeper here?

Mrs Winton gave her a cool look. 'Indeed, Madam. Mrs Morgan is the best of employers.' She tactfully withdrew before Diana could respond.

'Well, that put me in my place!' Diana said uncharitably. 'Who would have thought the straight-laced ice queen would melt?'

'She's a very good housekeeper, Mama. I imagine it was difficult for her at first, for Ruth had the run of the house. There were times when I thought they would throttle each other, but on the whole they get along very well.'

Diana nibbled the tasty scone. 'Are you happy?' The question surprised them both.

Gaby looked at her for a moment as if weighing the answer in her mind. 'Yes. The happiest I've ever been.'

'That's not to say you couldn't have been happy with someone of our own class.'

Grinning, Gaby replaced her teacup and saucer back to the tray. 'Actually, I don't think I would have.'

'Tosh!'

'Truly, Mama. He is kind and loving...'

'You live in a ramshackle farm house!' Diana protested in disgust.

'Mama,' Gaby gazed sadly at her, 'it matters naught where you live as long as you are with the man you love. Haven't you learnt anything being married to Father?'

'What do you mean?'

'Why did you marry Father, Mama? Tell me, did you love him? He was *your* social inferior after all.'

Diana squirmed. 'We aren't talking about me, but since you mentioned it, I would have thought you might all learn by my mistake! I married a man totally inferior to me; I did it out of spite to a controlling, unloving father. Yet, I hadn't been married more than a day before I knew of the dreadful error I had committed. I've lived in fear of my daughters doing the same ever since.'

Gaby gazed out of the window. 'I began meeting John to spite father, like you did to yours.' She turned back to her. 'But the difference is, I married him, not because of the baby as everyone thinks, but because he is kind and caring. He is right for me.'

With a snort, Diana shook her head. 'How can you love *him*? He's much older than you and nothing but a tenant farmer.'

'I know what he is, Mama, and I find it easy to love him. He's a good man who would die for our son and me. His social state means nothing to me. *My* social state means nothing to me. Yet, we have friends; good local people.'

'You cannot convince me, Gaby.'

'Then, I am sorry.'

Diana looked sharply at her daughter; the one she least really knew. It dawned on her this young woman was content in a way that she herself had never been. With a nod of understanding, Diana stood. 'I wish to ...' she cleared her throat, '*may* I see my grandchild?'

'I would like that very much, Mama.' Gaby smiled.

* * *

CHRISTMAS CAME and went at Woodruff House with hardly a ripple of excitement. As a family, they attended church, received the few visitors that dared to call and ate the traditional Christmas fare. The day before Christmas Eve saw Diana, with the girls by her side, giving out small tokens of appreciation to the servants. These gifts, wrapped weeks prior by Grace, also held wages. For ten of the staff it also held letters of reference. Lower gardeners, grooms, and kitchen staff, some having served loyally for years, found themselves without jobs. It was a distressing time that affected the whole house and plunged it into depression.

The removal of William, Felicity and Verity to London before Christmas helped Grace's state of mind, but no one else's. For their presence in the house had afforded some diversion. Without them, the events of a turbulent year crashed to the forefront of everyone's thoughts yet again.

'Is eighteen-seventy-one going to be better for us, Mama?' Phoebe asked on New Year's Eve, as they all sat in the drawing room waiting for midnight.

Diana sighed, looking mournfully into the blazing fire. 'I doubt it can be any worse.'

253

'Surely it's our turn for some good fortune,' Emma Kate grumbled. With no word from Mr Vincent, she was as miserable as a miser in a poorhouse.

'Shall I read to you all?' Faith suggested hopefully.

'Heavens no!' Phoebe protested. 'Why should we listen to tales of adventure to make us even more wretched?'

Grace smiled at Faith, acknowledging her effort. 'Shall we not have Phoebe play for us?' she said rising, making the others do likewise.

'I might as well,' Phoebe moaned. 'Who knows? The piano may be next on the list to go.'

Grace rolled her eyes at Phoebe's whine and walked into the hall. Sudden banging on the door halted her. Not waiting for Doyle, she opened it herself.

A man wearing a dark hooded cloak stood in the dim gloom cast by the hall light. 'I must see Miss Woodruff.'

'I am she.' Grace shivered as the night air touched her skin. Her family gathered in the hall behind her.

'I've come from Leeds. I have news of your sister.'

'Come in, come in,' Grace urged him, opening the door wider. 'What news do you have?'

The man removed his battered hat and nodded respectfully at the gathered women. 'My aunt, Fanny Bates, was called to a woman who we believe is your sister.'

Grace held up her hand to quieten them as they all spoke at once. 'Mrs Bates? She has Letitia?'

The young man nodded, his eyes serious. 'She was called out to a doss house this night, for she sees to the sick when they can't afford a doctor. My aunt got word to me that I had to come here as quick as I could. It seems your sister is very ill.'

'How ill?' Diana asked, her hand going to her throat.

'I'm not sure, but if my aunt thinks its urgent then I suggest you hurry.' His gaze went to each of them.

'I'll have Sykes round presently, Miss Grace.' Doyle had arrived without them knowing.

Grace nodded, as again they all began talking at once. Diana cried she was feeling faint and Faith told Emma Kate and Phoebe to take her upstairs.

'Partridge!' Faith called as the maid came up the hall. 'Have Miss Letitia's room readied and hot bricks put in the carriage.' The maid ran to do her bidding. Faith turned to Grace who donned her coat and gloves. 'I'm coming with you, Grace.'

'No, Faith, I need you here. You are the only sensible one I can trust.'

'But...'

'It's all right, Miss Faith.' Doyle came back into the hall dressed for outside. 'I'll accompany your sister.'

'Thank you, Doyle.' She kissed Grace's cheek and went outside with them as the carriage was brought around to the steps.

Sykes whipped up the horses as Doyle covered Grace's lap with thick blankets. She glanced at him, but in the darkness she couldn't make out his face clearly enough. Underneath the blankets, his hand groped for hers and held it. She accepted it gratefully.

CHAPTER 21

*T*he rumble of the carriage wheels sounded loudly in the slum quarters of the town. A half moon shone in the star-littered black sky, etching the town in long shadows. They passed revellers and private parties where the light and noise spilt onto the street, but the chill of the cloudless night kept most indoors. To many of the town's inhabitants, New Year's Eve was an ordinary night and tomorrow's start of another year gave them no cause for celebration. Nothing was going to alter their circumstances, no matter what the year date proclaimed.

A tomcat's cry rang out through the narrow lane as Doyle assisted Grace from the carriage. Back-to-back hovels lined either side of the lane. She lifted her skirts from the sludge-covered stone flags.

'This way.' The messenger showed them towards an archway between the houses. No glow of light filtered from windows to help them to find their way through the cut. Its limited width forced them to walk single file. The short passage opened onto a square yard bordered by rundown houses that seemed to lean against each other for support. Even in the shadowed gloom, the filth and waste was visible. A lingering stench assaulted their noses, making breathing unpleasant.

'Your aunt lives here?' Grace was alarmed to think of the dapper Mrs Bates living amongst such conditions.

'No, she lives a few streets away, she covers the whole area,' the man replied, opening a door. He waited until they were beside him in the dark stairwell. 'This is a place where people go who've a penny to spare for a bed.'

'A penny for a bed.' Grace shook her head as they followed him up the rickety stairs to the next landing. There, he paused, before opening another door and stepping back to allow Grace and Doyle to enter on their own.

'Oh my...' Grace breathed. She stared at the bunks of beds lining the walls and grouped in the middle of the room. Women and children lay huddled together; some coughed the phlegmy cough of the dreaded consumption. A few spoke in low voices, but most slept, letting their weary bodies get what rest they could. As Grace passed the beds, those awake clutched at their meagre belongings thinking they might be stolen.

'Put your handkerchief to your nose, Grace.' Doyle muttered. 'I hate the thought of you within the confines of this hideous house.'

A single lantern, suspended from a beam, issued a weak light. Grace walked on. Her eyes, now accustomed to the dimness, picked out Mrs Bates at the end of the long room. She hurried to her side, only to stop short upon seeing the figure on the bed. Stifling a cry, Grace bent low to stare at the woman on the bottom bunk. *Mrs Bates is wrong. This cannot be Letitia.*

'Nay, she's all right, Miss Woodruff,' Mrs Bates murmured. 'She still breathes.'

'Are...' Grace swallowed with difficulty. 'Are you certain?' To her, the figure looked like a corpse. That it was Letitia she completely doubted on first glimpse, but now she saw a vague resemblance. Her once beautiful sister lay on a stained gray blanket, her black dress dirty, ripped. Sores dotted the once creamy skin, now stretched tightly over prominent cheekbones. Thin white hands rested by her side, her fingers red and rough from the cold, fingernails torn. However, the greatest shock was Letitia's hair, shorn about her head no more than an inch long.

'I was waiting for yer ter come, before I did anything further.' Mrs Bates felt Letitia's forehead. 'I can tell yer now, a doctor will take a lot of convincing ter come here.'

'I want her home.'

'I don't think it wise ter move her, Miss Woodruff.'

'She can't stay here! She needs proper care, away from vermin and filth.'

The door opening at the far end of the room had them spinning around.

A large man with fleshy jowls stared at them a moment before striding down to them. 'Mrs Bates, what is going on 'ere?' He stopped at the end of the bunk. He peered with distaste at Letitia. 'Is she dead?'

'Are you in charge?' Grace accosted him. His odour nearly made her heave, and his flabby stomach spilling out over his trousers revolted her.

'These are my premises, yes.'

'Then you should be ashamed of yourself for allowing these women and children to sleep in such a disgusting environment!'

'Now listen 'ere,' The man's small eyes peered at her from his wide face. 'I do a good service fer these unfortunates.'

'A service?' Grace's voice rose. 'By charging them money they can ill afford to sleep in this rat infested establishment?'

The fellow swelled himself to his full height. 'If it wasn't fer me, this lot would be sleeping in doorways! Here at least, they're safe from attackers and the like!'

Grace was beyond reason. 'I'll have the police onto you, see if I don't!'

'Then it's on your head if they all die in t' snow!' He spat.

Their squabble woke the sleepers and a general mumbling broke out. One woman sat up in her bunk. 'Leave him be, yer silly cow! Can't yer see he's given us a place ter rest?'

Grace turned back to Letitia, who hadn't moved or even opened her eyes. 'I want to take my sister home.'

'Good idea,' the man huffed.

Grace pinned him with a stare. 'But I'll be back! And when I do, this place better be fumigated, whitewashed and clean blankets issued.'

'Nay!' He objected. 'Yer think I'm medd of money?'

'It's either that or the police called! It wouldn't surprise me you run other ventures within these walls.' Grace gave him a contemptuous stare. 'Now, get some light onto those stairs, so we don't break our necks.'

Grumbling about militant women, he left the room to do as she asked.

'Stand aside.' Doyle shouldered his way past the two women, took his coat off and placed it over the frail creature on the bed. Deftly, he picked Letitia up and cradled her to his chest. 'Come Grace.' He strode ahead with his burden as the church bells tolled throughout the town heralding a new year.

FAITH CLOSED the library door gently, as everything in the house was now done in quiet since Letitia's return some six weeks ago. She went along the hall, into the parlour and through to the conservatory where she knew Grace would be. Hidden behind tall palms, she found her by the workbench, potting an orchid. 'Dearest, there's damp in the library. It's on the far wall, in the corner. I've asked Partridge to clear the shelves. I ll need to be inspected.'

'Blast!' Grace thumped the dirt into the pot harder than she ought.

'I'll have Doyle see to it.'

'Poor Doyle is worked too hard as it is.'

They heard the distant tinkle announcing a visitor at the front door. Grace groaned. 'Mr Swindale.' She took off her dirty gloves and untied her apron.

'Do you want me to be with you?' Faith asked, as they walked back through the parlour.

'Thank you, no. Mama said she would sit in on the interview.' Grace managed to say before gliding into the drawing room and greeting the solicitor. 'Shall we make ourselves comfortable in the study, Mr Swindale?' Grace then turned to Doyle. 'Ask Mrs Woodruff to join us, please.'

'Certainly, Miss.' Doyle bowed and left them.

Once seated in the warm study, with its cheery fire glowing, Mr Swindale opened his leather satchel and took out many sheets of paper. Grace watched his efficient shuffling and placing of the paper upon the desk. He seemed nervous, jittery, which was not unusual for Swindale, yet today he appeared worse than normal. 'Is there something troubling you, Mr Swindale?'

His pale eyes peeped wearily from behind his glasses. 'We have much to discuss today, Miss Woodruff. Will your mother be joining us soon?'

His grave tone increased Grace's anxiety. 'Is there something I should know before my mother arrives, sir?'

Suddenly, Swindale leant back in his chair and sighed deeply. He looked very old and tired. 'I have sent for Mr Ross. I cannot stem the tide another day.'

Fear clutched at her throat. 'Tell me.'

'The death of your father and the disaster at the colliery has made investors wary of your father's businesses. Many have distanced themselves from any Woodruff owned companies. Orders have dropped from the factories.'

'Don't they know of Mr Ross?' Grace asked.

'He's not here all the time, Miss. He is not meeting the businessmen of Leeds and surrounding areas to keep the flow of contact open. They see him as some member of the family that visits now and then from London. It isn't enough to instil their confidence.'

'But we have you as well.'

Mr Swindale shook his head. 'I'm not a businessman. I have no power to buy or sell your father's interests. Only Mr Ross can do that.'

'Can I do it?'

'You?' Swindale frowned. 'Not possible. The executor is Mr Ross.'

'So, I must sit here helpless?' Grace stood and paced the floor. 'It's not right, Mr Swindale. Mr Ross is busy with his own life; he cannot be here at all times. Yet, I am.'

'Miss Woodruff, even if you were given the power, not many men would do business with you anyway. In fact, you being a woman would only drive them away faster.'

'What ridiculous standards men have!'

'Maybe so, but that is the way the world works.' Swindale took a handkerchief out of his breast pocket, and then taking his glasses off, he meticulously wiped them over.

'Is there nothing I can do, Mr Swindale?'

He glanced up from his task. 'Sell everything. Live in a simpler way, somewhere else. In town maybe.'

'No!' Diana stood at the door with a determined expression. Swindale rose as she entered the room, while Partridge followed her carrying a tea tray. Once the maid left, Diana turned on the solicitor. 'We will not sell, Mr Swindale. Therefore, I suggest you go back to your office and think of another plan to get us out of this mess.'

'I've tried everything I know, Madam.' Swindale accepted a cup of tea from Grace. 'You must realize understand I alone cannot keep this family solvent.'

Diana sat stiffly on her chair. 'We will not sell this estate.'

'An estate of this size cannot be maintained by the remaining businesses.'

'The estate keeps itself!' Diana argued.

Swindale shook his head. 'No, it doesn't Madam, and it hasn't done for some time.'

'He is correct, Mama,' Grace intervened when it seemed that Diana was about to debate further. 'The rents, the yearly sales of the livestock and crops are not enough to keep the estate viable now. We've always needed the profits from our other businesses to keep the estate in its position of grandeur. Now they have been sold, or are making little profit, the estate is suffering.'

'But we have let staff go, and cut back on our expenditure! We've had no new dresses for six months!'

'It is not enough, I'm afraid, Mrs Woodruff.' Swindale collected a few sheets of paper and handed them to Diana. 'These lists will show you the present income and expenditure for the estate.'

Diana hurled the papers onto the fire. 'No list shall sway me!' She stormed to the door but turned back dramatically to the little solicitor. 'I will never sell!'

Swindale turned his gaze from the black and flaming papers to Diana. 'It is not your decision, Madam.' He gathered up his remaining papers and satchel. 'Your husband's Will was clear. All decisions concerning the estate and businesses rest with Mr Ross.'

Triumphant, Diana glowed. 'There your argument is lost, Mr Swindale, for William will never make us sell.' She flounced from the room.

The solicitor peered at Grace over the rim of his spectacles. 'He has used great amounts of his own money already to keep creditors away.'

Grace brought her hands together under her chin in deep thought. 'He had no money until his marriage.' Her eyes widened as she realized his meaning. 'He used his wife's money?'

'It is his money now, Miss Woodruff.' Swindale's gaze darted away. 'I reveal too much. Mr Ross will be angry.'

An overwhelming sense of humiliation filled her. 'We've been living on Felicity's money ...' Grace felt the bile rise to her throat.

'Miss Woodruff, it's Mr Ross's money and he used it to keep your family from going under. He is a gentleman, and takes care of his own. You must not censure him on this. He was thinking of you all and did the only thing he could do. His married state meant he could do much good to his own affairs and those of his family. It's quite a natural thing to do.'

'Are you telling me that without his input of money after his marriage, we would have lost what businesses remained to us?'

'Yes, and more likely the estate as well.'

His words were like a physical blow to her stomach. She reeled, staggering back towards the nearest chair and sunk onto it breathing heavily. Her mind was numb; refusing to comprehend the debt they owed him, owed Felicity. Tears stung behind her closed lids, but she denied them release.

Some minutes passed by in strained silence until Grace gave herself a mental shake, pushing all thoughts of William and Felicity to the back of her mind. She would deal with that later. Now, her family's future must, for once, be firmly decided. For too long she had let the present state of affairs linger. Well, no more! It was she who had cared for them all for years, not her father, not her mother and definitely not William! She would rather burn this house to the ground than live on Felicity's money. 'If we were to live more frugally, maybe close up most of the house and cut all staff, except perhaps one or two would that work?'

'It would help, certainly,' Swindale agreed with haste. 'I have written to Mr Ross about the sale of more of the estate's land. The south quarter around to the western boundaries cover many acres. It's favourable farming land and should bring a good price.'

'How can we keep the house, if not the estate?' Grace was

clutching at straws, she knew, but if they could redeem something, however small, it was better than nothing.

'I have thought of that. If Mr Ross agrees, then all the
surrounding parcels of arable and woodland can be sold,
leaving the house, outer buildings and say twenty acres.
Enough land to grow crops for the few beasts you'll retain. If
we can achieve a good price then you might be able to maintain
a Mrs Hawksberry, housemaid, one gardener, and carriage
driver.'

'An enormous change for us all,' Grace said, her voice barely
audible above the crackle of the shifting logs in the fireplace. Her
thoughts were racing ahead. Such a transformation in their lives
was not going to be easy, but it could be done. She would make
sure of it. 'By doing this will the house then be unencumbered?'

'Yes. Hopefully. What profits are made will be enough to
sustain the family and house. Unless there is a fall in the market.'

'Good. Then it will be done.'

'It will?' Swindale looked at her strangely as if doubting her
word.

Grace's gaze was steady and cool. She knew what he thought.
'There will be no more tantrums and tears, Mr Swindale. I shall
begin the changes immediately.'

* * *

GABY LET herself into Letitia's bedroom. The room smelt of sick-
ness. It was airless and the sharp aroma of carbolic soap stung
her nose. A low fire burned even though the day was mild for the
end of winter. Walking over to the bed, she saw Letitia was
awake. 'Dearest.'

Letitia turned lifeless eyes towards Gaby.

'How are you?'

'Alive.'

Gaby sat on a chair placed close to the bed. 'Grace tells me you are getting better every day. Indeed, you look much better since I saw you last week. I'm so pleased.'

'Are you?'

'Of course.'

'It would have been best had Grace not searched for me. I didn't want to be found. If I had wanted to stay here, then I would never have run away.'

'Are you telling me, you would rather be out living on the streets at the mercy of riff raff and the weather? What nonsense! I don't believe you for a minute.' Gaby dismissed her protest like an annoying fly.

'And the alternative is this life, is it?' Letitia sneered. 'This house is full of soul destroying blackness.'

'No, it's not, dear sister. The only soul destroying blackness in this house is in here.' She jabbed sharply at Letitia's chest. 'You see no beauty anywhere. Look around you, Letitia, open your eyes to the love of your family. Take delight in the simple things.'

'Like a flower? Or a painting?' Letitia mocked her. 'Not everyone can settle for a life like yours, Gaby.'

Gaby brushed away the stinging comment with ease. 'Oh, Letitia, maybe marriage to a farmer is exactly what you need!' She laughed. 'That and lots of babies!'

'You disgust me.'

Gaby became serious. 'But, Letitia, I'm happy. I have nothing much really, except the quiet love of a good man and a baby who depends on me.' She bent closer to her afflicted sister. 'Everyone needs to be needed. It's a good feeling. I suggest you try it.'

'It's a little late for me to be a martyr, I think,' came her tart reply. 'I'm damaged goods.'

Gaby gave her a wry look. 'Don't try any of that talk with me, Letitia, it won't work. You might have the rest of the family running after you, but not me.'

Letitia's surprise registered on her face, before she scowled. 'You always did say what was on your mind, Gaby.'

With a laugh, Gaby bent and kissed her cheek. 'Then we are alike, dearest.'

'Go away. I don't want your merry smiles and sisterly love.'

'Oh, stop feeling sorry for yourself, Letitia. Your selfishness is boring.'

Letitia gasped. 'Don't you dare...'

'Dare to what, speak the truth? Don't you like it? Well, I don't care.' Gaby smiled sweetly to take the sting out of her words. She stood and whipped back Letitia's bed covers. 'In fact, I insist you get up and dress. Come down stairs and play with your nephew. He doesn't even know you!'

'The baby is downstairs?'

'Yes, being thoroughly spoilt by Mama.' Gaby grabbed Letitia's hands, pulling her up. She then went into the dressing room and flung open the wardrobe doors. 'What would you prefer, a dress or skirt?'

'I'm not going downstairs, Gaby.' She plucked at her nightgown. 'I...I cannot do it.'

'Nonsense!'

Letitia put a tentative hand to her hair. 'My hair. It's disgustingly short.'

'Yes, it is, but it'll grow. I can't believe you sold it.' Gaby brought out two skirts, one blue, and one deep green. 'Your face is pale and drawn, too. Thankfully, you've added some weight to cover those protruding bones.'

'Gaby, why aren't you wearing full mourning?'

Gaby grinned wickedly. 'I'm glad you noticed.' She held up both garments. 'Now, which do you want?'

'But it hasn't even been six months yet since Father's death.'

With a sigh, Gaby laid the skirts on the bed. 'I'm still in black, Letitia.' She indicated her black skirts and short waist jacket, though underneath she wore a plum-coloured blouse. 'However, I'm not a hypocrite. I don't mourn father.' She sniffed with disinterest. 'I never did.'

Letitia tilted her shorn head in thought. 'Nor I.'

Sitting on the edge of the bed, Gaby held Letitia's hand. 'Grace is trying very hard to keep the family together and the house going, dearest, she needs our help. The mine is still unsold and Grace spends all her free time at the pit village. She's even set up a soup kitchen there, and has been actively seeking new jobs for the workers wherever she can. So, I think it's time for you to help ease her worries here at home.'

'I can't...'

'You can. Grace was there for you when you needed her. Never did she give up on you. Now, it's your turn to think about someone other than yourself. I have learnt to, so has Faith, and we need you to even the score, for Phoebe is as self-indulgent as Mama. Heather thinks only of distancing herself from this tainted family. And Emma Kate thinks only of marrying Mr Vincent, after meeting him again when she and Phoebe spent the last month with the Ellsworths in Kent and London.'

'What use am I to anyone?' Tears, long suppressed, ran down Letitia's pale cheeks. 'I feel so worthless. I can do nothing right.'

'Nonsense. You are worth much. Your family loves you dearly.'

She choked on a sob. 'I've caused so much pain.'

'Nothing we can't overcome.' Gaby hugged her frail body tight.

'I'm sorry, Gaby, so terribly sorry.' At long last, Letitia cried, acknowledging her profound unhappiness. Gaby held her and let her ache ease.

CHAPTER 22

*G*race walked into the dining room and greeted her sisters as they ate breakfast.

'Good morning, Grace.' Emma Kate replaced her teacup upon its saucer. 'Heather sent a note saying he arrived safely last night. Mr Vincent comes today.'

'Indeed, Emma Kate. You have reminded me hourly for the last few days.' Grace smiled while adding bacon and eggs to her plate from the sideboard. She waited for Doyle to pull out her chair before sitting down next to Letitia. 'However, you and Mama shall have to entertain him without me. I've much to do this morning.'

Emma Kate's eyes widened. 'But this is very important, Grace. I'd like you to be here.'

Grace sighed as she poured a cup of tea. 'I'll do my best to be home in time, only I cannot promise.'

'What keeps you so busy today?' Faith asked.

'I'm going to the pit rows to find two girls to help Mrs Hawksberry.' Grace looked at Doyle, for it was he who brought to her attention Mrs Hawksberry's increasing infirmity since the extra staff was laid off. 'Hopefully, their parents will let them go for merely bread and board alone.'

'Pit girls?' Phoebe cried in horror. 'Mrs Hawksberry will never allow it.'

'Mrs Hawksberry is in pain more days than not from her legs, so she'll be grateful.'

'But will those girls be?' Letitia injected quietly, looking at her plate.

Grace frowned. 'In most cases, yes. The two girls I have in mind are sisters living with fourteen other siblings in a two-roomed cottage. I think their mother will not mind having them gone. I cannot give the girls a wage as yet, but I will send food baskets every week to their family.'

'Can't you send Doyle to do this errand and stay here to greet Mr Vincent?' Emma Kate whined.

'No, for that is not all I must do,' Grace said between mouthfuls of crispy bacon. She finished her tea and rose. 'Give my regards to Mr Vincent, Emma Kate. Invite him again for tea tomorrow and I'll see him then.'

Faith rose also and turned to Grace. Her face wore an inquisitive expression. 'What is happening with the storage barn at the end of the stables? I walked along there yesterday and found it to be a hive of activity.'

Grace hesitated. She stared at each of her sisters. 'I'm turning it into a school room.'

'A school room?' The sisters echoed each other.

'Yes, and before you ask, it's to benefit the children from the pit rows.'

Phoebe threw her napkin down. 'What possesses you to do such a thing? Mama will not allow the house to be overrun with pit children!'

Placing her hands on the back of her chair, Grace gave Phoebe a cold stare. 'They'll be in the barn, *not* in the house—'

'But why?' Emma Kate asked in confusion. 'Those children are wild. They cannot apply themselves to learn anything.'

'What a ridiculous notion, and it's beneath a reply.' Grace strode from the room.

Faith turned on Phoebe and Emma Kate. 'Where is your charity? You both should be ashamed of yourself, and you, Emma Kate, why one day you may be *Mrs* Vincent and that role will include being charitable to your husband's tenants. You could learn a lot from Grace.'

'I do charitable work,' Emma Kate refuted. 'But I don't live and breathe it as Grace does. Besides, Mr Vincent only has a house beyond York, not tenants. Although his father does.' Emma Kate was thoughtful. 'The Vincent family may or may not be charitable people. I had better find out before revealing too much of Grace's work. What do you think, Phoebe?'

Faith rolled her eyes as the two sisters discussed Mr Vincent again for the umpteenth time that morning. She was glad to leave the dining room and go upstairs. There was at least two hours before the appearance of the said man. Two hours in which she could read Jane Austen.

* * *

GRACE PULLED the dogcart to a halt at the end of the first row of houses. Spring was sending out tentative signs of its impending emergence. Melting snow dripped from trees and rooftops and, in places, patches of bright green grass poked through the mud.

Gathering her skirts off the ground, and grabbing a bag she brought with her, Grace made her way down the lane to the door of number three. She smiled to three women standing on a doorstep gossiping. A cool nod of their heads was their response and Grace turned back to the door with a sigh. These people weren't openly aggressive anymore, but neither did they trust her. She was startled when one of the women addressed her.

'Is it true, yer startin' a school fer our kids?'

'Yes. Yes, it is. The barn at Woodruff House is nearly ready. I wish to start next week.'

'Don't know why yer botherin'. You'll not get anybody.'

'Then that shall be a great shame.' Grace frowned. 'I think the children of these rows could lead the way in showing others that it doesn't matter how poor you are, you can still learn to write your name. It will benefit their futures, should they attend.'

'What future? Your lot made sure we don't have a future,' another woman called out.

'There are other jobs besides working down a mine.' Grace knocked on the door of number three. The last thing she wanted was to get into an argument.

The door opened, and Hilda Ferris squinted at her visitor. 'Aye?'

'Mrs Ferris. I was wondering if I could have a word?'

'Whorra about?' Her eyes narrowed suspiciously.

'May I come in?'

The Ferris woman opened the door wider, allowing Grace to enter. The stench of unwashed bodies in the closeness of the small room nearly knocked Grace off her feet. She quelled the need to put her handkerchief to her nose. Numerous pairs of eyes stared at her from different positions around the hearth. Dirty faces and ragged clothes adorned thin limbs of children of indiscernible ages. Opening the bag she brought, Grace showed the children the oranges within. With a smile, she gave the bag to the child closest and turned her attention to Mrs Ferris. 'I've come about your two eldest daughters.'

'Oh? They done summick?'

'No, nothing, I assure you.' Grace quickly appeased her. 'I would like them to come work in the kitchen at Woodruff House. Only, I cannot pay them a wage, but they will have food, clothing, shoes and board. Also, I will send you a basket of food each week.'

Mrs Ferris scowled. 'No money?'

'No, sorry.'

A child sidled up with orange juice slicing dirty streaks down his chin. 'Can I have the bed ter meself then, Ma?'

The child received a clip behind the ear for his troubles. 'No, yer bloody can't! Now, go git Alma and Minnie.'

Presently, the two girls came in grumbling about cold fingers and frozen toes from collecting water from the well down the lane. Their mother quickly told them the news of their employment. Astonished, both girls looked at Grace with wide eyes glowing from pale faces.

'You will be treated well,' Grace told them, hoping they would not become hysterical. With relief, she saw the girls smile and turn to each other in excitement, before quickly dashing off to gather what few possessions they had.

Grace stepped outside and appreciatively breathed in. The crisp fresh air was like nectar to bees, intoxicating. The three women opposite looked at her and she smiled. Allowing the girls to say goodbye to their family, she went up to the old dogcart and replaced the empty bag under the seat. The ride home would be tight, for the dogcart really only held two people, but the girls were slight, and she was sure they would fit.

After a final wave, the girls ran up the lane and stood behind the cart waiting, for Grace to move on.

'Oh no, girls. You shan't walk behind. Come and sit here beside me. There's room.'

Giggling, the girls scrambled onto the seat, and with a little squeal as the horse lurched forward, they turned to wave goodbye to the pit rows.

Once they had negotiated the track up onto the flat fields, Grace relaxed and turned to the sisters. 'So, how old are you both, and who's who?'

'I'm Alma, and I'm fifteen.' The girl at the end of the seat spoke up first.

'And I'm Minnie. I was fourteen last week,' the other added shyly.

'Well, I hope you both enjoy being at Woodruff House.'

'Oh, we will, Miss Woodruff. Anything is better than home.' Alma nodded wisely. 'Or working on the slag heaps.'

Grace hid a grin. She relaxed and gently flapped the reins. A sudden wrench, and a loud crack sent the dogcart sideways. They screamed as one side of the cart hit the ground with a teeth-shattering thump. Grace found the breath knocked from her as both girls landed on her. One wheel rolled some feet away and came to rest on the grass. Frightened, the horse shied and tried to bolt, dragging the broken cart along the track. The girls screamed again and hung onto the seat. The hard, wet ground brushed Grace's cheek as they were hauled along. One-handed, Grace pulled on the reins to steady the horse, while she also tried to hang on. Gradually, they jolted to a stop wedged in a muddy ditch by the side of the road.

As their senses cleared, they heard shouting and running behind them. Gingerly, Grace glanced back, trying not to move in case the horse bolted again. A man ran towards them.

The girls were above her, gripping the seat for dear life, their eyes wide in pale faces.

Moving to sit up caused pain to shoot up her arm from her wrist. 'Girls, are you all right?' she croaked.

'Yes, Miss Woodruff,' Alma mumbled, leaning up away from her sister, who was squashed between them.

In a scatter of stones, George Walters skidded to a halt beside the lopsided dogcart and knelt down beside Grace. 'Is anyone hurt?'

'No, I don't think so, Mr Walters,' Grace mumbled, easing her shoulder from where it was jabbed hard into the ground.

'Can you help me out, Mr Walters?' Alma asked.

'Right, lass.' He lifted Alma from the cart while the horse rolled its eyes in terror. 'Now you, young Minnie,' he instructed, as Alma stood shaking by the roadside. When both girls were free of the cart, he moved around to Grace.

He took the reins from her stiff fingers, tied them to the dogcart's front rail, and then gently put his hands under Grace and lifted her bodily.

The pain from her wrist made her cry out as Mr Walters adjusted her weight in his arms. 'Where do you hurt, Miss Woodruff?'

'My wrist,' Grace whispered, cradling it against her chest. She glanced up and found herself staring into his deep green eyes. At close range, she noted the green was darker around the iris. Fine crinkles creased the corners of his eyes, indicating he either smiled or squinted a lot. He returned her stare boldly, and she was shocked when her stomach tightened.

'Can you stand?'

She nodded, acutely aware of his strong arms holding her, supporting her against his broad chest. He smelt of soap, and his hair was damp. She had an insane urge to run her fingers through it. He gently stood her upright and she hated the break of contact. 'Thank you.'

He took out a folded handkerchief from his trouser pocket and dabbed it gently against her cheek. 'A few scratches,' he murmured.

Breathless at his feather-like touch, she willed herself to stand still and not give in to the weakness of her wobbly legs.

'Girls, come and stand by Miss Woodruff,' he ordered, before going to give the horse the once over. Satisfied that the horse had come to no harm, he un-harnessed it from the shattered cart. 'Can this horse be ridden?'

Her mind was in a whirl and her heart thumped like a drum. Something primal and intense awoke deep inside. Her senses were attuned to his every movement, his every word. 'Yes. Apples can be ridden.'

'Right then,' he swung himself up onto Apple's back, 'I'll go on to Woodruff House and let them know.'

Grace blinked, desperate to clear her head and summon her dignity. Why on earth had she reacted to him holding her? He of all people! He made it plain he didn't like her, had been barely civil to her on the few times they met. Confused and a little scared by her fascination of him, she directed her feelings into anger, an emotion she knew very well and one she felt safe using. 'You expect us to stay out here in the open and wait?'

'What do you suggest, then?'

'The girls and I can walk to Woodruff House. Thank you for your help.' She dismissed him in a brusque tone.

Grace waited for him to dismount and then nodding to the girls to retrieve their belongings, she walked past him with her head held high and took the horse's bridle with her good hand.

'Alma, why do you and Minnie go to Woodruff House?' He forestalled them, ignoring Grace.

'To work, Mr Walters. Got set on t' day.'

Grace turned back. 'Come Alma, Minnie.' She pinned him with a frosty stare. 'Good day, Mr Walters, and thank you again.' She inclined her head in a way that would have made Heather proud.

'I'll take the horse for you, so you don't hurt your wrist anymore.' He marched up and grasped the bridle. Without waiting for them, he made for her home.

They walked in silence for half a mile. The throbbing ache in her wrist made Grace grit her teeth with every step. The girls' excitement of an hour before had dwindled. Grace looked at their pale faces and felt sorry for them. No doubt, their thoughts had turned to what lay ahead.

Head bowed, she stole a glance from beneath her lashes at his long legs. His work boots were well worn and in need of repair, but they were clean. The dark brown trousers he wore fitted his lean muscles comfortably, and again Grace swallowed. *What is wrong with me! Why do the most unsuitable men affect me? And why do I think of him as the handsome George Henry and not the dismissive Mr Walters!*

Unintentionally, she had learnt a little about him while on her many missions to the pit rows. He was a loner, and a bachelor, who was friend to all but didn't seek company. Quiet and intelligent, he persuaded as many men as possible to attend the Mechanics' Institute in Leeds, of which he was a member.

Cresting a small hill, they saw the rooftops of Woodruff House nestled amongst the trees below them.

Mr Walters paused with the horse. 'You feeling all right, Miss Woodruff?'

'Yes, thank you.' Grace walked on. His presence unnerved her, made her think of things she shouldn't.

By the time they reached the drive to the house, the girls were falling behind, and Grace felt weak from pain. Her wrist had swollen badly.

Near the front steps stood the Ellsworths' carriage. Purposely, she led the little group around to the back of the house. Johnny came running to take.

The kitchen's soothing warmth welcomed them. Wearily, Grace sat at the large table. 'Mrs Hawksberry, some tea for Mr Walters and the girls, if you please.'

'Nay, Miss, what's happened ter yer?' Mrs Hawksberry wobbled over for a closer inspection.

'I've simply hurt my wrist, nothing to worry about. Mr Walters helped us.'

Mr Walters' tall frame and quiet authority dominated the room. 'She'll need the doctor.'

'Nonsense.' Grace shook her head at Mrs Hawksberry, warning her not to argue.

Mrs Hawksberry turned her attention to the two girls. 'What's yer names?'

'I'm Alma, this is me sister, Minnie.' Alma whispered. Both girls looked around in awe.

Mrs Hawksberry turned to her one and only helper. 'Tekk this pair upstairs to Hopeland. They'll need a bath and burn their clothes,' she uttered in disgust. 'God knows what they carry.'

Grace forced a weak smile at the girls. 'You both have new uniforms waiting on your beds. When you are finished, come back down for your meal. Your work starts tomorrow. Mrs Hawksberry will instruct you.'

'I'll get some linen to strap that wrist,' Mrs Hawksberry said, going out with them.

Mr Walters took a step. 'I'll be off too, Miss Woodruff. Good day.'

'Thank you, Mr Walters. I am grateful for your help.' Their gazes met and held for a fraction longer than necessary. He glanced across the room as the door opened and Doyle stepped into the kitchen.

'Grace? Mrs Hawksberry says you've...' Doyle faltered on seeing the other man.

'I'm fine, really.' Grace reassured, turning in her seat towards him. 'A sprain, I think. The dogcart broke an axle and tipped us out. But...'

'Who was he?' Doyle asked, coming closer.

Spinning about, Grace found Mr Walters gone. *What a strange man he is.* Tightness filled her throat. A wave of emotion she couldn't name, threatened to engulf her. *Shock. It's just shock.* Yet, a longing to race out the kitchen and call him back was hard to ignore. She breathed in deeply. 'Oh ... him. He's Mr Walters. He helped us.'

Doyle knelt in front of her. 'I'll send for the doctor.'

'Don't fuss, Doyle!' Grace snapped. When his expression changed to one of hurt, she leant forward to cup his cheek in her hand. 'I'm sorry,' she whispered, before breaking into sobs that shook her body.

· · ·

GRACE FOUGHT boredom as her mother ranted, yet again, about the schoolroom. They stood in the hall, as Diana waited for the carriage to arrive from the stables, for she, Emma Kate and Phoebe were to visit Heather and discuss the wedding. Mr Vincent's proposal came at a welcomed time; it gave the family something else to talk about besides Grace's devotion to the lower classes.

'Are you listening to me?' Diana demanded.

Grace turned her wandering attention back to her mother. 'Yes, Mama. Have you finished? I wish to go about my work.'

'Your work?' Diana's head snapped forward, her eyes narrowed. 'Teaching filthy, scabby-faced urchins is not the kind of work suitable for you.' She tugged on her white kid gloves with a scowl. 'I allowed it at first, for I thought it to be a passing fancy, but I should have known with you nothing is so easy. Haven't you learnt your lesson from the incident with your father's bastard!'

'Don't you dare, Mama!' She felt an angry flush colour her cheeks. 'Daniel Thomas was my brother and I loved him. He was the one good thing in my life.'

'Nonsense! You have a great deal to be grateful for. You have looks, intelligence *and* you could have marriage proposals from men of quality if you only made an effort. Look at how well Emma Kate has done. At least two of my daughters have managed to respect their family.'

'Mama, I don't wish to receive proposals. Besides, I enjoy this particular work and it's doing some good.'

'Good?' Diana barked. 'What good can come from riffraff knowing their letters? I'm telling you, this will cause trouble. You mark my words. The selfishness in you is outstanding. You think nothing of your family, nor your sister's recent good fortune.'

'Of course I'm happy for Emma Kate.' Grace tried not to let her temper rule her. However, her mother's ignorance and her uncharitable views of others less fortunate drove her to despair.

'Mama, my teaching the children does not interrupt your life in any way.'

'It certainly does!' Diana stamped her foot like a petulant child. 'From my very own windows I see scum running through the gardens. I heard Johnny found them raiding the vegetable gardens!' Diana straightened her collar as Emma Kate and Phoebe descended the staircase. 'So you see, Grace, as much as you think you can make a difference, sometimes these things simply do not turn out.'

'I will make it work, Mama. Many people have proved the lower classes can be rather intelligent when given the chance to learn. A number of society's finest have given their time and money to better the lives of the poor. I thought you would find it creditable to advocate my work to your friends and show them we, as a family, are not frightened to embrace the poor wretches of this world.'

Stunned at the speech, Diana blinked rapidly for a moment. 'You aren't becoming a secret Reformist are you?'

Grace rolled her eyes skywards. 'No, Mama.'

Diana raised an eyebrow suspiciously. 'I wouldn't be surprised.'

'I'm keeping the school open, Mama, and the children will not disrupt the gardens again, I promise.'

'They shan't have the chance,' Diana threw over her shoulder as Doyle came to open the door for them. 'I have written to William to come and put a stop to it. He will arrive presently.'

'William is coming? Why was I not informed?' Grace thundered.

Diana turned on the top step as her two daughters entered the carriage. Ignoring Grace, she continued with her tirade. 'It was bad enough you teaching a few of the little brats, but now it has grown to a whole roomful *and* you have Faith helping you! *That* I will not tolerate.'

'Mama...'

Once inside the carriage, Diana leaned out of the window. 'And, dear daughter, this is still my house and I shall invite whomever I please!'

Grace watched the carriage roll away and sighed heavily as Doyle came to stand beside her. 'Does she not understand how much good it does, not only for the children but for us, too? This schoolroom has given Faith, Letitia and I something worthwhile to do. Letitia's interest has been so encouraging. Have you noticed the colour in her cheeks lately?'

'Yes, I have. She is looking well. But your mother has no idea Miss Letitia spends time in the schoolroom. She only just became aware that Miss Faith does.'

'I'll not give it up.' Grace went back inside and retrieved her shawl from the small cloakroom. 'I'll be in the school room should anyone need me, Doyle.'

She ran lightly down the steps, across the lawns and around the back of the house. She had thrown herself into teaching the children, most of whom didn't even want to be there, but attended because of the one bowl of broth each child received at the end of the morning's lesson. Yet, despite their sullen acceptance of her attempts to educate them, she had found teaching a wonderful experience.

The April sun shone through the branches of the fruit trees in the orchard. Spring blossom budded in profusion along the gnarled limbs. Beneath the rows of trees, a carpet of meadow grass and flowers vied for the sun's rays. At intervals, a lone ladysmock opened its petals, but the best show was still a week or two away. Then, the whole two acres would be a living ripple of colour and scent. Grace reached up to sniff appreciatively at the new tender buds of apple blossom. A surge of energy bubbled inside.

A deep longing to ride came over her. She missed her horse and cantering along the countryside's roads. Riding was once her means of escaping a house too full of complex females and her father's bullying. Without that little freedom, she felt suffocated. Turning swiftly, she strode for the stables. Johnny sat outside the stables polishing a piece of harness. He looked up at her approach and smiled.

'Johnny, saddle up a horse, if you please.'

He stared at her and the smile froze on his lips. 'There's only Flinty in't stall, Miss. Mr Sykes has Apples and Ginger for the carriage horses now. That's all we have left.'

'I am aware of that, Johnny.' She stemmed her impatience, but was itching to go. 'Flinty will do then.'

The boy's face fell further. 'Er...He's been really bad tempered. Mr Sykes has tied 'im ter the stall ter improve his behaviour.' The lad reddened. 'He's mad for the fillies, if you get me meanin', Miss.'

'He'll be fine.' Grace dismissed his concern. 'Oh and Johnny, I don't want the side-saddle. I'll use my father's saddle.' She left him open-mouthed and marched along to the schoolroom situated at the end of the next long building.

A few children, early for lessons, had gathered and were playing about.

'Children,' Grace greeted them with a smile. She spied Faith crossing the courtyard and went to meet her. 'Faith, I have to go out. You have the children this morning.'

'Alone?' Faith's eyes widened. 'I cannot do it alone. The boys refuse to listen to me, and Tommy Burke enjoys baiting me.'

'If they don't behave send them home. Missing a bowl of Mrs Hawksberry's broth will pull them into line. Speak with authority, Faith. I know you can do it. Letitia will help. She only has to scowl at the boys to quieten them.' Grace turned back to the stables, anxious to be on her way.

'But what shall I teach them?'

'Work on the alphabet with them. If all else fails, read to them. They enjoy that.' Grace picked up her skirts and ran. Desire to be free from the house and its responsibilities ran through her veins like molten lava. Her footsteps on the stone flags matched the chant in her brain. Must get away. Must get away.

Johnny led the large Clydesdale stallion out of his box. Near the mounting block he tightened the girth. 'Eh, Miss, he's not been worked for a few days. He'll be a handful,' he warned. 'He's not used to a saddle, he's a plough horse,' he added in panic, as though she was a stranger to the estate and didn't know all the livestock they owned.

Grace lifted her skirts high and leapt from the mounting block onto the saddle. Thrusting her slipper-clad feet into the stirrups, she grabbed the reins. 'Gee up there, Flinty.' At her urging, the spirited young horse trotted out of the yard and into the low fields behind the stables.

Johnny watched them go with a mixture of awe and envy. He turned as Faith came to stand beside him. 'You missed her, Miss Faith. She was in a frightful hurry. She didn't even change her clothes or put boots on.'

With troubled eyes, Faith followed the progress of her sister astride the horse's broad back as they climbed the hill beyond the fields. Grace was as tight as a coiled spring and it frightened her. *What will it be that shall set her off?*

* * *

Grace let the stallion have his head. She was past caring if this was a wise thing to do as he tore along the narrow winding tracks across the hills behind the house. They scattered sheep and cows with scant regard to the offspring the animals carried or the newborns at their feet as they made their way to Whin Moor. Despite his size and weight, the horse pounded his way over the heather and bracken with speed, while she merely hung on, surprised at her own horsemanship in staying on the large horse.

After half a mile, Grace reined Flinty in and let him pick his own way up the bridle paths. Behind them the estate faded away, along with the villages of Scholes and Barwick. On the west horizon, the Pennines butted proudly skywards. To the east lay Potterton and beyond that, Black Fen.

They went as far as Wothersome, before they rested. She sat back in the saddle and scanned the countryside. Dry stonewalled fields made a patchwork of colour stretching for miles around. Blocks of thick woodland and squat clumps of gray stone farm buildings broke the landscape of undulating pastures. With the sun warm on her back, Grace breathed in the sharp, clear air. 'Let us never go home, Flinty,' she spoke into the quiet surrounding them. The horse's ears twitched at her voice and she smiled.

Presently, they made their way down to the edge of the village of Thorner. Hunger pains rolled in her stomach while the sun shone on her bare head, but she was disinclined to go home yet. Not wanting to encounter people, Grace steered Flinty off the main paths and headed back south towards Saw Wood. Shortly after entering the wood, they found a trickling beck at their feet. Flinty snorted, pulling at the reins.

Sliding off his back, Grace led him to the water's edge to drink. The deep shade of the wood was cool to them both, but comfortable. When the horse wandered off to nibble at clumps of spring grass, Grace found a flat rock and sat.

She scooped up a handful of clear, cold water and drank thirstily. A bird's call, high above, rang out. In the rushing water, minuscule fish darted, and Grace watched them in fascination. Nature's beauty provided a soothing balm from the thoughts that plagued her mind.

Slight movement out the corner of her eye caused her to glance up. She gave a start, as across the beck, near hidden amongst the trees, stood a man. He walked closer, out of the shadows, and a burst of sunlight through the branches shone on his face.

George Walters stood staring at her in surprise. With a giant leap of his long legs, he jumped the water and landed effortlessly some feet away. A thumping tattoo of Grace's heart caused her breath to quicken. He came closer and looked down at her. She swore his green eyes could see into her very soul, such was the intensity of his stare.

'I never expected to see you here.' He spoke in a deep, solemn voice.

'I came...I was riding.'

His gaze lifted to the horse beyond, before returning to frown at the black day dress she wore, the slippers peeping out beneath it. 'Your wrist is better?'

'Yes, completely.' She found it impossible to tear herself away from his gaze.

Walters turned to glance along the beck. He seemed to hesitate. 'There's a wide pool further up. I'm off to tickle some trout.'

Grace nodded like someone struck dumb.

He walked several paces, and then turned back. 'Care to watch?'

'Er, yes, very well.' She stood and went to gather Flinty's reins.

'Can you sit and not talk or move for minutes on end?' he asked sharply as she neared him.

'I'm sure I'm capable,' her retort was equally acute.

'Well, this is my dinner. I'll not be going back to a table full of food like some.'

Grace seethed. 'Do I have to apologize for the differences of our stations?'

He raised an eyebrow. 'Not at all, Miss Woodruff, just as long as you know food is not taken for granted by many.'

'I am aware, Mr Walters,' she said tartly, stepping behind him as they moved on.

They walked some way before the beck rounded a bend and opened out into a large, deep pool. Along the bank, the tree roots hugged the soil. Here, he laid down the bag slung over his shoulders. He took off his thin, short coat and rolled up the sleeves of his shirt. Grace diverted her gaze from his brown, brawny arms. It seemed he spent plenty of time in the sun during summer to allow his arms to be such a deep shade. Her stomach tightened in familiar awareness.

Grace sat on a moss-covered log and watched him lie on his stomach at the edge of the water. Many minutes passed before he ever so slowly slid his arm into the water without making a ripple. Once his whole arm was submerged, he neither moved nor spoke. The patch of sunlight she sat in was warm and throwing her head back, she closed her eyes to its rays.

From his position, George Henry allowed himself the luxury of looking at her. The creamy column of her neck invited to be kissed. Her glorious chestnut hair having escaped its holdings during her ride, now tumbled down her back, making her appear like a sixteen-year-old maiden. As she relaxed, the worried strain from her face. She was delightful, fine featured and delicate. The coolness of the water sent his arm numb, but his mind and body came alive, painfully so. He shook his head at his own stupidity and in one quick movement jumped to his feet, startling her.

'Did you get one?' Grace asked innocently, sitting straighter.

'No.' He strode to his bag and hoisted it across his shoulders. He reached for his coat, avoiding her questioning gaze. 'I must be goin'. Good day.'

'Oh, really?' Puzzlement furrowed her brow. She stood, bewildered by his quick actions.

He walked away, only to stop suddenly. He ached to turn around and drag her into his arms, but what good would it achieve? It would only heighten his passion for her and likely earn himself a slap. No. She was off limits to men like him. He sucked in a breath and, without turning around to look at her one last time, strode into the trees.

CHAPTER 23

William stepped to the window, teacup in hand, to wait for Grace's return. Behind him, Diana and Felicity chatted amiably. Their voices grated on his taut nerves. His journey north from London with Felicity had been tense. Remonstrations and accusations had flown between them without pause. That Felicity accompanied him was startling enough, but to have her rant at him with words and tears at every opportunity almost drove him insane.

She refused to believe his explanations that visiting the Woodruffs was necessary. Her rages had turned to sullen bouts of misery until the carriage came to a halt at the front steps of Woodruff House. He was astonished, on entering the house, to find his wife instantly become charming and likeable as she greeted the women. The amazing ease with which she could change her demeanour never failed to surprise him.

He turned now, to hear Felicity nearly purring in rapture as she spoke of their marriage and forthcoming child. The girls all told him how lucky he was to have such a gracious wife. He forced a smile. The teacup trembled only slightly as he placed it on the tray. 'If you'll excuse me, ladies, I shall retire to the study and the account books I know await me there.' Bowing to Diana, he refused to meet Felicity's eyes and left the drawing room.

William sighed in relief on making it into the hall without his wife calling him back on some pretext or other; a habit she delighted in, much to his frustration. At the study door, he saw Grace emerge from the back corridor and his heart missed a beat.

'William. I see you disregarded my instructions.' Grace gave him a quelling stare as she paused in front of him. 'You *did* receive my letter?'

'Actually, I've come to ask its meaning. Why do you wish not to see me anymore?'

'You need to ask?'

'Grace, I've told you...'

'You've told me nothing I want to hear, William, you never did. Do not make any mention of you divorcing Felicity to me. I won't be a part of it and I do not thank you for adding this pressure to my life.'

He slumped. 'I made a mistake. I admit that now. However, we still have a chance.'

Grace shook her head. 'No, we don't.'

She made to pass him, but he shot out a hand and stopped her. 'I love you.'

Tenderness filled her eyes and she sighed. 'There was a time when those words would have been enough to make me die for you.'

'Grace...'

'No, William.' Grace raised her chin. 'You are married with a child on the way to bear your name.'

'Yes, but we can be together. Felicity has a price, I know she does.'

'And your child?'

He wiped a hand over his eyes in weariness.

'I do not love you as you would wish me to, William. I realized that some time ago.'

'Good God, look at you two,' Felicity crackled from behind them. A look of madness twisted her beautiful features. 'It's like a scene from a Shakespearean tragedy!'

They sprang apart. Grace turned on her heel and disappeared along the back corridor.

Rounding on his wife, William felt an urge to link his fingers around her porcelain-white throat and squeeze. 'Go away, Felicity, before I say or do something that isn't gentlemanly.'

She laughed liked someone deranged. 'You? A gentleman?'

Phoebe and Emma Kate came noisily towards them, begging Felicity's opinion on the hymns to be sung at Emma Kate's wedding.

As the girls drew Felicity off, William entered the study and closed the door. All anger vanished as he leant his back against it. Like a fog creeping over the moors, despondency cloaked him. Fear clawed at him, a fear he couldn't shake, but he knew what it was. He lifted his hands up and they trembled.

* * *

'Now again! A. B. C...' Grace walked behind the seated children who sang out the alphabet. She smiled as the little ones stumbled over the sequence, and tapped a boy's hand with her cane as he sat picking his nose. The barn was terribly stuffy in the heat of June. The summer sun shining outside made the children fidgety. Grace knew of their longing to be away enjoying it; she wished it for herself, too.

A sudden rush at the door faltered the children's recitation as Johnny bounded into the barn. 'Miss, yer wanted at the house.'

'What is it, Johnny?' Grace frowned. 'Has there been an accident?'

'No, Miss. Mr Swindale is waiting for you in the study.'

She instructed one of the older girls in the class to take over, and after warning the boys to behave, hurried over to the house. On entering the study, she nodded in Swindale's direction. 'I wasn't expecting you today.'

He rose to greet her. 'I apologize for the inconvenience, Miss Woodruff, but it is urgent business I bring.'

'Oh?' Grace sat down behind the desk as Swindale passed her a sheaf of papers.

'Kendleton Colliery has sold.'

Relief and surprise flooded her. 'Wonderful! Oh, well done, Mr Swindale.'

'The sum offered is under the evaluation we had taken of the mine, but we are in no position to be choosy.'

'I agree.'

'Mr Ross signed the final papers and I received them this morning. They are those there before you. The new owner takes control Saturday, the first day of July.'

'Very good.' Grace scanned the papers. 'Anything else?'

'Indeed there is, Miss Woodruff, and it's not all good.'

Her heart plummeted.

* * *

Doyle stood on the front steps of the house as the carriage wheels crunched to a halt on the drive. He assisted the women into the house, noticing the red eyes and damp handkerchiefs. After taking Diana's gloves and parasol, he turned to help Grace. 'Is Miss Emma Kate safely away?'

'Yes. She has married and gone with her husband.' Grace's golden eyes told him of the sad farewell. 'We shall take tea in the drawing room, after we have changed.'

'Very well.' Doyle gave a small bow.

The Woodruff women plodded upstairs and for once Diana's or Phoebe's chatter didn't accompany them.

Grace washed and changed, but lingered in her room. A restlessness sent her from window to bed and back again. Lifting aside the lace curtains, she looked down on the head gardener putting his back into digging over a garden bed that once held flowers but would now grow vegetables. Raising her eyes, she scanned further afield to the pastures her family once owned.

With a light thump, her forehead rested against the windowpane. She felt old. The secret inside her begged to be told; there could be no more delay. Emma Kate was married and away to a new future; so one less would be hurt. Straightening, Grace gathered what strength she had left and left the room.

In the gallery, she encountered Hopeland.

'Oh Miss, I was coming to get you. Mrs Woodruff is taking tea in her sitting room and wishes you to join her.'

Grace entered Diana's rooms and found her remaining sisters talking in subdued tones. Her heart weighed heavy. Accepting a cup of tea from Faith, she took it to the window and looked out. A fine summer's day brightened the landscape.

'I thought Gabriella seemed a little distracted at the wedding, didn't you Grace?' Diana asked, inspecting the oatmeal biscuit she held.

'I believe she was feeling off colour,' Grace replied without turning.

Diana wrinkled her nose. 'Oh? Well, I do hope she hasn't passed anything onto the rest of us.'

'I doubt it, Mama. What she is suffering from none of us shall catch. She is with child.'

'Oh, my!' Diana squealed. 'How splendid, and so soon.' However, the glee fled from her face as quickly as it came. 'I do hope Mr Morgan treats Gaby with some respect, she isn't like one of his breeding cows.'

'Mama!' Phoebe pealed with laughter.

'I'm sure he loves Gaby very well, Mama, and will treat her accordingly.' Grace sipped her tea.

'This house is becoming rather empty, don't you agree?' Letitia said in a near whisper. 'Such a big house for the five of us.'

'Nonsense,' Diana barked. 'We shall be quite happy.'

'Actually, Mama, Letitia is right. This house is too large for us now. We cannot afford it.' Grace walked back to the group. 'Mr Swindale can no longer find ways of keeping us financial.'

Diana reared back as though struck. 'What are you saying?'

Grace took a deep breath and knew she had to tell them the truth now. 'We must sell Woodruff House.' The collective cry that arose from her words would be heard downstairs she knew.

'I'll never allow it!' Diana snapped. 'I shall speak to William!'

'I've already corresponded with William. He, Mr Swindale and I have devised a plan to prevent complete bankruptcy. Part of that plan is to sell this house.'

Faith stood somewhat shakily. 'Is there no other way?'

'No. We've tried everything.' Grace turned to her mother who appeared ready to faint. 'Mama, please don't distress yourself too much. Provisions are made; none of us shall be begging on the street.'

'Ruined! Ruined!' Diana wailed. 'We are ruined and shall be buried in paupers' graves! I cannot bear it!'

'Mama.' Grace stepped forward ready to slap the rising hysterics out of her mother. 'We are not ruined, just reduced in circumstances.'

'My bed! I must go to my bed,' Diana keened like a toothless old witch in the dead of night.

Shaking her head, Grace left Phoebe and Faith to deal with her and escaped the room.

In the gallery, Letitia hurried to her side. A look in her dangerously over-bright eyes stopped Grace in her tracks. 'Letitia?'

'I can't go.'

'Go where?'

'Wherever you and William want to send me.' Her soulful gaze pinned Grace and Letitia's grip on her arm hurt. 'I'll die if you do.'

'Darling,' Grace prised Letitia's thin hand off her arm and grasped it between her own, 'we are not sending you anywhere.'

'I have to stay here … It's not safe out there for me, you understand?' she implored her. 'I can't manage out there.'

'Listen to me, no one is sending you away. Why would you think so?'

Letitia stepped back, her eyes widened in fear. 'Mama hates me. I've seen how she looks at me, Heather too. They think I'm disgusting. They discuss me like some repulsive insect.'

'No, dearest...' Grace hesitated.

Letitia laughed like a madwoman and then abruptly stopped. 'You think you are so clever, but you're not. You don't know me!'

'What are you talking about?'

Wrapping her arms around herself, Letitia inched away. Her gaze darted along the gallery as though looking for an outlet. 'I swear to you I haven't touched a drop of anything for days!'

Stunned, Grace froze. 'Days? What do you mean days? You've been home for months.'

Letitia clapped both hands over her mouth.

Grace advanced on her. 'Have you been drinking since your return?' She grabbed Letitia by the shoulders. 'Tell me!'

Lowering her hands, Letitia grinned. 'I tricked you. I'm sharper than you'll ever be.'

'Oh no, please …' The anger died instantly, and Grace's hands fell from her sister. 'Where did you get it? I forbid it in the house. You have no money.'

'And you have no imagination, Grace.' Letitia was triumphant.

'But you've been so…'

'Sober?' Her mood swung to being snappy and secretive. 'How would you know how I've been?'

'I've kept an eye on you. Never have you seemed under the influence of alcohol. You've been quiet, sometimes unpredictable and temperamental, but that's your nature. Not once did I see evidence …' Grace shook her head in bewilderment. 'I don't understand. I've seen you teaching the children …' Suddenly it dawned on her, and she felt paralyzed by its effect. 'You got the *children* to get it for you.'

An evil grin spread over Letitia's face and a devilish sparkle glittered in her wild eyes. 'You think I'd willingly spend my time with that lot of vermin?' She pranced around the gallery snickering. 'I'm no martyr of charity like you and Faith, dear sister.'

It was a catastrophe which Grace had not see coming. Dazed, she stumbled to her bedroom door and Letitia's laughter followed her. Grace glanced down at her hands and saw they were shaking. A red mist of sheer fury clouded her vision. Blood drained from her face as the urge to strike her sister took hold. Slowly, she turned, her eyes narrowed with spite. 'I'll never forgive you for this! I care little for where you go or what happens to you now.'

Frightened, Letitia fell to her knees to grab Grace's skirts. 'I'm sorry!'

Grace threw Letitia from her. 'I've tried, Letitia. I've forgiven your nasty ways and gone out of my way to help you, and yet you repay me by using innocent children. At this moment I never want to see you again!'

'You care more for a bunch of scum than for me, your own sister?'

Movement to the left caused Grace to turn her head. Diana, Faith, Phoebe and Doyle stared wide-eyed at them. 'Yes, look!' She screamed. 'Look, but don't help. Oh no, one mustn't dirty one's hands, must one! See, Mama, see what happens when you relinquish your motherly duties! This is what occurs when one is too weak to stand up to a lifetime of bullying. Father was to blame but he is not alone. *You* could have made a difference, yet it was easier to lock yourself away in your rooms, wasn't it?'

Grace stepped away from the pitiful creature on the floor. 'Well, Mama, now it's your turn to take care of your family.' She entered her bedroom and slammed the door.

CHAPTER 24

A gentle breeze billowed Grace's black skirts as she strolled over the fields to Morgan Farm. White, fluffy clouds sprinkled the blue sky and swallows soared before darting back to the treetops. Coming to a dry stone wall on the boundary of Morgan's fields, she paused to lean against it and fish in her pocket for her letter. It had come an hour before. The plain, cream envelope showed William's bold writing. A deep sigh escaped her as she turned it over in her hands. Deftly, she tore it open and read.

Dearest, Grace.

Two hours ago, my son was placed in my arms. A fine boy, the image of my father.

My heart is glad he is safe, an outcome I did not always believe would occur.

Please pass on to your mother and sisters this glorious news.

I have implored my mother to visit London again to see her grand-child as I believe it will be some time before we travel north again.

Swindale informs me not all is well at Woodruff House. I beg of you to write and tell me what new troubles have arisen. Your mother's latest letter informed me of Letitia's devilishness and I am in the process of

relieving you of that particular burden, but I shall write more of that
when I have further news.

Faithfully yours,

William.

'Miss Woodruff.'

Grace spun at the sound of the soft voice behind her. She stared open-mouthed at George Walters. His approach had been silent, typical of him. The unassuming aura he carried bespoke much of the man. His presence started a fluttering in her chest.

'Going for a walk?' he asked with a wry smile.

'Yes, to Morgan's Farm.'

Eyeing her with a quizzical turn of his head, he pushed both hands into his trouser pockets. 'You're closing the school.' It was a statement not a question. He made every word count.

'Yes. The house is for sale.'

He nodded. 'Shame.'

'I agree,' Grace murmured. 'We shall be sad to leave.'

'I was thinking of the children.'

'Oh, yes of course.' She blushed, he probably thought her self-centred. 'I will miss the children very much.' Her stammer deepened the flush, and she looked away. His aloof manner unnerved her. It made her want to think about him more than she cared to.

'Where will you go?' A sharpness entered his tone and his gaze was direct.

She lowered her lashes, feeling tongue-tied. 'We aren't certain …'

'You will be missed.'

She stared at him. 'I will?' A tiny, insignificant spark of something she couldn't name formed in the pit of her stomach. She was achingly aware of him and very much wanted his strong arms to hold her but then she didn't because it frightened her to acknowledge him as a man. She realized she highly respected him and wanted his good opinion. Yet, he seemed untouchable, unreal to her world.

'Aye.' George Walters stepped to the wall and leaned his fore-arms on it. His position was very close, but he did not glance her way. 'There's not many who will think of others beneath their station.'

Unreasonably, his words disappointed her. *Did she want him to miss her?* She searched for something to say. 'I'm...'

'The children enjoyed learning to write their names. I've seen the girls writing in the dirt. They've begun teaching each other.' He turned his intense, dark green eyes on her. 'One boy has asked to come with me to the Mechanics' institute.'

'Wonderful!'

'It's all because of you.'

'Oh, no...'

'Don't simper!' he scolded. 'It doesn't become you.'

Grace's eyes widened at his manner. 'I'm sorry.' She bristled at his brusqueness. No one ever spoke to her that way. Her chin rose. 'If you'll excuse me, I must be going.'

'You're a strange woman.'

Again, he had the ability to surprise. She hoped her cold expression showed him his comments were unwelcome. 'Strange?'

'Aye. Strange.'

'You are bad-mannered.'

'Not really. I speak my mind as I see it.'

'How am I strange?' She itched to slap his face.

'Not sure why, just are. I've never met a *lady* who can fit so well into the lower class.'

'Do you meet many *ladies* then?' She raised an inquiring eyebrow at him.

He smiled a secret smile. 'Ahh... that would be telling.'

'You are crude, sir!' She scoffed, spinning away.

Instantly, he seized her wrist and crushed her to him. With his other hand, he held her head still and bent to ground his lips against hers.

Caught off guard, her mind whirled as she pushed against him.

He raised his head a fraction to stare into her eyes. 'Don't fight me, sweet one,' his voice caressed. 'I would never hurt you.'

Startled more by his tender words than his abrupt embrace, Grace sprang from him. 'How dare you! What right do you have to behave in such a way? Is this how the working class men obtain their women?'

He leaned his back to the wall and sighed as if content, totally ignoring her. He chuckled, and then dared to laugh.

'What is so funny?' Grace demanded. 'Have you lost your mind?'

He edged away from the wall and came to stand a foot from her. Her eyes widened at his nearness. With a gentle hand, he cupped her cheek, rubbing his thumb softly over her bottom lip. His mouth lifted at one corner. 'Yes, I have lost my mind and I never want it back again.' He strode off, leaving her confused and breathless.

'Grace!'

Lifting her head at the sound of her name, Grace waved half-heartedly to Gaby coming along the path on the other side of the wall. After a last glance at the retreating figure of George Walters, she picked up her skirts and hastened to the gate further down. She squashed the urge to touch her lips where he had caressed them.

'Who were you talking to?' Gaby kissed her cheek and then linking her arm through Grace's.

'Um… Mr Walters, he's from the mine.'

'I've seen him before, I think, in church. He's so tall he stands out. A handsome devil, if I remember correctly.'

'Yes, I suppose,' Grace whispered. Her heart turned somersaults whenever she looked into those green eyes of his, so she guessed he had an attraction. She had to be careful for he had the power to reduce her to a quivering wreck of physical need. She mustn't fall into the same trap with him as she had done with Doyle.

Forcing the man and the feelings he stirred in her to the far recess of her mind, she summoned a smile. 'You shouldn't have walked this far.'

'Stuff and nonsense!' Gaby laughed. 'Besides, I needed a breath of fresh air and time away from Mrs Winton and Ruth. They are both in fine form today.'

'I thought they got along?'

'Oh, they do for the most part. However, some days I feel the need to hide all the knives just in case.'

They laughed together and the tension eased slightly from Grace's shoulders. 'How I envy you, Gaby,' she said wistfully.

Gaby squeezed her armed in concern. 'Your life will be happy one day, Grace, I promise.'

'You think so?' Grace gave a mock laugh. 'Letitia is locked in her room, Mama is impossible to live with, and Phoebe has disappeared to Heather's. Only Faith is willing to help make the house ready for sale.'

'Are you still teaching the children?'

'Yes, without them I would go insane, but all that will stop soon.'

'I wish I could help you more.' Gaby smiled sadly.

Grace impulsively kissed her cheek. 'You do help, by letting me come here every Sunday. The respite is wonderful, even if it's only a few hours.'

'When will the house be ready?'

'Next week, I think. Faith and I have organized for the excess furniture to be sold, and the rest will be packed ready for our move.'

Gaby bent to pluck a yellow wildflower. 'Has Mr Swindale found you a house to rent in Leeds?'

'No, not yet. It is a shame I sold my cottage. Anyway, Mama wants us to go to Scarborough and stay with cousin Verity until something can be sorted out. But can you imagine Verity's reaction to Letitia?' Grace pulled a wry face.

'I thought William was buying her a place in a gentlewoman's asylum in London?'

'Yes well, William is busy.'

'I understand. I felt so sorry for him on reading of his embarrassment in the newspaper a few weeks ago. Imagine Felicity, not only attending a ball heavily with child, but also leaving with an unknown man! It's rather shocking even for me.'

'Felicity gave him a son,' Grace stated unmoved.

'Really?' Gaby's face shone with delight. 'How lovely for William.'

'Yes. I am happy he has a son.'

Gaby stopped walking and faced her. 'I know William claimed your heart and then rejected you. It's grievous you didn't become a couple, but William is paying the price by being forever tied to Felicity.'

Grace nodded and was surprised when tears blurred Gaby's face before her.

'Oh darling, whatever is wrong?' Gaby asked aghast. 'Is it because of William or those at home?'

'I don't know.' She shook her head like a dog shaking rain off its coat. 'I'm not crying for William or Letitia or anyone! I'm crying for me, I think, and I so hate to cry!' Grace furiously wiped the tears with the back of her hand.

'You have earned the right.'

Grace put her hands to her cheeks. 'I'm so tired.'

'Of course you are, dearest. You've been everyone's support for too long.' Gaby held her tight. 'I *shall* do more to help you. I will write to William. After congratulating him on the deliverance of his son, I will then demand he secure Letitia in a good place to lighten your burden.'

'Heather says it's shameful to put Letitia in an asylum,' Grace spoke as they stepped in the direction of the farmhouse.

'What does Heather know?'

'Well, between her, Andrew and the rest of the Ellsworths, they know a lot apparently.'

'Heather was always such a mouse, then puff, she gets married and turns into a sagacious judge of righteousness!'

Grace grinned. 'True.'

'I say let Heather take in Letitia.' Gaby snorted. 'She deserves to do something worthwhile. She was appallingly rude to me last Sunday at church. That's the only time we see each other. Never does she come here.'

'Sadly, marriage has changed Heather.'

'Well, honestly, she always thought herself to be better than the rest of us. That I am having another child, and she still has none, irks her too.'

'Poor Heather.'

They reached the farmhouse and stopped in the yard to speak with John a moment. On extracting his promise to join them soon, they went inside to see the baby.

* * *

'There you are.' Faith entered the library. 'Mama's crying again.'

Grace glanced up from her inventory of the books. 'She never stops. Mama thinks hysterics will change the course of our future that if she cries enough the house will not be sold.'

Faith ran her hand lightly over the books stacked on the desk. 'I was awake all night last night.'

'Oh?' Grace moved along the bookcase.

'An idea came me and I tossed it around for hours.'

'What idea?'

'About the house.'

Grace paused to look at her sister. A tinge of hope mingled with Faith's usual serious expression. 'What?'

'It was a plan really. Silly now when I think of it.'

'Tell me.'

Faith swallowed. 'I thought we could turn this house into a school.'

'A school?' Grace's brow wrinkled. 'It's not possible. We'd need a lot of students to keep it profitable, and their parents won't pay to send them here when they can be put to work.'

'I wasn't thinking of the poor children,' Faith said in a rush. 'I mean a proper boarding school for young ladies.'

'Young ladies?' Surprise made Grace's voice higher. 'A boarding school for young ladies?'

'Yes, why not?' Faith blinked.

Putting a hand to her forehead, Grace stared. 'What an enormous proposal, Faith. You can't simply say, let's have a boarding school.'

'I know, but we can try. If we get William on our side, he can put up some of the money, and we can ask Mr Swindale to make sure all is legal and correct. We can have patrons to help finance the teachers' wages...'

'Faith! Faith, stop!' Grace shook her head and rubbed her temples. 'We have to sell the house because we cannot afford to pay our bills. How do you think we can manage a boarding school?'

'Wealthy, self-made men would be only too willing to send their daughters to a good boarding school to obtain an education.'

'You know that for certain, do you?'

Faith blushed. 'I've heard muttering to that effect, yes.'

'Where?'

'At the library in town, and ...' Faith's shoulders slumped. 'Well, if you must know I heard Heather's mother-in-law, Mrs Ellsworth, mention something some months ago.'

Grace pulled a face. 'Mrs Ellsworth?'

'Yes.' Faith straightened. 'Yes, indeed. She said that she herself was educated by French ladies at a boarding college in London, and that the north sadly lacked such refined places.'

'Do you think the world needs any more Mrs Ellsworths?' Grace grinned. 'I, for one, wouldn't want a school churning out prim, narrow-minded replicas of Mrs Ellsworth!'

'We wouldn't. Our girls would have the chance to learn everything, not only French and Latin and needlework, but Mrs Hawksberry could have classes on menus for fine dining. Our gardener could show the girls how to grow plants to fill their conservatories, we could fill the stables with ponies and let them ride over the fields on picnic days and go fishing—'

'Faith, no father will want their daughter fishing or digging in the dirt getting their hands dirty.' Grace down trod the idea.

'The aristocrats wouldn't, no, but merchant men from Leeds, York and Manchester will. The men, who only a generation ago didn't have a shilling in their pockets, but now own businesses with money lying idle *will*.'

'No, sorry, Faith, this is madness.' Grace walked back to the bookshelves.

'Why?'

Looking over her shoulder, Grace smiled despondently. 'It wouldn't work. For a start we'd need to alter some rooms upstairs for the dormitories, find teachers, patrons and pupils, and to do all that we shall need more money than Midas has. But finally and importantly, I don't want to do it.'

Faith's eyes darkened to flint with determination. 'Grace, I never want to marry, ever. You know that. I don't want to leave this house and be cooped up in some small terrace with Mama, Phoebe and Letitia. I want to do something worthwhile, and this is it. With the right people helping us, I know we can do it, or *I* can do it.'

Grace thought for a long time and then sighed deeply. 'What if I said yes,' she put up a hand to stop Faith from butting in, 'once you can show me it would be viable?'

'Good as done.'

'No, Faith, it'll be very hard convincing the community they should put money into this school.'

'It's not a school. It's a college.' Faith beamed. 'Woodruff House Ladies College.' She ran up and pecked Grace's cheek. 'I'm off to town to send a telegram to William. He has more money than he knows what to do with, so he can be the first patron!'

'Don't get your hopes up, Faith! You'll need a board of governors and...' Grace faltered as her sister ran out the door, almost bumping into Doyle, before disappearing.

'Miss Faith looks happy,' Doyle said, coming to Grace's side.

'Yes, she has some mad idea to turn this house into a ladies' college.'

'Really?' He looked impressed. 'I hope she's successful, then maybe we can all keep our jobs.'

'Well, you all have excellent references and the new owner might keep you on should we sell.'

'But I wouldn't be with you.'

'Doyle...'

'I know, I know!' He laughed at himself. 'We'd best not stray into those murky waters, hey?'

'No.' A glimmer of a smile wavered on her lips.

'Anyway, I came to tell you that a Mr Walters is here to see you.' Doyle frowned. 'He came to the front door too, not the back as he should have.'

The blood drained from Grace's face. 'Mr Walters?'

Doyle took a step closer. 'Yes. Why, what's the matter? Shall I throw him out?'

'Oh, no.' Grace moved quickly to the door to prevent her emotions from being displayed too clearly. 'I... I simply thought something bad had happened at the mine.'

Doyle hurried to keep up with her. 'But the mine is no longer yours.'

Grace stopped at the entrance to the drawing room. George

Henry was out of place standing amongst such finery in his rough country clothes. He wore no hat and summer highlights streaked his tawny hair. 'Mr Walters?'

'There you are.' He stepped forward and took her hand. 'I need you to come with me.'

'Why?' Grace drew back startled, though kept her hand within his.

'Who the hell do you think you are?' Doyle barged between them. 'Take your hands of Miss Woodruff at once!'

'Doyle, please, it is all right, really.' Grace soothed.

'Will you come?' George Walters stood totally unperturbed by Doyle's aggression; his gaze never left her face.

'Yes.' A glow of warmth spread through her body. Grace knew she would do what he asked without question, and went with him into the hall hand in hand.

'Grace!' Doyle exploded behind her. 'What do you think you're doing?' Taking her summer shawl off the hall table, Grace turned back to him. 'It must be important, Doyle, otherwise Mr Walters wouldn't come for me.'

'I don't like it.' Doyle seethed through his clenched teeth.

'I'll be back soon. Don't worry.'

They cut across the lawns and through a gap in the boundary hedge. Heavy clouds hung low, ready to spill their contents. Still, he was in no hurry, and thankfully for Grace, adjusted his long stride to suit her as they walked along the edge of fields waist high with wheat.

Soon, they crossed a lane and then climbed the hills towards the mine. At the top of the rise, where the lane forked left to the pit or right to the pit houses, he paused to let Grace catch her breath.

'You all right?'

'Yes.'

Squeezing her hand, he set off again taking the left track.

Grace asked no questions, not wanting to spoil the moment of being with him. She gave herself up to the pleasure of her hand being held in his large, rough one. Knots of tension formed in her stomach and her heart beat so rapidly it pounded in her ears. She shook her head in wonderment. This tall, silent man beside her never ceased to surprise her.

The shallow valley in which the mine nestled came into view, but George Walters steered them onto a rough, cart-made track over the next rise. Presently, they wandered down a rutted drive to stand before a two storey, red-brick house. From the outside, the house held a pleasant aspect. Its mullioned windows, numerous chimneys, and wide front door appealed.

He stood holding her hand and looking up at the house. 'Do you like this house?'

'It's a fine house.' Grace nodded, gazing at the small flowerbeds beneath the lower windows.

'There's three bedrooms, and a ladder leading up to the attic above. A good kitchen, scullery, parlour and a small dining room.'

Grace glanced at him puzzled. 'Whose house is this?'

'It's the mine manager's house.'

'Why are we here?'

'The owner of the pit got rid of that slimy coward who was the manager for your father.' He turned to her fully. His green eyes deepened to the colour of moss. 'I am now the new manager and this house comes with the position.'

'Congratulations.' Grace smiled with genuine warmth. 'I'm very happy for you.'

'The new owner is allowing me to make it over.' He indicated to the house. 'He's giving me what I need to make it modern. Eventually it'll have running water in the scullery and be fully painted and there will be new carpets. Are you sure you like it?'

'Yes.' She chuckled at his urgent insistence, amazed at his passion. She had never seen him so zealous. 'Anyway, it's your house, not mine. You are the one who has to like it, not me.'

'It's our house.'

Shock hit Grace like a blow as she digested his meaning. 'Ours?' she whispered, afraid to speak the word aloud.

'Aye.' He looked at the house and nodded. 'Once we're married, we can fix it to suit us. I'd like more gardens, especially vegetable gardens and you will want flowers...'

'Mr Walters...'

'George Henry.'

'P...Pardon?' Grace stammered.

'My name is George Henry. You're not to call me Mr Walters anymore.'

'I...You...' She tried desperately to form something sensible to say, but his words echoed in her brain. 'Married?'

'Aye.'

'We cannot!' She flung herself away from him, breaking the link of their joined hands.

He folded his arms. 'Why?'

'Why? Because we don't know each other.'

'You think I'm not good enough for you?' His terseness cut the air between them.

Grace gasped, her eyes wide. 'I'd never think that. Never.'

'But your answer is no.'

'This is madness! We've met no more than a dozen times or so, and you are asking me to marry you?' Dismayed by the warring feelings this paradox of a man wrought in her, she didn't know whether to run back home or sit in the dirt and howl like a child.

'Aye, why not?'

'How can you take it for granted we would suit?'

He shrugged. 'I simply know.'

'This is astonishing. You assumed we'd be married, just like that?'

'Look, either you do, or you don't, which is it to be?' His gaze never wavered, as though he didn't care either way.

'I cannot answer this minute!'

'Right. Well then, I'll leave you alone and get about my work.' He turned away and walked some yards before Grace's scream halted him fractionally.

'Why? Why did you do this to me?' She yelled, frantic. 'I hate you, *Mr Walters!* I hate you for giving me this option. I don't want it. Do you hear? I don't want to be in this situation!'

He walked away without answering her, without looking back.

CHAPTER 25

*S*weeping rain lashed at the windows of the carriage. William shivered inside his greatcoat although it was the end of July and until now the summer had been warm. He sighed heavily as the carriage rumbled into the drive of Woodruff House. Guilt was not a good travelling partner. Felicity's raging curses as he left their London townhouse for the station still echoed in his ears.

Doyle nodded to him on opening the carriage door and held an umbrella over them both. William ran swiftly up the wide sandstone steps and into the chilled house.

'William! Oh, dear boy!' Diana's wail rang throughout the hall as she descended the staircase. She enfolded him in a fierce embrace.

'Cousin Diana, good to see you.' He disentangled himself from her.

'You have come with news?' She implored him, helping him take off his outer clothing and handing it to Doyle.

'Yes.' William glanced around preoccupied. 'Where's Grace?'

'The weather has turned nasty, William, and we have no fuel for all the fires. My guests do not wish to come to a cold house,'

Diana whined, 'and Grace stubbornly refuses to open up the other rooms! Only the other day, Mrs Ellsworth and Heather...'

'Where's Grace?' William interrupted with a haggard sigh. Hearing Diana's complaints was the last thing he wanted.

Diana turned worried eyes to Doyle. 'Miss Grace?'

'In the study with Miss Faith and Mr Swindale, Madam,' Doyle answered.

'Get them at once.' Diana panicked. 'Quickly, Quickly. William has news for us all!'

'Calm yourself, dear Cousin. All shall be well.' William comforted.

'Shall it, William?' Diana waved her ever-present white handkerchief like a flag about her head. She squeezed out a long tear from the corner of her eye. 'A school, here, in my house! It cannot be borne! And Letitia! Oh my, I cannot go on,' she blubbered into his chest.

'I have taken care of it all, Diana, now pull yourself together.' His rebuke startled her into silence. 'Go and sit down and have some tea brought, while I speak to Mr Swindale and your daughters. We will join you soon.'

Amazingly, Diana did as she was told. 'Very good, William.'

Entering the study, William found its three occupants in conversation around the desk. He noticed Grace had lost weight. 'Good day, everyone.'

'William, I'm so pleased you could come.' Grace rose to receive his kiss, and then waited for him to shake hands with Swindale and kiss Faith. 'Is everything well?'

'As can be,' he nodded.

'I want to thank you, William, for all you have done.' Faith's gratitude was clear in her eyes.

'I was pleased to help, Faith. Your idea is a good one, and can work. Tell me what has happened so far.'

Faith shuffled under the great amount of papers littering the desk and came up with a list. 'Mr Swindale has taken care of all the legalities, which is wonderful, and we've had no opposition; well, very little. Some bigoted provincials thought educating girls a waste of time and money, but they were in the minority.' She gave a wry smile. 'Still, many great men of Leeds have opened their hearts and bank accounts to us,' she concluded happily.

'Brilliant.' William read the list before him. 'Any pupils yet?'

Grace sat forward and took up another list. 'Yes. Ten so far, starting in September, but we have four more families arriving next week to have a tour and meet with us. We interviewed three teachers yesterday, who have good credentials and experience.'

'Excellent. What about refurbishing and alterations?'

'Nearly done,' Faith supplied. 'Shall I show them to you?'

'No, not yet.' William smiled at her enthusiasm. 'I wish to speak privately with Grace a moment.'

'Oh, yes, of course.' Faith collected the papers off the desk.

'I must be on my way too,' Mr Swindale announced. 'How long are you in the north for, Mr Ross?'

'A day or two at most. I will come to see you later, if I may?'

'Certainly.'

Grace watched Mr Swindale and Faith leave the study before turning her attention to William. She noted the new liberal sprinkling of gray in his black hair, and the drawn lines biting deep around his mouth. 'How have you been?'

William shrugged, moving closer to the fire. 'I'm managing.'

'And the baby?'

He smiled into the flames. 'He's my shining star. I adore him.'

'I'm so delighted for you.' Grace smiled. She really was happy for him and hoped that one day she too would have a child. She moved near to the bell pull. 'Care for some tea?'

'Not yet.'

Studying him, Grace walked to stand by his side in front of the hearth. He wore loneliness like a cloak. Compassion and pity filled her. 'Felicity?' she whispered, staring into the fire.

Throwing his head back, William groaned with great pain.

When he lowered his head again, the firelight was reflected in the tears glistening in his blue eyes. He stepped away, going to the window to stare blindly out of it. 'I have found Letitia a place in a private clinic.'

'You have?' Grace asked, astounded, she had expected him to speak of Felicity not Letitia.

'Yes. It's in Nice, France. I own some property there and came across it on my last visit. It is far better than any I have seen in London.'

'Is it a comfortable place with caring nurses?' She looked at him. He'd gone white along his cheekbones, and a muscle jerked along his jaw.

William nodded. Coughing to clear his throat, he continued, 'It's like a home for them, not a hospital or a madhouse. Their problems are dealt with humanely. I inquired to make sure and and I met the matron, an Englishwoman.'

Grace sat down. William's manner and emotion frightened her.

'The matron's friends send her English newspapers; a touch of home. She recognized my name and asked me how Felicity was.' He paused to find his handkerchief and then wiped his eyes. 'You see she had read of mine and Felicity's marriage and of her recent exploits. She, the matron, held a special interest in her because Felicity was once her patient in an asylum in Cornwall.'

'A patient?' Grace gasped.

William stumbled to a chair like a man drunk. Resting his elbows on his knees, he hung his head. 'Felicity's father had her sent to an asylum at the age of fifteen until she turned seventeen. Afterwards, he allowed her to return home as long as she behaved like normal young women. All was well for a time, and then Felicity began to act strangely again, became demanding, highly-strung, rebellious and sullen. Her father had made a fortune and many influential contacts; he didn't want to be made to look a fool by having a mad daughter. Stupidly, selfishly, he decided to marry her off, virtually sell her, thereby completely giving the responsibility to someone else. Some money hungry fellow would either fall in love with her beauty, or failing that, enjoy being instantly rich. It was a foolproof plan and it worked, because I came along, desperately poor, and needing money to regain my family's former position.'

'Oh, William.'

'Yes, poor me.' He laughed mockingly. 'What a blind, money-grubbing ass I am.'

'You weren't to know.' Grace reached out a hand to him and he took it gratefully.

'I should have taken your offer, Grace, do you remember, in the kitchen? You said you would live in a cave with me.'

'I remember.'

'If only we could go back.'

Grace shook her head, heart-sorry for him. 'Don't, William, don't torment yourself with past mistakes. You have a son you must care for and...a sick wife.'

'I don't love her. I love you.' Agony wrote itself across his face.

'William...'

The study door crashed open and bounced against the wall. Felicity Ross stood in a raging fury in the doorway. Her hair hung in disarray the same as her clothes. Wild, passionate blue eyes glared. One hand was clenched in the skirts of her cream muslin dress, the other balled into a fist, which she thrust in the air. 'I knew it!'

Doyle, looking anxious, waited behind her in the hallway, ready to intervene if necessary.

'Why are you here, Felicity?' William spoke as though talking to a child, his body taut with tension. 'Why did you follow me? You should be home resting.'

'Ha! And let you come whoring?' She laughed crazily and the veins on her neck stood out. 'As soon as my back's turned, you come sniffing around her!' Felicity grimaced in Grace's direction. 'You slut!'

'Felicity, come and sit down, and we'll talk.'

'Oh no, dear husband, I have no wish to talk to you now, not when you demand it. Any other time you don't utter a word to me.'

'Where's the baby?' William asked, his face white.

'In the Thames!' Felicity shrilled, her face distorted with hatred. '*He* stood in the way, don't you see? You only wanted him, not me. I was no use anymore!'

William swayed. 'No, no!' He gripped the back of the chair for support. 'Tell me you didn't.'

Grace went to go to him, but Felicity pounced with a scream, pushing her back with one hand. 'Stay away! He's mine, not yours.'

In an instant, Doyle was in the room to protect Grace. He grabbed Felicity's arms, only to find her turn on him. Out from the folds of her skirts, Felicity flashed a knife and without pause, she thrust it into the base of Doyle's throat.

Grace screamed as Doyle fell to the floor with his lifeblood pumping from him in great arcs.

William flung Felicity to the other end of the room, sending the knife spinning into the air. It came down to thump the desk before falling to the carpet.

Grace collapsed beside Doyle. 'Doyle, dearest, lie … lie still,' she pleaded with him, cradling his head on her lap. His hands clutched at the wound in his throat and Grace covered his hands with her own, unsuccessfully stopping the blood from oozing out. Stricken, she blinked, fighting to understand the scene of William struggling with Felicity. The world had gone mad. She turned to the doorway, shrieking for Faith, her mother, Mrs Hawksberry, anybody.

A gurgling sound brought her attention back to the man in

her lap. 'Yes, darling, hold still. You'll be fine, just fine, lie still. We'll get help …' She kissed his brow. 'I'll help you, don't worry.'

Blood frothed in pink bubbles as air escaped Doyle's lungs. He was unable to breathe and losing the fight. With the last of his sapping strength, and grim determination, Doyle reached up a blood-coated hand to touch Grace's face. In his eyes, shone the love he held for her. The love, she knew, that had gripped his heart the moment he saw her at his interview.

Her mind silently screamed at the waste of such a good man. She bent down to kiss his hair. 'I know, dearest one, I know,' she sobbed. Her tears dropped onto his closing eyelids and mingled into his lashes. He shuddered, and then was still.

Grace was dimly aware of the yelling, the running, and the complete pandemonium overtaking the house. She rocked Doyle slowly, crying over him until she was lifted away from him. William caught her as her world went black.

* * *

GRACE HESITATED at the top of the staircase. The sleeping draught the doctor had given her the night before, still lingered. She had managed to dress without calling for Hopeland's help, and now had a burning desire to see Doyle.

At the bottom of the steps, she halted and listened. The drawing room stood empty, quiet. Muffled voices came from the study, drawing her. Standing in the doorway, she faltered. Faith and Gaby stood talking. Something drew her gaze; she didn't want to look, but there was no choice. A dark stain obliterated the carpet's pattern. Doyle's blood. A groan escaped her before she could stop it, and at once they were beside her.

'Where is he?' She croaked.

'Who? Doyle?' Gaby glanced at Faith and back again. 'He's at the mortuary.'

'The mortuary?' Her eyebrows dipped. 'Why? Why is he there and not here?' Pain shot through her and she winced.

'Because he's not family, dearest. So, he went to the morgue.' Faith took her hand. 'Come...'

'He was *my* family!' Grace sneered, cutting her with an icy glare. 'You had no right.'

'I thought it was best.'

Grace spun and pushed past her. 'I have to go to the mortuary.'

'No, Grace.' Faith took her arm and stopped her headlong rush. 'Doyle wouldn't want you to go and see him there.'

'I'm not going to see him. I'm going to bring him home!'

'It's not your responsibility.'

'Of course it is,' Grace cried. *Are they all mad?* 'It's my duty!'

Gaby shook her head. 'No, it's not. Doyle's uncle is taking him back to his home to be buried. He's collecting him today.'

'His uncle? Today? What day is it?'

'Come.' Faith led her into the drawing room and sat her down before asking Partridge to bring in some tea. Sitting opposite, Faith took Grace's cold hands in her own warm ones. 'Some tea will make you feel better.'

'I don't want to feel better.'

'Becoming sick won't bring Doyle back.'

Grace's stare was glacial. 'Did you contact Doyle's uncle?'

'No, the police did. They found letters and an address in Doyle's rooms. His uncle was listed as next of kin.'

With a nod, Grace turned away as tears threatened. It was all too unbelievable. 'W-where are the others?'

'Mama and Phoebe have gone to stay with Heather. Letitia is still locked in her room.'

'Mama didn't stay to help?' Grace snorted as Faith struggled to say something. 'That was a silly question wasn't it? What about William?'

'He's gone to London. You mustn't blame him, Grace,' Faith

whispered. 'It wasn't his fault Felicity came, just as he isn't responsible for her being unstable.'

'Is his son dead too?'

Faith shook her head. 'Felicity lied. The baby is safe and well.'

Grace shrugged her shoulders. No answer could explain the feeling of guilt consuming her. Doyle had loved her, cared for her every need, and she had rejected and used him. Now, she would never have the chance to say sorry and beg his forgiveness. Abruptly, she stood. 'I must pack.'

'Pack?'

'I am attending Doyle's funeral.'

'No, Grace.' Aghast, Faith grabbed her wrist. 'Enough is enough. It's all over. No one expects you to go.'

'I must pay my respects.' Grace took a step. 'I owe him that.'

'Owe him?' Gaby smiled with sadness. 'No, pet, let his family oversee it all.'

'Why must I?' Tears hung on her lashes. 'Why must I let him go? He was the one person who loved and helped me without asking for anything in return.'

'He was our butler, Grace,' Faith spoke. 'It was his job to help us, and his love for you caused him nothing but pain.'

'That is why I must go. To honour him.'

Faith and Gaby looked at each other before Gaby rose and took Grace's hand. 'Dearest, you have suffered enough. Let Doyle go to his family without the embarrassment of your presence. Do you think they, in all their humbleness, can mourn him with you standing beside them?'

'But...'

'Send a letter with his belongings or even have it delivered by Sykes and allow him to hand the letter over, but do not go yourself.' Enfolding her in a tight embrace, Gaby whispered, 'Doyle knows of your feelings and takes them with him. Now, we must think of the school. It has the power to bring Woodruff House back from the brink of devastation. This scandal cannot be leaked.'

Grace moved away to wipe her eyes. 'I'm tired of being strong, so very tired.' She straightened her bowed shoulders and faced her sisters. 'A good man died before my eyes... I'll be gone for three days.'

* * *

DIANA RECLINED on her plush velvet chaise lounge with a white handkerchief, sprinkled liberally with lavender water pressed against her nose. Her gaze narrowed as she regarded William opposite. 'How soon can we go?'

'As soon as you like.' William dejectedly rubbed his fingers along his jaw where the stubble of a new beard grew.

'Well, you must understand my position. I cannot remain here at Woodruff House, now it is to be a school. The very thought is outrageous. It's obvious Faith and Grace spare me no thought at all.' Diana grunted. 'It seems my wants and needs are never considered. No longer do I have a say in what happens to my very own house!'

'You only have yourself to blame, Diana. You've been too happy to let Grace take your role. Is it any wonder your opinion is treated with scant respect?'

Diana bristled at his cutting words, yet she held her tongue, for she knew William was the only one able to keep her in luxury. On no terms was she giving up his proposal. She cleared her throat. 'Your offer of a house in Nice is very generous, dear William. You are too kind.'

William inclined his head. 'I trust you shall be most comfortable there. Besides which, you'll have peace of mind being so close to Letitia.'

Her expression changed slightly at the remark. 'Indeed.'

'Still, Letitia won't be confined forever, and when she is

released, the villa will be a suitable place for her to live, as returning to Woodruff House is out of the question.'

'Yes, I see.' Diana sniffed with disapproval.

He frowned. 'I can set you up in Leeds if you prefer?'

'No, no. I am confident your villa in Nice is of adequate taste and style. Your mother informs me no expense was spared in its I. I dare say I shall adjust to the French lifestyle eventually.'

'When will Grace be home?'

His sudden question startled Diana. 'Oh, tomorrow I believe. She has been gone longer than she said.' She dismissed the question as unimportant. Her mind became full of the pleasures France could afford her. 'The Ellsworths have many friends in France, and spend a great deal of their time there. Indeed, I'm told a large British community live along the French south coast; is that true?'

Springing up from his chair, William squinted in puzzlement. 'Er...Yes, I believe so.'

'Of course it'll be nothing like home, but Faith implores me to take what valuable furniture, and other items we have left, with us, as they will not be needed in a school. So, with our comfortable and known belongings accompanying us, we shall not be too homesick.' Diana watched William pace the floor and her heart went out to him. 'Dear boy, please, try not to worry about your situation. You did a wonderful job hushing up the whole sorry episode.'

'Pardon?' he barked.

'The dreadful incident hardly made the newspapers.' She shivered dramatically.

'Felicity's father managed to control it, Diana, but even he, with all his wealth, cannot buy everyone's silence. Still, that is not my concern. I care little whether my name is splashed across every newspaper in the land.'

'But you must, William! Think of your son's future.'

'My son has a mother who is unstable and a murderer. Nothing can change that.' William's voice choked on emotion.

Diana rose and crossed to him, placing her hands on his arm. 'Why do you not take him away, William, and start again somewhere else where he won't be tainted with this? Come to France with us.'

'Running away won't change anything, Diana.' He shook his head. 'No, we shall go to Scarborough and live on the estate with Mama. There, he can grow surrounded by all the wonderful delights I knew as a child.'

Diana patted his arm with confidence. 'Ask Grace to go with you. She has always loved you.'

'No.' He drew in a deep breath. 'I lost my chance with Grace. She no longer holds strong feelings for me. No one can blame her for such a change of heart. Putting bricks and mortar before the love of a genuine person is a tragic mistake. Still, I made my choice and must live with the consequences.'

William kissed her cheek. 'In the library are all the documents for the villa and Letitia's place at the asylum. Once she is treated and well again, she can be released into your care. The villa is yours. I've put it in your name, and I've allowed an income for you and Phoebe as well. Good bye, cousin.'

William moved towards the door leaving Diana openmouthed in astonishment. He paused. 'I have given Swindale instructions about a large donation for the school. It'll thrive under Faith's vigorous control, I'm sure. Woodruff House will survive better as an institution of female learning than it ever would have as Montgomery Woodruff's home. Ironic, yes?' Quietly, he left the room, closing the door behind him.

* * *

GRACE SLIPPED the letter into the post box. She paused for a moment. Sending that letter to William was putting a seal on the past. She had written that he would always have her friendship and she wished him nothing but happiness with his son.

Feeling better, she turned and walked back to the waiting hansom cab. The porter deposited Grace's luggage on the rack at the back of the cab while Grace gave directions to the driver and seated herself inside the vehicle. She gazed at the busy traffic coming and going from Leeds station but didn't really see it.

Instead she remembered the scene two days ago of standing in the rain listening to the thudding of dirt sods landing on Doyle's wooden coffin. She'd watched, mesmerized, as small lumps of clay rolled down the coffin's sides to the grave bottom, where pools of water already gathered. The thought of Doyle, always so warm and full of life, now encased within his earthen prison made her want to cry out at the ugliness of it. Swallowing the bile rising in her throat, she turned away to stare out the window.

They passed small parks and open squares that trapped the warmth of the summer's day and brought out the townspeople to enjoy the Sunday break from their everyday toil. Couples strolled arm in arm, with children hopping and running about in carefree innocence. A nurse pushed a perambulator along the path by the road, and a small child's hand waved in the air. Grace's eyes softened, as she recalled the sweet gentleness of holding Daniel Thomas while he slept.

Suddenly, like a spark put to dry timber, a sense of what she needed to do came to her. Its effect was nearly physical such was the release it afforded and the calming peace that then settled over her. Yes, she knew what she wanted, the simplicity of a deep, nurturing love and a family of her own.

The cab trundled out of Leeds. Shop buildings, tenement housing, paved streets and people gave way to the hues and scents of the countryside. Bird song trilled above the crunching noise of the wheels. Hedgerows of flowering, perfumed hawthorn saturated the air. Grace let her senses soak it in with new awareness. For so long she had let the family's troubles rule her every thought, but not any longer. The shackles of responsibility were finally struck off, and now, unfettered, the freedom was intoxicating.

The light-heartedness didn't falter when the cab turned into the drive and Grace saw the chaos in front of the house. She told the driver to stop and climbed out. She waited while he handed down her baggage and she paid him. Slowly she walked towards the confusion.

Diana stood crying into her handkerchief, but managed, between bursts of tears, to direct Johnny and Sykes in the loading of the luggage. Phoebe went from one bag to another insuring all was perfect and nothing forgotten. While Letitia held back, content to silently watch from the side.

They all turned as Grace neared. Diana barged her way past the others to confront her. 'How dare you be so late on this day of days?'

'I am here now, Mama. You are all ready?'

'Well, whether we are or not is little concern to you apparently!' Diana snapped. 'You take yourself off to God knows where, without thought to me or your family, but then, your selfishness has always been paramount! Always had to have your own way. Are you counting the minutes until you are rid of us, so then you have full control of this house?'

With a sigh, Grace placed her bag by the wall and pulled her mother into a tight embrace, knowing the pain at leaving sharpened Diana's tongue. 'I love you, Mama, and I'll miss you, and we both know you'll enjoy France immensely. So, stop this nonsense.'

Startled into silence by the tight embrace, Diana sniffed and wiped her eyes. 'Yes, darling, I'm sorry for my harsh words, it's the thought of leaving you all.'

'You'll see us soon. I know William has put money at your

disposal, so there is nothing to stop you from coming back and forth across the Channel.'

Faith stepped forward and hugged her. 'Grace is right, Mama. There will always be a room for you here.'

Diana straightened, all vestige of tears gone. 'If you think I'll stay in a school, you can think again, daughter! I'm sure Heather has adequate room for me should I return.'

'Or you can come stay with me, Mama.' A twinkle of mischief entered Grace's eyes.

Four pairs of eyes stared in bewilderment at Grace; even Partridge, coming down the steps with the last carry-case, paused.

Diana raised an eyebrow. 'What on earth do you mean?'

'When I get married, you can come stay with me,' Grace explained.

They let out a breath and even nearly smiled at each other, secure in the knowledge Grace would never marry now William and Doyle were out of the picture. With sudden importance, Diana ushered Letitia and Phoebe to carriage. Dutifully, Grace followed, hiding the smile threatening to escape.

When at last all the luggage was strapped and stowed, Phoebe and Diana kissed Faith and Grace, waved to Mrs Hawksberry and the remaining servants, who stood on the steps behind the family to see them off, and entered the carriage.

Letitia kissed Faith and then with the slightest hesitation stood in front of Grace. 'I promise to become well, Grace. I'd like to return home one day, if not to Woodruff House then at least to England.'

'I've every confidence in you, Letitia.' Grace took Letitia's gloved hands in her own and squeezed them softly. 'It is a new beginning for all of us.'

A lift of her mouth was the closest Letitia had got to smiling in a long time. 'Can I write to you?'

'Need you ask?'

'I'm sorry, Grace, for everything. Do you forgive me?'

'Of course, you're my sister.' Grace kissed her cheek and released her hands. 'Be happy.'

'Come along, Letitia!' Diana instructed impatiently. 'We've Heather and Gaby to call on yet!'

Grace and Faith stood arm in arm, waving, as the carriage pulled away. The servants called out their goodbyes.

Once the carriage disappeared from sight, the gathering disbanded to return to their duties.

'Two teachers have arrived, Grace.' Faith eyes were bright with excitement. 'They're waiting in the drawing room. Come, I'll introduce you to them

'Faith.' Grace stayed by the door.

Turning to glance over her shoulder, Faith halted with one foot on the bottom step. 'Yes?'

Grace bent to retrieve her case, and then faced her squarely. 'I have to go.'

Puzzled, Faith frowned. 'Where?'

'I am to wed.'

The colour left Faith's cheeks and her eyes widened. 'Pardon?'

'I know it must come as a surprise.'

'A surprise!' Faith hissed, and then remembering the women, she asked them to excuse her before taking Grace's arm and leading her into the parlour. 'What in heaven's name are you talking about?'

'I am to marry George Walters.'

'Mr Walters!' Faith rolled her eyes. 'Have you gone mad? And what of the school? And me? I cannot do this alone.'

'Yes, you can, you will excel at it. Also, you will have three other women to help you, and the servants. You won't need me.'

Faith trembled. 'I tell you, I cannot do it without you.'

Grace placed an arm around her shoulders. 'Dearest, I'm only five minutes away by carriage. I will call everyday if need be, but I know you'll be all right.'

'Why have you not told anyone about this suitor?'

Grace chuckled. 'George is not the kind to be called a suitor, but he did express an interest in me, and after considerable thought, I have decided to marry him. I believe he will give me what I need, the love of a good, honest man.'

'But he does not know this as yet?'

'No. I'm going now to ask him.'

'It's been a long time since I've seen you really happy. I hope he knows what a treasure he will have in you.'

'Thank you.' Grace smiled.

Faith nodded with a resigned sigh. 'Well, at least I'll have you until your wedding day.'

'No, I'm *leaving* now.'

Shock rendered Faith speechless.

Grace kissed her pale cheek and wished her well. Going into the hall, she paused to stare around her home. She didn't need to say goodbye to everyone, for she'd see them again very soon.

Quietly, she opened the front door and walked down the steps to the drive. Hitching her bag more comfortably in her hand, head held high, she took the first step towards her new life.

She took her time walking across the fields, lingering to pick some wildflowers and watch the birds flying overhead. Eventually, she arrived at the track leading down to the manager's house.

Stopping for a moment, Grace stared at what hopefully would be her new home. Now she was here, apprehension tickled her stomach. A fretful beating of her heart made her breath quicken. 'Grace Elizabeth Woodruff, you have come this far, you might as well finish it.'

With determined steps she walked, bag in hand, down to the house.

He didn't answer her knock at the door and for a moment she faltered. She was certain his shift at the pit would be finished now. As manager, his hours would be long, but the lengthening shadows showed the afternoon sun was on its way down. Her confidence ebbed as she went around to the back of the house.

Rounding some over grown bushes near the house wall, she halted on seeing him.

How long she watched him might only have been minutes, but time felt suspended. His shirt hung on the pump and he wore only his trousers. Strong hands rubbed the cake of yellow soap thoroughly over his arms, chest, neck and back. Grace swallowed as her eyes followed his movements. Blood pounded in her ears. An ache of want, of a deep surging need, spread from her inner core.

She blinked suddenly as his hands stopped and she became aware he was watching her. Caught out and embarrassed, she strode up to him and placed her bag at his feet. 'That's all I have.'

His eyes narrowed with misunderstanding.

His silence frightened Grace even more. 'I own not a thing more.'

'Really.'

'Well?'

'Well what?'

Averting her eyes from his bare, soapy chest, Grace looked at the mud at her feet. 'Now you know that I have nothing, that I won't be making you a rich man...' She was crushed so tightly against his chest, her head snapped back and the words died in her throat.

'I never asked for anything but you,' he snarled.

Anger made his eyes blaze. It was the first time Grace saw past his quiet demeanour. His strength was overwhelming but exciting. His wetness soaked her clothes causing a sensation so intoxicating, she felt powerless to stand on her own. She lowered her gaze to the pulse beating at the base of his throat.

'Look at me,' he demanded in a harsh whisper. When she met his gaze, he pulled her even closer. 'Will I be enough for you?'

Grace nodded.

'Are you sure now?'

She raised her chin defiantly, glaring at him for doubting her. 'Will *you* marry *me?*'

His smile was slow coming, but it reached his dark green eyes.

Instinctively, Grace traced the tiny wrinkles fanning out at the corners. Relief flooded her as she caressed his bare shoulders and heard his intake of breath. 'Well?' She whispered. 'Care to take me on?'

He kissed her lips softly. 'Oh aye.'

ABOUT THE AUTHOR

AnneMarie Brear

Ms Brear has done it again. She quickly became one on my 'must read' list. –The Romance Studio

Australian born, AnneMarie Brear's ancestry is true Yorkshire going back centuries.

Her love of reading fiction started at an early age with Enid Blyton's novels, before moving on into more adult stories such as Catherine Cookson's novels as a teenager. Living in England, she discovered her love of history by visiting the many and varied places of historical interest.

Her books are available in ebook and paperback from bookstores, especially online bookstores. Please feel free to leave a review online if you enjoyed this book.

To receive AnneMarie's newsletter about her books, please go to her website.

http://www.annemariebrear.com

.

Manufactured by Amazon.ca
Bolton, ON

18705796R00196